TO CATCH A FOX

BY

TED COLBY

This is a work of fiction. Names, characters, places, and incidents are either the product of the author's imagination or are used fictitiously, and any resemblance to actual persons, living or dead, business establishments, events, or locales is entirely coincidental.

ISBN: 1-4107-3968-6 (e-book)
ISBN: 1-4107-3970-8 (Paperback)
ISBN: 1-4107-3969-4 (Dust Jacket)

This book is printed on acid free paper.

1stBooks - rev. 6/23/03

Author's Note

The Princes of this world appear to have a special anointing. Their individual and personal safety somehow is considered sacrosanct. It has become an acceptable alternative to bomb an entire country and an entire people back into chaos, yet leave their leader...evil though he may be...intact and safe from any assassin's will. It is he who molds the will of the many, yet he is left blameless and protected while the people are destroyed. Would it not be more appropriate to eliminate that one person to save millions of innocent people? The start of the Third Millennium, like the start of the First Millennium, has a philosophical and theological dilemma with which to deal...to sacrifice one man to save the many or to abandon the many in order that one man may live.

To catch a fox...one must be a fox

—*An old Russian saying*

Dedication

This book was essentially written prior to the events of September 11th 2001. On that day, the world didn't change so much as our view of the world changed. The world, partly as I have described it in this work, is the one that my grandchildren will inherit. I would have wished something better for them, as most of us would, but it is not to be. I don't believe that any one of us was directly responsible for the tragedy in the world, but neither were we directly responsible for preventing it. The people whom I have described herein are some of the best and some of the worst that mankind has to offer. Some of these people and the legacy they leave are those with whom my grandchildren must eventually contend. If they must inherit the fear, the pain, the danger, and the tragedy of this world, it is my fervent prayer that they will equally inherit the strength, courage, hope and most importantly, the faith to persevere and eventually overcome the evil that they find here and bring about a world reborn.

It is to all thirteen of them, Anita, Colleen, Daniel, Jeremy, Jessie, Martha, Mary, Nathaniel, Nicholas, Pete, Sarah, Stephen, and Zachary, that I most lovingly dedicate this story.

Prologue

USS Ticonderoga, CG-47
Position: 28 º 49' N, 50 º 56' E
Heading: East by Northeast; Azimuth 62º 16'
The Persian Gulf
Sunday Morning, 24 October 1999
09:12:43 AM Local Time

Captain Ernest Holloway, USN, had been at his station on the bridge of the *USS Ticonderoga* for almost twelve hours without a break. He had been in command of the ship for almost a year now and felt comfortable in his position as commanding officer and in his knowledge of the missile cruiser's capabilities and the status of his crew's training and effectiveness. Through his binoculars, he peered intently through the smoke at the bright flame of the last of four Tomahawk cruise missiles he had just launched as it disappeared over the horizon. It was headed northwest in the general direction of Baghdad. They had used both of the missile cruiser's fore and aft launchers and separated the launchings by three minutes each. He smelled the acrid odor of burned solid rocket fuel and it stung his nostrils.

"Good bye, Saddam," he said sardonically in a slow Southwestern drawl. "Good riddance, you asshole."

His instructions had been to allow a special team on board to modify the guidance systems of the missiles to search for and then lock in on a specific modulated frequency. The team had come aboard several days ago to complete the modifications to four of his Tomahawk missiles. Something out there would be broadcasting a homing beacon to the missiles; he didn't know what it was or who was placing it there. The TSSI, Top Secret, Sensitive Information message he had received early that morning had only given him a time, a general direction for launch and a frequency for receiving instructions…that was all. He had deduced from previous traffic and a personal visit from the head CIA contact for the Middle East, that there was specific activity to target the President of Iraq, Saddam Hussein, for assassination. Holloway's guess was that someone had finally been successful in planting a locator on the dictator so as to broadcast his position.

Dictators like Saddam Hussein have to think like a fox to assure their own survival. It is widely known that Saddam never sleeps at the same location two nights in a row and never announced where he will be at any time. Locating him has always been extremely difficult, especially for foreigners or those in Iraq who might wish to target him. Even close family members know little of the President's activities. Saddam trusts no one, including his own family. Two of his sons-in-law once defected. In a magnanimous show of forgiveness, he gave assurances for their safety to his daughters, but then had both men killed when they trustingly returned to Iraq. Now perhaps the means of his destruction was on its way. Operation Desert Fox had been a failure in any attempt to control Saddam, and in fact the dictator had used it to force a wedge between the United States and

Britain, and the Arab world. Saddam had pleaded the martyr's cause and eventually seemed to garner some degree of sympathy from his Arab neighbors.

"Let me know contact and detonation time," Holloway instructed the CIC, the Combat Information Center, as he turned around and started to leave the bridge.

"Aye, aye, Sir," came the response. As he departed, he heard the familiar, "Captain leaving the bridge," announced behind him.

For all the confidence he had in his position as captain and in his ship, Captain Holloway nevertheless felt a cold chill cross his shoulders as he climbed down the ladder to the deck that housed the Officers' Ward Room. The smoke still hung in the air and burned his eyes. He needed a cup of coffee and he needed to sit down. Hell, he needed more than that, but a shot of whisky was against regulations on this or any other U. S. Naval vessel. He had a maximum of one hundred and eight minutes, nearly two hours for the cruise missiles to reach either their target or their maximum range. He would know by then if they picked up the coded signal beacon and destroyed their target or whether they had fallen useless into the desert sand.

Holloway wondered what it might have been like to have been a person responsible for destroying Adolf Hitler before the madman had tortured and murdered millions of innocent people. Wasn't this the same thing? If Hitler had been killed before he had committed such atrocities, no one would ever have guessed that multitudes were destined to die at the will of a madman. In all probability, Hitler's killer would have been tried and convicted of the horrendous assassination of a promising and progressive new world leader. Holloway wondered if this would be what he might face. But in Saddam's case, Holloway rationalized, it was a little different; it was already widely accepted that he had gassed thousands of Iraqi Kurds; he also was a trained and accomplished assassin himself. Holloway shuddered again as he sank into the armchair at the head of the table in the wardroom.

"Morning', Capt'n. Coffee, Sir?" inquired the head steward, Chief Petty Officer Sam Monroe. He had heard someone enter the wardroom and had just stuck his head around the doorway to discover the ship's captain sitting there alone.

"Oh, yeah…thanks, Chief."

The steward retrieved a mug with "CAPTAIN CG-47" in heavy black letters on it from inside the stainless steel coffee center and filled it from the large chrome coffee urn on the shelf. He walked over to where Captain Holloway sat and placed the white porcelain mug on the table in front of his Skipper.

"Problem, sir?" he asked.

Holloway looked up, smiled, and said in a quiet voice, "Yeah…in a way it's a problem." Then he reached out with both hands and held the large warm mug. The heat of the mug seemed to flow through his fingers and up his arms. It was reassuring and healing. Slowly he looked up again at the ageless and kindly black face of the head steward. "Tell me, Sam, if you had just killed Adolf Hitler or Joseph

Stalin, considering all the suffering they have caused, how would you feel?"

The older, somewhat heavyset enlisted man thought for a moment before responding. "It's a heavy responsibility to be the cause of any one's death, sir," he replied slowly. "But those kind of people...those kind of people were the cause of a whole lotta trouble and grief in the world. Only the Lord knows for sure of blame, Capt'n, but if that's what troubles you, sir...for what it's worth, I'd say you did a big favor to all of us, and you should just rest easy."

"I sure hope so, Sam, I sure hope so...thanks."

"Will there be anythin' else I can get for you, Capt'n? Somethin' to eat, maybe?"

"No...no, Sam, thanks."

Left alone again, Ernest Holloway continued to ponder the potential results of carrying out his last instructions as he slowly sipped the hot coffee. Political assassination was, of course, not authorized since publication of a Presidential Executive Order. Each President since Johnson had reiterated that order. He could have refused his orders, that is if he had wanted to. He could have claimed that it was illegal according to well known standing executive orders. He could have, but he didn't. In his heart, he knew that if the launch were successful, it would have rid the world of a great evil. He looked at his watch; thirty-three minutes had passed since the launch sequence had culminated in the first missile heading down range. He would hear within the next hour and fifteen minutes.

It had been an early start to the day and he hadn't slept very well the first part of the night; his eyelids drooped and his chin settled on his chest as he dozed briefly. Holloway gave a start as the loudspeaker suddenly crackled out, **"Captain to the bridge, Captain to the bridge."** He pushed back his now cold mug of coffee and grabbed at his hat as he swung out into the passageway and headed towards the ladder thirty feet away. The expectancy of what might have just happened gave him more than enough adrenaline to quickly scamper up the ladder and down the passageway to the door of the bridge. He was through the door before the familiar, **"Captain on the bridge,"** was sounded.

"Target?" the Captain asked.

"Yes sir, it appears so," replied the Bridge Officer. "If it had been another eleven minutes, it would have reached maximum range. We have two confirmed detonations, sir. Pictures are coming in….now."

Holloway leaned on the u-shaped console that held an array of radar and missile control paraphernalia and screens; he concentrated on one of the monitor screens, waiting impatiently as the technician busily keyed in the commands for the pictures to start their sequencing. "Here is the last picture sequence of the first missile to detonate," acknowledged the sailor. The screen blossomed into light and showed the Iraqi terrain moving swiftly underneath the missile. Ahead in the distance there was a speck in the sky. The speck continued to grow larger until it was transformed into the image of an airplane. As the Captain and the Bridge Officer watched, the speck took on the unmistakable silhouette of a Russian-built Ilyushin IL-96, Russia's most modern passenger jet.

"Oh, my God, it's Russian…commercial. Musta come from Dubai," groaned the Bridge Officer.

"Contact AWACs and have them check with Fujairah International; see if they had any Aeroflots scheduled out of there that have left their flight plans," ordered the Captain. "What's its heading now?" he asked as an afterthought.

"Looks like it's flying on an azimuth of uh…three-one-five degrees, Capt'n," responded the technician. "It's also closing in on where the 36th parallel crosses the Iraqi-Syria border. That'll keep it just outside the no fly zone. If it then turns north, that bird'll be headin' straight for Moscow."

"Oh, shit," exploded the Bridge Officer.

Holloway was quiet; he didn't like the look of this…it should have been simpler. Saddam should have been located in one of his palaces or at some army headquarters, or in a convoy in the desert. Damn it, he'd been told that it was okay to fire. Hell, where'd that plane come from anyway, and why were his birds tracking it? Was Saddam on board? That really didn't bother him, but who else was on that plane? "Yeah. Oh, shit," he echoed.

The aircraft image grew and the missile tracked it as though it were a magnet. Below, the terrain came up closer and closer. Holloway yanked his handkerchief from his rear pocket and wiped the perspiration from his face as he stood staring at the screen. The statistics in a panel on the right side of the screen gave the speed and altitude of the missile as well as the distance to the terrain below it.

"It's closing in on terrain," warned the technician. "It's not losing altitude, the elevation of the terrain must be increasing."

There was a white flash and the portion of the screen showing the aerial picture turned blank.

"What happened?" demanded the Captain.

"Hard to say, sir. It was closing in on the plane and then it detonated. It could have hit the plane, but also it was only thirty feet above the ground at that point…it could have augured into a mountain in that area."

"Put on the next one," the Captain ordered.

Perspiration started to show on the forehead of the technician seated at the console keyboard. Holloway knew that having his Captain hovering over him was making the man nervous, but it was unavoidable. He placed his hand on the sailor's shoulder and quietly whispered, "Easy does it, son. You're doin' fine."

The technician quickly keyed in the instructions and hit the enter key. "Second missile on screen, sir….now," he announced.

"Heard anything from the last two missiles?" demanded the Captain. He leaned against the console and crossed his arms over his chest, staring at the screen.

"Nothing yet, sir, they have three minutes and six minutes respectively until maximum range is reached." The heat in the CIC began to be unbearable and Holloway looked over at the temperature gage. It was over a hundred degrees and rising.

"OK, now let's see what number two horse did." Holloway whispered. The screen activated and a similar sequence of terrain vanishing beneath the speeding missile flashed on the screen. The same plane could be seen in the distance and the missile seemed to be closing in on it, but at a lower altitude. Again, the ground proximity indicator revealed a rapidly decreasing distance between the missile and the ground. The screen went white and the proximity indicator read zero.

"We have number three detonation sequence now," announced the technician, quickly keying the commands into the keyboard. The familiar scene appeared on the monitor once more.

"Where the hell's that plane?" shouted the Captain.

"It doesn't seem to be interested in the plane this time," observed the Bridge Officer.

"Different target?" asked Holloway. No one answered. Holloway silently assumed that no one watching the screen knew the answer to his question. He leaned both hands on the edge of the console and watched the ground proximity indicator click off the narrowing distance to the ground until a white flash terminated the sequence once more.

Holloway straightened up and quietly observed, "That was certainly uneventful," then added, "Dump another million and two into the fiscal sewer." They waited quietly for three minutes.

"Report from AWACs, sir," announced the Bridge Officer. "There weren't any Aeroflot departures scheduled from Fujairah. Whatever it is, it didn't come from the Emirates."

"We have detonation sequence for the last missile at maximum range," interrupted the technician.

"OK, let's see the last horse," the Captain ordered; this time he took a seat in front of the terminal.

"Aye, aye, sir," the technician responded as he repeated punching in the set of instructions on his keyboard, hit the ENTER key and stopped to look over at the monitor. "Last round on screen, sir...now."

The terrain flew by beneath the missile. The screen showed no aircraft. The proximity scale clicked down slowly. Fifty–five, fifty, forty–five, forty... The range indicator showed a red dot, and the monitor beeped. A message appeared on the screen, "MAXIMUM RANGE: DESTRUCT SEQUENCE INITIATED." The screen went white.

"Damn," groaned Holloway as he swung away from the console and the monitor; he tossed the pencil he had in his hand at the blank screen of the machine. Quickly, he recovered his composure like the professional he was and turning to the technician quietly ordered him to do an analysis on the first two sequences to determine if either missile had locked onto the beacon and if either had hit the aircraft. "I'll need that information probably within the hour," he added, turning to walk out of the CIC.

"Another message from AWAC, Capt'n," the Bridge Officer called as Holloway was going through the hatchway. Holloway stopped and turned to face the Bridge Officer. "I'm afraid it's not good news, Captain. AWAC says that a diplomatic flight originated out of Baghdad about an hour ago heading for…Moscow."

The Captain simply stared at his Bridge Officer without replying. Fear tightened in his chest and he caught his breath. A question whispered in his mind once more. Who was on that plane? The Bridge Officer answered the Captain's silent question, "They say it was Prime Minister Primakov on that flight, sir."

The Captain muttered under his breath. "Oh, my God!"

As Captain Holloway left the bridge, his mind was bursting with questions. He considered what the next few hours, the next few days might hold for him. Had he indeed been responsible for the death of a potential head of state or at the least, a Russian diplomat? If so, what would be his future, now? Most likely, he guessed that he'd be sacrificed for the "good of the country." He reviewed the situation. Under orders that were Top Secret, he had sent out four "horses" to attack the Satan of the Middle East; it seemed for a moment as though he might be referring to the Four Horsemen of the Apocalypse and he grimaced at the thought. No need to be pretentious about this whole thing, he mused. But, what about the strange loss of target for the last two missiles? It could have been that the second one had totally destroyed the aircraft and the beacon. That was possible, except both of the last two would have gone to maximum range, not just the last one. The first one had a definite lock-on to the beacon; the second and third ones…maybe. He'd have to wait on the analysis…and hope.

If the beacon really was on Saddam, he wondered what the Iraqi President was doing on a Russian diplomatic flight to Moscow. He certainly didn't announce his plans to travel to another country. That didn't seem to make sense. Besides, Saddam rarely, if ever, left Iraq nowadays. Navy Intelligence would have known about it and warned him in that case. And who else was on that flight?

If the former Russian Prime Minister was indeed on board and the plane was downed by a US cruise missile, it could be interpreted as an act of war. Would he personally be responsible for starting World War III? This was beginning to get more unsettling by the minute and Holloway knew he'd have to come up with the right answers if he had missed his target with four horses; especially so if he had hit a friggin' Russian diplomat instead. Okay, the bottom line remained, did he kill Saddam or did he start World War III. "Ah, shit," he muttered to himself, shaking his head. "Sometimes, it just don't pay to get up in the morning."

Chapter One

The Color of Despair

Arroyo de la Miel
Costa del Sol, Spain
Late Sunday morning, six weeks earlier

Jack Deiter stood on the back porch of the villa overlooking the sandy beach that ran between the house and the sea. He leaned both hands against the railing; his head was bowed. He was dressed in a black tee shirt with black slacks and black Wellington boots. His mood reflected his dress. As he looked out at the waves crashing on the beach, he ran one hand over his shaved head and then brought both hands up to cover his face; he rubbed his eyes as though to relieve the tension; even alone, he felt he must keep his composure. John Remington Deiter III was not a run-of-the-mill person and not a man to come to tears easily. Today, though, was an exception. The sadness and tragedy that had stalked him most of his life was finally too much for even someone of his stature and fortitude to stoically bear.

In the imagination of his inner soul, he could even now see his Rose walking up the beach toward him, waving frantically in acknowledgment of his sudden presence. He imagined her breaking into her awkward run in the loose sand just to be with him all the quicker, her wild mass of dark red hair blowing in the wind. His fantasy finally ended with her throwing her arms around him and kissing him in the way she did when she was completely overcome with the love and passion that they shared. As the fantasy passed, tears ran down his cheeks and disappeared, as though embarrassed at the outward emotion, into the collar of his shirt.

At the age of fifty–seven, Jack Deiter was still a very active and athletic man with a catlike physique. The muscles that showed beneath his shirt had lost neither their mass nor their strength. His shaved head and sharply arched heavy black eyebrows gave him a fierce appearance; to women he was immediately attractive in a dangerous and sexy way. His high cheekbones and narrow eyes gave him a distinctly Eastern European, even Slavic look. Today, though, the strong shoulder muscles shook and his proud head no longer looked out defiantly at the world.

For a few brief moments, the long train of tragedies that had started when he was a only few months short of graduating from high school flooded through his mind. He had arrived home from school on that cold and gray afternoon in February to find both his mother and father unconscious on the floor of their home. His mother was pronounced dead immediately by the emergency squad, but his father, although technically brain dead, hung on for another week. Unknown to him at the time, both deaths had been orchestrated by their KGB handlers in retaliation for their betrayal of the Soviet Union to the United States. It was only last year that he learned about his parents' role as Soviet deep agents and their rejection of the Communist philosophy that was to cause their deaths. The official coroner's report indicated that they had died of natural causes, only the Soviets knew the truth.

Almost immediately following their funeral, he had been given an appointment to the United States Naval Academy at Annapolis through the auspices of his mentor, CIA Chief William Colby. He never understood "Uncle" Bill's concern or interest in this new orphan…until last year. He only knew that the CIA Chief appeared to be an old friend of his parents. The challenge of accustoming himself to the rigors of the Naval Academy cut short his grieving period and the years that followed at Annapolis were relatively happy ones. When one summer he met Sally MacIntire, he felt his life was complete. Within six months of graduation, he shipped out to sea. Sally remained in Alexandria, Virginia.

His first shore duty came after a year and he found himself being assigned to the Pentagon in Washington as Junior Aide to the Chief of Naval Intelligence. Two years later, he and Sally were married. Just a week short of their first wedding anniversary, Sally was tragically killed in a traffic accident while driving to Michigan to see her parents. All joy seemed to leave Deiter's life and he went through a full year of understandable, but agonizing depression.

With his required four years in the Navy finally over, he became restless and dissatisfied with life at sea and searched for a new challenge. He resigned from the Navy and with a scholarship and the last of the inheritance from his parents, he attended law school. The

Central Intelligence Agency recruited him barely a month before he graduated and following his initial schooling at Langley, he was assigned to the Rome office for a covert mission.

It was in Rome that Rose Spinelli first came into his life. At first, the memory of Sally was still heavy on his mind and he wasn't seeking a romantic involvement. As he began to know Rose, though, he once more fell in love. Within a year, the mission was complete and it was time to move on. Although Rose promised to meet him in Washington when she was finished with her next assignment, the reunion never took place and Deiter resigned from the CIA to begin work in the FBI's Department of Espionage and Counterintelligence. Deiter became engrossed in his work and although he dated periodically, he became totally dedicated to his work and being an inveterate bachelor.

Just last year, his life took yet another direction. While working on a new case, he needed the services of a Russian translator, someone who knew the nuances of the language like a native. He thought of Rose. She had been the best Russian linguist he had ever known. The CIA finally and reluctantly gave him Rose's current address only because it was an interagency request at a particularly delicate time of strained relations between the two agencies. The Senate was becoming annoyed at the infighting within the intelligence community and a refusal to provide assistance would have reflected badly on the Agency. During the intervening years since Rome, Rose had married...unhappily, as it turned out as she had divorced after only a few years. She had a grown son who was in law school and her new last name was McGuire. He decided to ask her to join him on the case if she was available. Their meeting again was as though the time that had passed them by simply didn't exist and they were able to take up where they had left each other so many years before.

The case they were working on revealed that Deiter's parents had left him a legacy worth many millions of dollars that had been kept in various bank accounts for use by Soviet deep agents. Only he had access to their accounts. The money allowed him to retire early from his position as Supervisor of Investigations for Espionage and Counterintelligence for the FBI and Deiter could spend more time with Rose. In fact, with any and all financial worries behind him, he had looked forward to spending the rest of his life with Rose...until today. He shook his head again in bewildered disbelief.

Just last night he had kissed Rose and left her at the airport in Madrid and then had driven home to the villa, arriving as day broke. She had insisted that she would be safe and that he had a long drive back to the villa and should start out early. He protested, but to no avail; she was a persistent and headstrong woman. He wasn't planning to fly back to Washington for another two weeks and had needed time to close up the villa until their return next spring. Rose was scheduled to stop enroute in New Jersey to pay a surprise visit to her parents in Upper Saddle River. She had intended to stay there the first week and then continue on down to Washington. She would spend the second week getting their townhouse on Prince Street in

"Old Town" Alexandria, Virginia cleaned up and ready for him to join her there.

A sudden screech of a seagull brought him back to the present. Only a few minutes before, he had answered the door bell to find the tall powerful figure of his long time friend Brigadier General Hank Henderson, Assistant Deputy Chief of U. S. Army Intelligence, standing there with a solemn expression on his face. Deiter had welcomed him with a light-hearted question.

"Hank, what the hell are you doing here? I thought you were still in Washington. You should have come earlier...I just put Rose on a plane last night for the States."

"I know, Jack" the combat hardened veteran replied in almost a whisper. "That's why I'm here. They had me take a Concord to Madrid last night."

"Who did? Why? What's happened, Hank?"

"The flight from Madrid to Newark went down in the Atlantic last night; it was destroyed by a bomb. There were no survivors...I'm sorry, Jack. God knows how sorry I am."

People handle the shock of the death of a loved one differently. Some scream or cry uncontrollably and some rail against someone or something whom they blame for the tragedy. There are others who simply accept it with an outward calm, a private silence, and their sorrow hidden from the world, while their inward soul screams out to Heaven. That's the way it was with Jack Deiter.

Deiter turned without a word and leaving his friend standing at the door, walked through the rooms of the villa, past the paintings still propped up against the wall where Rose had left them. She had bought them from an artist in Madrid only last week. He walked out onto the porch that overlooked the beach. Rose had so loved this place, the beach, the sun, and the water. Looking at the things she loved made it seem as though he was close to her, even now, as though death had not visited him again.

From the shadows behind the French doors leading out to the porch, General Henderson watched his friend in respectful silence. Henderson's craggy, rugged profile seemed somehow incongruous with his soft, gray sympathetic eyes. Of all people, he knew the sadness and grief that Deiter felt at this moment. During their college days, they had often shared each other's dreams, each other's ambitions, loves and heartaches. When they first met, Hank was a Cadet at West Point and Jack Deiter, a Midshipman at the U. S. Naval Academy in Annapolis. During the summers, both of them had reveled in the freedom from the harsh and demanding life at the Academies and the excitement of being together at Hank's parents' home in North Carolina. They delighted in filling their time with conspiracies of mischief, much to the dismay of Hank's parents. General and Mrs. Hodes Henderson, however, had fully accepted the orphaned boy as though he were one of their very own.

Unable to stand there anymore and watch the sadness play out in his friend, Henderson moved out onto the porch. "Jack," he said softly. He received no response. "Jack, they're certain that death was immediate for everyone aboard. Nobody, Rose included, felt anything. I know it's not much, but there was no pain, no waiting, no fear."

Deiter turned his head slightly and murmured, "Thanks, Hank, at least there's that." He hesitated, a sob choking in his throat; finally he asked, "Were there…were there any…any bodies?"

"No, nothing. It happened over deep ocean; over a mile down, the plane will never be recovered. The fireball consumed it completely." The General hesitated and then went on. "There were indications, however, that the cause was unmistakably a bomb that had been placed abroad the aircraft."

"Who…why did they do it?"

"I….we don't know yet, Jack, it was the act of terrorists, obviously, but exactly who and why hasn't been established yet."

"Do you think it was directed against Rose…or me?"

"I don't think so, Jack, there's no indications of that…not the same connections. This looks like an Arab thing…very possibly Iraq…Saddam Hussein in particular. Maybe it was Osama bin Laden who was involved, we really don't know, but it certainly doesn't look like a Russian thing."

That thought held a small bit of comfort for Deiter, but not much. If Rose had to die, at least something that he was involved with or somebody who had a vendetta for him didn't cause it. That seemed to ease his conscience somewhat. It didn't help the loneliness, however, nothing could at this point. As the truth sunk in, he wanted to strike out at the ignorance and bitterness that had caused someone to destroy innocent lives. If it were within his power at this very moment, he would destroy whoever or whatever was in anyway responsible her death; and he wanted to do it personally. Deiter clenched his teeth and grimaced as he again looked out at the scene that Rose had love so much. His eyes narrowed. "They'll pay for this," he whispered quietly under his breath. Although the words were private, General Henderson still heard him…and understood what his friend meant.

"I'm suppose to tell you that the CIA wants to talk with you," Henderson said.

"Oh? What the hell do they want?"

"It's something about the bombing," Henderson shrugged. "They know something more about it that they haven't shared with me. You remember Adams don't you?"

Deiter's shoulders visibly sagged. "Oh, shit, what does that fat asshole want now?"

"I'm sorry, Jack, I'm suppose to tell you that he wants to talk to you back at Langley and that it's about the bombing. They think you can help."

"How?"

"They didn't say."

"Kind of late, isn't it?"

"Don't do this to me, Jack. I'm only a messenger. You know I loved her too."

Deiter turned partly around and looked at his friend. "It didn't have to be, Hank," he said, shaking his head; he then turned back to look at the sea. "I think I'll sell this place, it was Rose who loved it so; I've got no use for it now."

Henderson sighed and leaned back against the railing with his hands in the pockets of his brown leather jacket and looked over at the man he had known for so many years. "Do you want me to leave, Jack?" he finally asked.

"I guess I need to be alone," Deiter replied quietly.

Henderson nodded and started to leave, but at the doorway he turned back towards Deiter. "Call me, Jack; I'm at the pension in the village." Deiter turned slightly and without expression nodded to his friend; he then turned back to look out upon the beach and the sea.

The sadness and despair were beginning to give way to something else, some other feeling. Deiter knew what it was and let its wave flow over him. He knew that over the eons of human existence, the soul and mind of man has been protected from the ravages of despair and grief by a metamorphic salve more commonly known as vengeance. Only after the metamorphosis is complete and has run its course, does the gentleness of the human spirit again gain prominence. Although the loneliness continued to eat a hole in his heart and probably would never ever completely cease, the flame of vengeance started to burn. The dark hatred grew and strengthened itself in his resolve. He promised himself…and Rose…that those who were responsible would pay and he knew he would somehow find a way to do that. Tomorrow he would contact his friend, but for now, it was time to concentrate on giving form to the feelings he was developing. The tragedies of the past had hardened his resolve to act on the pain it had caused him. This time, perhaps, there would be a personality, a physical body, an individual whom he could find and upon whom he would wreak his vengeance. It was suddenly quiet again, very quiet. It was past the time for tears. Even the sea gulls had stopped their incessant crying and silently circled the lonely beach that stretched between the villa and the sea as though they too were silently searching for a love lost…for Rose.

Hank Henderson walked slowly down the pathway that meandered from the villa to the small road leading to the village of Arroyo de la Miel; the crunching his shoes made on the crushed shell surface of the path was the only sound he heard. He walked to where he had parked the car he had rented at the train station in Seville upon arrival from Madrid earlier that morning. As he opened the car door, he paused and looked back up at the house and imagined his friend still standing on the back porch overlooking the beach and the sea. He shook his head and suddenly felt a twinge of nausea. He sighed and slipped into the driver's seat and closed the door. It was only about a ten-minute drive back to the village and the pension, but Hank drove it slowly; now he was in no hurry. He knew his friend, Jack Deiter, well enough to know that he had no other recourse but to wait until Jack was ready to let another person back into his life. Until then, the man he loved and called his brother would think himself to be the only person left on earth. Hank knew him very well indeed.

As he drove, Henderson thought back to days that, maybe weren't any simpler, but they seemed to be a lot more carefree. At the Academy, he and Jack thought that someday they would be able to influence the whole world. There were, of course, the very good times when they were in the company of pretty girls who were deliciously impressed by the uniforms of West Point and Annapolis. In retrospect, it seemed that each of the girls was prettier than the previous one; and each one of them was delightful and charming. This companionship continued even after they graduated from their respective academies. After their initial schooling, Jack had joined a carrier task force as junior officer aboard a destroyer escort, while Henderson had been given a platoon in the 3rd Battalion, 187th Airborne Infantry with the 101st Airborne Division at Fort Campbell. He later commanded a company in the same battalion in Vietnam where he was awarded several medals for heroism including the Silver Star for gallantry in action. Several rounds of AK–47 fire in his abdomen and thigh had cut short his tour in the Far East combat zone and he was shipped back to finish his recuperation in North Carolina. He had been somewhat surprised when Jack resigned from the Navy after his obligatory five years, but it didn't change the respect he had for his friend.

When Henderson was sent on a covert assignment to Rome for Army Intelligence, he was delighted to find that his CIA contact would be his old friend John Remington Deiter, III. That's when he first met Rose. She was Jack's partner and their cover was that of Russian agents. Hank never fully understood why this would be the best cover for a CIA operative, but he didn't question it; Don Adams of the CIA had set it up. Rose spoke and understood Russian like a native; Jack looked like a Russian and could converse passably in the language; his accent sounded more Chechen than anything else, but he was credible. He had noticed that Jack and Rose seemed to hit it off well together. At times, Hank had wanted to warn them that their personal lives might compromise their mission, but they kept their senses about themselves and were able to pull it off.

It was Rose, he guessed, who was the first to become worn out with the deceptions and intrigue. One day, she was there, the next day she was gone. While he didn't mention her absence to Jack, her partner didn't seem to be concerned at all, so Hank dropped it. A few months later, Jack also dropped out of sight and apparently returned to the States. Hank simply assumed that the two of them would eventually meet again and pick up where they had left off. He never dreamed that it would take more than two decades for them to finally get back together. Sometimes in life, two people are meant to be together; he concluded it was that way with Jack and Rose, no matter how long it took, they'd be together.

Later, he would continue his career in the Army and find considerable successful in his chosen profession. Jack was snapped up by the FBI and joined their espionage and counterintelligence branch.

Over the years, and through his dedication, integrity and leadership, he rose to the rank of Supervisor and was posted at the headquarters in Washington. Somewhat later, Jack and Rose finally met again and it seemed as though his old friend had at last got it all together. They had been happy this last year since they had found each other again. Hank paused and thought a moment; Jack and his first wife, Sally were married only a year when she died in a traffic accident. Now it was Rose. It had been barely a year since they were married. He knew his friend was thinking the same thing. Oh, God, why did this have to happen?

Hank Henderson pulled his rental car into the courtyard of the pension. Earlier, he had just thrown his bag into the room he had rented and quickly driven out to where Jack's villa was at the shore without bothering to unpack. He looked at his watch; it was nearly noon. He knew that it would probably not be today that Jack Deiter would get in contact with him, so he considered what he would do with the rest of the day. As he passed the desk in the lobby, he noticed an English newspaper on the counter and snatched it up on his way to his room. He tucked it under his arm and mounted the steps to the third floor. He found the room essentially as he had left it and threw his two-suiter luggage onto the bed, pulled the light brown suit from the bag and hung it on its hanger on a rod behind a heavy brown cloth curtain. The rest of his clothing, he placed into a small set of dresser drawers, and his toilet articles he placed on the sink on the far wall. His room didn't have the advantages of a toilet or bath, but he had roughed it before in Europe and kind of liked the quaintness of it. He stood at the window for a minute looking outside at the rooftops at the center of the village. It gave him a peaceful feeling and he understood why people here were so friendly. Finally, he stripped off his shoes and grabbing the newspaper, he flopped all of his six-foot-two, linebacker frame onto the bed. He felt tired from the "redeye" flight and the encounter with his friend, but he needed to relax before he could get any meaningful rest.

The newspaper's headline announced the crash of Continental flight 63 from Madrid to Newark, New Jersey. There were speculations about a terrorist bombing and there was mention of at least 198 Americans aboard plus 25 Spanish citizens. Three of these came from Madrid where the newspaper originated; it gave their names. No names were listed for the Americans aboard. Hank knew that Rose had been one of them; that's what Adams had told him. It was amazing how quickly the firm had learned about the bombing and the fact that Rose was aboard. They certainly have their fingers into everything, he observed to himself. He knew also that Jack Deiter would need to handle his own grief, and that most certainly he eventually would. Now, he just had to wait for Jack to get back to him. The newspaper slipped from his hands and he drifted off to sleep.

It was early evening when he finally awoke. It took him a few moments to acclimate himself to his surroundings, then he sat up and stretched. Hank had to admit to himself that he felt quite a bit better now. He rubbed his chin and decided that he needed to shave before he wandered out to find something to eat. A change of shirt, some comfortable shoes, a wash cloth scrubbing of his face and neck and a shave made him feel like a new man, ready to search for supper and a drink…but not necessarily in that order. He had visited Jack and Rose here once before, and they had gone to a couple of very fine taverns that had not been entirely infested with tourists. He remembered also that the food was inexpensive and very good. He threw on a light jacket, headed down the stairway and strolled out into the darkening streets. The night was cool and he hadn't walked far when he spotted the first establishment that Jack and Rose had introduced him to previously. He recalled that both of them seemed to be great friends with the owner; and the owner, in turn, was completely captivated by Rose. The sign over the doorway read *"Casa de Paraiso"* or House of Paradise.

Henderson opened the door and went inside. The interior of the small bar was only a little brighter than the streets outside, but Hank found a wooden chair next to a rough-hewn table in the corner and sat down. As his eyes became accustomed to the darkness, he began to examine the gallery of framed pictures adorning the mud colored walls; they all were intended to be some sort of endorsement of the restaurant by famous people. The owner looked up from his newspaper, then folding the paper, he laid it down at his table and walked over to where Henderson sat with his elbows on the table and his hands clasped in front of him.

"*Buenos noches, Señor,*" he said as he came up to the table. He looked down and squinted at the tall American. "Señor Henderson, is it you?" he asked, a smile creeping to the lips of the swarthy and wrinkled old man as he wiped his hands on his apron.

"Hi, Juan," Henderson replied with a returning smile, "its me...how've ya been?"

"Wonderful, Señor, but why are you here alone; where are your friends, Señor and Señora Deiter tonight?"

"You haven't heard, then, I take it?" Henderson asked, turning his head slightly but riveting his eyes on the elderly gentleman.

"Heard what, Señor?"

"Did you read about the plane going down?" Henderson asked, motioning toward the newspaper that the man had just placed on the table.

"Si, Señor, it was terrible...such a loss."

"Even more so, Juan. Señora Rose was on that flight."

It took a few moments before the connection finally hit the old man and then slowly he turned around a chair from the next table and sat down facing Henderson. He placed one hand over his lips and simply stared at the tall man until tears began to find their way down the wrinkled, brown cheeks. He made the sign of the cross three times and lowered his head. After a few moments, he lifted his head again and looking straight at Henderson asked, "Where is Señor Deiter now?"

"I left him at the villa; he wanted to be alone for awhile."

17

The old man nodded his head in understanding and then pulled himself to his feet and said, "I will bring you some wine…may I join you?"

"Of course, my friend, of course."

The evening progressed through several glasses of wine and a plentiful platter of mussels and other seafood followed by more wine. Juan Maranda was a truly warm and caring individual. It was clear that he had been, in his own way, very much in love with Rose; Hank understood that they all had in some way or at some time been in love with Rose. Juan then described the last time that he had seen Rose and something about it began to arouse Henderson's interest. Juan related that Señora Rose had talked to another American in the tavern only three days ago. He described the man as being large and heavyset with a black and white speckled beard; Juan didn't seem to have liked the man at all. Somehow, the description sounded like Don Adams of the CIA, but Hank knew that was impossible; the old man was obviously describing someone else. Juan said that they had talked about some terrorist group from the Middle East. The names were all Arabic sounding and were strange to the ears of the old man. It was almost midnight before Hank was able to tear himself away and stumble back to the pension. Something bothered him, but he couldn't put his finger on it. He had consumed too much wine and was too upset about the happenings of the last two days to make much sense about anything for that matter.

It was the pounding on the door that finally awakened Henderson the next morning. It persisted even though he tried to ignore it. He finally threw off the bedclothes and, dressed only in his underwear, shuffled towards the door of the room. He turned the lock and opened the door a crack to peer out. Standing there in the bright sunlight was a man dressed in a black leather jacket and black pants; the man's shaved head gleamed in the early morning sun and his eyes were steel-gray slits under heavy black arched eyebrows; they looked like the eyes of an Arctic wolf. The features on his face suggested a Slavic heritage. The tight-fitting jacket failed to hide a muscular, feline physique; both hands were stuffed into the jacket pockets…it was Jack Deiter.

"Going to sleep the rest of your life away?" Deiter asked humorlessly.

Henderson opened the door for his friend and then turned back and stumbled towards the unmade bed. He flopped down on the bed on his back and throwing his arm over his face to shield him from the early morning sun, closed his eyes again. "Didn't expect you so early," he remarked quietly.

"We've gotta lot of work to do."

"We?" Henderson asked opening one eye and staring at the figure standing at the end of the bed.

"You're more than just a messenger boy, Hank; even the Army doesn't allow messenger boys to wear stars," Deiter retorted, referring to Henderson's rank of Brigadier General.

The other man chuckled slightly, "I don't think they could find anyone else with guts enough to come and tell you. They needed your help, but were afraid to ask for it."

"They have it...but only if I call the shots. I'm retired from the FBI and don't work for the CIA...I'm very independent...freelance."

"I think that's fairly close to what I told them you'd say," Henderson responded matter-of-factly.

Henderson washed, shaved and got dressed as Deiter waited. Nothing was said between them. Henderson noticed that Deiter was staring out of the window at the village and the red rooftops of Arroyo de la Miel stretching out before him. He knew that Deiter had developed a fondness for this village and knew that he'd miss it. But he also knew that Deiter had now commissioned himself to a mission that he recognized would take him close to death. He knew that his friend was resigned to it, with any and all the repercussions it may cause. He realized that in the frame of mind that Deiter had carefully constructed throughout the previous day and that night, that death didn't enter the equation. Everything and everyone he had ever loved was already gone and he only anticipated the opportunity to join them. Henderson had expected that, but the knowledge that it had occurred was troubling to him, nevertheless.

It took awhile for the reservations to be confirmed for the next flight out of Madrid to Washington. The phone at the tavern was the only private one around. It was early in the morning and Juan Maranda was only glad to be of some assistance; he closed the tavern.

Henderson worked the telephone to the embassy in Madrid and Deiter sat talking with the old man in hushed tones. Finally, Hank hung up the phone and turned to the two men sitting at a table across the room. "We're confirmed on tomorrow's flight out of Madrid."

"Good," responded Deiter. He turned back to the old man. "Look for a buyer for the villa," he said quietly. The other man nodded sadly. They shook hands and Deiter stood up. Juan placed his hands on the taller man's shoulders and then he made the sign of the cross and said, *"Via con Dios, mi amigo, via con Dios."*

Deiter cupped the old man's cheek and replied. *"Via con Dios."* After a long pause, he quickly turned around and walked out of the door without looking back.

Henderson watched as his friend walked out of the tavern. He then walked up to Juan and expressed his thanks to the tavern owner and followed his friend into the street and back to the pension.

It was almost noon before the two men had finished taking care of any final tasks. Henderson then drove them both north out of the village in his rented car and headed towards Seville. The road wound snake-like across the brown fields surrounding the village. It would be at least six to eight hours before they would arrive at the airport at Madrid and check into a hotel. The ride was mostly in silence and the scenery was storybook in its magnificence. Only century-old stone walls and an occasional fortified ruin broke the expanse of golden fields.

Deiter sat gazing blankly out of the window at sights that he recalled had elicited squeals of delight from Rose on their trips along the same road. They passed through the city of Ronda replete with its quaint medieval charms. He remembered that driving through the town had been especially delightful as Rose discovered each new and exciting detail. The city was set perched on the edge of a cliff overlooking the expansive countryside surrounding it. As they drove pass Spain's oldest bullring, Deiter casually mentioned to Hank that the structure was the site of the first bull fight in 1785; Rose had told him that a couple of months ago when they had visited there. He could still visualize her reading it from the book that she held in her lap while sitting cross-legged beside him in the car. Deiter noticed that Henderson winced as he eased the car across the narrow four-arched bridge of Puento Nuevo. Far below, he could see the white-capped river raging through the gorge. He smiled to himself recalling that he had felt the same way the first time he had crossed that bridge; Rose had teased him about it.

Two hours later, the two men pulled into the flight departure lane at the Seville airport. It was another two hours before the flight to Madrid took off, but in less than an hour and a half after that, they found themselves in a taxi heading towards the airport hotel in Madrid. Their flight to Washington via Newark was scheduled to leave at noon the next day. They would have an unavoidable two-hour layover in Newark and would finally touch down at Dulles International at 5:35 p.m. Eastern Daylight Time.

Deiter dreaded the anticipated long period of inactivity on the flight. It would provide too much of an opportunity to remember and dwell on the flight that only a few days ago had ended so tragically. Would every moment of the flight only bring increasing loneliness and feelings of despair to him? He tried to think of something else.

The takeoff was uneventful and the routine of the flight was well underway before Deiter started to recall once more, most clearly, what it was like to know and to love Rose and be loved by her in return. Deiter knew full well why there was an intense feeling of closeness to Rose at this time. It was the knowledge that the flight he was on was following the same great-circle path that her flight had taken and that at sometime during the flight they would pass over where she now was. He wondered if he would know when that time came. He wondered if somehow she would communicate that she was near. He closed his eyes and the fantasy of seeing her running up the beach toward him played once more in his mind. He sat up quickly and shook his head; no, it wasn't going to help matters to dwell on something that no longer could be, that was now gone forever. He recalled how long he had struggled over Sally's death. Deiter didn't fall into love easily, but when he did, he fell hard. This time, he thought, he would try to put it behind him and be thankful for the time he did have with her. The night before, he had developed his resolve toward vengeance and now he must develop an even stronger resolve to keep his depression in check. He knew that the combination of danger and depression often could be fatal. He knew that he had to be in top condition if he ever wanted to be successful in what he now assumed was his final destiny…avenging his wife's death.

Chapter Two

The Mission

Dulles International Airport
Tuesday afternoon, October 5, 1999

The Continental 747 eased down toward the runway, touched twice and braked to a final stop at the turn to the taxi way leading to its berth some distance from the terminal building. After a few minutes, a shuttle car snuggled up to the door of the aircraft and the passengers began to transfer into the conveyance. The shuttle rolled away from the aircraft and plodded back towards the terminal. After arriving at the main building, Hank Henderson and Jack Deiter picked up their bags and walked through green double doors past the customs counter. Henderson showed his credentials to the customs official and indicated that Deiter was with him. Both were motioned quickly through to the outside landing. Henderson spotted a black limousine and headed for it. A limousine driver dressed in a black uniform hurried up to meet him and grabbed his luggage. The driver gave a glance at Deiter and appeared to contemplate whether or not he should overextend himself by taking the other man's luggage too. He thought better of it, turned and hurried toward the car. Deiter shrugged, looked at his friend, muttered something about "damn brass" and continued walking toward the limousine carrying his own luggage. Henderson smirked.

It was a few minutes past seven o'clock that evening when the limo bounced down the cobblestone hill toward Deiter's town house on Prince Street in Old Town Alexandria. The slippery stones that glistened in the light of the street lamps seemed to upset the driver and hampered his ability to control the plush limo as he piloted rather than drove it down the street. The car lurched uncontrollably down the antiquated street. Earlier, they had dropped Hank Henderson off at his home. Deiter figured that it was just protocol to deliver the General to his quarters before getting rid of fellow travelers even though it would have been closer to have stopped in Alexandria first.

Finally, thankfully, the driver stopped the limo in front Number 125. Deiter climbed out of the rear seat of the oversized automobile, pulled out his luggage and slammed the door behind him. He then waved to the figure in the front seat, indicating that the driver was now free to leave. Happy to be out of the swaying and bouncing conveyance, he smiled as his eyes fell on the familiar British Racing Green Jaguar XK8 convertible parked in front of his townhouse door. The license plate read simply "DEITER." It had been almost three months since he'd driven it and he missed the exhilaration it gave him. He assumed that someone, probably Hank, had called ahead to notify Deiter's assistant, Conley, that he would be arriving. Conley would have known to get the car from the garage where he normally stored it when away for extended periods of time, and park it outside the house. He was glad to see the car, as he'd need it in the morning.

Deiter's home was one of the very few things besides his Jag on which he prided himself. The building was one of about a dozen on that side of the block and was generally the same age as the others. Built in the early 1740's, it was two and a half stories high, brick, with the original black, working, wooden-slatted shutters on the windows. The door was of a dark gleaming natural mahogany with highly polished brass fixtures. A heavily carved oval framework was set in the middle of the door and contained a large brass door-knocker in the form of a fox's head. An oval plaque on the left side of the entrance identified it as an original registered building in the Colonial section of Alexandria. The flickering glow coming from a pair of matching brass lantern-styled lamps set on either side of the door was warm and inviting. He had bought the house back in the seventies when he was first assigned to the Washington area; later, when he and Sally were married, she had moved in with him. After Sally was killed, he remained there alone. More recently, he had asked Rose McGuire to move in with him while they were working on a case together, and finally, they made their home there after they were married. There have been many happy and wonderful times here in this gracious home, he thought as he slid the key into the brass plate in the door. Why did they have to end so tragically both times?

Deiter unlocked the front door and stepped inside; he normally would have quickly headed for the alarm shutoff switch located down the hallway and around the corner, but tonight Conley was there to greet him. Following their wedding last year, he had hired Conley to see to the upkeep of the house and take care of any business or personal affairs that needed attention while he and Rose were in Spain. Of course there was also Sam, Deiter's large, sleek black Persian cat that needed someone for company and care in his absence.

Conley stood in the middle of the hallway peering over a pair of reading glasses perched on the end of his thin straight nose. He was a slight man in his early seventies. His hair was a stalk white, with a flowing cowlick above a pinched, but pleasant face. He was dressed in a nicely form-fitting charcoal-black suit with a silver and black striped tie. He wore a white handkerchief in his breast pocket. Conley had lost his wife to cancer a little over a year ago and was looking for some kind of work to keep his mind off his loneliness, yet not be overly stressful for a man of his age. Deiter and Rose had immediately become fond of the old gentleman.

"Welcome back, sir." Conley offered. "I'm so sorry to hear about Mrs. Deiter. General Henderson called me about it before he left to go tell you. If there's anything I can do, sir."

"Thanks, Conley. I'll be here for a few days and then…then I don't know exactly, but I'll be gone for some time, I'd guess…probably out of the country. If you'd just continue as usual, I'll let you know as much as I can in advance of what my plans will be. Right now I want to just get a sandwich and relax for awhile before bed. It's been a long flight and a long day."

"I understand, sir. I'll fix you something and bring it into the study for you. Leave your luggage here, sir, and I'll unpack it for you."

Deiter hung his overcoat on the rack next to the door and walked through the pocket door on the left side of the main hallway that led to his walnut paneled study. The light from recessed lamps in the room's upper corners dimly lit the study and his stereo was offering the lively stains of Mozart's aria, *"Der Vogelfänger bin ich ja"* from **The Magic Flute**. The combination seemed to mellow the air and slightly brighten his mood. He removed his suit jacket, removed his tie and unbuttoned his shirt collar. He noticed that his black knit sweater was folded neatly on the back of his large leather easy chair, he tossed his coat and tie on the chair and he pulled the sweater over his head. Now, he finally felt that he was at home.

The study was Deiter's private sanctuary and reflected the personal tastes of its owner. In the center of the room was a large, heavily-carved, double-pedestal walnut desk; sitting on the left side of the desk top was an antique brass adjustable student lamp that had been electrified. Between the two windows that looked out onto Prince Street was a simple table supporting a three-foot scale model of a four-masted man-of-war that Deiter had built from original plans some years before. Otherwise, the room was sparsely furnished in keeping with the age of the house. A Chinese red oriental rug covered most of the polished hard wood floor. Shear curtains hung over the windows set off by a dark crimson velvet cornice and floor-length drapes that could be closed during the winter months to keep out the cold wind that sometimes blew up the cobblestone street from the Potomac River. The wall opposite the windows contained a built-in floor-to-ceiling polished dark walnut bookcase. A brass ceiling rail ran across the entire top of the bookcase to support the matching walnut, sliding ladder hanging from the end of the rail in the far corner. The bookcase was half-filled with an elegant array of collector's editions and several knickknacks of personal memorabilia. On the adjoining wall stood a cabinet of Queen Anne design that housed his bar supplies. He headed for it.

After pouring himself a "Jamison" Irish whiskey in a small Old Fashion glass and tossing in several ice cubes from an ice bucket that Conley had thoughtfully filled earlier, Deiter flopped down in his overstuffed dark brown leather covered chair. A large, long-haired, silky black cat immediately pounce onto his lap. Sam's master was home and he wanted to show his appreciation.

"Miss me, guy?" Deiter inquired of his companion. "I guess so." Deiter looked over at his desk and noticed a blinking red "1" on his answering machine. He stretched across the desk and hit the blue button next to the light.

"Jack…Don Adams," the machine responded in a slow, measured and deeply resonant voice that hinted of a hoarse whisper. "Sorry to hear about Rose. Uh…we have to talk. I'll be meeting with Henderson tomorrow morning about nine o'clock…my office. Do hope you can be there. It's…very important…has to do with Flight

63." There was a click and the machine added its own message in a metallic voice, "End of messages."

Deiter could picture the corpulent figure of Don Adams leaning back in his chair and scratching his graying beard while he droned into the speakerphone. Deiter had expected something like this. Adams didn't give a damn about Rose or him for that matter. The years had not softened his dislike for the CIA bureaucrat, but at least it was a beginning to finding out the answers to what had happened to the flight, and to Rose. He sat back and savored another mouthful of the cool and soothing amber liquid, washing away the sound of Adams' voice.

He must have dozed for a few minutes, because he was brought back to awareness by the sound of the pocket door to the study being slowly slid open. Conley's slight frame was silhouetted in the doorway. "Sir," Conley said in a hushed voice, "I fixed you a snack to eat."

Deiter stood up, causing the cat to seek more stable sleeping accommodations elsewhere. Conley set the tray he was carrying in the center of the walnut desk. "Is there anything else I can get for you, sir?" he asked.

"You've done more than enough, thanks, very much. I just got a call. I have to be at the CIA at nine tomorrow morning. I don't know what'll happen after that, but I'll let you know."

"It'll take a good hour to get there at that time of the morning," Conley replied, "I'll fix you some coffee and something to eat at seven, if you'd like, sir."

"Thanks, that would be great."

Conley said good night and left the study. Deiter looked at the tray and saw that his "snack" was shrimp scampi over linguini with Italian bread and a glass of Chianti. A small tossed salad was on a separate plate. This man was certainly worth every penny he was paying him, thought Deiter. He sat down and took his first mouthful and washed down the delicious bit of food with a sip of the dry, but full red wine…yes, Conley was a real find, indeed.

Wednesday morning, October 6, 1999

As the sunlight started to creep across the window frame and into the bedroom, Deiter absently reached his hand over to touch Rose. His hand landed on an empty pillow and it brought him suddenly back to reality. He half raised his head, squinted at the electric clock on his bedside stand, and finally forced himself out of bed. It had been relatively early when he had turned in, but the effects of the last two days had finally affected him, and he had slept throughout the night. In a few minutes, he had showered, shaved and was beginning to feel human once again. His mind raced in contemplation of the things he thought he might have to do today, yet they would all depend on what happened at the CIA. At seven o'clock sharp he was downstairs sitting at the dining room table reading the newspaper that had been placed next to his coffee at the table. He browsed the newspaper as he sipped a fresh cup of coffee. Five minutes later, Conley walked in with a serving of Eggs Benedict, orange juice and toast.

At seven forty–five, Deiter, dressed in a black turtle neck sweater under a charcoal gray sport jacket over black wool slacks and carrying a black trench coat slung over his arm, left the front door of his townhouse and slipped behind the steering wheel of his Jaguar. The machine roared into life, and Deiter pulled it away from the curb and maneuvered it carefully over the cobblestones until he reached smooth roadway at the bottom of the hill.

The most direct way to get to Langley, Virginia and the CIA Headquarters from Old Town Alexandria is to drive north up the George Washington Memorial Parkway along the western bank of the Potomac River. Deiter drove around the block and headed up King Street to where it intersected with the GW Parkway. For Washington, the traffic seemed light, and he made good time. He passed by Reagan National Airport just as a lumbering 747 was straining for altitude. He thought of Rose again and Flight 63. The drive was relatively pleasant and gave Deiter time to consider what he would say to Adams. Deiter drove past nearly a dozen joggers who were exercising on the trail that parallels the highway, passed under Chain Bridge Road and came to the Turkey Run turn off opposite the entrance to the CIA campus. He had made this drive countless times before and he had a feeling of *déjà vu*. Turning right and around the jug-handle, he followed a half-dozen cars as they approached the main gate leading into the complex.

Deiter stopped the Jag opposite the right side of the guard building in the center of the road. A guard dressed in a white uniform shirt with gold badge and a gold trim on his medium blue pants stepped up to the car; he leaned down to look at the driver and asked for a pass. Deiter gave the guard his name. He waited as the guard moved his finger down a list of names. Deiter's gaze shifted to the twin set of red steel curved barriers across the roadway ahead of him and the double row of tire slicers. The barriers gave the impression of giant twin snowplow blades set across the road. Things had changed since he had last worked for the CIA; apparently they were expecting someone to ram through the entrance with a ton of explosives or something equally drastic. Maybe it was because they were such a friendly bunch here, he mused to himself. The guard's finger stopped halfway down the list.

He grunted and said, "Here it is, Mr. Deiter; you are visiting Mr. Adams, is that right?" Deiter nodded. The guard asked for identification and Deiter pulled his wallet from his rear pocket and produced his driver's license. The guard grunted again and straightened up. At a signal, the first of the barriers disappeared into the ground along with the long row of knives aimed at his tires and Deiter shifted into first gear and crossed the barrier. As he drove close to the second barrier, it descended into its hole and he crawled past it. He could see in his rear view mirror as he drove away that both barriers had returned to their original position.

The sprawling expanse of the Central Intelligence Agency Headquarters complex can't be seen from the main highway. Deiter drove up the long rise in the road leading to the center of the complex, ignored the directions to the expansive parking lot that rivals only the Pentagon, and drove up to the VIP "visitor" area in front of the Administration Building and parked. He proceeded up the walk towards the main entrance and stopped momentarily at the statue of Nathan Hale outside the Old Administration Building. Deiter had always admired Hale and the story of the man's unabashed patriotism. He then walked briskly to the main entrance of the New

Administration Building (or the NAB as it was affectionately known) and into the reception area.

The building itself gave the modernistic appearance of a bird in flight; the architecture consisted of a series of curved roofs. His guess was it was supposed to be an eagle. At the oblong reception desk sat two women. One was in her early fifties and the other must have been no older than thirty-five. Both were rather striking and it somewhat amused Deiter that the Agency had a way of selecting people for the most menial positions using criteria exclusively of their own; hardly an equal opportunity employer, but they easily got away with it. The younger woman had a full head of brunette hair and a little too much makeup for Deiter's taste. She was very attractive, though, and was the first to notice Deiter. "Yes, sir?" It was a question not a statement.

"John Deiter, to see Don Adams," he said.

She didn't look at the list of names in front of her, but picked up the telephone and hit three buttons on the pad. Deiter guessed that if the receptionist knew Adams' number from memory, that the bureaucrat had done well in the last few years working for the "firm." She waited a few moments for someone to answer and then said, "There's a Mr. Deiter to see Mr. Adams." She paused. "Yes, of course." She hung up the phone and looked up at Deiter with a slight smile.

"Mr. Adams would like for me to escort you to his office right away." With an even wider smile and coquettish tilt of her head, she said. "Would you follow me, sir?" Deiter nodded, but as he followed the pleasantly built young woman, he observed to himself that something had changed recently. The last time he was here, he was forced by Adams to cool his heels in the reception area. Adams hadn't allowed him up to his office, but instead sent a clerk to give Deiter the information he had requested. Yes, sir, something was up all right, and it made Deiter very suspicious. Unfortunately, he still didn't have the slightest idea what it was.

Deiter followed his guide through the double doors and into a waiting elevator. She pressed the button for the third floor and stepped back. The doors closed and less than a minute later they were entering the reception area of the Director, Central Intelligence Agency. The receptionist slipped her plastic card into the slot next to the large double wooden door; it made a buzzing sound and she pressed down the brass handle on the door and indicated that Deiter should go through the entranceway. Deiter noticed that there were several private offices surrounding the rather plushly appointed reception area. The receptionist went up to the secretary's desk and announced that she had John Deiter with her. The secretary, who was a very pretty brunette with long hair almost to the middle of her back and an infectious smile, acknowledged Deiter with a nod and pressed a button on her console while picking up the phone.

"Mr. Deiter's here, sir," she said into the phone as though she were whispering into a lover's ear. "Yes, sir." She put down the instrument and motioned Deiter to follow her. They walked to the office door at the far end of the reception area and she knocked twice on the door and opened it to allow Deiter to enter. As he passed her, he noticed that she wore a distinctly pleasant perfume that matched the smile she gave him as he entered the room. Unconsciously, it made him nervous.

"Jack," General Henderson called out. "Come on in."

Deiter noticed that there was only his friend and Don Adams in the office. Henderson was standing next to Adams' desk. Adams, on the other hand, was sitting at his desk looking to Deiter like a pompous walrus. He wore a wrinkled brown tweed sport jacket with a limp red handkerchief stuffed in his breast pocket. Deiter's couldn't hide his dislike for Adams and he could tell that Henderson knew what he was thinking. Henderson rolled his eyes and looked up at the ceiling. Adams failed to take notice.

"Morning, Hank," Deiter said. He then looked back at Adams. Adams remained seated at his desk, but finally leaned forward, wheezing in the process, and extended his hand across the desk. Deiter took it, pumped it once and then dropped the plump, limp rag of a hand and plopped himself into one of two overstuffed green leather chairs that faced the Assistant to the Deputy Director. He next turned to Henderson and extended his hand smiling slightly. Henderson grasped the extended hand and squeezed it as though to say "mind your manners," and then took his seat in the other chair.

A thought crossed Deiter's mind. This man sitting in front of him was responsible for the first time that Rose left his life and now, somehow, he was involved the second time that Rose left him. Deiter recalled that, not long ago, he and Rose had discussed how and why they had failed in their attempt to meet again once her mission was over. They had planned it so that even if the "no-contact" rules of the CIA might try to prevent it, a definite place and time had been set up before she left Rome. Later, when her mission was extended, she had asked Adams to explain to Jack why she couldn't make the meeting. Adams lied when he told her that he had lost track of Deiter and knew nothing of his whereabouts. That led to almost twenty-five years of their being separated from each other. Last year, it had taken an official FBI inquiry to get Adams to provide Rose's location and status.

The reason for Deiter's hatred for Adams went even further. His parents had taken on new identities when they became deep agents. When they died, he had no ancestors and without the life he had planned with Rose, he now had no children…no descendants. He was a generation to himself, no past family and no future. Why this miserable excuse for a human being felt that he needed to control and interfere with other people's lives totally escaped Deiter's comprehension, and he despised the man for the misery he had caused in his life.

There was an awkward silence for a moment as all three men looked at each other. Adams then lowered his eyes and broke the silence by clearing his throat. "Ah, Jack…" he began, his voice a low, raspy and resonating whisper reminiscent of the *Godfather*, "As I said before, I offer my condolences. We think we have a positive lock on the main operative who placed that bomb." He paused to see if that elicited any reaction. Seeing none, he continued. "We have a definitive link with Iraq. It seems as though Saddam himself was in on the planning of this one. There was an American on the plane who had been on the UNSCOM Inspection Team. He was particularly disliked by the leadership of Iraq." He waited again before continuing. Deiter's eyes narrowed at the reminder of his loss, but he had expected that this would be the topic of conversation, so he remained calm. Adams continued.

"There is more to this than just a bombing of a plane with Americans aboard," he quickly added, "uh…as bad as that may be. Tomorrow, General Henderson will show you what we've found out about Saddam's plans to cause worldwide catastrophes with weapons that he currently possesses and with the means to deploy them." Adams picked up something that looked like a TV remote and pointed it at a panel in the wall. The panel slid aside, uncovering a large screen. He pushed another button and the scene of a building came into view. He started to flip from one slide to the next. Pictures of launch vehicles, stores of canisters of biological agents and chemicals flew by in rapid succession.

"We got these pictures from the Schweizer RG–8A; that plane can detect anything we tell it to and can even pinpoint people inside buildings. It was able to record the times and locations of transfer of nuclear and biological weapons to launch locations. We gave the information to the UN Special Commission's Inspection Team, but they haven't been able to get back into the country since then to check it out; it's doubtful that they would have been given a chance to search that building anyway. The Iraqis have the capability to cause a lot of destruction in the Middle East. Not only that, we now fully expect that they'll attempt to contaminate the water supplies of New York City and Los Angeles with anthrax to bring their war to the American mainland. If those are the only strikes, we'll be lucky. They can easily smuggle a nuclear weapon into New York or San Francisco on any tramp steamer they want to contract." He stopped and allowed that information to sink in. "This is a sick man, Jack."

"And what's the cure for a sick man?" asked Deiter, stroking his chin.

Adams paused and looked over at Henderson; he then looked back at Deiter, raised his massive eyebrows, scratched his mottled, gray-streaked beard and said, "You are Jack, you are." Deiter was unmoved. "There's a plan that's been in effect for some time," continued Adams. "We've just found out that our contact has initiated the sequence, and we can now take advantage of it. The window is short, though, and we can't waste time."

"To do what?" inquired Deiter.

"Assassinate the President of Iraq," came the quiet reply. Deiter was still unmoved and he knew that Adams could see it. "Saddam Hussein was the one person who we believe was directly responsible for what happened to Rose," he reminded Deiter.

From someone else, this would have been a battle cry, a rallying call, but from Adams, it fell hollow. Deiter understood that the President of Iraq was a dangerous man and that most probably, he was responsible for directing that the bomb be planted aboard Flight 63, but coming from Adams, somehow it lost some of its impact. Something else bothered Deiter, why after all this time was the government going back to the Kennedy days when it was open season on heads of state like Fidel Castro? Clinton, for all his indiscretions, had not seemed the sort to begin assassinating world leaders again.

"You're zeroing in on Saddam; why do you know it's him?" Deiter observed. "Why not bin Laden? Or Arrafat for that matter, they're all terrorists of one type or another. My personal choice is bin Laden; he and his al Qaida really are into that kind of thing. With his worldwide organization, he has contacts everywhere. Saddam is kinda stuck in Iraq after the '91 war." Deiter looked over at Henderson. "What do you think, Hank?" he asked.

"Jack, what I think personally is immaterial; this is a CIA initiative," Henderson replied. "Officially, no one else in the government knows anything about it…that goes for the President, as well. They have to be in a position to deny any knowledge of it. If all goes well, it'll look like a stroke of luck that Saddam was just in the wrong place at the wrong time, and it'll allow an opportunity for a more moderate government to assume control. This initiative is being justified under the policy section of the Congressional bill called the 'Iraq Liberation Act of 1998'. It may stretch the intent a bit, but not too much. I have some other information that I'll share with you tomorrow as to why it's got to be this way."

"Everything's in place," Adams interrupted," but we need a man on the ground in Baghdad to complete the last piece of the plan. That's where you come in."

"I don't speak Arabic," Deiter interjected.

"No, but you speak passable Russian and that's even better," Adams returned. "Your cover will be as the new Russian member of the UNSCOM Inspection Team. In fact, Iraq in a way helped us by demanding another Russian be placed on the team as a precondition to allowing the inspections to resume." He paused to chuckle to himself and then continued. "And, we already have arranged it. With the new 'Russian' member, the team plans to go back into Iraq six weeks from now; they'll be staying in Amman, Jordan and you can join them there. We plan to fly you and General Henderson to Rome for any last-minute briefings and then you go on to Amman alone. Henderson will fly to Kuwait to monitor the operation. The team will travel from Amman to Baghdad overland by convoy a couple of days after you join them."

The talk of posing as a Russian caused Deiter's thoughts to suddenly think back to the long hours over the past year that Rose had coached him in speaking and reading Russian. When he had found out about his heritage, he had been eager to find out more of it. He felt that it would be absolutely necessary for him to be conversant in the language of his ancestors in order to comprehend fully his ethnic background. She had been an expert and dedicated teacher, and he had learned quickly. It had been as though the language had been there all along waiting for a signal to be released into his conscious memory.

"I'm on my own, then?" Deiter asked.

"Yes, you call the shots. As General Henderson warned us, that's the way you wanted it, so that's the way we'll play it."

Deiter thought it over for a few moments and then looked over at Henderson with an unspoken question on his face. Henderson did a slight shrug as though to say, "It looks okay to me."

"All right, so far...so good," Deiter replied to Adams. "Tell me more."

Adams keyed the remote and the picture of a .45 caliber semiautomatic pistol came on the screen. Deiter's eyes rolled up at the ceiling, but he said nothing.

"What we have here, you may recognize," Adams continued.

"Oh yeah, I recognize it all right; it's a special M1911 ACP pistol that was ordered for FBI's exclusive use from the Springfield Armory. A damn good weapon; no other company could compete with it. This one's got a match barrel and bushing, Novak night sights, target trigger, and a lowered ejection port. It's also tough; it did great on the Abuse Test," Deiter interrupted.

"Absolutely," added Adams, "but it's been taken one step farther. A personal identification chip has been installed in it to prevent anyone except the owner from firing it."

"That technology isn't perfected yet," observed Deiter.

"Oh, you're right, of course, but thanks to the anti-gun lobby, most people think it is now state-of-the-art," Adams replied with a smirk.

"What's this got to do with the plan?" asked Deiter.

"You'll see. We'll come back to this a little later." Adams pressed a key on the remote and a scene of Saddam Hussein came onto the screen. He was smiling and was surrounded by what appeared to be equally smiling and adoring soldiers. "You'll notice something about this shot; the only one with a weapon there is the President, himself. Everybody else is unarmed. That is normal operations. He fears assassination so much that no one, not even a family member is allowed to be armed in his presence."

"Okay, I seem to remember reading that somewhere." Deiter left his remark as though it were a question.

"The weapon that I showed you earlier would be just the type of thing that would impress the dictator, particularly if it were presented to him as a gift from an adoring and politically connected friend."

"Makes sense. Who's that adoring friend? It sure as hell isn't me." Deiter responded.

Adams chuckled a second time. "No, I dare say. But he does have an admirer in this Country...Louis Farrakhan. The Reverend Farrakhan has already been approached and was very receptive to the idea."

"Farrakhan's working for you?"

Adams chortled at that suggestion, "Oh, no, nothing like that, but a contact whom he trusts, has been…uh, recruited, so to speak. The man's a bit weak minded, but useful. It seems that he made a mistake a while back and with a bit of convincing on our part, he was encouraged to play along. He isn't one of our people, no. We just have in our hands something he values very much…his freedom. Farrakhan thinks that the whole idea was thought up by his friend as a way to further ingratiate himself with the dictator and has no idea of our plan."

"So we get Saddam a gun that he can use to protect himself and that nobody else can fire, and we get Farrakhan to deliver it to him. Frankly, I don't see the benefit."

Adams was almost gleeful at this point as though he were allowing Deiter to be the straight man for his performance. "That's what everyone's going to think," Adams continued. He squirmed in his chair. "Have you kept up with the science of Global Positioning Systems or GPS?" Deiter didn't respond, but looked sideways towards Henderson, and Adams continued. "We can place an electronic chip in the weapon that will be tied into the power system that regulates the owner identification circuits. It will be undetectable in that circuit. We will know exactly where Saddam Hussein is any time we activate it." At this point, Adams was on the edge of his seat in anticipation of explaining the last piece of the plan. "When it looks like he is safely away from any highly populated area, we will launch cruise missiles to destroy him," he huffed.

"And where do I come into this pretty picture?" Deiter asked quietly.

"Farrakhan will depart the States with a version of the weapon that he has purchased privately. Once he's in Baghdad, our version of the weapon with the GPS beacon must be swapped for his copy. That's where you come into the picture. You won't be searched on your way into the country for two reasons; first, you'll be a member of the UNSCOM Inspection Team, but more importantly everyone will think that you're a sympathetic Russian placed on the team at the demand of the Iraqi Government."

Deiter didn't like it, but it all sounded like it might work. He supposed that he didn't like it because it was Adams' plan and it sounded brilliant; well, maybe devious would be a better description. But, he had to give the devil his due; it looked very good indeed. One thing bothered him, though, and he voiced it. "Why not substitute the gun here in the States rather than wait until it's in Iraq?"

"Good question, Jack, and the answer is simply that Farrakhan has already purchased the weapon and we don't know where it is. We think that you'll have a better chance to locate it in his hotel room in Baghdad than we will in the headquarters of the Nation of Islam. Also, we are precluded from operating within the borders of the United States; that's the domain of the FBI, as you'll recall." Deiter realized that the last part was a subtle and camouflaged dig at him for accusing the CIA of interference several years ago.

"I want to hear more about the fingerprint-activated gun and more about the GPS chip," Deiter said.

Adams squinted at the remote that he still had in his hand and pressed two buttons. On the screen, a commercial demonstration for the A236 video DSP chip manufactured by Oxford Micro Devices, started to play. It showed the application of biometrics to store in memory the fingerprints of one or several authorized users of the weapon. The user is identified immediately prior to firing. Further, the highly miniaturized user authorization system is built entirely into the weapon and requires no external radio, key or any other devices; a quick sweeping of one's finger across the fingerprint sensor frees the weapon to fire.

"Somehow, I'd still rather have a piece that works all the time. I've never given up my weapon and doubt I ever will. Nevertheless, it should impress someone who is as paranoid as Saddam," Deiter said, after the demonstration finished. "How about the GPS?"

"That's something I know you've had experience with," replied Adams. "We've come up with a more modern approach then the one you remember…and the beacon is, of course, a much simpler one. When activated by a specifically modulated frequency, it transmits a brief signal that can be detected by a monitor. It also transmits its precise location as determined by satellite triangulation. Each of four cruise missiles will be modified with a transmitter and monitor to periodically interrogate and home in on that signal and nothing else."

Deiter contemplated the plan and its possibility of success. It seemed feasible. The sticking point was getting the modified weapon switched in Baghdad. That was his responsibility. So, it seemed as though the whole plan did center around him. Okay, he thought to himself, as long as I'm in charge, I'll play the game.

"I'll need an in-depth cover; history, family, education, references, that kind of thing." Deiter said in answer to Adams' unspoken question. "I'll also need someone who's been on the team for a long time who'll recognize me as an 'old friend' from college days, or something along those lines, and he has to make it look good. I want to be given every bit of credibility. I can't take a chance that someone will spot me as a plant."

"Considerate it done," replied Adams quickly. "That's easy."

"I'll need to stay at the same hotel as Farrakhan; can you do that?"

Adams thought for a moment. "It'll be arranged, somehow. Usually the inspection team stays together at the same hotel, one that the Iraqi government strongly suggests. I think our contact at the Nation of Islam may be able to influence where they end up staying."

"I want to have firepower with me too. That'll mean getting it by the border and any checkpoints I may run into."

"The gun that you'll switch will be inside a piece of UNSCOM nuclear radiation detection equipment. We can also put something additional in there for your own protection. The team usually keeps their equipment with them in the hotel rooms to make sure it's not compromised or destroyed. You can get access to it whenever you need to."

"The gun needs to be an exact replica of the original; I assume that can be arranged. Do you know the serial number?"

"Their civilian version of the weapon has a serial number of CRG 169. We have one of the original batch of 258 that were ordered for the FBI; it was stamped FBI 169. We re-stamped it before we implanted the chip. A pretty good job, if I do say so."

"I certainly hope so," Deiter muttered under his breath.

"We've already started building your cover. It should be completed by late this week. Farrakhan is scheduled to arrive in Baghdad on Saturday, November 20th. The switch needs to be done within 24 hours. You need to be well established by that time so you can have a comfortable run of the hotel facilities. I suggest that you leave here no later than the middle of November for Rome. The inspection team is now scheduled to reenter Iraq next Friday. I expect you'll fly to Amman a couple of days before that to join the team. We'll have your double fly from Moscow to Rome just in case they check up on you. It wouldn't do for a Russian to originate his travel in Rome. You can switch places with him at the hotel."

Deiter tried to think of anything else that he might require Adams to set up for him, but his mind went blank. He had to assume that everything had been thought of to reinforce his cover and the mission's success. He looked over at Henderson and raised his left eyebrow as though to pose a question.

"I can't think of anything else at this point to cover, Jack," Henderson replied to the unstated question.

Deiter nodded his head and stood up. "Call me when the cover is set up and the documentation is ready," he said to Adams. "I'll need some time to rehearse."

"I'll let you know as soon as it's ready," Adams replied.

Both Deiter and Henderson left the office without a formal good-bye to Adams. The two men did nod and smile at the secretary on their way out to the elevator, but nothing was exchanged between them until they had left the reception lobby and were walking down the pathway to the visitor VIP parking area.

Hank's black limousine was waiting and the driver was holding the rear door open for him. Deiter finally spoke. "Do you think everything is on the up and up?" he asked.

"I have no reason to think otherwise," Hank responded. "Why?"

"I never have trusted Adams."

For a moment, Henderson almost told his friend about what the tavern owner in Spain had told him about Rose's mysterious companion who sounded like a reasonable description of Adams. He rejected the idea as pure speculation and probably counterproductive in view of Deiter's obvious dislike of Adams.

"I'll be in touch, Hank," Deiter said as he offered his hand.

"Right, Jack...I'll give you a call early tomorrow. Oh, Adams did tell me to ask you to keep a low profile until this thing's over. He was concerned that somehow, someone might get a picture of you and the press would want to publish it. That would put you in danger. He said that no mention that Rose was on that plane should get out, including you or anyone else contacting her parents.

Deiter frowned. "I was going to call them this afternoon. Rose wanted to surprise them by showing up for a visit. She intentionally didn't tell them she was coming. I think they deserve to know that their only daughter is…" He couldn't finish it.

"It'll only be three weeks at the most, Jack; then you can contact them in person."

Deiter still didn't like it, but he could understand the reasoning. He felt his anger starting to burn so he just nodded, turned on his heel and walked over to his Jaguar. He didn't have a plan for the rest of the day, so he decided to go back to Prince Street. He suddenly felt exhausted. Something about all this still bothered him and he had to think it out. Besides, it would be well to get his estate in order; he didn't know what the next few weeks would hold for him, but it wouldn't be like having a safe desk job somewhere. He also had to prepare something to notify Rose's family…just in case he didn't make it back either.

Chapter Three

The Pentagon

125 Prince Street
Alexandria, Virginia
Thursday morning, October 7, 1999

Deiter had repeated the routine of the previous morning and was sipping his coffee at the dining room table while reading his newspaper, when he heard the phone ring once. He assumed correctly that Conley would have answered it. In a moment, his assistant walked through the doorway to the kitchen holding a cordless telephone in his hand.

"It's General Henderson, sir," he said in a hushed tone.

Deiter held out his hand for the phone, thanked Conley and cleared his throat. "Uh, good morning, Hank."

"Sleep well?" returned Henderson and then adding without waiting for a reply. "Can you make it in to the Pentagon this morning, Jack? I have something that might explain some of the 'why' questions you had yesterday…both spoken and unspoken."

"Sure, what time?"

"Nine."

"You got it. Where are you located?"

"I'll have my aide, Captain Wilson, meet you at the main entrance. You can't miss the red hair. You can park the Jag on the plaza just outside; I'll make arrangements."

"Fine, I'll see you at nine sharp."

Deiter hung up the phone just as Conley brought him his breakfast.

After having eaten a leisurely breakfast and read the newspaper, Deiter put on his overcoat and went out onto Prince Street. He clicked the button on his key ring and the Jaguar responded by unlocking its doors. He climbed in behind the steering wheel and locked his seat belt across him. It was almost eight–thirty and he knew that it would take almost a half-hour at this time in the morning to get to the Pentagon. The Jag roared into life and he swung it around the corner heading back up King Street. Traffic was moderate and it wasn't more than fifteen minutes before he turned right off Interstate 395 towards the Mall entrance to the Pentagon. He slowed as he hit the plaza area next to the main entrance and after a short conversation with the guard at the plaza entrance, he slid the Jag into an empty parking place at the extreme end of the restricted parking area. Deiter locked the car and proceeded across the plaza to the large main entrance to the Pentagon.

Deiter walked through the large double doors and came upon a busy reception area with an oval shaped reception desk. He looked around at the numerous civilian guards in dark blue uniforms, but none of them seemed ready to be of any real assistance. No help here, he said to himself. Hank had said his aide would be there. He didn't see any Army Captains about with red hair. As he was about to head into the open hallway to scout the way up to Henderson's office by himself, he heard a very pleasant high-pitched voice behind him.

"Mr. Deiter? Mr. Deiter?" the voice repeatedly questioned.

Deiter turned around and at first didn't see anyone. He then looked down to see a short, very attractive young female Army Captain with long dark red hair. She was looking up at him expectantly.

"Yes, I'm Jack Deiter," he responded.

The woman seemed to wilt as she realized that she had finally contacted her prey.

"Thank goodness, I'm Captain Janice Wilson, sir, General Henderson's aide. I'm here to escort you up to his office," she said with a very large smile.

"I'm happy to see you, Captain," Deiter replied, also smiling, "I wasn't really looking forward to the great safari into the bowels of the Pentagon trying to find Hank's hideaway."

The Captain laughed in a liquid, lilting way that reminded him of Rose and she said somewhat seductively, "You can follow me, sir. I promise not to get you lost." Then she winked and turned to head for the door to a set of stairs.

Both of Deiter's black eyebrows raised up at the same time. "She winked at me!" he mused to himself and then smiled broadly. Deiter followed her and as they walked up the stairs to the next floor, he noticed that the tight fitting slacks showed off the excellent physical condition of the modern Army. He also stored in his "to be used later" memory files that his friend Hank seemed to be surrounding himself with nice looking women. There had to be something there he could use to plague the General with at a later date. He chuckled to himself.

Upon reaching the third floor, Captain Wilson turned left to head towards one of the inner rings of the Pentagon. The walls begun to shed their green paint and were replaced by walnut paneling. Paintings appeared, hung inside the panels. Deiter could tell that he was entering the inner sanctum of the military structure of the country. They approached a guard post with a Military Policeman dressed in a Class A, green uniform standing beside a small desk. The Captain flashed her identification, which was on a cord around her neck, and indicated that she was Deiter's escort and the two of them were passed on by with little fanfare. They had only gone a short distance when she turned right into a paneled doorway. The gold raised printing on the right side of the door read, "Office of Army Intelligence." A pretty civilian receptionist hardly looked up when Deiter and the Captain walked in. Jan Wilson headed straight for an office door on the other side of the reception area. Emblazoned in embossed brass lettering on the walnut panel was "Assistant Deputy Director, Army Intelligence." Under it in smaller letters was "Brigadier General Henry H. Henderson."

"Jack, come on in," Henderson said as the door was opened. The Captain held the door as Deiter went inside and closed it behind him leaving the two men alone inside.

"Quite a place you have here, Hank." Deiter said looking around, his hands in his pants pockets.

"Don't start now, Jack," Henderson replied holding his hand out to Deiter, a broad smile on his face.

Deiter returned the smile and took the outstretched hand. He looked around and sat in one of the two overstuffed leather chairs in front of Henderson's large mahogany desk. Behind and to the right side of the general were two flags trimmed with gold fringe. One was the national colors and the other a red flag with a single white star in it, Hank's personal flag to signify his rank. A round plaque about two feet across with the seal of the Army Intelligence Corps emblazoned on it was directly behind the desk. The darkly paneled room had numerous plaques and memorabilia on the walls and a mahogany cabinet on which was placed a set of finely bound books between West Point bookends; an original 21 inch Remington bronze of "Rattlesnake" was at the opposite end.

"What's really going on, Hank?" Deiter asked.

"Care for coffee?"

"Yeah."

Henderson pressed a button on his desk and ordered two coffees.

"Something doesn't ring true about all this, and I think you know it, Hank."

"What you probably don't have an appreciation for right now, Jack, is the status of our combat readiness," Henderson started. "Let me show you something. Here's a statement that was made before the House of Representatives' Military Readiness Subcommittee of the Committee on National Security by Colonel John Rosenberger in February of this year. I've known John for a number of years now, and he's the best man I know of to give a realistic look at our readiness to go to war." Henderson handed Deiter two typewritten pages and sat back to wait while his friend finished reading it.

Deiter took the document and sat back in his chair. The statement started off with a description of the Colonel's qualifications and experience in the Army. It then concluded that from his observations, the United States Army currently lacked the ability to perform in combat. Most of the reasons given were due directly to lack of funding, the use of combat troops on "peacekeeping" missions, reductions of force, but not mission, and generally the cause of the problem was identified as the incompetence of the Executive Branch of the government, the Presidency in particular. Deiter read on:

"The reason for this decline in war fighting ability is not elusive in my view. What I observe at the National Training Center is a great Army, filled with terrific soldiers, suffering from an inability to train at every level with the battle-focus and frequency necessary to develop and sustain its full combat

potential. What I see is an Army reeling from the effects of decisions imposed upon it externally and internally: a sustained shortage of leaders and soldiers; high personnel turbulence created by an imbalance of force structure and national requirements; less-experienced leaders produced by a decreasing amount of time to serve in critical leader development positions; insufficient money at every level of command to train as a team of teams at the frequency necessary to sustain combat proficiency at home station; expanding peacekeeping operations which quickly erode war fighting knowledge, skill, and ability, creating a growing generation of young leaders who don't know how to fight as members of a combined arms team; increasing numbers of soldiers diverted from combat training to perform installation support services, back filling cuts in the civilian work force and severe cuts in contractual support; and an absence of time and opportunity to focus, in a predictable fashion, on battle-focused training."

Deiter looked up at Henderson and observed, "We've got too many 'police' type missions and no real time for combat training. You can't do both. Besides, soldiers make lousy policeman, don't they? When you're taught to damage property and kill people, it's hard to develop any real people skills."

"You got that right," the General responded softly. "The only part of the Army that's been saved is the Special Forces and that's only because they were Jack Kennedy's favorites and the current administration knows that they'd be castrated if they fucked with them."

Deiter smiled at his friend's candor and went back to reading the script of the testimony. The Colonel's testimony ended with the following admonition:

> *"Mr. Chairman, speaking for myself, it is a hard thing to watch my Army, the Army that delivered the outcome of Desert Storm, the Army I and many others sacrificed so much to create from the ashes of the Vietnam War, slowly deteriorate from the conditions we've been compelled to endure the past seven years. Anything this Committee and Congress can do to help us reverse these conditions would be welcome and exciting news for the troops. I thank you for the opportunity to speak to you today and I stand ready to answer the committee's questions."*

Deiter put down the papers and looked up at Henderson. "What are you trying to say, Hank? It looks like the Army can't fight its way out of a wet paper bag."

"That's pretty much it. I'm not much of a politician, but we've been handed a bunch of shit details in the last few years. The high command has been handpicked by Clinton and they and the other hand wringing, liberal assholes have led the Army that we had finally built up after Vietnam down a pathway to destruction. None of them know a Goddamn thing about the military and they quite frankly couldn't care less about it. Jack, we're in a helluva fix in the world today in general. The bottom line is that we couldn't pull off another Gulf War right now. Even if all of the rest of the countries that helped us at that time were to send in the exact number of troops and support, **we** would fall flat on our ass. When you have a draft-dodging womanizer in charge, it's real hard being a soldier."

Deiter quietly let his friend rail on; he knew from experience that there are evil or conscienceless people out there who would always take advantage of the weakness' they find in others. This, he also realized was particularly dangerous when it came to leaders at the national level. He respected the frustration of his friend and knew the comments he had just heard came from the heart and were never to be repeated to anyone else. Like Colonel Rosenberger, it would mean the end of Hank's career for such criticisms to be heard in public.

"Jack, as much as I personally find the assassination of a head of state distasteful, there is no alternative at this point. I need to tell you why so you'll understand. Here is the joint intelligence evaluation as to the current ability of Iraq," Henderson continued as he handed Deiter a bright orange folder with the words TOP SECRET across the front. "We're convinced that they currently possess at least five nuclear weapons, each of them with at least a twenty-kiloton capacity according to the number of Russian weapons that can't be located or are unaccounted for. Add to that a goodly quantity of military grade VX and anthrax, and the delivery means with which to destroy the state of Israel at least and extend this terrorism to the rest of the world, the US and Great Britain in particular, and we've got a problem. You do realize that if Saddam did launch a first strike, and I mean a deadly strike, say on Israel, the rest of the Moslem countries wouldn't lift a finger and we'd have to go it alone…if we could."

He let Deiter digest what he had said and then went on. "Saddam Hussein has no qualms about destroying his own people or his own country; he has no qualms about destroying the rest of the world either. I'd almost give a metaphysical characteristic to what we know about him. Nothing that we know of accurately describes him. To compare him to Hitler or Stalin or Mao is only to compare the numbers of human beings who were eventually slaughtered under their directions; it doesn't fully describe the person. Sociopathic, I guess, is a good clinical diagnosis, but very dangerously so. Whereas someone like bin Laden is a zealot and rich enough to finance terror, always a bad combination, Saddam borders on the edge of reality; if his actions promote a worldwide conflagration, it wouldn't bother him at all. That's what we're dealing with, Jack. He is an egotistical madman of mammoth proportion who grew up as an assassin himself."

"And what about Osama bin Laden?" Deiter asked. "Individual acts of terrorism are his stock in trade; he and Arrafat are of the same ilk. I thought Saddam liked to send in his goon army to invade other countries to add to his empire, while bin Laden is the one who delights in making simple terror rapes on the innocent to exercise his egotistical will."

"Wait until you see the rest of what I've got," Henderson replied. "I don't necessarily disagree with you, though. That guy's dangerous too." He thought for a moment and then, looking away from Deiter, he added, "Unfortunately, we know that they've combined efforts, and we may be in just one helluva fix." Henderson hesitated again and then turning back around, he leaned forward to continue. "Jack, terrorism is being given lip service by this administration, and that includes the likes of bin Laden. Hell, the Commander-in-Chief himself has entertained pro-Hamas, and other pro-terror Islamic groups at the White House for the purposes of raising campaign cash. What in God's name are we expected to do?" He then answered his own question. "We...the intelligence community and the military have got to act before it's too late. The first step is Saddam, the next will be to root out every friggin' terrorist cell and destroy its leadership and then every one of its operators."

Henderson stood up and walked over to the window. When he turned around, the look on his face disturbed Deiter. "Jack, what I'm about to tell you hasn't yet been published anywhere. I know you remember the 1993 bombing of the World Trade Center. And you probably were aware of the assertion that the mastermind was a 27-year-old Pakistani by the name of Abdul Basit. Well, just recently, we were able to confirm that Jim Fox, the FBI's chief investigator at the time was absolutely right. It wasn't Basit; it was Ramzi Yousef, an Iraqi intelligence agent. We found Yousef's fingerprints on Basit's file in the Kuwaiti police headquarters."

"How'd that happen?"

"The how is easy to explain. Yousef must have had possession of those files during the Gulf War when Iraq occupied Kuwait. That's the only explanation. These files were doctored by Iraqi intelligence so that Yousef was able to assume Basit's identity. How could a man in just three years grow four inches, put on 35 to 40 pounds, develop a deformed eye, develop smaller ears and a smaller mouth, age substantially, and go from a computer programmer to being computer illiterate? What that means is that it wasn't Basit, but Yousef who planned the attack on the World Trade Center and it was Iraq, not some radical student who was the really responsible. This is just a continuation of Saddam's war against the United States and I'm convinced that the Clinton administration knows that, too. Flight 63 was just his next attack on the United States."

Deiter shrugged his understanding and began to flip through the material that he had been handed. There were pictures and bills of laden and eyewitness accounts and confirmations of incidents. It all added up to a very dangerous situation for the whole world.

"What about the other alternative?" Deiter asked.

"Which one?" Henderson countered."

"What about financing an opposition to Saddam? You know, setting up some ambitious or begrudged demagogue to stir up a revolution and let the Iraqis solve the problem for us. There are several that come to mind. General Najib al-Salhi or General Fawzi Al Shamari are two favorites. If you need a civilian, then the head of the Iraqi National Congress, Ahmad Chalabi could be tagged."

"That's been thought of already and after a great deal of research, we rejected it. I'll tell you why. The first two are mavericks from the Iraqi military, who might fit the bill, but they need to be inside the country and they're not; neither is Chalabi. Anyone we 'choose' will look like a US puppet and won't be accepted by the Iraqi population." Henderson paused for a moment, walked over to his desk and sat down. He leaned forward with his elbows on the desk, his hands clasped together in front of him and his mouth buried in his fists. Henderson considered just how much he could tell Deiter. Finally, he said. "Just recently, we've concluded that any attempt to bolster a challenge to Saddam would be totally useless and probably only end up giving him another propaganda victory. Any opposition must come from a coalition of the various minority sectors and definitely not from inside the ruling Baath Party. Since the Gulf War, Saddam has purified his party AND his family. Any rumor of a challenge within his group would be detected immediately and eliminated. The various minorities don't have anything in common except their fear and hatred of Saddam; that's not enough to build a real coalition for a responsible future for Iraq. With Saddam gone, there would be an opportunity for one of the three you mentioned to return to Iraq and form an opposition to the Baath Party in the leadership void.

There's something else too. Our 'friends' in the rest of the Arab world don't really want to weaken the power of any potential ally against the Iranians. This is still an Arab-Persian mutual dislike problem that's just as real as the Moslem-Israeli problem and has lasted thousands of years."

"So, back to Plan A," Deiter replied with a wry smile. "What about Iraq's threat internationally? Just how bad is it?"

"Glad you brought that up, Jack," Henderson responded handing another file to Deiter, "Earlier this year, Dick Butler, who was chief of the UNSCOM inspection team, wrote this letter about an Iraqi chemical plant that was converted by Saddam from a vaccine production facility for livestock to a biological warfare plant. Large quantities of the biological warfare agent botulinum toxin were produced, and research was conducted on viral agents including camelpox, enterovirus 70, and rotavirus. That was in 1995. Iraq admitted to that after being confronted by the evidence. Even though the team supervised the destruction of 28 pieces of equipment identified by Iraq as having been used in the production of the biological warfare agents, 40 major pieces, originally imported for the production of hoof-and-mouth disease vaccine remained because they hadn't specifically been linked to agent production. We're quite positive that they're still producing agents and the pictures in that file prove it."

"Anything else?" Deiter asked quietly, as he leaned back in his chair.

"Yes, one more thing," Henderson added, picking up another folder. He hesitated before handing it to Deiter. "You have the right to know this."

Deiter took the file and opened it. Inside was a copy of a letter from the Iraqi high command outlining a plot to seek retribution on a former member of the UNSCOM Inspection Team who uncovered the information about Saddam's treachery. The woman who was his contact within the Iraqi government was going to be with the UNSCOM man on Flight 63 from Madrid to Newark on October 2nd. A special team was dispatched from Baghdad to Amman, Jordan and on to Madrid to arrange for planting a bomb on the plane. Both a copy of the original document and its translation were the first documents in the file. Deiter looked at Henderson with a look of incredulity on his face.

"Where the hell did you get this?" he asked.

"Adams. This stuff is CIA developed. We don't have the contacts that they have."

67

"Do you know who they got to do it? Set the bomb, that is?"

"While it could have been anyone. There's been a helluva lot of those guys being trained at bin Laden's terror camps lately. We've got their pictures and their names; they were Iraqis."

Deiter went through the rest of the file. There were still-shots of video tapes made in the baggage area of the Madrid airport that showed when and how the bomb was planted in the luggage to be loaded onto the flight. There were three black and white still shots of the two men who deposited the bomb. One was acting as lookout and the other was setting the device and closing the top of a large suitcase. They were then identified in additional documents as the agents who were dispatched from Iraq.

The last item was the initial results of an investigation as to the cause of the loss of Flight 63. Although the black boxes were never located, the last communications with the flight indicated that an explosion had occurred in the forward hold of the aircraft and that there was no response to the controls. Apparently the smaller explosion triggered a massive explosion of the fuel cells. The passengers knew nothing until they were incinerated. Finally, he came to a passenger list that listed the two people who were the targets of the terrorists. Deiter quickly scanned the rest of the list and stopped at the entry that read "Seat 6-A, Rose Deiter – USA."

Deiter slowly closed the file and handed it back to the General. He stood up and walked over to the window. Outside he could see the brightly-colored trees of the park in the center ring of the Pentagon below him. There was a woman standing next to a bench talking with a man. She reminded him of Rose. Deiter was thankful that his friend was letting him have a few moments in silence to sort out his emotions. He and Hank seemed to always know when either of them needed something. He guessed that's what made them like brothers. The words he had read on the last sheet of paper kept coming back to him...Rose Deiter – USA. In some way, it was final; it was closure. Up until then it had been only a bad dream. Now, he couldn't just wake up, reach over and touch her; now it was final. He turned around and looked at his friend sitting there sadly staring into space. He shook his head again in total disbelief.

"I'm sorry, Jack," Henderson said, in reply to the query on his friend's face, "but you needed to see what was in that file. I got it from the CIA yesterday. It was hard for me too."

Deiter cleared his throat and asked hoarsely, "Where do we go from here, Hank?"

"Why, to Baghdad, of course," his friend replied.

Ted Colby

Chapter Four

Setting the Lure

Cairo, Egypt
Friday afternoon, November 20th, 1998
One year earlier

The Sheraton Heliopolis towered seventeen stories over tree-lined Uruba Street in the Heliopolis section of Cairo. The view from the seventh floor gave a spectacular panorama of the ancient city. The Honorable Minister Louis Farrakhan stood looking out of the window at the view smiling. This afternoon, he would meet once more with Iraq's Deputy Prime Minister Tariq Aziz at the Arab League's headquarters in Cairo. With him would be the League's Secretary-General Esmat Abdel Meguid. During the meeting, he would take the opportunity to reiterate his call for a lifting of the UN sanctions against Iraq and extensive restitution by the United States and Great Britain to compensate for the chaos they have criminally wreaked on that sovereign country. As before, he will call it terrorism by a much larger country and military force against a struggling third world country. Among the long list of topics he hoped to discuss with Aziz was a proposal made to him by his friend Abdel Kadan Muhammad to present the President of Iraq with a very special handgun from the Nation of Islam. The weapon was designed to preclude it from being used against its owner and so further protected Saddam from harm.

71

Aziz would be able to advise him if this would be acceptable to the President and make the proper arrangements. If so, they would purchase the weapon and customize it for presentation. First, he would confirm his third visit to Baghdad next year in November or December and his hopes to talk directly with Saddam Hussein.

A quiet serenity came over him as he stood there looking out over that ancient city. Farrakhan started to reminisce on his life and tried to bring the present into perspective. He was born Louis Eugene Walcott on May 11, 1933, in Roxbury, Massachusetts and was reared in a highly disciplined and spiritual household. He was raised solely by his mother and had learned early in life the value of work, responsibility and intellectual development. He recalled how she had taught them about the plight of black people and about their struggle for freedom, justice and equality. Even before he was six years old, he was given a violin and began years of formal training totally financed by his mother's hard work as a seamstress and housekeeper. By the time he was 13, he had played with the Boston College Orchestra and the Boston Civic Symphony. The next year, he won the Ted Mack Amateur Hour. He also earned an athletic scholarship as a sprinter and attended Winston-Salem Teacher's College in North Carolina where he delighted in and excelled in English.

It was February 1955, he recalled, that was a turning point in his life. After listening to a talk by Elijah Muhammad, he joined the Nation of Islam and left a promising career in music. Within three months of the death of Malcolm X ten years later, Farrakhan was appointed by Elijah Muhammad to Temple No. 7 in New York City. Later, he was to assume the leadership of the Nation of Islam and bring it to a position of respect and admiration. His success was evidenced by mosques and study groups in over 80 cities in America and Great Britain, and a mission in Ghana devoted to the teachings of the Honorable Elijah Muhammad. He understood well that it was he who was the catalyst that had projected the Nation of Islam into its prominent role on the national and international stage. He had fully taken the tenets of the Muslim faith to heart and in turn he had been well rewarded.

Farrakhan's thoughts were interrupted by a knock on the door. He heard his bodyguard go to the door and allow someone to enter. Finished with his reverie, he was just turning around when his friend greeted him with a question.

"Louis, are we all set?" asked Abdel.

Farrakhan smiled and welcomed his friend by placing his arm around the man's shoulder. "Yes. So I'm told, we're to get a private meeting with Aziz and I'll ask him about your idea for a gift to the President. You are planning on being there, aren't you?"

"I'd better. I've got all of the design details in case Aziz wants to know the more technical stuff."

"I'll take the opportunity afterwards to talk to the press. We won't mention anything about the weapon, though. That's better kept secret until we get to Baghdad next year."

"Whatever you think is best, Louis. You know better about these kinds of things."

Both men sat down and discussed the other topics they wanted to bring up at the meeting. Abdel realized that Louis had known and trusted him since they were very young men and still had the names they were given at birth. Abdel, on the other hand, felt uneasy about his role in what was to be a purposeful deception of his friend.

Abdel fully suspected that Saddam might be insane and that a more rational leader should be allowed to rule Iraq. That's what the men from the CIA had told him when they questioned him about some of the transactions he had made. He never really understood why they were involved. He would have expected the FBI, maybe, but not those people. They scared him; they told him that unless he did what they wanted, he would spend the rest of his life in prison. He believed them. People like them operate outside the regular law-enforcement systems. But then, what they wanted him to do wasn't all that terrible; in a way it sounded almost patriotic.

In any event, it was difficult to understand his friend's continuing relationship with people like Iraq's Saddam Hussein and Libya's Moammar Gadhafi. He didn't dare question him about it, of course; to do so might bring his loyalty into question. In the long run, Abdel thought, it would be better for their cause and the world if Saddam were replaced. Louis would never ever guess the truth and there was no way of him finding out. In the end, the weapon would be destroyed and no trace of his deception would ever be known. More important, they wouldn't put him in jail.

At three–forty–five that afternoon, the cream colored Mercedes limousine was waiting at the hotel main entrance. Abdel and three bodyguards accompanied Farrakhan as they left the building and slipped into the large plush car. It was only a five-minute ride to the Headquarters of the Arab League, and they arrived with ten minutes to spare. At the main entrance of the League, Farrakhan and his entourage were met by the Secretary-General's senior aide and escorted into an elevator and up to the third floor. One bodyguard was left in the lobby and the other two stayed with the limo. Although he had seen the building before, Farrakhan still marveled at its design. He understood that simplicity itself often speaks of great power and wealth. The reception area of the Secretary-General was simple without all the trappings and decorations of the Western culture. There was no mistaking the wealth that created the structure, however. The senior aide asked the two men to wait and knocked on the large ebony paneled double doors leading to the inner office of the Secretary-General. He went in and closed the door behind him. In less than a minute, the door opened again and the aide nodded to the waiting pair and beckoned them to come in.

As Farrakhan walked into the large room, he could see two figures sitting in a small conversation area at the far end. There were four chairs around a small coffee table. Deputy Prime Minister Aziz sat on the left and Secretary-General Meguid on the right. The newcomers were escorted across the large empty expanse of the room and toward the seated men. As they approached, both men stood up and smiled. It was Aziz who first showed recognition of the Honorable Minister Farrakhan. He approached him and the two embraced briefly.

"My friend," Aziz said, holding the taller man at arm's length and looking intently at him. "It has been almost a year since we met in Baghdad. Tell me, how is your health? We heard that you were not well."

"I am feeling fine now," replied Farrakhan. "Thank you for your concern." He then shook hands with the Secretary-General and introduced Abdel Kadan Muhammad as a long time friend and confidant. The four sat and a servant brought coffee and placed it on the table. When the man had left, it was Aziz who opened the conversation. The list of topics that Farrakhan had committed to memory were addressed one by one. Finally it was time to discuss his visit to Baghdad next year and the proposed gift.

"I'd like very much to meet with the President on my next trip to Baghdad," Farrakhan began with a confident smile. The discussion had been going well, and it looked as though this would be the time to broach that topic. "My friend Abdel Kadan has suggested an intriguing gift that I would like to present at that time to solidify our friendship and concern for the President and the people of Iraq." Aziz smiled, but said nothing. Farrakhan motioned to Abdel who opened a small thin leather folder he was carrying and selected several sheets of paper.

"We notice that the President usually carries a sidearm," he began. "There is a technology that now exists in the United States that would allow such a weapon to be fired only by its owner and no one else. Also, a semiautomatic has been developed exclusively for the Federal Bureau of Investigations that is the most accurate and yet reliable one available anywhere. We can have it modified to accept a fingerprint identification sensor that, after the President has programmed it, will allow only him to fire it." While he talked, he presented the full color pictures and specifications of the weapon to the Deputy Prime Minister.

"Very impressive," remarked Aziz. "The President, as I'm sure you are aware, appreciates unique weapons of all kinds. I think that he would be very pleased. I cannot totally guarantee that he would be available for a personal meeting, but let's see what the political climate is at the time." He paused to look at the papers once more and then continued. "I assume that I may have these? It may help make such a meeting possible. When do you propose such a trip?"

"At his convenience, of course." replied Farrakhan. "It will take us perhaps six months to complete the modification and obtain the weapon. Perhaps next September or October would be a possibility."

"I will let you know within a few weeks," replied Aziz, smiling. "Now, I must talk with the Secretary-General in private. It has been good to see you once more. I do hope that your third visit to Baghdad will be possible next year, and I will argue your case to the President personally."

Farrakhan and Abdel stood up and shook hands with the Secretary-General and Aziz and left the room. They didn't speak until they had left the League Headquarters and were in their limousine heading back to the hotel. Farrakhan was pleased at the outcome of the meeting and leaning toward Abdel quietly said, "I think that your idea went over very well. In fact, I think that it should guarantee a personal meeting with Saddam Hussein next year; thank you, my friend."

Abdel smiled and shrugged modestly. The lure seemed to have been just what was needed; that part of the plan had now been placed in effect. All that was needed now is for their visit to be approved and the gun delivered to Saddam. Abdel sighed and leaned back into the soft cream colored leather of the limousine.

Chapter Five

All Roads lead to Rome

Fort George Meade, Maryland
National Security Agency
Tuesday morning, November 16, 1999

The sleek silver unmarked Boeing 727 sat patiently waiting for the last of the passengers to arrive. It was parked on the tarmac some three hundred feet from the gate of the Headquarters of the National Security Agency at Fort George G. Meade, Maryland. The CIA doesn't like to draw attention to its transportation system, much less advertise it. Using the NSA strip for this kind of operation appeared to be the prudent course of action. It was nearly ten o'clock when a black stretch limo passed by the entrance gate and took the connecting road leading to the ramp area. It sped by three smaller planes tethered to the tarmac and finally came to a stop in front of the hulking Boeing 727.

Two men climbed out of the car and quickly clambered up the stairway ramp that was placed against the front door of the airplane. A uniformed chauffeur hustled four pieces of luggage from the limo to a waiting crew member at the bottom of the ramp. Once inside the plane, Deiter saw that a young blond woman was waiting for them. On seeing him she quickly came up to him and threw her arms around his neck and buried her face in his shoulder. He put his arms around his friend and held her for a moment.

"Jack, I'm so sorry. Hank told me about Rose," she whispered.

"Thanks, Charlie," he replied, holding her back to look at her. "I'm glad you were able to come with us. You're the only one I know of except Rose who knows Russian like a native. Besides, this mission is for Rose and she would be happy to know you were here."

"I know that, Jack," she answered placing her hands on his shoulders and looking into his eyes, "but you do know realize this isn't going to be any vacation. Between now and when you leave for Amman, you're going to spend a lot of time perfecting your Russian, and I'm here to make sure that you sound like the real McCoy, if that's the right comparison. I'm certainly not going to take a chance on you getting jailed or something worse in that horrible place just because your Russian sounds phony." She pushed him back and smiled at him.

"Thank you very much," Deiter replied in Russian, returning the smile.

"Good for starters, kid, but until we get there, we speak only in Russian, unless you need to talk to Hank, of course," She added with a smirk and nodding to the tall man who was stuffing a piece of luggage into the overhead rack. The passengers quickly found seats and settled down for the long journey.

For about two years, "Charlie," Charlotte Ann Waggner, had worked for Jonathan Banks, Inc. a Washington-based think tank. It was better known as JBI, and had been the mainstay of the intelligence community for almost a decade. It had achieved a considerable reputation as being one of the finest firms of its kind in the country, if not the world. Charlie was tops in her field, which was the translation and analysis of documents written in Russian. Recently, she had worked on a case with Deiter, Rose and Henderson involving Soviet deep agents. Her father, up until last year, had been a senior staff member of the United States Senate Intelligence Committee and had been with the Senate for over three decades. He also was a lifelong friend of Jonathan Banks, the founder of JBI.

Everyone seemed to be charmed by Charlie. She was a confident, green-eyed, pretty blond who was absolutely in charge of her life. At 5 foot 5 inches and 115 pounds, she was, at the grand old age of 35 years, firm, athletic, strong, while not muscular, at the prime of her life; the world was a challenge, and she was intellectually brilliant...but of course she knew all that. Her routine at the gym kept her in top shape, which was just what she considered perfect, 36–26–36. A female with masculine interests, she could be one of the guys and yet alluring at the same time. She kept her blond hair cut short; it fit her lifestyle better. Her high cheekbones and a pretty slender nose that was almost on the verge of being turned up, were inherited from her mother, but her straight and sensitive lips, which seemed to always have a hint of a smile or smirk, as though she was hiding some seductive secret and about to let it out in delight, were copies of her father's.

As the only child, Charlie was both doted upon and challenged by her parents. She had attended private schools while growing up; she was a Girl Scout, which she enjoyed, and played soccer throughout her secondary school days. At George Washington University, she became a gymnast and placed first in overall competition during her junior year, but had to drop out after breaking her left arm in an unfortunate fall during practice the first part of her senior year. In compensation, her father taught her to fly and she earned her private pilot's license before graduation. Her love for her father made it easy to share his interest in sports and the excitement of life. To any male seeking to court her, Charlie was a challenge indeed. She was surely a prize, but the cost of obtaining, to say nothing of "owning," her was simply too much of a challenge for most men.

As soon as the aircraft had reached altitude, Deiter could see that Charlie wanted to begin his tutoring. "Okay, Charlie, what's first on the menu?"

"To start off with," she said, handing Deiter an envelope containing several pieces of paper and some 8 by 10 inch photographs, "you are Dmitri Andreiovitch Kolyushkin and you graduated from the Lenin School of Engineering, that's in Moscow, in 1961, and you received a doctorate at MIT in 1992. You were fraternity brothers with Alex Carter, the number two guy on the UNSCOM Team. He will recognize you. Now introduce yourself in Russian."

"My name is Kolyushkin, Dmitri Kolyushkin," Deiter replied in Russian.

Charlie squinted her eyes at Deiter. "Very funny, Mr. Bond, very funny indeed," she replied flatly to his attempt at making it sound like the introduction usually reserved for the fictitious British spy, James Bond, 007. "Russians don't talk that way and you know it very well." She leaned back in her seat and tilting her head, looked at Deiter. "I gotta feeling this is going to be a really long trip," she finally added, shaking her head. Deiter only grinned at her.

During most of the flight, Hank Henderson slept curled up with a blanket over him in a set of three row seats; it was his solution to listening to the less than interesting conversation in Russian between Charlie and Jack Deiter. By the time the flight began to descend in preparation to land in Frankfurt for refueling, Jack's accent, although not disappearing, sounded more Chechen than American. Rose had insisted on Deiter learning Russian as spoken in his ancestral land rather than classic Russian. The seat belt sign came on and the pilot's voice came over the loudspeaker to announce their immediate arrival at Frankfurt with a warning to stay seated with seat belts fastened. The giant aircraft bounced hard twice and finally rolled to a stop at the end of the runway amid a complaining roar from the engines in reverse. The flight attendant's voice came on the loudspeaker and announced in a sarcastic voice, "We ask you to please remain seated as Captain Kangaroo bounces us to the terminal." In unison, everyone voiced their concurrence with her critical evaluation of the landing.

The stopover in Frankfurt lasted only an hour, but provided an opportunity for the trio to stretch their legs and get some fresh air. The sense of going back to Rome held a number of mixed feelings for Deiter. They located a nearly deserted bar in the Frankfurt, Flughaven lobby and ordered a round of drinks. By Deiter's calculation, it was only six p.m. Washington time, and it would be almost midnight in Rome. Conversation was slow and each one of the group seemed preoccupied with his or her own thoughts.

It had been in 1972 when Deiter had last been in Rome. He had been working for the CIA as an undercover operative with Rose. Their mission was to unmask a Soviet espionage ring that was accessing and transferring NATO classified information to the Soviet Embassy. The leak was thought to have come from a U.S. Army source and their Army Intelligence contact had been Hank Henderson. Deiter looked around the lounge and the airport lobby; he noted that it had really changed a lot since he last waited for the connecting flight that would take him back to the States so long ago. Had it really been so long ago? He looked out the window at the road leading to Frankfurt and began to recall his last visit to the Eternal City. He was deep in thought when he suddenly became aware of someone standing behind him saying something to him.

"Jack, we have to get back aboard... Jack?" Charlie persisted.

Deiter grunted, gulped down the rest of his drink, and followed her out into the lobby and down a flight of stairs to the tarmac. They climbed aboard their flight and settled themselves again for the next leg of their journey. Deiter felt a sudden weariness come over him and begged off any more of Charlie's Russian lessons. He located a barely comfortable bed made up of two seats in the rear of the aircraft, grabbed a pillow and blanket from the overhead compartment and nestled himself down on the bed. He could faintly make out the distant voices of Charlie and Hank in the front of the cabin. The voices dropped off as he drifted into sleep.

"Rose...Rose," he muttered quietly to himself, "Where are you, Rose...my love?"

"Jack, wake up...Jack, damn it, wake up!" she said anxiously.

"What, who...? Rose, where've you been?" Deiter stammered out.

"We've triggered the source of the leaks and have another theft of documents," she exclaimed.

In his dream, Jack Deiter raised himself up from the sofa in his apartment where he had fallen asleep over an hour before and grabbed Rose Spinelli by the shoulders. He pulled her down to him and kissed her fully on the lips.

"What the hell was that for?" she finally asked softly after they had relaxed from their passionate embrace.

"Just overcome by seeing you, I guess," he replied with a sudden embarrassment. "I musta had a bad dream. So, what the hell's going on?"

The aircraft suddenly hit some air disturbance and jerked Deiter wide-awake. Had he been dreaming or had he really just kissed Rose? It took a few seconds for reality to reestablish itself in Deiter's mind.

When it did, he wondered if returning there again had caused him to have that short dream. Deiter guessed so, yet it caused him to begin recalling the details of the last few hours of the mission and the last few hours he had been with Rose only to have her disappear for the next twenty-five years.

For several months, Deiter and Rose had been cultivating relationships with the suspects in the investigation. The primary suspect was Brigadier General Wallace Thornberry, US Army, who had been sent to Rome from his previous assignment in Germany. It had been seriously rumored that he was pulled out of a troop command assignment because of some sexual indiscretions with the wives of his subordinate officers. A strange situation in light of the fact that his wife, Jacqueline, was an extremely beautiful and charming lady; and that description didn't even begin to describe a grace that made grown men wilt.

Rose had flirted with the General at a private tennis and swim club initially and had been successful in gaining his attention. That wasn't, in Deiter's opinion, a great feat in that General Thornberry was continually "on the make" for any good looking female, single or married. Rose simply was the next luscious morsel that happened along. Deiter and Rose had a special relationship, and he was privately jealous of her assignment. He rationalized that his job, to seduce the General's wife, Jacqueline, was a "safe" situation, but the reverse was not true, or so he believed. He never voiced this to Rose, of course; to do so would have been "unprofessional." Nevertheless....

Prior to coming into the assignment, they had learned that both the General and his lady had relationships to some degree with two Soviet agents. Both agents had been arrested by the Italian authorities, but nothing could be substantiated and the two agents were deported from Italy without any fanfare. If either Rose or Deiter could establish a situational relationship with either Thorneberry, and if they could substantiate where the leak was and which Thorneberry was responsible, that would end that part of the investigation.

Deiter turned over restlessly in the seat-bed on the aircraft. He had dozed briefly, but soon found himself reliving the last few hours of his mission in Rome.

Deiter was sitting on the roof of a four-story stucco building across the street from the athletic club that was frequented by the General. He leaned back against the brick chimney as he focused his binoculars on a fifth-story window across the street. Rose and the General had entered the room about five minutes before. Rose had planned the meeting with a request for something "really interesting" from the General. Deiter checked the earpiece that was plugged into a receiver/recorder he had nestled between his feet. Periodically, the sound-activated device came to life to provide a continuing saga on what was happening inside the apartment.

"Where's your wife tonight?" Rose asked.

"A child welfare meeting of some sort...something like that. I'm suppose to be at a joint strategy meeting with the Italian military." he chuckled.

"Is it an all night affair?"

"Would you like it to be?" he responded. In his mind, Deiter could see her smiling coyly. He also noticed that she was now speaking with just the slightest Russian accent. Nice touch, he thought.

"I am so impressed with what you do, Wallace. The whole world is being protected by what you do. You know so much about the Western plans to defeat the Eastern nations."

"No, dearest, I'm afraid you don't understand. We're only defending ourselves." She moved closer to him and slid her arms around him and kissed him on the lips.

When they finally parted, she said something that escaped Deiter's hearing. The General suddenly dropped his hand from her breast and reluctantly moved away from her. He turned and walked over to a briefcase resting on the table. Rummaging through the papers, he came up with a package encased in a cream colored envelope. He withdrew it from the briefcase and handed it to Rose who took it and opened it. Inside were several dozen pink sheets of paper, each marked with a "NATO TOP SECRET" stamp. She scanned them and then refolded the package and placed them back inside the envelope. She slid the envelope inside her large leather purse. Smiling, she turned towards him and cradled his head in her hands as she kissed him.

"Now it is time," she whispered seductively.

Upon hearing the code words, Deiter tore the earpiece from his ear and punched the warning button on his transmitter. Several agents of the Italian Security Police and the U. S. Army Intelligence were waiting to break into the apartment occupied by the couple. He clamored down the stairway and across the street. Three agents whom he recognized were already at the elevator and he joined them on their trip up to the fifth floor. At the doorway to the apartment, Deiter traded glances with Hank Henderson, who was standing next to the doorway and smiled.

"She did it," Deiter remarked, lifting his eyebrows and smiling.

Two bodies crashed in unison against the door and it gave way. Deiter was first to get to the bedroom. Henderson picked up the purse with the evidence. The General pulled himself up from the bed with as much indignation, bluster and bravado as he could muster without wearing his pants. Rose swiftly slipped off the bed and moved out of the bedroom and into the bathroom. She closed the door behind her.

"Bring him back to the base," Henderson instructed the other two agents. He looked at Deiter. "She OK?" he asked.

"You go ahead, I'll stay with her." Henderson nodded and left the apartment following the other two agents and the General, who was now in handcuffs.

Deiter walked to the doorway of the bathroom and waited. After a moment he said, "Rose?" There was no answer. "Are you OK?" No answer. "I love you, dearest." The door unlocked, then it slowly opened.

Rose stood in the doorway of the bathroom, tears streaming down her cheeks and her bottom lip was quivering. Her eyes were red. "Why did you take so long?" she asked.

Deiter moved towards her and enfolded his arms around her, burying his face into the side of her neck. "I'm sorry, Rose, I came as soon as you gave the signal. I'm sorry, darling, I'm sorry."

Deiter led Rose from the apartment and down the hallway to the elevator. She was sobbing quietly. The elevator door opened, and they stepped quickly inside and Deiter pressed the button for the lobby.

"We don't need to go back to the shop tonight. It'll hold 'til tomorrow. Let's get you home," he whispered. She silently nodded in reply and as soon as the elevator opened to the lobby, they hurried out the door and into the street.

Deiter had learned that night just how fragile Rose could be and how much she wanted and needed a secure and trusting relationship. It wasn't that Rose was weak, she had proven herself too many times. But, when it came to violating a personal and intimate relationship, even in the line of duty, she couldn't do it. He respected and loved her for that and felt good about his decision to resign from the CIA and apply to the FBI or go into private practice so that she wouldn't need to put herself in that situation again. A week later, she told him that Adams needed her on one more assignment, but that after that, she would join him. They made their plans to meet at *Masterson's*, an upscale restaurant in Old Town Alexandria, near Washington. It was to be at eight o'clock in the lounge on Christmas Eve. Deiter had waited until past midnight that night and finally left a message with the bartender with his telephone number if she ever arrived that night. She never did.

The jolt of the aircraft hitting the runway pavement of the Leonardo DaVinci International Airport near Rome suddenly brought Jack Deiter wide-awake. He threw the blanket that had been covering him onto the back of the seat behind him and swung his legs into the aisle. Strangely, he could still smell Rose's perfume and he felt her closeness to him. Looking towards the front of the airplane, he noticed that his companions were seated, waiting for the plane to come to a stop. As the plane taxied towards the arrival slot, he put on his shoes and made his way forward.

The bright early morning sun streaming through the opening initially blinded Deiter as the door to the aircraft swung open. He could see that a stairway ramp had already been rolled up to the doorway. Deiter stared out towards the familiar terminal; for some reason he almost expected Rose to be there waiting for him. He was shaken out of his reverie by a voice behind him.

"Let's get going; time to daydream later," Henderson muttered as he swung his garment bag under one arm and, grabbing one of Charlie's bags that had been placed next to the door, elbowed his way past those standing in the doorway of the aircraft and ambled awkwardly down the ramp ahead of them. A black limousine sat near the end of the ramp, and Henderson headed for it followed by the other two. A cool breeze from the Mediterranean Sea met them as they climbed down the ramp. A uniformed driver quickly grabbed the luggage from the passengers and indicated to them that they should quickly get out of sight behind the darkened windows of the limo.

The ride to the safe house took only about twenty minutes. They left the airport and headed east along route E80 towards Rome, then the driver turned on the exit ramp leading to the west lane of Grande Reccordo Anulate, the divided highway encircling Rome. They continued for about seven kilometers and took the second exit ramp that led south on Via Laurentina and back out into the countryside on a road that Deiter and Henderson knew only too well. They traveled about a kilometer along the tree-lined narrow road and turned right on a much smaller road that led to a large villa surrounded by a twelve-foot stone wall. At the stone gateway, they stopped momentarily while the ornate iron gate swung open. The limo rolled on through and pulled up in front of the main entrance to the house. The three passengers piled out of the car. Deiter looked up at the impressive entrance to the villa and smiled. It hadn't changed a bit, and somehow that was comforting. Again he had the feeling that Rose would come bounding down the stairs and throw her arms around him. They had spent several weeks at the villa before he returned to the States; it was a time during which they had seemed to be so much in love. My God, he thought to himself, is she really dead or not. These ghosts seemed to reappear at the damnedest times. The driver informed them that he would take care of the luggage and that they were to go inside to the study where they would be informed what was to happen next.

The main hallway of the villa had high ceilings and tapestries hanging on either side. Deiter led the way down the hallway and opened the double mahogany doors to the study at the end of the hallway. The study was everything one might imagine of a nineteenth century library. On both sides were bookshelves containing entire collections of books. Deiter suddenly recognized that he had unconsciously patterned his own study after this one. There was a conversation cluster containing several sofas in front of an elaborately columned white marble fireplace. Standing in front of the fireplace was a very dignified gentleman of about sixty–five; his right hand placed sportingly inside his jacket pocket. He had white hair styled over the ears in a very European fashion. His brown tweed jacket had dark brown leather suede patches on the elbows and a shooting patch on the right shoulder. A blue and maroon paisley ascot and dark brown trousers finished off his casual, but elegant attire.

"Good morning," he said in a deep baritone voice while smiling and opening his arms in a munificent gesture. "Please make yourselves comfortable. My name is Ashton Woods and I've been asked to bring you up to date on the latest information we have on your project. Oh, but first, would you like some coffee…or something stronger, perhaps?" He gestured toward a Empire Period mahogany side-bar on which stood several three-liter chrome carafes of coffee and tea and several bottles of liquor, glasses, ice and cups.

As soon as the three travelers had each poured a cup of coffee and seated themselves, Woods continued. "Things are not as we had hoped; we had thought that the UN would be allowed back into Iraq to continue its surveillance and inspections. In fact, this was scheduled to happen within the week. This is not the case, however."

"That's what I suspected all along," said Deiter quietly.

"The project's still on," retorted Woods enthusiastically. "You're still going to Baghdad, Mr. Deiter, but as a representative of the Russian government, only the Russians don't officially know it."

Deiter was skeptical; he rolled his eyes and voiced his objection. "Just how in hell's that going to be accomplished?" he asked sipping his coffee.

"It already has been," Woods replied softly with a slight self satisfied smile. "It's, uh, just a bit...complicated, but there's something that the Russians want. Right now they're fairly hung up in Chechnya, as you well know. They want information that we have and are quite willing to negotiate for it. There are those in the Russian government who will know who you are, but they only have a faint idea of why you want to go to Iraq incognito. They've no idea that you want to effectuate the assassination of Saddam Hussein."

"That gives me a comfortable feeling," interjected Deiter sarcastically.

"It's the best thing under the circumstances, and it's also very fortunate that the Russians are in the predicament in Chechnya they're in right now."

"Wonderful," muttered Deiter, looking over at Henderson and raising his black eyebrows. His friend averted his eyes and looked back at Woods. Deiter suddenly felt uneasy.

"You're to negotiate for additional oil sales in exchange for food," Woods continued. "At least that'll be the story. You'll not actually meet with the Iraqi representative, but you will be able to stay in Baghdad for nearly a week. They will keep you waiting for an audience with the Minister of Trade as is their habit. That will be their own undoing. When the switch is made, you'll have a ready excuse to leave, stating that they don't appear serious about negotiating and you need to return to Russia to get new instructions from your government."

"How do I get weapons past security at the Rome airport or once in Iraq?" Deiter asked.

"You'll carry them in a diplomatic pouch that will be properly sealed and marked by the Russian government. The security of the pouch will be honored and so will your diplomatic status."

"That doesn't make me feel much better. I don't understand why the Russians are so damn accommodating."

"You will in time, but right now you'll have to take my word for it that they're very eager to be accommodating for the favor that we're doing for them...unofficially."

"What's our schedule now?" asked Deiter.

"We have a couple of days before all of the connections will be in place. Mr. Farrakhan is not due in Baghdad until Sunday. We know

95

he's booked at the Baghdad al-Rashid Hotel and I have made reservations on Saturday for a certain Russian diplomat by the name of Dmitri Andreiovitch Kolyushkin. By the time you leave here, you'll have the proper papers, diplomatic pouch, and Russian clothing. The Russian government will have sent a special message to their Embassy in Baghdad to expect you. Your double will make the trip from Moscow to Rome on tomorrow's flight. He'll stay overnight at the Sheraton Roma Hotel only 20 kilometers from the airport. That's when the two of you will make the switch."

For a quickly made-up change in plans, it didn't sound half bad. Deiter even felt more comfortable with this version. It might be better to do this than connecting up with the inspection team. Going through those checkpoints even under the UN's protection would have been tricky at best. You never can tell what some ambitious guard might pull.

"You've all had a long journey, why don't you take a few hours to rest. We do have time and you must be at your best," Woods concluded. "There's a suite upstairs prepared for you and your luggage has already been delivered there. Good luck and we will be speaking more tonight after dinner."

The upstairs suite was quite spacious. It included a common area, a kitchen and three separate bedrooms coming off the common area. It didn't take long for the inhabitants to claim their separate domains and settle in. Hank had an itinerary of people whom he had to contact, meetings which had to be held within the next two days, and a list of items that must be obtained. But now, for a few hours though, it was time to rest.

It was almost two o'clock that afternoon when the Americans finally started to emerge from their separate rooms and assemble in the common area of the suite. Hank came out a few minutes before the rest and was reviewing the many documents and schedules that he had downloaded on his laptop computer. He was finally prepared to brief his two sleeping companions whenever they awoke.

Deiter was the next to wander into the common area and upon seeing Henderson seated before his computer, he sat down beside him.

"What's going on?" he asked.

"I've got a time table and some maps for you. It looks like Farrakhan is on his way from the States to Cairo right now. After a stopover in New York, his flight's scheduled to go to Jordan. He changes flights in Amman and flies on to Baghdad. He's booked at the Baghdad al-Rashid Hotel and we've got confirmation on that as well as your reservation." Hank responded without looking up from the monitor screen.

"Looks good, so far," Deiter observed cautiously.

"You're booked on the Friday flight out of Rome for Amman, Jordan. You'll transfer planes and fly to Baghdad from there."

"And my look-alike?" asked Deiter.

"He's flying from Moscow to Rome today, then he'll check in at the Sheraton Roma. We can't be too careful. After you arrive in

Baghdad, you'll have almost two full days to play like the diplomat and scout out the hotel before Farrakhan arrives."

"Do you have anything definite on Farrakhan's schedule or Saddam's, for that matter?" asked Deiter.

"It looks like Saddam's got Farrakhan cooling his heels for a couple of days before he graciously grants the gentleman an interview," Henderson quipped sarcastically, as he leaned back and stretched his arms above his head. "Farrakhan's scheduled to have an audience with Aziz the day following his arrival and then be escorted around the country to show him all of the damage that's being caused by US and British bombing. You can bet Iraq will get some great publicity on it. Then when Saddam's good and ready, he'll meet with him. We don't know the exact time and probably won't until it's too late. That's why you'll have to make the gun switch as quickly as possible."

"I understand," said Deiter as he stood up and headed for the kitchen. He suddenly was hungry. "Hey Hank, did you notice if they stocked this place with something to eat or do we have to call room service?" he hollered over his shoulder from the kitchen.

"Look in the fridge," Henderson replied, without looking up. "There's also a microwave. I'd guess that room service here is at a minimum."

Deiter opened the door to the refrigerator and bent down. There was beer, vodka, scotch and a variety of soft drinks. He opened up the freezer side and noticed an assortment of frozen dinners. He selected a frozen cheeseburger, tore open the corner as the directions showed and placed it in the microwave oven. The box told him to set it for eight minutes, which he did, and went back into the center room opening a bottle of Italian beer.

As Hank saw him coming out of the kitchen, he said, "It looks like we have another visitor going to Baghdad this Friday, a former Russian Prime Minister."

"Which one? They change 'em so fast, it's hard to keep track," Deiter replied, sitting down next to Hank on the sofa and looking over at the screen of the laptop on the coffee table.

"Yevgeny Primakov; as Russian Foreign Minister, he became good friends with Saddam," Henderson replied. "He's probably thinking about running for Prime Minister again or to replace Yelsin and is trying to look international for all the folks back home. It's said that Saddam gave him almost a million dollars for his help in the Iraqi nuclear weapons program."

"I bet he's also trying to needle the West by playing games with the big trickster himself."

"It shouldn't cause us any problems," Hank replied thoughtfully. "It may even cause a good diversion. He's staying at the Baghdad al-Rashid Hotel as well…just one big happy family."

"Good morning again, anything happen?" a sleepy female voice interrupted.

"Just reading the latest on our little junket," replied Deiter.

Hank sat back and smiling broadly interrupted the conversation, "Looks like our friend Jack'll have company on his trip to Baghdad." Deiter looked at him expectantly. "A young lady by the name of Anna Borisovna Cheklenov will be accompanying you. She's your aide."

"My aide? I don't like this. Who the hell is she? She doesn't know me either; this isn't going to work," said Deiter in exasperation.

"Oh, that's something I haven't had a chance to tell you yet," Charlie explained excitedly. "Woods told me just after we broke up downstairs that I'd be going along with you, just in case you got in trouble," she teased. "I…am Anna Cheklenov. They thought that a woman would give a little more credibility to the mission and be less threatening. Besides, I speak better Russian than you. Don't you agree?"

"I bet Adams thought that one up," muttered Deiter shaking his head.

"Chauvinist," Charlie retorted, wrinkling up her nose and then breaking into a broad smile. Deiter could see that she was thoroughly excited with the thought of going on her first covert assignment and he didn't want to spoil her enthusiasm.

"Well, if I've gotta have a skirt tagging along, I'm glad it's you," he responded in a John Wayne imitation. "At least you speak the language." Charlie hit him on his arm with her fist. Deiter responded by placing his arm around her shoulder and saying, "Glad to have the company, Charlie."

The hours passed slowly as the three went over the information that Woods had provided and the statistics that Henderson had downloaded earlier from the Internet. It was almost seven that evening when Deiter stood up, stretched and moved over towards the windows. He leaned against the drapes covering the edge of the window and looked out over the well-manicured garden at the rear of the villa. There was an extensive herb garden with a fountain in the center; the entrance was an arbor with flowers and vines enveloping it. Deiter remembered it very well and through his sorrow, he managed a smile in the remembrance of the times when he and Rose had walked in that very same garden. He looked up at the moon just rising above the tree line to the east. The two of them had watched it dozens of times. The window was open and the breeze felt cool on his face. It was still daylight, although the shadows had grown long, and there was a quietness in the air that wasn't altered by the gentle breeze.

Deiter remembered how she had been so beautiful and vibrant. He closed his eyes and whispered quietly to himself, "Rose." When he opened his eyes, his glance returned to the scene below and he suddenly noticed a figure standing at the entrance to the garden under the arched trellis. The figure either hadn't been there before or he just hadn't noticed; he didn't know which. It appeared to be a tall woman with long dark wavy hair; she was dressed in a long white flowing gown. He thought he saw a deep redness to her hair as it reflected the late-day sunlight. She moved onto the pathway in the garden and

Deiter gasped. It was Rose, the way she walked, he was sure of it. Deiter turned and bolted from the room leaving his bewildered friends staring after him.

"Jack," shouted Henderson, "What the hell's the matter?" There was no reply as Deiter disappeared down the hallway.

Henderson looked at Charlie for a moment and then jumped up and followed his friend out of the suite and down the hallway. By the time Henderson reached the garden gate, he found Deiter leaning against the trellis, his head bowed, and his hands shoved into his pants pockets.

"Jack, what was it? What'd you see?" Henderson asked, coming up to him and putting his hand on the other man's shoulder.

"Rose."

"What? You saw Rose? Jack, that's impossible," Henderson grasped Deiter's shoulders and slowly said in a softly spoken whisper, "Jack, Rose is dead."

"Then why do I keep seeing her?"

"I can't answer that. Oh, I'll give you some psychological explanation, if you want it, but frankly, Jack, I don't know. Are you all right with this assignment, Jack?"

"I'll kill that bastard, Hank, I <u>will</u> kill him," he said with determination. "No one should get away with something so wrong, so devastating."

"It's gonna happen, Jack. It's gonna happen," Henderson said, in a desperate attempt to comfort his friend. They both turned and slowly headed back towards the villa. Deiter grabbed Henderson's elbow.

"Don't tell Charlie," Deiter whispered, his eyes showing the intensity of his feelings as he looked the other man directly in the eyes.

"Of course not, Jack. This thing with Rose is just between you and me."

As they approached the French doors, which led onto the patio from the house, they both noticed Ashton Woods standing in the doorway.

"Is anything the matter?" Woods asked.

Henderson was the first to reply with a question of his own, "Are there any other 'guests' here?"

"Why?" responded Woods.

"I thought I saw someone I once knew," said Deiter.

"Our guests are usually not discussed," came the reply.

"But, in this case?" Henderson countered. "More specifically, is there a tall woman with red hair?"

"Why yes, there is," replied Woods, hesitantly. "You may have seen Anna Marie Noviskova. She is assisting us with what I referred to previously as the *quid pro quo* we have with the Russian government."

"Then she's Russian?" asked Henderson.

"Oh, most assuredly," replied Woods with a wry smile. "Well, she's from Grozny, which I suppose, is technically Russia. That group will be leaving tonight."

Henderson and Deiter looked at each other, and then Deiter brushed by Woods and entered the house. Henderson nodded to Woods and followed his friend.

To her credit, Charlie didn't ask any questions when the two men returned to the suite. She had a distinct talent for sensing when it was best to say nothing. She figured that if it was important to the mission, one of the men would have said something. They didn't. She looked at her watch; seven o'clock, no wonder she felt hungry.

She wondered aloud what their hosts had planned for meal arrangements when a knock on the door interrupted her monologue. Deiter was over at the window looking down at the garden once more and Henderson had just gone to the kitchen for a beer. She looked at both of them, shrugged, and headed for the door. "That's OK, I'm not doing anything; I'll get it," she said to anyone who wanted to listen. She opened the door to find a cart of food and a young, attractive Italian man standing there beside it. He smiled and gave the impression that he didn't speak English. It was obvious that this was dinner. He pushed the cart into the suite and over against the right wall of the common area next to the large dining table. Charlie thought that he would place the servings onto the table or make some effort to serve the meal, but the man immediately turned, handed her an envelope and left the suite without saying a word.

The envelope wasn't addressed to anyone in particular, so Charlie tore it open. Inside, there was a note from Woods telling them that there would not be any need for a meeting after supper and that they would meet tomorrow morning at 8:00 A.M. downstairs for breakfast. "Looks like we have to serve ourselves," she announced as she set three places at the table and moved the food dishes from the serving table to the dining table. "Come and get it, and if you want something to drink other than wine, get it yourself."

The mood of the trio was improved by the sumptuous dinner that included a bottle of very nice Italian red wine. It was almost eight–thirty by the time that they had finished and were stacking the residue back onto the cart. Charlie headed for her room to read and Hank took the laptop computer into his room to see if he could hook up the modem to the phone extension next to his bed. Deiter first pushed the dinner cart into the hallway and then wandered back over to the window again and looked out over the garden. There were no lights at the rear of the villa and he could see the stars very plainly. He turned and headed for the door to the suite again thinking that a walk in the cool night air might make him more inclined to sleep that night, particularly after the experience earlier in the evening.

As Deiter walked down the hallway, he came to a window overlooking the front driveway and the road leading through the gates to the Italian countryside. A long black limousine was parked in the middle of the driveway in the front door to the villa. A uniformed driver stood next to the limousine's back door, between the car and the front steps to the villa. Deiter leaned against the wall next to the window and watched. He was there only a few moments when several people appeared at the main doorway and bustled down the three stairs to the driveway and hurried over to where the limo was parked. The driver opened the rear door to the car and then quickly walked around to open the other rear door. The two men wore dark beards and were clothed in long white flowing Arabic dress. They were followed by a woman dressed in a traditional burqa; her head and face were covered with black cloth. She was the last to enter the car, and rode in the front seat next to the driver. The limo sped down the driveway and disappeared through the iron gates that closed automatically behind them.

Jack didn't quite know what to make of the incident, but he was familiar with covert operations and the secrecy and stealth involved. Anyway, it didn't appear to have anything to do with his mission and seeing the woman in the garden, whomever she was, only reminded him once more of what his own personal reason for this mission was and of its importance to him. Deiter stared after them for a few moments and then turned, jammed his hands into his pants pockets and slowly walked back to the suite and to his own room; a walk in the night air had suddenly lost its appeal.

Chapter Six

On to Baghdad

Leonardo DaVinci International Airport, Rome
Friday morning, November 19, 1999

The Lufthansa flight rose gently as it sped down the runway. As the wheels noisily found their berth beneath the wings, the plane veered right slightly and headed for Amman, Jordan. From Rome, there were no flights directly to Baghdad, Iraq, and hadn't been for some time. With exception of official government sponsored flights, those who wanted to get to Baghdad stopped first in Amman, Jordan and transferred to a smaller airline. The flight over the Mediterranean Sea was uneventful. This part of the journey was the least dangerous and the sights below held Charlie's interest as she looked at the wondrous scenery. After a meager breakfast of rolls, jam and coffee, the drone of the engines finally lulled her to sleep. Deiter hadn't said much that morning and was reading a Russian language newspaper; he seemed engrossed in the articles. The luncheon meal was finally served and as the crew was busily retrieving the remnants of it, the plane's captain announced that they were beginning to descend into Jordanian airspace.

The landing was unspectacular, but adequate, and both "Russians" departed the airplane and sought out the means for the next leg of their journey. At the end of the long line of airline counters in the terminal, they found the counter advertising their next mode of transportation in both English and Arabic…TransJordan Air.

TransJordan Air was one of only a few airlines that flew regularly into Baghdad. It was a small company with only five aircraft, and it took advantage of the fact that most of the larger airlines didn't want to risk flying to Iraq or were registered in countries such as Britain and the United States that forbade travel to countries such as Iraq. For these small airlines, it was, although somewhat risky, also quite lucrative.

Flight 1243 was to depart in two and a half hours for Baghdad. About twenty minutes prior, the call for first class passengers was made over the loudspeaker system, first in Arabic and then in French and then in English. Deiter and Charlie boarded the small aircraft and found their seats immediately in the front of the aircraft. A Russian dignitary needed the prestige of flying first class in order to keep up appearances even though first class only meant the forward section of the cabin area.

The flight departed without incident, and as soon as the seat belt sign was turned off, Charlie stood up and walked through the cabin to the rear of the airplane. It wasn't that she expected something to happen on the flight, it was just a precaution. When she returned, she plopped herself into the seat next to Deiter and whispered in Russian that it looked secure, as far as she could make out. She hadn't recognized anyone in particular that might be a threat. Deiter smiled and sighed in relief in the knowledge that he had a companion who was so totally competent.

Deiter turned towards her and thanked her in Russian. During the rest of the flight, they discussed many things, but always in Russian. It was improving his command of the language and securing their identities as well.

Woods had briefed them that morning as to what to expect in Baghdad. There were rumors of a United Nations vote to consider lifting the sanctions if the UNSCOM inspectors were allowed into the country and given leeway to check certain areas. Deiter doubted that Saddam would give such permission to anyone who had demonstrated their ability to ferret out his secrets. With nothing new in the works, it would mean that the current plan was still in effect and that inspection teams from the UN would not be allowed into the country. Saddam had another agenda.

Charlie turned and peered through the window of the airplane at the countryside beneath them. The terrain below looked much like some parts of the southwestern United States, except for the lack of any signs of habitation. As a pilot herself, she noted that their altitude was considerably lower than that she was used to and guessed that it was some kind of security measure to prevent observation of "secrets" by foreigners. "Paranoid assholes," she thought to herself.

She glanced over at Deiter who was leaning back in his seat with his eyes closed. She studied his face. There was so much strength and character written in those craggy features and heavy black eyebrows.

Ted Colby

She also saw, in this moment of relaxation, a gentleness she hadn't really noticed before. That gentleness made her wonder if he might be dreaming of Rose. The thought immediately saddened her as she recalled once more the tall flamboyant red-haired beauty she had known. Could someone like that really be dead? She wondered if immortality comes only by way of the remembrances of those still alive, and if so, is it still immortality? We remember; we see again in our mind's eye, in our imagination, the persons we once knew and it can, at times, seem to become a sort of reality. While she really didn't believe in ghosts, is that still true after the death of the person? She also knew that something had happened at the villa the previous evening and that neither Jack nor Hank had mentioned anything about it. It must have been something quite significant, nevertheless; she was sure of that. She also was fairly certain that if it pertained in any way to the mission, they would have said something to her about it. They hadn't, though; they pretended as though nothing had happened. She had watched from the window as Hank ran up to Jack who was standing next to the trellis and saw how they had talked briefly before returning to the villa. She had also seen them talking to Woods as well, yet they had mentioned nothing about it to her. Later, she had opened that message from Woods explaining that there was no need for a meeting that night. Why the change in plans? Did it have something to do with what had happened earlier? She felt uncomfortable again and looked back at Deiter. The strong yet peaceful and serene look on his face reassured her that whatever had transpired, it had nothing to do with the mission or her safety. She sat back again and relaxed.

Deiter stirred and shifted position in his seat. The drone of the aircraft's engines lulled him into semi-consciousness once more. The harmonics of the noise sounded at times like a telephone ringing at the other end of the line…that sound, silence, the sound once more, silence again…over and over.

In his mind, he was seated on the sofa next to his bed in a hotel room near the Newark Airport in northern New Jersey. Deiter looked at his watch; it was now a little past nine o'clock in the evening. That day had been spent visiting the FBI's New York Field Office…just to check in, and the City's 20th Police Precinct to pick up evidence in the murder espionage case he had just been assigned. After he had finished the supper that he had ordered through room service, he decided that it was time to contact Rose. He placed a call to the number he'd been given for Rose's home, but there was no answer and the answering service came on the line, instead. Deiter hung up; he didn't want to leave a message, he wanted to speak to her.

For the last several days, she had come into his mind or he had seen women who reminded him so much of her. Why after all these years would he begin to remember Rose Spinelli…oh yes, it was now Rose McGuire, he had almost forgotten that she had been married for a short time many years ago, but had kept her married name even after the divorce. From very Italian to very Irish; with her red hair, she could pass for the real thing either way. Deiter had felt truly compelled to contact Rose. The excuse he gave to himself and others was that she would be the perfect person to help on the most recent case he'd been given. He needed someone who understood all the nuances of Russian, even its humor. He didn't know anyone, outside of getting a Russian national, who could do that better than Rose. He had been informed that she now worked for a law firm in Upper Saddle River, New Jersey. The firm had a lot of international dealings, most recently with Russian firms who wanted to do business with the United States. Undoubtedly, she did all of the firm's legal translations.

He looked back at his notebook and found Rose's work number at the law office. It was Friday night, but perhaps she was still working. Most likely, she was out on a date, though, he guessed dejectedly. Deiter sighed and punched in the work number, anyway. The phone rang three times and he was about to hang up when a woman's voice answered in a weakly whispered question, "Yes?" Rose told Deiter somewhat later that she thought the phone call was from her boss, Aldridge Mason, wanting to come over that evening on the pretence of business and then pressing to spend the night. She very badly wanted to end the repressive relationship, but didn't know how; the last thing she wanted to do that night was to spend it with Mason.

"Rose?" Deiter asked tentatively.

"Yes, who is this?" she responded.

"Rose, it's been a long time, I know, but I hope you'll remember me. It's Jack…Jack Deiter." He paused. "You remember, your contact in Rome in...uh, '72 or '73, I think; yeah, that's it 1973. We were recruited at about the same time by Don Adams." He was about to ramble on further when she suddenly cut him off.

"Jack, you old scoundrel," she bantered, "Where've you been?"

"Me!" he exclaimed, slightly exasperated. "Do you know what I've been through and how much it's cost the Bureau to locate you?" He quickly added, "The 'Company' isn't very cooperative in helping us locate some of their past, and ...uh, best operatives. One has to do a lot of arm twisting." He paused for a moment and then continued, "Say, Rose...can you spare a few minutes? I need to talk with you. I've got a proposition you might be interested in that goes back in a way to the old days, but a helluva lot more promising and financially more productive. How about dinner tomorrow night? Your place...it's more private. You used to do a great Stromboli."

"A proposition is it? After a quarter of a century, out of the blue, you me call on a Friday night, at work, with a proposition?" Rose replied.

Deiter mentally kicked himself. Why did he have to use that word? Had he lost all finesse in speaking with women? His mind raced to find the right words; he started to sweat and he put his hand up to wipe his forehead. Suddenly, as he was about to say something, probably wrong, the voice on the other end of the line answered her own question.

"I'm kidding, Jack, I'd like that...and Jack...it's really good to hear your voice again; you don't know how much I've missed it, and

113

right now I need… Oh, never mind, I'll tell you all about it later. Tomorrow night, then. Six? I'll be looking forward to seeing you."

The phone went dead; slowly Deiter replaced it on its cradle and leaned back on the cushions of the sofa. "That seemed to go well," he muttered to himself. "Yeah, right, only it wasn't my fault it did," he reminded himself. He had even remembered her voice after all these years. Yes, it was Rose…really Rose. He realized that he was too pumped up, he'd never get to sleep now. Deiter climbed into his running clothes, left the hotel, and followed the same running trail that the hotel clerk had described to him the night before. When he returned a half-hour later, he was more composed and immediately went to bed. As he lay there in bed, the memories of Rose started to flood back to him. He recalled even the smallest detail of their time in Rome and he drifted off to sleep with a smile on his face for the first time in over twenty years.

Deiter shifted position in his seat on the aircraft and his face brushed against the fragrant hair of his sleeping companion in the seat beside him. He inhaled the intoxicating perfume and began dozing once more. A series of vignettes cascaded through his dreams.

Even on a Saturday, the roads were filled with cars, but it was just six o'clock when Deiter drove up to the brick split ranch at 136 Princeton Court. He tucked the bottle of Chianti under his arm and walked up to the front door.

Deiter wondered what he would say to Rose as she opened the door. It would be she who opens the door, wouldn't it, he asked himself? The nervousness returned once more. "Oh, shit," he muttered to himself. He pushed the doorbell and heard the sound of the chime coming from inside the house. It seemed like hours, although it was only seconds, and the door opened.

What Deiter saw standing in the doorway was a slightly more mature version of the person he remembered as Rose, but she was, in a way, even more beautiful. He didn't know what to say, so he said what was then on his mind. "My God, do you just keep getting more beautiful? Where'll it ever stop?"

"Jack, you'll never change; at least not that part of you, thank God." She smiled broadly and stepped though the doorway toward him, throwing her arms around him. Their lips met in a long kiss, arms tightly encircling each other and for a moment the years since their last meeting vanished as though they were only yesterday. The evening ended with Deiter going back to his hotel room and kicking himself for not taking Rose's unspoken invitation to stay the night at her place.

The next day, though, he picked her up and drove up the Hudson River to West Point. When he was a Midshipman at Annapolis, he had spent several months at the Military Academy with Hank Henderson as an exchange student and he thought of no more romantic a place to bring his newly re-found love. After a romantic stroll along the scenic Hudson River and a casual picnic lunch, they spent the night at Thayer Hotel and returned the next day to Saddle River so that Rose could pack up some of her clothes before heading for Virginia. She told him about the repressive relationship in which she found herself and Aldridge Mason's possessive nature and vicious temper. They decided not to let anyone know where she would be and deal with Mason after the case was finished. Until then, she would stay with Deiter in his townhouse in Alexandria.

The details of the case flew by in Deiter's semiconscious recollection and progressed finally to very happy scenes at their villa in Costa del Sol and shopping tours throughout Spain and Morocco. He watched as Rose enchanted the street venders in Madrid and cheered at the bullfight as though she were at a football game back home. He loved to watch her. The change in pitch of the engines brought a brief moment of panic to Deiter as he envisioned the aircraft suddenly pummeling downward toward the ocean. He awoke with a start and a feeling close to panic filled his entire being. He took a deep breath, which made the feeling subside.

He noticed that Charlie must have dozed off as well; the distinct difference in the sound of the engines of the small jet must have awakened the pilot in her because she quickly sat up and looked out of the window. Deiter followed her gaze. The signs of civilization beneath the plane, when added to the change in the sound of the engines, let them know that they must be descending on the airport in Baghdad. The plane suddenly veered right and the sound of the wheels being lowered from their in-flight position confirmed his conjecture.

"Looks like we've arrived," he whispered hoarsely in English. Charlie smiled in return and nodded. Deiter now seemed to feel more relaxed and in control once again.

The landing was straight in and sudden. The reverse engines roared and braked the aircraft to a sudden stop. Quickly, the pilot turned the plane to the right and headed for the international terminal of Saddam Hussein Airport. Deiter had the feeling he was entering a combat zone in the way the aircraft swung into the traffic pattern and the suddenness of its landing.

After a ten-minute wait for the baggage to be unloaded from the plane, they proceeded to the customs area and selected their luggage, which was piled onto several low benches. They queued up behind three other passengers who appeared to be traveling together. Deiter guessed that they were Iraqi by their speech and dress. An officious customs official scarcely looked at their four pieces of luggage and waved them through. "I guess they are more concerned about what goes out of the country then what comes in," Deiter remarked to Charlie in Russian.

"At least this won't take too long," she replied softly as she walked up to the customs agent who had seemed so cavalier toward the Iraqis ahead of them. The sound of Russian being spoken seemed to change the attitude of the agent, however, and he instructed them in a crude sort of sign language to open all of their luggage and stand away from the counter. He held out his hand and gestured impatiently to indicate that he wanted their passports and visas. They both handed the papers to the agent who proceeded to conduct a through inspection of their passports, their diplomatic credentials and finally their personal baggage; the latter search took fully fifteen minutes.

The diplomatic pouch containing the weapons that Deiter had requested and the replacement gun meant for the Iraqi President was the subject of a rather heated discussion among the custom officials. Deiter had kept it handcuffed to his left wrist and refused to give it to the agent. In the end, it was not searched or x-rayed.

Although they seemed to be singled out for special attention, their situation as Russian diplomats appeared to hold some influence with both the customs agents and the military that were ever present at the airport. Deiter guessed that this was just some sort of low-key message from the Iraqis to the Russians that they could have been more difficult if they had wanted. An Iraqi army officer came in to discuss the delay with the head agent, gave a curt order, turned and left. The head agent shrugged, turned and walked over to Deiter and Charlie; he then gave them a sign that they could pass, impatiently waving them through as though they were the ones causing the delay.

As Deiter and Charlie exited the customs sector through a set of heavy, green double doors leading into the main part of the terminal, they were confronted by several men in black suits as well as a tall Iraqi army major with the markings of an aide or liaison officer. A heavyset, but very dignified and obviously Russian man stepped forward towards Deiter with his hand outstretched.

"Good day, Dmitri Andreiovitch, it's a pleasure to meet you. My name is Boris Ivanovich Ulanova," the man said in Russian.

Deiter was still irked at the attitude of the Iraqi customs agent and without smiling curtly thanked the Russian for his greeting and grasped his hand briefly. He then in turn and introduced Charlie as Anna Borisovna Cheklenov, his aide.

"Welcome to Baghdad, both of you; we will escort you to your hotel and tomorrow afternoon, after you have rested, we will speak in more detail about your mission."

At this point, the Iraqi major stepped forward with an irritated look on his face at being upstaged by the Russian, and introduced himself as Major Mustafa Mussula, an aide to the Assistant Deputy Economic Minister. "After you have settled in your hotel," he continued in Russian, "I will send you word as to where and when we will discuss your proposed meeting with the Minister." He then turned and without waiting for an answer, left the group and rapidly headed for the exit leading out of the terminal.

"Friendly," Deiter remarked sarcastically to Ulanova.

The Russian took Deiter by the arm and smiled as he led the way towards the parking lot.

"There are times when we must treat our friends as though they were children. I was wrong, perhaps, not to have given him a more central role in our meeting, but then again....he will also know his place now on the international level; you understand, this is Russian to Russian...that is an important thing for them to know as well."

119

"But of course," Deiter replied, smiling for the first time.

"It was, of course, an insult to send such a low ranking person to meet you," Ulanova whispered.

"I thought that, as well," Deiter responded, "They don't seem to be much in the mood to talk." Privately, Deiter was very thankful for the arrogant reception; it would better suit his purpose.

Deiter liked the Russian, though; he was open and unassuming, and most of all, he seemed honest. Did he know Deiter's true identity? Deiter wondered.

Outside the terminal, a black Mercedes was parked near the end of the area reserved for the pickup of passengers. It was the only private automobile parked there, which said something about the current tourist trade in Iraq. An abbreviated line of rather shabby looking taxis was parked along the side of the curb. The Russian contingent busily deposited the luggage inside the trunk of the car and with the exception of Ulanova, vanished back into the terminal. Deiter and Charlie took advantage of the automobile's open rear doors and climbed into the back seat. Their Russian host quickly joined them and closed the door behind him. A previously unseen group of people from across a large, relatively empty parking lot, pushed toward them. The first contingents of the crowd had reached the opposite curbside and had stopped. Deiter could see cardboard signs now which seemed to appear from nowhere, some were in English and others in Russian and French, The driver quickly slid in behind the steering wheel and put the car in gear. The Mercedes pulled out onto a nearly empty road leading from the Saddam Hussein International Airport to the al-Rashid Hotel in the Karkh sector of Baghdad.

"That was the 'unofficial' welcoming committee for all foreigners. They want to make sure that everyone knows of the sanctions that have been imposed on them. We try to either ignore them or get out of their way," Ulanova remarked.

They drove for about five miles before the area began to take on a more urban appearance. Deiter and Charlie said nothing to each other during the entire course of the trip. As they drove down the wide street, they began to see multi-story buildings rising up along the highway and the traffic became more congested. Most of the cars and trucks were of an older vintage, but the number of Mercedes and other luxury cars indicated that at one time there had been a significant amount of wealth in the city. The desolation of the streets and buildings and the vacant look in the eyes of the people spoke of a change that been forced upon them. Finally, they passed through Zawra Park, crossed 14th of July Street and turned into the entrance to al-Rashid Hotel. They were greeted by the bell captain as they pulled up at the main entrance. It was apparent that they were expected. Ulanova spoke with the solicitous doorman, turned and walked over to where Deiter was standing.

"I reserved a room for you when I heard that you would be coming. There is also a room reserved in the name of Anna Cheklenov; I was not quite sure of the particular 'arrangements' I should make…uh, for your convenience," he added with a sly smile and shrug of his shoulders.

"Two rooms is both appropriate and in good taste," Deiter replied smiling. "I would not like to endure the reaction from my aide should it be any different," he added glancing over at Charlie, who was waiting at the entrance to the hotel with the bell captain.

"Very good then. If you will go to the desk, they will provide you with the room keys. I wish you a good day, Dmitri Andreiovitch. I will be in contact with you tomorrow." Ulanova handed his business card to Deiter and added, "Should the Iraqi major contact you first, please let me know what he has to say. My home number is also on the card; you may call me at any time."

"I'll do that, and thank you for your hospitality, Boris Ivanovich, you have been more than helpful," Deiter concluded. The two men shook hands, and the Russian climbed into the back seat of the sedan and instructed the driver to leave. Deiter turned and escorted Charlie through the hotel entrance and over to the desk.

"May we have the keys to the rooms reserved for Kolyushkin and Cheklenov," Deiter inquired of the desk clerk as he handed over both Russian passports.

The clerk briefly looked at the documents with a disdained disinterest and handed both keys to the bell captain, saying the room numbers in Arabic as he did so. Deiter nodded a thank you and followed the bell captain to the elevator where Charlie was waiting beside a cart that held their luggage. On the way up to the fifth floor,

Deiter looked at his watch. With the two-hour time difference between Baghdad and Rome, it was almost six o'clock in the evening, Baghdad time. He hadn't eaten much of his lunch aboard the flight to Amman and suddenly he felt hungry. Turning to Charlie, he said in Russian, "Would you want to try some room service? I didn't realize the hour."

"Good idea, I really don't want to venture out after dark here until I get used to the place."

"Meet me in my room in half an hour. I'll order up something in the mean time." She nodded her agreement.

The elevator came to a halt and the bell captain handed a key to Charlie while he set her bag on the floor. He then pushed the cart off the elevator and headed down the hallway towards Deiter's room. Charlie shrugged as though to admit that she now understood the status of a woman in this country. The elevator door closed and proceeded up to the sixth floor.

After the bell captain had busied himself for the requisite amount of time required for a tip, Deiter placed a couple of coins he had been given at the safe house in Rome into the man's hand and turned away. The bell captain left the room, shutting the door behind him. Deiter placed the secondary lock in place on the door and proceeded to unpack his luggage.

Now he was in the lair of the fox, he mused to himself. Here he was, traveling under false credentials…not only as a Russian, but a diplomat as well. He didn't know how much the Russian who met them at the airport knew about the project, but he didn't, or rather couldn't trust him even though he tended to like him. He looked around the room. "I can't believe that they, whoever that might be, didn't put a bug in the room…microphones anyway; perhaps a camera as well," he mused to himself. If Charlie were to have dinner with him here, he'd have to warn her about that possibility. He began a methodical search of the room.

At exactly six–thirty that evening, there was a knock at the door of Deiter's hotel room. He unlatched and opened the door to find Charlie's beaming face; she was in an excited state that had her almost bursting at the seams. Deiter put his finger to his lips in a move designed to warn her to watch what she said. She nodded her understanding and slipped into the room. Deiter was the first to break the silence.

"Want a drink before the room service arrives?" he asked in Russian signifying that there was some reason not to speak English.

"What do you have?" she asked in reply.

"Only *Jameson*…Irish whiskey…sorry, no vodka; and there's no ice either, but it's probably safer without it anyway; the water is questionable."

"Only a couple a' fingers," she replied with a smirk. She obviously seemed to be enjoying the playacting. Deiter motioned her into the bathroom and closed the door behind them. He turned on the water in both the sink and the shower.

"I checked this room and think it's OK, but the noise of the water is just in case. I found a bug in the phone and the lamp; oh yes, the balcony is bugged too," he explained.

"I was going to tell you the same thing. Should we complain to the manager or the government?" she asked with a giggle.

"Although this may be a pain in the ass, it's better to know where the bugs are rather then complaining about them and then having to search for new ones all over again. We can always go outside if we need to talk about the mission. Maybe it could even be useful if we need to send them on a wild goose chase."

"Right now they probably think we're taking a shower together; should we give them something to talk about or play it straight?" she joked.

As a reply, Deiter turned off the water, opened the door and poured two drinks in the glasses on the counter, offering one to Charlie.

"Supper should be up shortly," he said with a grin.

They sat in the two overstuffed chairs that had been provided near a table in the room and spoke only about the flight and made up some small talk about the pending talks about oil sales. A knock on the door interrupted them. Deiter went to the door, unlatched it and opened it to allow a waiter to push in a cart with two dinners placed on it. The waiter maneuvered the cart towards the table and parked it there as he looked at Deiter with an impatient and disdainful expression on his face. Deiter curtly thanked the man and then turned his back to him.

"Let me serve you supper," he said to Charlie in Russian, completely ignoring the waiter. Disappointed and shocked at the lack of a tip, the waiter turned quickly and left the room. Deiter walked over and latched the door behind the man.

"I don't like unwarranted arrogance," he responded on his way back.

"Hope you're not counting on any more room service," Charlie giggled. "I don't blame you though, the guy acted like an asshole."

"I think that's the attitude we can expect...even as Russians," Deiter said.

They paused for a moment, looked at each other and reflected on what they had just said. It was open and honest, but was it enough to incur the wrath of the Iraqi government. Deiter made a face that seemed to indicate that it was all right. Charlie nodded and sat back in the pillows on the sofa and relaxed. Keeping a phony conversation going was tougher than she thought. She had to think about it; she hated being spied upon and listened to.

Deiter served the meal on two plates, and both of them ate it as though they were starving.

"Tomorrow, we'll see how we can begin negotiations on the oil project," Deiter interjected into their lapse of conversation, and setting the course of conversation. She quickly grabbed onto the meaning of the opening and responded.

"Whatever you need me to develop for the negotiations, please let me know," she said.

The meal finished and conversation being progressively difficult, Charlie said goodnight and left to return to her own room. Deiter put together the remnants of the dinner on the tray and pushed the cart outside the door and parked it in the hallway. He closed and latched the door behind him. Tomorrow would be a busy day and he felt that he needed sleep. He would have to fully explore the hotel without raising any suspicions.

Ted Colby

Chapter Seven

The Switch

al-Rashid Hotel, Baghdad, Iraq
Saturday morning, November 20, 1999

Deiter woke with a start; it took him a few moments to acclimate himself to his surroundings in the hotel room. When his wits finally came to him again, he sensed that he had been wakened by a noise at his door. He listened. Nothing. Looking around the room, he noticed that the sun had not yet risen, but there was a lightness just beginning to chase away the shadows of the night. He looked at his watch; five–thirty. He stretched his arms above his head and then threw off the light bed sheet that had been the only covering he had needed during the night. It was going to be a busy day if his guess was right that Farrakhan would arrive at the hotel today. He needed to scout out the hotel and find ways of getting around the elevators from one floor to another without being spotted or raising suspicions. He guessed that the early morning would be a good time to establish himself as a familiar fixture with the hotel staff.

It took him less than five minutes to change into his running outfit. He wore a black sleeveless cotton tee-shirt with matching black running shorts and white running shoes. The shirt had the Russian double eagle crest on it in gold. Around his head he slipped on an old and shabby white terry cloth headband adorned with the hammer and sickle emblem of the Soviet Union and the letters CCCP. Many people in the world still were unaware of the nuance that the Soviet Union had broken up and consisted only of the loosely connected remnants of the former world power. There were those in Russia who still yearned for those "good-old-days." He knew that the Russian visitor to Baghdad this day, former Prime Minister Primakov, was reported to be one of them. It wouldn't hurt if he innocently displayed a low-key reminder of the old days of glory, should he be noticed. Deiter wrapped a towel around his neck, locked the door of his hotel room behind him and walked down the hallway to the stairway leading to the lower levels of the hotel.

The stairways were deserted as he guessed they might be at this early hour and he had a chance to inspect the locking mechanisms of the doors and note the time it took him to climb down each floor. The locks were mechanical and could not be centrally locked…that was good. He would need to know how much time he had to travel between floors when it came time to break into Farrakhan's room to swap the CIA version of the M1922 ACP pistol with the GPS device embedded in it for the one the Reverend was going to present to Saddam. From the fifth floor, it took him less than ten seconds to reach the floor below. At that rate, he could easily descend to the ground floor in less than a minute. He calculated that it would take him three times that to climb to the fifth floor. He didn't know how many stories there were to the hotel and would have to find that out. The stairway was dark and dank smelling. Deiter guessed someone was habitually using it for a urinal. The walls were gray unfinished cinder block and retained the mold and various smells that permeated them. The single low-wattage light above the door leading to the hallways on each floor was encased in a corroded metal cage. No other lights were in the fire well. On the fourth floor, he opened the door and looked out into the hallway. It was empty. The room configuration on either side of the hallway was identical to his floor. He repeated this routine until he reached the ground floor. No surprises so far. He quietly opened the door to the ground floor and stared directly into the face of an Iraqi soldier sitting back in his chair sleeping at a table opposite the doorway. By the look of his uniform and scarlet beret, he was obviously a member of the Republican Guard. This was a surprise. Deiter swung open the door with a flourish and approached the soldier, waking him with a start.

"Hello there, how goes it? Do you speak Russian?" Deiter inquired loudly in Russian as he held onto the edge of the soldier's desk and practiced deep knee bends as though warming up for a run.

There was no answer from the surprised soldier who obviously was shocked to see the powerfully built bald headed man dressed in black suddenly bursting through the door and confronting him in Russian at this time of the morning. Deiter nodded as though to convey his understanding that the poor befuddled man didn't speak Russian. As he headed down the hallway in the direction of the lobby, he waved his hand and called a goodbye over his shoulder to the befuddled soldier.

Deiter crossed the lobby and approached the desk in hopes that someone there spoke either Russian or English. No one was at the hotel's main desk, but the doorman who helped them with their luggage the evening before was seated behind the concierge desk and Deiter went over to him.

"Do you speak Russian?" Deiter inquired of the bellhop in Russian. There was no response other than a shrug. Deiter then asked him if he spoke English.

"Yes sir, I speak some English," the man responded quickly.

Deiter considered this one to be a cut above the average and certainly brighter than the soldier he confronted in the hallway. "Wonderful, we can speak in English then," Deiter added with a generous smile. "I'm looking for a good path to follow for my morning run; do you know of some place?"

The man pulled out a sketch map of central Baghdad; it was obviously one for the general use of tourists to find their way throughout the city and he possessed a plentiful supply. He indicated the location of the hotel and a green patch labeled Zawra Park just across 14th of July Street from the hotel. Deiter thanked the man and was about to leave when he turned and asked him if any Americans or other Russians would be arriving at the hotel today.

"Both," the man replied smiling. He was obviously pleased to express his knowledge of English and the fact that he might be considered important enough to know of the arrivals and departures of distinguished guests. "As you must already know, Prime Minister

Primakov is due to arrive this morning about ten o'clock," he added knowingly. Deiter nodded, indicating that he knew about the arrival of the Prime Minister. "And an American Moslem leader will be here just after noon for a visit with our beloved President." Deiter didn't want to arouse suspicion by pressing the issue any more, so he thanked the man again, left the hotel and headed for the park.

An hour later, Deiter had completed his run through the park and had examined the hotel from a distance noting the number of floors, configuration, and access routes. On his return, he circled the hotel to memorize the structure from all angles. Satisfied, he reentered the lobby. This time the arrogant desk clerk was at his station, and the bellhop was nowhere to be seen. Deiter walked directly to the elevator and pushed the button for the fifth floor. Once inside the elevator, he also pushed the button for the eighth floor, three floors above the one on which his room was located.

After a brief pause at the fifth floor, the elevator finally groaned to a stop at the top floor of the hotel and the door slowly opened. Deiter looked out into a hallway that was very different from the ones he had seen previously. For one thing, the hallway was almost twice as wide and there appeared to be only four doors leading to what Deiter guessed were plush suites. One hallway went the entire length of the hotel and it was crossed in the center by a hallway running at right angles to it. The elevators were at the conjunction of the two hallways. The configuration allowed for four separate apartment suites, none of which were adjacent to each other. Each had complete privacy for the occupants and the opportunity to easily observe anyone lurking in the hallways. Deiter noticed the presence of two rotating cameras above the elevator door. Quickly, he backed into the elevator and pressed the button for the seventh floor. The door slid shut and the elevator creaked and groaned down one floor. Deiter left the elevator and quickly slid through the fire exit door into the stairway; he then walked back up the stairs to the entrance door to the eighth floor. Then he noticed the two black cables coming through the wall near the ceiling, just to the left of the door. The cables ran down the wall of the fire well to somewhere many floors below, perhaps the ground floor or the basement. He opened the door slightly and looked up at the cameras mounted on the wall above the elevator door and confirmed what he had guessed. The cameras apparently were a recent addition and the cable went from the cameras, along the wall to a point above his head; he slowly closed the door and retraced his way down to the seventh floor. On opening the door to the hallway, he discovered that the layout of this floor was identical to the ones below. The stairs down to the fifth floor were like the ones lower down, but smelled less of urine. On each floor he paused to look through the doorway to check the configuration of that floor. All of the other floors were set up identically to the one he occupied. On reaching the fifth floor, he walked down the hallway and returned to his room, bolting the door behind him. He looked at his watch; it was seven o'clock.

Deiter showered, shaved and dressed in his black turtleneck shirt and black slacks. From the closet he pulled out his charcoal gray sports jacket with the black suede leather patches on the elbows and a shooting patch on the right shoulder and set it on the bed. He would wear that when he went out later. He now had a very good idea of the layout of the hotel. His guess, at this point, was that Farrakhan would occupy one of the four suites on the top floor of the hotel, maybe the Russian would be housed there as well. He had to gain more information on when the suites would be empty so he could make the swap of weapons. He remembered the bellhop in the lobby and decided to see if he could get more information out of him. Deiter was deep in thought when the telephone on the bedside table rang twice, startling him.

"Da," he barked into the receiver.

"Hey, good morning to you, too," Charlie replied in Russian.

"Sorry, guess I was deep in thought," Deiter replied.

"Plans for the day?" she asked.

"Why don't we take a walk in the park across the highway? I was out earlier and it was delightful," he suggested.

"Could we get something to eat there…a cup of coffee at least?" she asked.

"We can return to the hotel for that later."

"Seven–thirty?"

"Yes, in the lobby."

"Whatever you say," she replied. Deiter hung up the receiver.

135

At exactly seven-thirty, Charlie met Deiter in the lobby and together they dodged the unexpected traffic as they crossed 14th of July Street toward the park. Charlie was dressed in a three-quarter length khaki skirt with a safari jacket to match. Her brown boots reached almost to her knees...the tops were hidden by the bottom fringe of her skirt. Her short blond hair was covered with a scarf that complemented her ensemble and gave her a jaunty and adventuresome look, yet in keeping with the Islamic dictated decorum. She walked beside Deiter with her arms clutched about her waist, warding off the chill of the morning. Whereas the days in the Near East were warm this time of year, the temperatures in the early morning were sometimes quite cool. As Charlie strolled along the cinder pathway in Zawra Park with Deiter, she remarked upon the obvious English influence in the way the park was laid out and in its selection of vegetation. The path circled the pond in the center of the park. Waterfowl frolicked on the shoreline as they passed by. As soon as they were safely away from anyone who might be listening, Deiter returned to their previous conversation, again in Russian.

"I did a reconnaissance of the hotel early this morning. The top floor is divided into four suites; I think that our mark will be up there. I can get on to the floor by way of the stairs in the fire well, but there are cameras in the hallway of that floor."

"How'll you get by them?" she inquired, as she stooped down to look at some bright-red flowers growing along the pathway.

"The cables for the cameras run down the fire well stairway; they can be cut, of course, but I think that this would be a good time to try a bit more sophisticated approach. If we cut the cables, they'll be looking for the person who did it and we don't want to arouse suspicion against us."

"What then?"

"Hank gave me a gadget that could be called a scrambler, I guess. It's battery powered and generates spurious signals at low voltage and can be used in a number of different applications. It plays hell with a telephone or a TV set or a radio and is hard to identify. I can insert one of the probes from the device into each cable and it'll disrupt the signal enough to hide my move into the suite. Once inside, I should be relatively safe; I doubt if they have a camera in there any more than in our rooms. When I'm through making the switch, I can remove the device and seal the holes in the cable. No one will be the wiser. Most importantly, they won't have surveillance transmission while it's connected."

"Won't they send someone up there to investigate?"

"Right, but if the elevator door is jammed open, it'll force them to run up the eight floors. I can leave something common in the door to the elevator that will look as though it was dropped accidentally and jammed in the sliding door. I timed how long it'll take for them to run up and at the worse, this should give me a full five minutes. I'll have even more time if they try to fix the problem with the cameras before deciding to pay a visit to the top floor. I don't think they'll want to report a lapse in observation if it didn't pan out to be something they could really point to as the reason. Also, I'm banking on the fact that none of them really wants to run up eight stories for any reason."

"Okay, sounds good, what can I do?"

"We can stay in touch with our cell phones; if you hear them clambering up the stairs, you can warn me. We can take the elevator down and evade them."

They had completed a circle around the park and were standing on the sidewalk directly across from the al-Rashid Hotel. A cream colored limousine had just pulled up to the entrance of the hotel and a contingent of what appeared to be African-Americans exited the vehicle and proceeded to pull luggage from the trunk, placing it on the sidewalk so that the bellhop could load it onto a cart. Standing apart from the rest of the group was a tall, thin, solitary figure. The man watched the activity of the others with an appearance of detachment.

"Farrakhan," Deiter said quietly. "Let's get back to the lobby and find out what floor they go to."

The two of them hurried back across the wide width of 14th of July Street, dodged a couple of cars that were speeding down the roadway and followed the group who had arrived in the limo into the hotel lobby. Deiter picked up a newspaper from the wire stand just inside the doorway to the lobby and dropped a coin in the slot. He opened the newspaper and studied it intensely. The couple slowly drifted toward the elevator. An excited and exasperated bellhop, the one Deiter had spoken to earlier, was fussing over the stack of luggage and hanging clothing bags on his cart as he maneuvered it toward the elevator. He looked over at the man in black and smiled as though to indicate to Deiter that he had been right about the group's arrival. Deiter smiled back and nodded in acknowledgment of the man's important status and went on reading the newspaper.

It took very little time at the desk to finalize arrangements as an Iraqi official who had accompanied the group in the limo was expediting the check in. This time, however, the arrogant desk clerk was overly solicitous. "Hypocritical worm," Deiter murmured to Charlie under his breath. In less than two minutes, the group, minus the Iraqi, was on its way to the elevator. Deiter and Charlie stepped aside and allowed them to crowd into the green-paneled box. When they were in place, the door slid shut and they disappeared from sight. Deiter and Charlie watched the lighted numbers change as the conveyance moved up the building...3rd floor...5th floor.....7th floor...and finally the 8th floor. There was a pause. Deiter pushed the UP button and waited. In a few moments, the numbers started to reverse themselves...8, 7, 6, 5, 4, 3, 2, L. The light above the elevator blinked on and a chime sounded as the door slid open and Charlie and Deiter quickly stepped inside. As Deiter didn't have time to employ the ruse of stopping at an intermediate floor this time; he pressed the "8" button and the elevator slowly started its groaning slide up the building once more. As they reached the 8th floor, the elevator slowed and finally jerked to a stop. The door slid open and Deiter poked his head out and quickly scanned the hallways. At the end of the hallway on the left, he saw the bellhop closing the door to a suite and start to walk back towards the elevator pulling the cart with him. Deiter jerked his head in, confident he had not been noticed, and pushed the button for the 6th floor. The door closed and the device groaned down two floors and stopped. Both Deiter and Charlie walked out into the hallway and headed straight for the door to the fire well. They walked down one flight of stairs and out into the hallway of the 5th floor. Quickly, they walked to Deiter's room and went inside, locking and latching the door behind them.

Charlie plopped herself down onto the sofa against the wall of the room and sighed loudly. Deiter put his finger to his lips and smiled. Charlie nodded in understanding…the bugs.

"I'll be back in a minute," Deiter announced, as he indicated she should follow him as he headed for the bathroom. Charlie quietly followed him. After Deiter had turned on both water faucets in the shower and closed the door, he whispered, "Farrakhan's suite is the one on the opposite side of the hallway to the left."

"What now?"

"Wait until they leave. How many of them did you count?"

"Farrakhan and three others."

"That's what I counted too. My guess is that they'll be allowed to rest for a few hours and then be taken around the city to see the damage done by the American and British bombing. That will prime them for their visit with Saddam. While they're out, though, I'll have time to locate the gun and replace it."

"How can we know when they leave?" Charlie asked.

"Wait here, I'm going down to chat with our bellhop friend; maybe he'll know something."

Deiter turned off the water faucets and went back into the main room. He grabbed his sport jacket from the bed and left the room as Charlie walked to the window and peered down at the street below. She could see the front of the building, the park across the street and the entrance to the hotel. She perched herself on the windowsill and watched.

In about twenty minutes, Deiter arrived back at the room. He wore a smug smile.

"Who's canary did you eat?" Charlie asked as she sat on her perch, her arms around her knees.

"Saddam's, I hope," he replied in a self-satisfied way. He knew the reference would be missed in the translation if anyone were listening. He went into the bathroom and Charlie followed him. After turning on the shower, he said quietly, "The bellhop says that the limo is due back at two this afternoon. That's when they're due for a tour of the city. Looks like my guess was right."

"That's five hours from now; is there anything we can do in the meantime?"

"Get ready," he replied.

Deiter went over to the safe in the closet, unlocked it and took out the diplomatic briefcase he had carried handcuffed to his wrist on the airplane. Inside was, among other items, the handgun he would be exchanging for the one in Farrakhan's possession. He placed it on the coffee table in front of the sofa. He took out a small black plastic box about the size of a computer floppy diskette with electronic chips embedded into the top. It had two wire leads coming out of one side; each end of the wire leads terminated in a solid pin. He next took out another semi automatic pistol, this one in a small black holster. He checked the magazine to make sure it was loaded and there was a round in the chamber. This he placed in his belt and slid it around to fit in the small of his back. He reached back into the briefcase and pulled out a second weapon somewhat smaller than the first. He checked it and handed it to Charlie. She nodded, placing it in the inside pocket of her jacket.

Deiter walked over to the small television set on the table and turned it on. It was set to the government news station and an announcer was excitedly talking and gesturing. He examined the rear of the set. A cable originating from a plate in the wall was attached to the antennae. Placing the small black box on the table next to the television, Deiter placed first one lead and then the other against the cable junction. Each time he touched the junction, the LED lamp on the device blinked red and the television screen went to snowy static. When he lifted the lead, the announcer returned with his animated monologue. Deiter looked over at Charlie and smiled as he placed the black box into his pants pocket and returned the television set to its proper position.

"Now we wait," he whispered.

They sat in silence; Charlie sitting in the window and Deiter on the sofa. Each one was deep in their own thoughts as they waited and watched.

It was noon when Charlie wildly motioned to Deiter to come to the window. She pointed down towards the hotel entrance. Another limo had just pulled up to the curb, and several men had stepped out of the rear door and were standing on the sidewalk. Deiter recognized one man immediately from newspaper articles, former Russian prime minister Yevgeny Primakov. He motioned to Charlie to keep watch on the scene below and then pointed towards the ceiling and to himself conveying the fact that he was going to go up to the eighth floor. Charlie nodded her understanding.

It took Deiter only about a minute to climb the six sets of stairs in the fire well up to the eighth floor. He eased open the door and looked down the hallway towards the elevator. No one was in sight. He waited with the door cracked open. Five minutes passed before he was rewarded by the light flashing on above the elevator and the chime sounding. Four men and the now familiar bellhop exited the elevator and started down the hallway in Deiter's direction. He eased the door shut and flattened himself against the wall. The group passed by the fire exit and continued down the hallway. Deiter took a breath and slowly eased the fire exit door open again. At the end of the long hallway, the last of the group of men was just disappearing through the doorway. Primakov's room was at the opposite end of the hallway from Farrakhan's and on the opposite side of the hallway. Deiter closed the door and returned to his room.

When he opened the door of the hotel room, Charlie was still at the window. He motioned for her to come with him and they both left the room and headed for the lobby. Once outside on the sidewalk, they would be able to talk once more. They headed southeast across Yafa Street and down towards the Unknown Soldier Monument. Deiter figured that he would have at least another two hours before they had to be back in their hotel room to wait for the Farrakhan party to depart on their tour. Besides, he had promised Charlie some breakfast earlier that morning, and it was almost noon.

"Looks like all of our parties have arrived at the hotel, and we know which rooms they are in," remarked Deiter.

"Not a bad morning's work," Charlie reflected.

"How about some coffee?"

"I thought you'd forgotten. You know what I'm like without coffee in the morning."

They easily found a small cafe on 14th of July Street and sat outside at a small table. By now the day had warmed up slightly, but they chose a place in the sun. The waiter brought them coffee and after some sign language and bits of English and Russian, he managed to understand their needs and brought some rolls with a sweet jam made from some unknown berry. Charlie dove into it with enthusiastic relish. Deiter realized privately, and with an uncharacteristic smile to himself, that she was a real asset to the mission and that he was fortunate to have her with him.

Deiter laid out his plan for Charlie and they discussed each contingency. First, they would assure themselves that all four of Farrakhan's party were out of the room. From the hotel room window, they could count them as the group entered the limo at two o'clock that afternoon. They would both walk up from the fifth to the eighth floor where Deiter would place the scrambler on the cables. As they walked passed the elevator, Charlie would press the call button and as soon as the elevator arrived at the eighth floor, Charlie would place a tour book of Baghdad in the doorway of the elevator, which would restrict its closing. Charlie would purchase the book on their way back to the hotel room. She would then wait at the fire well door while Deiter picked the lock and entered Farrakhan's room to search for the gun. Both would keep track of the time from the moment they place the scrambler on the camera cables - five minutes - then, they would have only another three minutes if she heard sounds in the stair well. They would be in constant contact through their cell phones.

If sounds were heard in the stairway, they would disengage and take the elevator to the fifth floor and return to their rooms. There would always be another time to try again. If she didn't hear any activity in the stairwell, that would mean that the government agents either were not really observing the eighth floor hallway or that they were still trying to clear up the video image electronically. Either way

145

it would mean that Deiter had more time to search for the weapon. Everything had been thought out to the last detail…Deiter hoped.

They headed back along 14th of July Street to the hotel so as to be there at a quarter to two. In the store just off the lobby, Charlie purchased a thick tour guide to Baghdad…in Russian, of course. They returned to Deiter's hotel room and waited. Charlie perched herself in the window and watched the activity at the entrance to the hotel; Deiter relaxed on the sofa.

At five minutes before two o'clock, Charlie motioned to Deiter that something was going on below at the entrance. Deiter went over and followed her silent advice to look down at the street below. A limo had just pulled up to the curb and was waiting. The driver and another person who had arrived in the limo were standing on the curb next to the car.

As they watched, two men left the entrance to the hotel and stood by the limo. Deiter guessed by their appearance that they were of Farrakhan's entourage, probably his bodyguards. Two other men, one of them was Farrakhan, walked from the hotel entrance to the limo and climbed into the vehicle. Immediately the Iraqi standing near the limo climbed into the vehicle, as did the bodyguards and the driver. The limo pulled out of the circle in front of the hotel and onto 14th of July Street. The coast appeared to be clear for the next move.

Deiter and Charlie did a silent high-five congratulation ritual and headed for the hotel room door. Deiter eased the door open and waited for Charlie as she slipped past him into the hallway and then he quietly latched it behind them. They entered the stairwell and hurried up to the eighth floor. As they had planned it, they stopped on the stairway entrance to the eighth floor and Deiter implanted the leads into the two cables from the observation cameras. A red LED on the front of the box above each lead blinked on indicating it had made contact with a circuit.

They looked at their watches to confirm the time, and Deiter led the way through the doorway of the fire well and walked down the hallway leading down to Farrakhan's suite. As they passed the elevator, Charlie pushed the button to call up the elevator. She waited as Deiter continued on down to the doorway of Farrakhan's suite. As he was picking the lock to the door, the elevator arrived with a chime of the bell. The door of the elevator opened and Charlie slid the tour book in line with the door's line of closing. In a moment the door closed until it hit the book and then stopped. Charlie cast a glance down the hallway towards Deiter just in time to see him open the door to the suite and disappear into the room, closing the door behind him. She walked back up the hallway again and opened the door to the fire exit. She leaned over the stairway and looked down to see if there was any activity below…nothing. Charlie stood in the open doorway listening for any sound to come up from the stairwell and to observe both the hallway and the stairwell.

Once inside the suite, Deiter quickly walked through all of the rooms to make sure that he was truly alone. There was no one there. He looked in the logical locations for electronic observation or listening devices and at first didn't find any. Either they used more sophisticated means or these accommodations were exempt from government spying. Deiter doubted that, even the President's own family was spied upon. In the table lamp, he found the usual bug and left it undisturbed. So far, so good, he thought to himself. Now to find the damn gun. He thought of the safe that normally was located in the hall closet in most of the rooms. He quickly found it. It was open and unused. Okay, they didn't believe in safes. Where else?

He started searching the first bedroom. The expensive set of luggage probably was Farrakhan's. He checked the identification tag. It read *Louis Farrakhan* and included the address of the Nation of Islam. Deiter guessed that the gun must be in some sort of presentation case. It would be tacky to simply give the Iraqi president a gun with nothing to signify what it was and who presented it to him. Would Farrakhan leave it to someone else to secure the presentation box or would he keep it close to him? He searched everything in the room, but couldn't find the gun or a presentation box anyplace. Where else? He looked at his watch. He had two minutes to go.

Adams had said that someone was working for the CIA on Farrakhan's staff, someone who was a close friend to the leader of the Nation of Islam. It was he who suggested the presentation of a handgun to Saddam. What was his name? Had Adams mentioned it? Deiter doubted it. He walked out into the main living room of the suite and looked around. There were three other rooms coming off the main living room. He chose the one next to Farrakhan's room and walked into it. There were several pieces of luggage scattered on the bed and on the floor next to the bed. Deiter checked the nametag on one piece. It read *Abdel Kadan Muhammad.* On the desk near the window was a package wrapped in brown butcher paper. Deiter picked it up. It was fairly heavy and addressed to Muhammad care of the al-Rashid Hotel, Baghdad, Iraq.

The tape on one end pulled back fairly easily as though it had been opened previously and retaped. Deiter slid the contents of the package through the opening. It was a small black lacquered wooden box with a brass plate on the top. The Iraqi president's name was engraved on the plate along with the acknowledgment of the Nation of Islam. He opened the box. Inside was a semi automatic with a black finish. The box had a recessed space for the weapon and another recessed area that held a fully loaded clip of ammunition. Deiter quickly removed the weapon from its location in the box and replaced it with the one he had in his pocket. He wiped the gun carefully before placing it in the box to remove any latent fingerprints. It was an exact copy; well, it appeared to be an exact copy. Deiter smiled to himself and replaced the box inside the paper wrapper, making sure the tape reattached to the paper. He set the package back on the desk and quickly walked to the doorway of the suite and quietly opened the door.

Outside in the hallway, all was quiet, and no movement could be seen. He left the suite and closed the door behind him. Charlie saw him as he left the suite and motioned him that all was clear. As he passed the elevator, he reached down and picked up the tour book that was wedged in the opening and continued down the hallway to where Charlie was standing in the fire exit doorway.

"Got it," he whispered as he slid past her into the stairwell. Quickly, he pulled the scrambler from the cables and pushed it into his coat pocket. Then, with a coin he rubbed at the pinholes in the cable where the leads had been pushed in until no indication of them remained. "Done," he remarked, and both of them started down the stairs to the fifth floor. There was no sign of activity in the stairwell and they quickly made it to their floor and to Deiter's room without seeing anyone. Once in the room, Deiter took off his jacket and flopped on the bed; Charlie collapsed on the sofa and both of them smiled at each other in mutual congratulation of a job well done. No one would know that the weapon had been swapped. Deiter looked at his watch, it was two–fifteen.

Although the weapons had been exchanged and the one in Farrakhan's room was the one with the homing signal in it, Deiter's job wasn't complete. He still needed to make contact with the Navy after he was confident that the weapon was in Saddam's possession. Hank would now be in Kuwait and waiting for his signal. Deiter figured that it wouldn't be until tomorrow that Farrakhan would meet Saddam Hussein and present the gun to him. He needed to keep a low profile until then and wait until he was sure that the dictator had the gun on his person, then he and Charlie could leave.

Something suddenly seemed to bother him and a shiver went down his spine. He pushed himself up from the bed and walked over to the window. Looking outside, he could see the bright street in front of the hotel reflecting the mid-afternoon sun. The traffic had eased somewhat and he looked down the street in the direction of the cafe where he and Charlie had sipped coffee earlier in the day. He could just make out a figure sitting in the very chair that Charlie had occupied earlier. His skin suddenly became cold and clammy; the bright sun caused his eyes to water so that he no longer could see the figure clearly. At that moment, though, he was once more dramatically reminded of his reason for being here in the first place. The copious amount of red hair was all that he could make out to identify the woman sitting there at the cafe. He closed his eyes for a moment and then opened them again. The figure was nowhere to be seen. He closed his eyes again and thought to himself, the seeds of vengeance have been planted, and soon she would be avenged and *that* man would die. He so wanted to pull the trigger himself, to watch him die, to see him breathe his last breath on earth.

"What's the matter, Jack?" Charlie asked cautiously. "You look like you've seen a ghost."

"Maybe so," he replied softly. "Maybe so."

Ted Colby

Chapter Eight

Discovered

al-Rashid Hotel, Baghdad, Iraq
Sunday morning, November 21, 1999

Deiter rolled over in his bed and closed his eyes again. The sun was brilliant through the window and persisted in waking him. He finally opened his eyes and looked around the room, trying to recall what had happened the night before. He and Charlie had gone to dinner in a restaurant that had been suggested by the familiar and now quite friendly bellhop. It was past eleven o'clock when they had returned to the hotel and he had seen her safely to her room on the sixth floor. Deiter had returned to his room and immediately gone to bed. That night he had dreamed of Rose and the vision he had seen earlier that afternoon. In his dream, though, he had walked up to the woman at the table in the cafe and spoke with her. She didn't recognize him at first, but he persisted and then she...she simply vanished. Deiter shook his head and pushed himself out of bed.

Today had to be the day when Farrakhan would present the gun to Saddam. He wanted to be ready when this happened. Yesterday, Farrakhan's group had been shepherded around Baghdad so they could be suitably indignant at all of the damage done by American and British bombings. Would the Iraqis want to prolong the tours for another day or would they want the press coverage of the meeting with Saddam to glean the propaganda advantage now rather than risking any adverse feelings that might be generated by additional delays? Deiter guessed that the Iraqi government would want to act swiftly to gather all of the political advantage they could. He quickly showered, shaved and dressed. He switched on the television to see if he could get any information from the newscasts and sat on the sofa facing the screen. He looked at his watch; it was just after 8:00 A.M. A news clip showed a crater caused by a bomb dropped by an American aircraft. The scene changed to a view of the ruling council around a table with Saddam addressing the group. None of the conversation could be heard over the voice of the newscaster, but it looked like a video bite that had been dubbed in for emphasis. Saddam appeared to be conveying a calm response to the incident and indicating that he was in total control of the situation. The reassurance to the Iraqi public came off as false to Deiter, but he knew that the population would perceive it differently. "Another mother-of-all-threats," Deiter muttered to himself.

The next scene drew Deiter's interest. It showed a group of African-Americans being escorted through some recent smoking ruins. Farrakhan was very obviously in the lead of the expedition as he gestured about him at the desolation. Deiter couldn't make out what was being said, but the next scene showed a shot of Saddam; the scene then switched to something entirely different. That certainly seemed to be some indication that the group would soon meet with the dictator to further capitalize on the propaganda advantage. Timing would be all important now.

Deiter decided to stroll down to the lobby and see if he could locate the friendly bellhop. He stepped out of the elevator as it opened on the lobby level and spotted the little man busily arranging luggage on a cart. Deiter walked over to him.

"Good Morning. Someone checking out so early?" Deiter asked causally.

"Yes, the Americans will be leaving this evening after they meet with the President," he replied.

Deiter expressed surprise. "Really? That seems strange to be leaving so soon after they arrived."

"Apparently, the President has business in Basra. Following the Americans, he will meet with another of our guests later in the afternoon."

"Oh, you mean our former Prime Minister?" Deiter asked.

"But of course," was the man's reply. "I understand that the Russians will be departing tomorrow morning. I am suppose to arrive at work very early in the morning to assure that they make it out to the airport on time for their departure."

"Why so early?" Deiter asked.

"I really don't know except that they want to get back to Moscow sometime during the day."

Deiter again felt that he had pushed the poor man to the limit of his knowledge and bidding him good-bye, turned and returned to his room. No use arousing suspicion at this point. As the elevator door closed, he saw the man moving the luggage through the main entrance to the hotel toward a cream colored limo parked outside.

Back in his room, he walked over to the window and peered down at the street below. He could clearly see the parked limo with the driver and Iraqi escort standing beside it. They appeared to be waiting for the group to arrive from the top floor. Deiter couldn't see the bellhop so assumed that the luggage had already been loaded. Something about the sudden meeting and departure bothered him, but he couldn't put his finger on it. As he watched, the four Americans came through the entrance and piled into the limo, followed by the escort and the driver. The limo pulled out into the traffic and disappeared down the highway towards the Presidential Palace. Deiter went over to the television set and turned it on.

There was a knock on the door and he unlatched the lock and cracked it open. Charlie stood there in a black suede jacket over dark gray wool slacks; a gray plaid scarf was around her neck and flowed down the right side of her jacket. Deiter made a mental note that she looked exceptionally perky and pretty this morning; he also liked the color of her ensemble. He swung the door open and motioned her in with a nod of his head and closed and latched the door behind her. He motioned to the television set.

"Interesting news," he said guardedly. The newscaster had just started repeating the top stories of the day that Deiter had seen earlier. "I think we should wait for awhile before we leave the hotel."

Just as she was about to inquire why, the story of the visiting Americans played on the newscast and she looked up and smiled at Deiter. She understood that they were waiting until conformation from the television that the meeting between Farrakhan and Saddam had taken place; they could then notify Hank and complete their plans to depart Baghdad. She settled herself on the sofa, drawing her legs up beneath her and facing the television set; Deiter changed locations and leaned back in a chair next to the bed; they waited and watched.

On the noon broadcast the story unfolded about the meeting between the Reverend Farrakhan and the Iraqi president. After the newscaster finished his introduction, the camera switched to a scene of Saddam and the leader of the Nation of Islam smiling and chatting. No mention was made of the weapon, but Deiter noticed that the black lacquer box with a brass plate on it that he had handled earlier sat on a table between the two men. The transfer had obviously been made, but the presentation must have been considered a private affair and not one to be publicized. Deiter went to the telephone and dialed the local Baghdad number he had been given by Henderson when they were briefed earlier. An answering machine responded and Deiter left a message.

"The fox is tagged," he said and broke the connection temporarily. Next, he picked up the folder with his airline ticket and punched in the number for the airline that was listed on it.

"My name is Kolyushkin and I wish to confirm return reservations for myself and my aide Anna Cheklenov on the seven–fifteen evening

157

flight to Amman, Jordan, tomorrow," he said. He gave the airline clerk the number on the ticket, received confirmation, thanked him and hung up the phone. "Done," he said. "What do you want to do for the rest of the day?"

"See the city," Charlie shrugged.

"Let's go," Deiter replied with a grin.

The Presidential Palace
Baghdad, Iraq
Early Sunday afternoon, November 21, 1999

The cream colored limo pulled away from the curb in front of the steps to the Presidential Palace. The two passengers in the rear seat of the limo were in high spirits as they chatted excitedly. The Honorable Minister, Louis Farrakhan, and his friend and aide, Abdel Kadan Muhammad, had just concluded a private meeting with the President of Iraq, Saddam Hussein and the excitement of that moment was still very much with them.

"I'm fully convinced, my friend, that it was in part because of you that this has been such a successful trip," remarked the Minister.

"No, Louis, I'm sure that the President would have seen you without the gift," Abdel replied.

"Oh, I didn't have a chance to tell you," Farrakhan continued. "Prime Minister Aziz mentioned to me just now that we'll be accompanying the President on his trip tomorrow to Basra. He will be flying there by helicopter."

Farrakhan noticed that Abdel paled visibly at the new change in itinerary. His friend was not meeting his eyes, but was looking down. In a shaking voice, Abdel asked, "Must we go?"

"Absolutely, it would be extremely rude to turn down the President's request, and besides, it's too late now." He reached over and lifted the other man's chin with his hand. His eyes narrowed. "You're not afraid of flying. What is it?"

A look of panic now filled Abdel's face. Farrakhan noticed the obvious desperation as the man blurted out, "I don't think it's wise to fly with the President…especially if it's in, or near the no-fly zone. That's all."

"No, that's not all. I've known you too long; what's the matter?" The steel cold eyes bore into the now shaking man, and Farrakhan's hand bit into his friend's arm.

"They forced me to do it; forgive me, Louis."

"What did you do? And who are 'they?" Farrakhan demanded.

"The CIA," he replied, drooping his head.

"What did you do for the CIA?"

"They intend to kill Saddam Hussein."

"Tell me everything or I'll leave you for Saddam's people to deal with," Farrakhan warned the now devastated and whimpering man.

In less than five minutes, Farrakhan knew the entire plot to assassinate the Iraqi president. The fact that he was the one who had delivered the means of that assassination was incredible to him. He also realized the incredible embarrassment this would be to him back home if it was ever discovered that he was involved would be minor compared to what would happen to them here in Iraq. Saddam would not deal gently with them even though neither he nor the others were in any way culpable. He thought quickly of what he must do. It's doubtful that if the assassination went through that he would ever be linked with it. He also doubted that any of his group would be implicated. The problem centered on the possibility that the Iraqi government would somehow detect the homing device. If it were detected, he would never get out of Iraq alive. When would the attempt to kill Saddam happen? He was due to be with the President during most of the rest of the day and possibly into the evening. Being in Bosra would be an advantage to the cruise missiles; it was virtually in their back yard. All of them might end up dead along with the President. He had to warn Saddam. He directed the limo to return to the Presidential Palace.

Ted Colby

Chapter Nine

Damage Control

al-Rashid Hotel, Baghdad, Iraq
Early Sunday afternoon, November 21, 1999

At the entrance to the hotel, Deiter asked the now more than friendly bellhop to call a taxi to take them to some of the well-known sights of Baghdad. The man responded with the suggestion that his brother-in-law would be very glad to escort them around Baghdad for a slight fee, to cover the expense of the gasoline, of course. Deiter consented and within fifteen minutes he and Charlie were in the back seat of a black 1986 Mercedes heading for the business and shopping center of Baghdad. The afternoon progressed pleasantly, and the two walked most of the streets in the downtown district.

By six o'clock, they were both famished and ready for a glass of wine and something to eat. Their driver and escort had promised to pick them up at the restaurant that he had recommended at ten–thirty and drive them back to the hotel. Left on their own, they meandered slowly to the restaurant and spent the next few hours over dinner and drinks.

A few minutes before they were to meet their ride back to the hotel, they left the restaurant and wandered across the street to look at several television sets that had been left on in the window of an appliance store. The perpetual newscast was showing and it looked like the one they had watched earlier. The scene changed and after an introduction by the announcer, Deiter saw the former Prime Minister, Yevgeny Primakov, standing proudly next to the dictator; they were posing for the cameras shaking hands. Apparently, this had occurred sometime after the meeting with Farrakhan.

Just then, Deiter noticed two things on the screen that made him sick to his stomach. The first was Saddam himself. Although he was armed as usual, it was not with the gun that Farrakhan had provided him earlier; it was a Chinese 9mm with an ivory handle. The second thing he noticed was that sitting on a table behind them, between the two chairs they were to occupy, was a presentation black lacquer box…the one he had seen before in Farrakhan's suite. Now, instead of the brass plate, there was a large brass seal; Deiter guessed it was that of the Republic of Iraq. He gripped Charlie's hand.

"Look on the table," he whispered to her. "The box is the one with the gun in it. What's it doing there?" Deiter almost dared not to think of the obvious answer to his question. They watched transfixed as the scene played out before them in triplicate on the three television sets in the window. Although they couldn't make out what the Iraqi announcer was saying, the dictator turned and picked up the box and presented it to the former Prime Minister who graciously opened it, admired the contents, turned it toward the camera, and finally closed it again. It was the gun that had been switched earlier that day; Deiter was sure of it. Primakov tucked the box beneath his left arm and shook Saddam's hand one more time before the two of them took their seats in the two chairs provided. Saddam was smiling broadly now as though he had just accomplished something deliciously evil.

"Oh, my God," Charlie gasped. "Primakov's got the gun."

Deiter nodded slowly and solemnly whispered, "And he wants the world to know about it, too."

At that moment, they were startled out of their concentration by the sound of a horn behind them. They turned around to see a black Mercedes parked across the street with its lights on. They turned back once again to look at the television sets in front of them just in time to see a final shot of the two men seated with Primakov proudly holding the black box on his lap. They hurried across the street and piled into the back seat of the car.

It took nearly a half-hour for the car to reach the hotel and for them to get up to Deiter's room. On the way up in the elevator, Deiter quietly told Charlie that he would inform Henderson by way of the telephone drop he had used earlier and that they would then need to either steal the gun or somehow get it away from the Russian. If the assassination attempt went wrong and a Russian diplomat was killed by a US Navy cruise missile, it could be the spark necessary to start a war. At this point, Charlie didn't need the explanation; she understood the situation perfectly, but she nodded her understanding anyway. Upon reaching the room, Charlie switched on the television and turned the sound off. Deiter grabbed the telephone and pulled it as close to the door to the bathroom as possible and then turned on the shower. He punched the number he had memorized into the phone and waited. After two rings, a beeping sound came from the receiver followed by a recording in Arabic. He tried again with the same results. The number had obviously been disconnected; by which side, he couldn't know. "Damn!" he exclaimed as he hung up the telephone. He removed the electronic bugs from the telephone and the lamp and threw them off the balcony and into some bushes. He couldn't extract the one on the balcony, so he smashed it with the heel of his shoe.

"We have to get to Primakov," he whispered. "I'll try to see him here at the hotel, otherwise, we'll have to find some way to get aboard the plane he's taking back to Moscow."

"Let's just head for the plane. If we try here and fail, we may not get another chance."

Deiter thought about it a moment and replied, "You're right. Let's get to the airport. Once there, we can look for a way to board the plane. Under the circumstances, I don't think we have any real responsibility to check out of the hotel; besides, that might attract attention. Let's just get a taxi and go. Do you have anything in your luggage that you can't replace?"

"I'd love to replace all of it," she said, smiling.

"Good; pick out anything you do want to keep, and let's give the impression we'll be going out on the town again."

"You are so romantic," she said with a flip of her head as she headed for the door.

"What did I say?" he asked, as he picked up the diplomatic pouch containing the guns and scrambler they had used earlier.

"I always love a considerate and gentlemanly invitation to a party," she replied.

Deiter just shook his head. An idea then struck him and he quickly turned back to Charlie and asked, "Wait, do you think our friend from the embassy, Boris Ulanova, could help us get aboard Primakov's plane?"

"It could be worth a try. You might tell him that there's an emergency at home and that you would return to Baghdad within...say, 48 hours, but needed to get back to Moscow by tomorrow night."

"Wonderful idea," he responded.

Deiter retrieved the card that Ulanova had given him from his wallet and dialed the number. He waited as the phone rang three times and then clicked as it was answered by the sleepy voice of an Iraqi servant.

"I must to speak with Ambassador Ulanova, now!" Deiter instructed. He waited.

"**Da?** Ulanova." the reply came after a few minutes.

"Boris Ivanovich, this is Dmitri Andreiovitch, I need your help."

"What is it?"

"I have just been notified that I must return to Moscow...a family emergency. I have booked a flight for tomorrow night, but fear that I may be too late."

"But what can I do?" Ulanova asked.

"I understand that former Prime Minister Primakov is due to fly out tomorrow morning early. If I were to catch a ride with him, I could be back in Baghdad within 48 hours. Any meeting with the Economic Minister would not happen until then, anyway."

"A family emergency, you say? Yes, I would dare say so; I saw the newscast. I'll see what I can do. The government plane is still parked at the airport. You go there and wait; by that time I will have made arrangements."

"Thank you, Boris Ivanovich; I will be taking Anna Borisovna with me as well."

"Yes, I would hope so." The phone went dead and Deiter returned it to the receiver.

"He knows." Deiter said to Charlie quietly. She nodded. "Okay, change of plans, Charlie. Pack your bags and let's get out of here."

"I was looking forward to buying new ones," she said in mock disappointment.

A quick chat with the friendly bellhop and a healthy tip produced a taxicab, and they were on their way to the airport. It took almost forty–five minutes to get through the traffic and up to the terminal at the airport. It was past midnight as they walked up to the International Desk. The flight departure board indicated that no Aeroflot flights were scheduled to fly out until the next evening. Deiter went up to the counter and asked if anyone spoke Russian. A young woman replied in broken Russian that she spoke a little.

"Wonderful," Deiter responded. "We are suppose to join the Russian contingent aboard their flight back to Moscow tomorrow morning early. Can you help us?"

"That is a private national flight that is due to depart at four–fifty tomorrow morning. It's not due to board until shortly before that."

"We were suppose to catch an earlier flight, and had already checked out of our hotel when we were asked to join former Prime Minister Primakov on his return. He told us to meet him here at the airport. We have no place to go for tonight. Where is the airplane now?"

"It is on the tarmac outside of Gate Number C," she replied.

"We'll go to the gate and wait for them," he responded. "Thank you".

The passenger counter at Gate C was dark as they walked up to it. Deiter looked through the window of the terminal and spied the sleek modern Russian jetliner parked about fifty yards from the terminal on the tarmac. The plane was dark and only a minimum of lights illuminated it. Somehow, they needed to get aboard and await the contingent that was with Primakov. It was better than the uncertainty of waiting in the terminal.

"Wait here in case someone tries to contact us at the gate," he whispered to Charlie. "I'll see if I can find anyone aboard the plane."

"What about the luggage?" she asked, envisioning having to struggle with the four pieces they had between them.

"I'll come back up here for it."

169

Deiter slowly pushed the door to the exit open, looked through the crack, then slipped through the opening and disappeared down the stairway. Charlie watched through the window as he walked out onto the tarmac and around the darkened plane. A ramp with a set of stairs was pushed up to the forward hatch of the plane. Deiter walked up the stairs and rapped on the door. Inside the plane, a light came on in the window just behind the set of cockpit windows. A few moments later, the front hatch at the top of the ramp cracked open, and Charlie could see Deiter conversing with someone inside. Charlie wondered what line Deiter was thinking up this time. The door closed again and Deiter turned around and gave a short wave to Charlie standing at the window of the terminal. Deiter waited for almost five minutes until the door opened once more. This time, Deiter turned and clambered down the ramp and walked swiftly for the lower level door to the gate.

"We're on board; let's go," he announced as he came through the gate and commenced to pick up his luggage.

"I don't dare ask what you told them," she remarked.

"Better you don't," he chuckled.

Moments later, both of them were settled in plush seats aboard the aircraft pulling blankets around themselves and adjusting their pillows. The lights in the cabin were then dimmed by the onboard crew.

"So far, so good," Deiter whispered to Charlie in English. "I do hope Boris does his thing and clears it with Primakov's contingent."

"Can't worry about it now; we've only got a couple of hours left to rest." she observed as she turned over in her seat to face the window.

They immediately dozed off to sleep.

Ted Colby

Chapter Ten

Flight to Moscow

Saddam Hussein International Airport
Baghdad, Iraq
Early Monday morning, November 22, 1999

A thud and a clanking sound came from the front of the airplane as the door was opened; it finally awakened the two recent passengers aboard the Russian aircraft. Both Deiter and Charlie sat up expectantly, blinking at the light coming from the overhead lamps of the cabin. Considerable activity seemed to be occurring in the front of the aircraft, and they fought to ignore it at the same time they sought to regain their consciousness and perspective.

"Show time," whispered Deiter.

Charlie was now fully awake and alert. She nodded.

The hefty man with a pudgy face and glasses who was walking down the aisle of the airplane was immediately familiar to Deiter; he was the man they had seen on television standing next to Saddam Hussein the night before, Yevgeny Primakov. Deiter stood up and stepped into the aisle to greet him.

"Hello, Mr. Prime Minister, my name is Dmitri Andreiovitch Kolyushkin. I would like to present my aide, Anna Borisovna Cheklenov."

"I am very pleased to make the acquaintance of such an enchanting woman," Primakov said, as he took her hand and kissed it.

"Thank you for the complement." Charlie replied coyly, yet graciously.

"Please accept my thanks for allowing us to accompany you back to Moscow," Deiter said.

"Um, I understand that there was a personal emergency that required your immediate return," responded Primakov.

"Yes, it was quite unexpected."

"You are welcome to share this citizen's transport."

Primakov nodded to both of them and returned to the more spacious seats in the midsection of the aircraft and settled himself in the swivel seat reserved for him. Within ten minutes, the aircraft was rolling down the runway and into the airspace over Baghdad...destination, Moscow.

Deiter knew that from this time on, every minute counted. He considered how he would approach Primakov about the gun. He knew a little about the former Prime Minister. He knew that the man spoke both English and Arabic and could be a skillful, charming and even non-ideological diplomat when he needed to be. He remembered that Primakov was not his original name; he had been born Yona Finkelstein, a Jewish identity he had lost as a child and then rejected as he grew older. When he worked for the Soviet KGB, he counted himself a friend of Saddam Hussein's. He still resented American "hegemony" and thought Russia deserved to be treated as a great power. He also opposed NATO's expansion and the belt-tightening demands of the IMF, the International Monetary Fund, which he was convinced was a tool of Washington. But to the Western world, especially in the intelligence community, Primakov was still a known quantity, a pragmatic and hardheaded pursuer of what he perceived to be Russian national interests. He had served as a spy master and then as a hard-line foreign minister. As Prime Minister, he would likely move Russia leftward, with more government management of the economy. Although he had rejected being thrust into the role of President before, as Prime Minister he would be welcomed by the Communists as well as the moderates. As Deiter evaluated it, he concluded that this was a man who would listen first and react after applying reason and the self-interest of the Russian Republic. He decided that there was no more time left to think. This was the time to act. He retrieved the diplomatic briefcase from beneath his seat, stood up and walked forward to where Primakov was seated.

"Please forgive me, but I must talk to you in private; it is of the utmost urgency," Deiter began. He sat down in a jump seat facing the former Prime Minister and fixed his gaze on him; his steel gray eyes riveted on the man opposite him. "I am an American. I am a fraud. I am a spy. All of our lives are in immediate danger and I need your help now." Deiter waited for a reply to his confession.

"You speak Russian well," Primakov said quietly, "For a spy," he added in English. "We'd better speak in English. Tell me, why all this charade."

"I will be totally honest with you because there isn't much time," Deiter began. "I work for the CIA, and I planted a device on the President of Iraq that would locate him wherever he is and target him for death in an attack by cruise missiles. Unfortunately, he no longer has that beacon. He transferred it to you after he found out that it had been planted on him."

"Well now, that *is* quite a story…if it's true."

"It's true all right," Deiter replied, taking the handgun from the briefcase. "Here is the original gun. You have the one with the beacon in it." He handed the gun to Primakov.

The Prime Minister placed the gun on the seat next to him and reached down to pick up the box that he had placed under the seat in front of him. He opened the box and withdrew the weapon inside. Picking up the gun he had placed in the seat, he inspected them both.

"They appear to be identical," he announced.

"Not quite. Look at the serial number carefully. There has been a change in the first three letters; it was re-stamped. The original letters were FBI, not CRG."

"I see. They are slightly smudged. It's cleverly done, though."

"Then you believe me?"

"Well, let's not go quite that far," chuckled Primakov. "Now that you have convinced me that there are two identical guns, what's this all about?"

"At this very moment, there is a cruise missile ship that is firing at the signal that this weapon is sending. We are in immediate danger of being blown out of the sky."

"I think that to be a very serious thing," Primakov replied. "What do you propose we do about it?"

"Throw the gun overboard; get rid of it, now!"

"An assassin who misses his mark is now seeking to save the life of another?"

"An assassin who missed his mark is now hoping to save the life of someone who that mark has in turn condemned to death," Deiter responded. "Your death was never my intent or that of my government."

Primakov thought for a moment. He didn't doubt for a minute that what this man had told him was probably true. But that Saddam Hussein was guilty of conveying the instrument of his violent death to him in a false act of friendship was hard to accept...or was it? They had known each other for a very long time. He had believed that it was indeed a friendship built on mutual trust. What would be the purpose in Saddam wanting him dead? Maybe it wasn't personal, perhaps he was just a target of opportunity, and the long friendship meant nothing to Saddam. It may be that Saddam felt that in a war between the United States and Russia, Iraq would gain some benefit. Could the President of Iraq really be as evil as many had portrayed him to be? He shrugged back into his seat and closed his eyes for a moment.

"Keep this gun as a momento," Deiter said, as he handed one of the weapons to the Prime Minister. "Ditch the other; it has no value to you. Why else would I want you to do this?"

The argument finally found fertile ground. If Saddam had intended to kill him to further his own ambitions, and if he were to survive that attempt with no outward indication of the attempt, then Primakov reasoned that the upper hand would be his. Saddam would never be sure if his suspicions about the weapon were true or not. This would put the Iraqi at a disadvantage.

Primakov took the gun from Deiter, pulled himself up and walked toward the door to the pilot's cabin. He handed the gun to a crewmember and gave him instructions. The man looked bewildered, but opened the door to the cabin and disappeared inside. Primakov walked slowly back to his seat.

"It is done," he said simply as he sat down.

The engine noise lessened, and the front of the aircraft began to slope downward. Deiter glanced out of the window and saw that the ground was getting closer as the aircraft lost altitude; the flaps on the wing were fully extended. Obviously, the pilot was attempting to lessen the effect of the wind and air pressure when the portal was opened to fling the gun into the slipstream of the plane. One minute…two minutes…three minutes…passed slowly. Deiter kept saying to himself that they needed to hurry up the process; the cruise missiles could be on their way. The nose slowly regained its horizontal position once more and Deiter noticed that the plane had slowed considerably. He looked out the window again and saw that they were traveling at less that 1,000 feet above the scrub brush on the parched desert beneath them. A sound like the rush of air escaping came from the front of the plane; it lasted only a few seconds and then it stopped as suddenly as it had begun. The nose of the aircraft eased up and the engines increased in volume.

"There is only one gun now," Primakov said with a sly smile. He stretched back into his seat and added, "But then, there really was only one gun. Don't you agree, Dmitri Andreiovitch?"

Deiter nodded, stood up and started to walk back toward where Charlie was waiting expectantly. He had almost reached his seat when suddenly the plane shook violently and an explosion was heard coming from somewhere outside the aircraft. Deiter looked back at the former Prime Minister who had turned around and was looking directly at him as well. Primakov nodded, smiled and turned back around.

"I'd call that timing," he whispered to Charlie as he regained his seat next to her.

"You could have given us a slightly larger safety margin, you know," she replied.

Deiter smiled at the deliberate understatement and whispered back, "Primakov knows everything; I don't know what he'll do now." He then shrugged and added, "We did save his life, for whatever that's worth."

"From what I know of him," Charlie offered, "he'll let us play out the scene…but keep a good eye on us. He knows that he is the only other person who knows about it, and we certainly won't let the cat out of the bag. At this point, he has everything to gain by playing the game and nothing to gain from exposing us."

"I agree. When we get to Moscow, we've got to get to the embassy. It's the only place we'll be safe. We can even change our identities if it's necessary to get back stretching out in his seat and closing his eyes.

Chapter Eleven

The bin Laden Connection

Sheremet'yevo Airport, Moscow
Monday afternoon, November 22, 1999

The sleek, modern Russian aircraft touched down easily on the long runway of Moscow's Sheremet'yevo Airport and taxied to the terminal. It was just after noon, Moscow time. He knew the next few minutes would mean the difference between freedom and possibly even death. It all depended on how Primakov handled it. Deiter and Charlie waited until most of Primakov's party had departed the aircraft before they picked up their luggage that had been placed in the row behind them and started towards the front of the aircraft. As they neared the front exit door, they saw Primakov standing there alone waiting for them. The door to the pilot's cabin area was still closed, and Deiter assumed that this was to be a private conversation with the former Prime Minister.

"Where are you and your beautiful aide destined for now, Dmitri Andreiovitch?" the Prime Minister asked.

"Home, I should hope," replied Deiter cautiously. "I wish to thank you again…for a number of things," he added.

"Is it over, now?" Primakov asked, lifting one thick eyebrow over the rim of his glasses. The old KGB agent seemed to feel some sense of camaraderie with the two spies who saved his life and very possibly prevented a tragic and horrific war.

"As far as I know…at least for the two of us." Deiter replied.

"That's good. I think that you know why I will not reveal your secret. At this point, it is better it goes undiscovered. If I were you, I would find a way to your embassy as quickly as you can; sometimes the streets of Moscow harbor all sorts of people with less than good intentions. I cannot say that the situation will not take an unfortunate turn that would make me change my mind about reporting the incident. You do understand?"

"Perfectly, and we do plan to do as you suggest. I understand fully." Deiter paused and added, "Thank you, Sir."

Primakov smiled and stretched out his hand towards Deiter. "I do hope we'll meet again under more pleasant circumstances," he said. Turning to Charlie and taking her hand, he kissed it once more and said, "And you, my dear, I will be devastated should I not see you again." He turned and walked towards the door to the airplane; when he had reached it, he turned and said, "Wait a few minutes, I'll be clear of the aircraft and any inquisitive people who will undoubtedly be following me. Goodbye, Comrad Kolyushkin.

Deiter nodded his understanding and added, "Goodbye, Mister Prime Minister, and thank you again." As soon as Primakov was gone, he looked over at Charlie and said, "Is he a diplomat or not?"

"He could charm the honey off a bee," she replied with an exaggerated Southern accent.

"Likes the ladies, too," Deiter added with a grin.

"Oh, shut up, you're just jealous because you don't have the knack; he's very charming."

"Suave," Deiter muttered. "But I like him. What you see is what you get."

"And we had better get to the embassy as he recommended," she replied with an affected sternness in her voice. Deiter rolled his eyes.

They waited fully five minutes for the entourage to clear the aircraft and enter the terminal. When it looked clear, Deiter and Charlie grabbed their luggage and made their way down the stairs of the ramp. They slipped into a doorway leading from the tarmac to the terminal and walked down the main terminal walkway.

"Apparently, VIP planes don't have any customs inspections here," Deiter observed, as they walked towards the exit and the taxi pickup strip.

"Nice for us," Charlie replied.

"I can't believe this went off as well as it did," Deiter said.

"I thought you'd be disappointed that Saddam didn't find the wrong end of a cruise missile."

"I gave it my best shot for the time being; the guy's lucky, it won't last forever. Someday, he'll get his, even though it's not today…and not from me."

At the taxi pickup area outside the terminal, Deiter and Charlie climbed into a taxi and gave directions for the American Embassy. Thirty minutes later, they were pulling up in front of a building with a plaque containing the American eagle. They paid the driver with the last of their combined Russian rubles and went inside.

"That was easy," Charlie whispered to Deiter as they moved through the main reception hall of the Embassy.

"Without Primakov, we'd have been part of the gulag clientele by now," he responded.

They walked up to a desk where a stern looking Russian woman was seated.

"We would like to see the Ambassador or the Chief of Mission Security right away," Deiter instructed the woman.

"I'm afraid that is impossible," she replied officiously. "That will require an appointment."

Deiter looked around and spotted a Marine standing next to a set of double doors, which looked as though they led to the inner part of the embassy. He ignored the woman and walked over to the Marine.

"My name's Deiter; this is Waggner. We're CIA and need to get asylum now," he whispered to the man sternly. "Give the head of security our names. We just got in from Baghdad."

The Marine reached over and picked up a wall-mounted telephone. He punched in two numbers and waited. When a reply to the call came on line, he drawled in a distinctly Southern accent, "Need to speak to the Colonel. Ah've got two here who say they'ah CIA." He waited several seconds and said, "Deiter and Waggner." He waited for a reply, and suddenly his face lighted up, "Roger that, suh." The Marine turned back to Deiter as he hung the phone back on its bracket.

"Follow me, suh. Uh, you too, ma'am."

Deiter and Charlie followed the Marine through the double doors and down the hallway. At the end of the hallway, they stopped at a door marked, "Security." The Marine knocked on it. Behind the door came the command, "Come." The Marine opened the door for the two visitors and indicated that they should enter. They did.

"Welcome to Moscow, you two; I gather your trip was comfortable." Ashton Woods was standing next to the large wooden desk in the center of the room; the nameplate on his desk read "Head of Security." He was smiling generously and genuinely appeared to be glad to see them.

"Ashton Woods? Isn't Moscow a bit out of your element?" inquired Deiter. "Last week you were stationed at the safe house in Rome."

Woods laughed. "You're right, Mr. Deiter. I was visiting my counterpart here in Moscow when I heard we might have missed the target with the cruise missiles. When Saddam came on television from Basra, I knew it. Our contact in Baghdad then left a message that said he had been asked to secure a ride for the both of you to Moscow, so I stayed here hoping to contact you. I heard you flew up here with Primakov...really? But, forgive my manners, please be seated. You must be exhausted."

"Under the circumstances, I think we lucked out rather well," interjected Charlie, as she plopped herself down on a large sofa that was obviously Russian-made.

"Tell me about Primakov; what happened?" asked Woods enthusiastically.

"He knows all about the attempt on Saddam," Deiter responded as he walked over to join Charlie on the sofa.

"And he let you go?"

"Primakov's a bit more complex than we might have realized. He finally came to the conclusion that Saddam was willing to have him killed if it meant a war between Russia and us. He now knows that the 'friendship' between them meant absolutely nothing to Saddam. He figures that he now has an upper hand over his former 'friend.' Saddam doesn't know whether the gun presented to him was really a beacon or not. Primakov also has a clearer view about his old 'friend' and will be more careful of him in the future. A positive for us."

"So, in a way, your mission did have positive results even though Saddam wasn't killed."

"Yeah, right," Deiter said, settling next to Charlie.

Now that the mission was over and they were safely in the embassy, Deiter began to realize that the devil he sought to destroy had, in the end, escaped his wrath. In one way, he felt a sense of total failure in his mission to revenge Rose's death; as though he had let her down. He had so wanted to wreak his personal vengeance upon the man who had caused her death…but he had failed. For that, he felt totally emasculated, dejected and helpless. There was something deep inside him, though, that felt relief that it wasn't his actions that were the key to a man's death. Had Saddam deserved to die? Certainly, but even under these circumstances, Jack wasn't feeling comfortable with being the one directly responsible. Too many years in the Bureau, he guessed, had given him respect for life.

"I think I know what you're thinking right now, Jack," Woods observed, "but there's more to this than what you've been led to believe. The original CIA evaluation wasn't all together correct, no. And, it now appears that there was someone more directly responsible; someone who is even now being sought by both the Russians and us...Osama bin Laden. Saddam knew of the plan to destroy Flight 63, but it was bin Laden who masterminded it and carried it out; it most certainly received the full approval and support from Saddam. He was far from blameless."

Deiter could see where this was probably leading and didn't like it. Were they just playing with him once more? Another thought came to mind. "Does General Henderson know what's going on, now?" he asked Woods.

"General Henderson will be here by noon tomorrow. I understand he'll attend the briefing for Don Adams at 1400 hours who's due to arrive late tonight from Washington.

"Adams is coming here?" Deiter asked, with an obvious disappointment in his voice.

Woods nodded, "About midnight," he confirmed.

Deiter's eyes grew cold; he shook his head. "No, you don't. Get yourself another boy, Woods. I'm through. I won't go to Afghanistan; the Taliban hates Americans and Russians and I'm not too fond of them either."

"But, he's not in Afghanistan, Mr. Deiter, he's here in Russia…in Chechnya, that is…Grozny, or just outside it." Woods let that news sink in for a moment before continuing. "The Russians want him as badly as we do and are eager to cooperate. He is known to be helping the Islamic rebels in Chechnya and that poses a threat to the Russian Republic. Why do you think you're here…and alive now?'

"Saving Primakov's life certainly helped."

"Yes, Primakov, of course. As you said, he didn't know about the attempt on Saddam until you told him, but he has known about the bin Laden connection we have for some time. It was his old KGB contacts that first led to our knowing that a certain contact who had once helped bin Laden in the 1970s might be able to convince him to come to Chechnya to continue his personal jihad there."

"I'm still not convinced. I'm not sure why you guys didn't realize that the real danger was bin Laden; I told Adams that the whole thing smelled of bin Laden, but he was sure it was Saddam. Now he's sure it's bin Laden. Do you see my problem with all this? I'm not sure you guys know what you're doing. Maybe you have another agenda."

Woods sighed and sat down on the desk. He thought for a moment and finally said, "Yes, Mr. Deiter, we want to get rid of both of them, and we are not fussy about how it's done." He paused and then brightened up and said, "But, why don't you two get settled upstairs and we'll talk about it later. I know you must be exhausted."

Deiter pushed himself up from the sofa and headed for the door. Charlie got up and followed, but stopped and turned back towards Woods and nodding, mouthed the words "it's okay" and continued out of the door after Deiter.

The upstairs suites set aside for dignitaries were spacious and comfortable. This particular one had two bedrooms and a central living room area; their luggage had been placed in their respective bedrooms, allowing both Deiter and Charlie some time alone to settle into their accommodations. After unpacking, Deiter flopped onto the double bed and closed his eyes. He needed to sort out his feelings

The diverse emotions that spun around in his head presented an increasingly confusing picture. It was impossible to choose the right thing to do at this point. He had wanted so badly to finally put an end to the hurt and sadness in his life. He thought that being a part of causing the death of the one responsible for what happened to Rose would somehow be a catharsis that would free him. It wasn't happening.

Now, a new evil had suddenly appeared; apparently the one who was really responsible for Rose's death. When would it ever end? Could he ever again believe what he's told? Who could he ever trust again? Was Osama bin Laden the one, or was he just the next one on the list that they wanted him to kill?

Deiter stopped his self-harangue and considered a basic fact about himself; he simply wasn't an assassin. Someone was trying to make him into one, but he didn't take the role of an assassin easily and never could. So what would he do? He wanted the person who was responsible for Rose's death to pay for it, and his desire for vengeance had been overwhelmingly great, but at the same time, he couldn't see himself any more as the executioner. He had spent too much time with the Bureau to take human life without the due process of law. There had to be another way. Planting the device on Saddam seemed to be a significant step away from pulling the trigger, but maybe it wasn't in reality. Maybe even that would be a direct act of murder. He had killed before, when it was necessary. He was more used to bringing in a perpetrator to face a court, a judge and a jury. He sighed heavily in recognition that he knew what he had to do. He doubted that the CIA, Adams or even Hank would be happy with his decision, but he knew what he'd have to try. If they wanted his help, it had to be his way.

As Deiter had done so many times in the past when faced with a difficult decision, he let his mind wander on every fact he could recall concerning the background of the problem. He lay there on his bed with his hands clasped behind his head and his eyes closed…a thousand facts and memories swirling through his head. Several hours had passed since he had first stretched out on the bed when he was interrupted by a voice at the doorway to his room.

"Penny for your thoughts?"

Deiter turned his head and smiled up at Charlie. "Do you really want to know?"

"Yes, matter of fact," she replied seriously.

Deiter swung his legs around and sat up on the bed. "I was just going over in my mind what went on down stairs and how this whole thing comes together."

"It's past noon, come on out here and I'll fix you a drink. You look like you could use one," she said as she turned to head for the bar in the common room.

Deiter stretched and finally got up and ambled out into the next room to find Charlie busily getting them both a drink from the bar. He wandered over to the sofa and collapsed on it.

"They have Jamison's, isn't that your poison?" she asked. "How'll you have it?"

"On the rocks, Charlie, thanks."

Charlie crossed over to where Deiter was sitting with two highball glasses in her hands and put one down on the coffee table in front of the sofa on which Deiter was sprawled. She sat in an overstuffed chair opposite the sofa. Holding up her glass, she proposed a toast. "Here's to whatever you now have in mind, Jack Deiter."

"I wish I knew, Charlie, I wish I knew."

Deiter watched as Charlie raised her glass to her lips and let the cool whiskey flow down her throat; she drew in a deep breath as the warmth flowed through her. She leaned back and tilting her head as she squinted her eyes, "Okay, Jack, what's the problem?" she said, "You know you can trust me."

"It's not simple, Charlie. There are a lot of things involved here. First, I haven't been trained as an assassin. I'm not one. As much as I would like to see Saddam...or bin Laden blasted to hell, I'm really not the one to do it. I guess I've been in the Bureau too long. We've been conditioned to handle things differently. I could kill someone in the heat of a firefight without blinking an eye. But, to seek someone out just to kill him, especially when it's not a matter of immediate danger to me or someone I care for, well, that's just not me."

"What about Chechnya? When Woods mentioned it, I saw a sudden change come over you. What's that all about?"

Deiter took a long, slow sip on his Jamison. He then stood up and walked over to the window and looked out with his back toward Charlie. His thoughts went back to what Woods had said downstairs. The very words themselves, Chechnya...Grozny, once again conjured up in his mind a myriad of faces, scenes, memories, and emotions. "Charlie," he began, "is there such a phenomenon as inherited memory in humans, you know, the kind they call instinct in lower animals?" He didn't wait for a response. "Well, this sort of thing seems to be happening to me right now and has for some time. You know something of my family's heritage from when we worked together last year; it seems that I've filled in a lot of the voids in my knowledge of that heritage through some sort of instinctive imagery of inherited memory."

"I know that your parents were originally Soviet deep agents planted in the United States sometime in the sixties," she responded. "Their names were John and Constance Deiter, as I recall."

"That's right, Charlie. I learned something about their early years together in Grozny from my "Uncle" Bill, William Colby; he was then Director of the CIA. You might say he kinda took me under his wing right after my parents' death, although I never understood why. He sent me a letter, which was to be opened after I graduated from Annapolis. It explained where they had come from and that they had illegally immigrated to this country. Their names were different then. But, it was only last year that I learned about their original purpose in coming to America and about the training they'd received from the KGB. As deep agents for the Soviet Union, they had been thoroughly conditioned on how to insert themselves into the American landscape. Their past had been created for them complete with documents, momentos, ancestors and even other living 'family' members. For awhile, they had been some of the most important and deeply planted agents of the Soviet Union. That was until they came to realize that their son could have a real future in this country living in freedom. They defected to 'Uncle' Bill."

"Weren't they killed because they defected?"

"Yeah, in a way I guess they were patriots to the country that offered them a new a way of life. On the other hand, the Soviet Union turned out to be quite ruthless when it felt betrayed. Or maybe it was just the "Russian" psyche, I don't know. Anyway, after their death, their secret lay hidden for several decades. Last year, when I discovered the truth, I began to wonder about the history of my newly realized ancestral homeland. I never had the opportunity to go there, but I researched everything I could lay my hands on. I took to the Russian language like it was always inside me just waiting to come out. My lineage is Russian, but my heritage is Chechen. I was lucky to have Rose to tutor me. I found out that my ancestors had fought with the Cossack regiments that sided with the Red Army during the revolution of 1917. Later, my family was settled near Grozny by the Moscow government as a part of the Russification of the land. Although my father was Russian, my mother was Chechen. I guess because of that, I sympathized not only with the Chechen Moslems who claimed the land, but also with the essentially Christian Russians who had been transplanted there; it had become their homeland as well."

"What caused all this hatred between the two factions?" Charlie asked.

"Well, like many other places in the world where different cultures clash, Chechnya is a shared homeland. It's claimed by more than one people, neither of which seem to be able to bring themselves to share the land or live in peace. Sometimes it's hard to understand this mutual hatred unless one's part of it. Violence begets violence and repeatedly opens old wounds so that the bleeding continues all over again. Lives become decimated by righteousness, revenge and retribution and that perpetuates the killing and the renewed hatred it breeds. Each new atrocity is coveted by the perpetrator as a victory and by the victim as a badge of courage. Under such circumstances, it would seem doubtful if anything could stop the continuing carnage."

"You realize that Chechnya isn't alone in this regard, Jack," Charlie observed. "Other places in the world have had the same problems and beg the same questions. Will the Irish factions ever be able to live together and find peace? Will the Jews and the Palestinians ever live as brothers and as mutual descendants of Abraham? Is there ever going to be forgiveness between the Bosnians and the Albanians? In each case, both sides have committed atrocities against the innocent. Both have returned blood for blood with no forgiveness or understanding. Hatreds that were spawned over five hundred, a thousand or even two thousand years ago were jealously coveted over the centuries and have little chance of being snuffed out by anything except mutual destruction or total war against a common foe. Such a thing happened in Yugoslavia years ago. They banded together against the Nazis. At times, that foe has been the State, or a vicious tyrant, or an invading army, but whenever this anomaly occurred, it was always something so important that it broke their concentration on the series of hatreds for their neighbors and they worked in harmony.

"To a lesser degree, Charlie, it happened in Chechnya during the Second World War. Old grudges were, for a time, set aside while both sides worked against the common foe. They shared a mutual hated or fear. Then, when Stalin suddenly reversed himself and believing that the Chechens were siding with the enemy, he broke all allegiance he professed to have with the Chechens. In return, they welcomed the invaders as liberators. Later, they were to be betrayed again; this time by Hitler. Between World War II and now there was a peace of sorts. More recently, though, both Yelsen and Putin vowed to destroy the Chechens completely."

Both of them were silent for awhile. In his reverie, Deiter wondered about the fate of his ancestral homeland and the chances that all parties could eventually live in peace. He considered this new assignment of his and how he would eventually deal with the two factions there. He would have to gain the trust of the rebels in order to locate and capture bin Laden. He knew that it wouldn't be easy and he was going to be challenged in the process. There was a finite difference in how he would be perceived by both sides. But, Osama bin Laden was even more of an outsider in this conflict then he was and he guessed that the Chechens would not trust the Arabian fully even though they wanted his money and what it would buy them. They knew that bin Laden hated the United States, but they also knew that Chechnya had received hundreds of millions of dollars in aide from the Americans while the rest of the world, even the Arab nations, had provided them almost nothing. Most particularly, bin Laden's own country, Saudi Arabia, had offered only a bare half-million to help the badly war-torn land seeking independence. Although the Chechens were Moslem, they were Caucasian and not Arabic. It would seem that an American with a Chechen background might have more credibility there than anyone else. Deiter considered that carefully in formulating his plan of action.

Finally, Deiter walked over to the table next to the sofa and picked up the telephone. He looked at Charlie and shrugged, "I think I've made up my mind," he said quietly. Charlie looked quizzically at him as he asked the operator to be connected to Security. The phone rang three times. "Woods," finally came the response.

"Ashton? Deiter. Say, I have a proposition for you; are you interested?"

"Why don't you come down and we'll discuss it?"

"Don't expect too much."

"Let's talk about it," Woods concluded.

Deiter slowly hung up the telephone and looked up at Charlie. "I don't know what's going to come of this, but whatever's decided, you know you'll be the first to know. Charlie just nodded and watched as he left the suite and closed the door behind him.

Moscow; the American Embassy
Tuesday morning, November 23, 1999

Charlie pushed the button in the elevator for the first floor. A few minutes ago she had been wakened by a call from embassy security and informed that she was expected in the office of the chief of security as soon as possible. It seemed strange as she was still recuperating from the mission, but she guessed it was something new concerning Iraq. She hadn't seen Jack Deiter since he had left to talk with Woods the afternoon before. She had been worried about him, but decided that he would be true to his promise and let her know what the next step was going to be. Right now, she wanted to get a flight back to the States and put this behind her for awhile.

The elevator came to a stop at the ground floor and Charlie quickly stepped out into the hallway. She walked down to the office of the Chief of Security, knocked on the door and waited. After what seemed like a long pause, she heard a low male voice telling her to enter. Charlie swung open the door and sauntered inside, closing the door behind her. She had expected one of the embassy staff or even Ashton Woods, but as she turned back towards the center of the room, she saw a Russian colonel standing with his back to her, his hands clasped behind his back; he was looking out the window. He is dressed in a dark blue uniform; his visor cap and his shoulder boards were trimmed with the light blue piping of the FSB, the Federal Security Bureau, the successor to the infamous KGB. Her first thought was that she was being turned over to the FSB as a spy. She quickly thought of her alternatives, some means of escape, logical alibis…anything. In the back of her mind she damned the lack of security of the Embassy as well as the dubious loyalty of the CIA to its operatives. Charlie steadied herself as the colonel slowly turned around to face her. She stared into the face of Jack Deiter.

"Damn it, Jack, you scared the shit out of me!" she exploded. "What the hell are you doing in that godforsaken getup?"

"I'm going to Chechnya," he replied quietly.

"Where'd you get the monkey suit?" she asked, still visibly shaken.

"Primakov," he answered with a smile. "I think the old boy's taken a shine to me. You know, the old ex-spy mutual admiration society…that sort of thing."

"You still scared the shit out of me!" she reiterated, collapsing into the sofa in front of the desk.

Deiter took off his hat and, placing it on the desk, sat down next to Charlie. "I'm sorry, I didn't think about the effect the uniform might have."

"Damn right," she replied in a sulk. Charlie began to recover and suddenly realized the impact of what Deiter had just said. She recouped her control. "Chechnya?" she asked.

"Yes," he began, "I know that bin Laden's supposed to be there, and that he's now the prime suspect in the bombing, but in the end, it was the draw of the land and my heritage there, I guess, that was too much for me to resist. I've got to go and to do whatever I can. I'll get bin Laden, believe that."

"Oh, I believe you think that, all right, but are you really going to assassinate him?"

"No, I'm going to take him alive and bring him back to Moscow…initially, to face charges in Russian courts…that's the deal I struck with Woods. I've been a cop for too long, Charlie, I've got to go with my conscience and my past training. Actually, I think he'd be safer in a Russian gulag than in the US Federal Prison system. At least he won't be let out on a technicality by some fuzzy headed judge and he sure as hell won't escape from there."

"But why are you going as a FSB colonel? Why not just infiltrate?"

"They thought I'd have a better chance getting through the lines as FSB. Once in position, I'll change clothes and make contact with someone who's knowledgeable about the movement of the rebels. I'll still be getting information from the CIA contact there who'll set up the confrontation."

"Need any help? Anna Borisnova's still willing and able," she asked with a grin and a flirty swish of her dress over her crossed legs.

"You know I would, Charlie, but it's too dangerous," he replied. "I can fake it as a FSB colonel for awhile, but they travel alone, sorry. A female aide would soften my image."

"Do you know who your contact is?"

"All I know is that it's a woman…maybe the same one we saw in Rome."

"Oh, you didn't tell me about her," she replied guardedly, her mouth in a barely perceptible smirk.

Deiter seemed embarrassed as he stuttered, "Yeah…well there was this woman whom I saw from the window…who looked like…," he broke off his explanation.

"Like Rose?" Charlie asked.

"Yeah, but she wasn't. I'm convinced of that now," he said shaking his head. "It was just a similarity, that's all…and the light was poor and my imagination was working overtime, I guess."

Charlie sat back in the sofa and Deiter knew she was thinking about the incident when Jack and Hank suddenly ran out of the room in Rome. She now knew why they didn't say anything when they returned to the room. He knew she would still think it was a strange coincidence, however. Was he going to Chechnya just to see if the contact might really be Rose? Was this the real reason? If Rose were really dead and she if was killed in the airline crash and that was a fact, could he be just running after a ghost?

"When are you going?" she asked.

"Probably tomorrow morning. I have to get used to this uniform and acting the part of a FSB colonel in the meantime."

Charlie was quiet.

"You okay?" he asked.

"I don't have a good feel about this, Jack," she said cautiously.

201

"Neither do I," he responded, "but it's the only way."

Charlie leaned over and wrapped her arms around Deiter...he responded. After a moment, they slowly relaxed and moved apart.

"I'm sorry," Charlie said. "I didn't mean that as it might have appeared. I'm just so worried about what might happen...my not being there, I guess, makes it worse."

"Don't be...sorry, that is," Deiter replied. "Charlie. I know that you're concerned and that you care what happens to me. I really thank you for that. You're a very special person. That's why Rose felt so close to you. She knew how sensitive you were."

"Can I help?"

"Stay with me during the briefings today; see if you can pick up anything I might miss."

She nodded and pulled herself up from the sofa. "Let me know when and where," she said as she walked over to the door. She paused and looked back at Deiter, smiled, and left the room closing the door behind her.

Deiter slowly rose from the sofa and moved towards the window. He stood there for awhile thinking. A mellow sadness enveloped him. He sighed and leaning his hands against the window frame looked out at the Moscow skyline. His frustrating failure in Iraq, the near catastrophe he had help create, his moving once more into the unknown in Chechnya. Was anything in his search for Rose's killer going to be any more productive?

He somehow doubted the story of bin Laden being the primary cause of the downing of Flight 63. He'd been misled before by Adams; why not now? Yet, for the most part it made sense. All probabilities now pointed to bin Laden's being in Chechnya. It would have been just the type of thing in which he would get involved. His hatred for the United States was equal to his hatred for the Soviet Union or Russia; it was all the same to him. He had fought the Soviets in Afghanistan and was at first deceived and then betrayed by the Americans, or so he claimed. With the Taliban being pressured to turn over bin Laden to the Americans so that he could be tried for the murders and the destruction of their embassies, it would be safer for him to be beyond their control. If matters became any worse, the Taliban could always claim, and truthfully so, that he was no longer in Afghanistan and that they knew nothing of his whereabouts. He would find ready friends among the Chechens who would want his money and his connections to buy more modern weapons. This all seemed to make sense, yet Deiter knew that the national policy was not usually developed on such flimsy suppositions, but rather on hard facts and personal observations.

Deiter wondered about the Russian woman whom he mistook for Rose. Were the men in Arab dress he had seen in Rome colleagues of bin Laden? Could it have been bin Laden himself who shared the safe house in Rome with them? If so, the Arabian terrorist may not have realized that he was in an American CIA safe house. That would have been, as Jimmy Durante used to say, "a revoltin' development" for bin Laden if he had ever found out who the landlord was. Yet how better to get bin Laden into a situation and place where he would feel entirely safe in the company of fellow rebels, and allow a chance at assassination or capture by either the Russians or the Americans. But, if that were true, why didn't the Americans simply capture or kill bin Laden in the safe house?

Deiter thought he knew the answer to that one. If bin Laden could be lured to Chechnya and captured there in the act of sabotage and complicity with the rebels, there would be no legal wranglings to interfere. Capturing him in Italy might have opened a political can of worms that the CIA didn't want to touch. It was well known that if tried in a court in the United States or Russia, bin Laden most probably would have faced the death penalty. Capital punishment was not very popular with most European governments and if extradited, they would most certainly require assurances that he would not be executed. Putting bin Laden in prison would only be a reason for more terrorist activity to force his release; that would be unacceptable. Bin Laden had to die, one way or the other. The war in Chechnya could also provide something positive for the Russians and one that would fit with the American priorities as well; the neutralization of Osama bin Laden might lay the groundwork for future cooperation between the Americans and Russians in dealing with worldwide terrorism. In recent years, Russia had itself felt the sting from some of the same terrorists who had long plagued the West. Deiter wondered who had thought up this scenario. The poetic justice, the complete irony of the plan had Don Adams' signature written all over it.

Suddenly, the thought of Adams brought something else to mind, something that Rose had told him about a year ago, when they had met once more after losing track of each other for over twenty years. Because of her linguistic abilities, Rose's last assignment after she left Rome in 1974 was to arrange for and complete a secret sale of arms to the new Afghan government of President Mohammed Daud, a former prime minister who in 1973 ended the monarchy of Mohammed Zahir Shah, abolished all royal titles including his own and proclaimed a republic. The arms deal was supposed to provide the new government with enough strength to protect itself against pro-Soviet leftists. Washington had not only condoned it, but the CIA actually promoted the arms transfer. At that time, it was the thing to do to thwart any potential move by the "Evil Empire."

Rose had become friendly with the Afghan group and had eventually traveled extensively in what would become the Taliban controlled parts of Afghanistan. There, she had met many of the people who would eventually become the Taliban. To them, she was a Chechen who was interested in establishing an independent nation of Chechnya. At that time, she also had met bin Laden, he was an intermediary to the Afghans from Saudi Arabia. She also met many others who would eventually end up in prestigious positions in the Taliban militia. After she completed the job, she went back to Washington.

She was suppose to have returned directly to the States from Rome and had planned to meet Jack Deiter at that time. It was to be at exactly six o'clock on December 25, 1974 for a Christmas Eve dinner in a little pub in Alexandria. They had frequented the bar while in training at the CIA School. They knew that they may not be able to contact each other while one or the other was on mission and relied on this specially arranged tryst to be a safeguard against not being able to communicate and losing contact with each other. At the appointed time, Deiter had arrived at the place and waited until long after midnight. At the time, though, she was still in Afghanistan finishing up the arms deal with the new government. When she didn't show up, he was devastated, yet he assumed that she had made other plans or had met someone else.

When Rose finally returned to the United States in mid January of 1975, she inquired of Don Adams about Jack Deiter. But, Adams had lied convincingly and told her that Deiter had suddenly resigned and claimed he knew nothing of her former partner's current whereabouts. Rose too, then resigned from the CIA and returned to her parent's home in Upper Saddle River, New Jersey to begin a new life for herself. She had never really trusted Adams' explanation, but proving that he lied would be impossible and there was certainly no other way of finding Deiter.

Deiter wondered if the Russian contact he saw in Rome could possibly be a lookalike substitute for Rose in order to act as a contact to get into bin Laden's camp. Could Rose's death been an unfortunately timed flaw in Adams' plan? One he had tried to fix by use of a double? Maybe there was something even more sinister that was going on as well. Deiter wondered if...suddenly he straightened up as though he had been shocked; his eyes stared, wide open, incredulously. Could Adams have...oh, my God, Deiter thought. Even Adams' mind couldn't be that twisted...or could it?

Ted Colby

Chapter Twelve

Complications

The American Embassy
Moscow
Tuesday afternoon, November 23, 1999

The room was not that large; apparently they had not expected too many people would be in attendance. In fact, only ten people were authorized to attend this briefing and be privy to the project. It was twelve-forty-five in the afternoon, and Ashton Woods looked anxiously at his watch. He paced nervously back and forth at the head of the oval mahogany conference table. Seated at the table in the twelve dark brown leather arm chairs were the American ambassador to Russia, Walter J. O'Sullivan; Brigadier General Hank Henderson of U. S. Army Intelligence; Don Adams of the CIA; Colonel General Andrei Konykov of the Russian Federal Security Service (FSB); Andrew J. Donavan, the U. S. Embassy's Chief of Security; James K. O'Reilly, the CIA's Chief of Mission for Russia; and Deputy Assistant Premier for Internal Affairs, Yuri Sarkorosov, who represented the interests of the political factions of the Russian government. Colonel John H. Kosty, Military Attaché to the Embassy, sat in one of the upright chairs that lined the two opposing walls of the room.

Ambassador O'Sullivan had just been appointed to his position earlier in the month and was still feeling his way around. He was a mousy looking man with a thin mustache and gaunt face that gave him an older appearance than his 54 years should deserve. In fact, he looked very much like a character out of a 1938 gangster movie. The President, whom he had known at Oxford and whom he had admired greatly for his stand against the war in Vietnam, was only happy to appoint his former colleague and friend to fill one of the most important diplomatic posts in the world. But the type of activity he had just been briefed on, and was probably about to sanction, didn't sit very well with him. He had been a stanch supporter of the Democratic Party for many years and in his various capacities within the Party, had done things that might even have been termed illegal or at least unsavory, but he had also been careful. That, of course, had been in New Jersey where he knew the State and how it operated; it was also at a time when he was well connected to people who would protect him. He was out of his protective element here in Russia. This activity, while it might be extremely beneficial to the United States and might even build a closer link with Russia, could backfire. If it did, it would be a tremendous embarrassment to him. He knew very little about this agent that Woods and Adams were foisting on him and he had never trusted the CIA during the many years he had been involved in politics. He knew also that for all his loyalty to the President, if anything went wrong he would be the one hung out to dry. The President didn't take heat for anyone. After this meeting, he would know better how to handle the situation. He squirmed nervously in his chair and looked up at Woods with a face that had impatience written all over it.

Colonel General Andrei Vladimirovitch Konykov was a thick, but not overly heavy man. He had a kindly face and looked somewhat like a stereotype of a simple, benevolent Russian grandfather. The intense intellect that sparkled forth from his dark eyes, however, immediately discounted that notion. He was five and a half feet tall and wore his dark blue uniform as comfortably as though he had always been an officer. On his chest, he proudly wore the red ribbon and medal of Hero of the Soviet Union, the Order of the Red Star, the Valor Medal for action in Chechnya, and the Chechen Campaign Medal as well as the Medal for Afghanistan. Konykov had started out in the enlisted ranks of the Soviet Army when he was only seventeen and had shown so much promise that he was sent to study for his commission at the Officer's Training School. After a tour of duty in the Soviet Armored Corps, he was transferred to Army Intelligence. The KGB soon became aware of his uncanny ability to sift through the chaff of a complicated situation and focus on the crux of it. He was solution-oriented and displayed an intense appreciation for timing and the ability to choose individuals on sight who would provide him success in his missions. Once initiated into the KGB, he quickly rose through the ranks. When the Soviet government was in its last throes of existence, he was among the first to side with those who prevailed. When the FSB was created out of the remnants of the KGB, he was chosen to serve in one of the top power positions. He viewed the Interior Ministry with complete disdain for harboring whom he considered were lazy holdovers from the obsolescent Communist regime. Yuri Sarkorosov, the Deputy Assistant Premier for Internal Affairs, was the personification of Konykov's complaint with the MVD.

Sarkorosov had a somewhat feminine face; it was round, pudgy and smooth. Surrounding it was a large shock of white hair. He was well dressed and looked like the consummate bureaucrat, which of course he was. Sarkorosov was invited to this meeting simply out of protocol; the MVD had a strong presence in Chechnya and his assistance could be extremely helpful to the mission; his interference, on the other hand, could be devastating to the mission. Sarkorosov had been a bureaucrat of the Communist Party for over thirty years. Until the demise of the Soviet Union, his future had been pretty much confirmed in the hierarchy of the Party.

This war with Chechnya was a confusing and frustrating interlude for Sarkorosov. He simply did not understand the Chechen situation. As far as he was concerned, the Chechens were nothing more than a stupid and rebellious people who did not appreciate the attributes or conveniences of a more advance form of government. He thought that way when the government he served was Communist and he thought that way now. He had never been to the Caucasus region and really never intended to travel there if he could help it. The people there were little more than savages as far as he was concerned. Even the czars had experienced problems with those people. Time after time, the Russian government, both czars and Communists alike had relocated the troublemakers to Siberia. Unfortunately, time after time, these same people had returned one by one, family by family, back to the land that they imagined was some sort of homeland for them. They were animals, not rational human beings that could accept their new status and remain in the outlands of the Soviet Union to make something of themselves and serve the State. They had a strange and unacceptable attraction to this particular mountain region and continued to maintain their own backward customs. They were an odd race of people, he thought.

Except for Don Adams, the rest of the American contingent seated at the table looked as though they were fairly competent and eager to push forward with the plan. Adams wore his usual wrinkled tweed jacket and filled the large leather chair at the conference table as though it were wrapped around him. The collar on his off-white shirt was dark where it hit his beard and neck and was turned up at the ends. He looked like he had just arrived by air and had not had the opportunity to rest or clean up before the meeting.

In comparison, Hank Henderson, who had arrived on the same flight, looked rested and was dressed in a neatly cut dark suit that looked recently pressed. His white shirt was fresh and set off the black, gray and gold regimental tie that spoke of his West Point background.

Andrew J. Donavan, the U. S. Embassy's Chief of Security, and James K. O'Reilly, the CIA's Chief of Mission for Russia looked as though they might be brothers. Both were initially recruited into the government through the FBI and had served apprenticeships together with the Bureau. When the position of Chief of Security came open, O'Reilly, who was already assigned to the Embassy, recommended his old friend for the job.

Colonel John H. Kosty, Military Attaché at the Embassy, came to his position with the new Ambassador. He had recently been promoted and his Russian language background and graduate degree in Political Science from Columbia University were all that the Ambassador needed to pressure the Army into reassigning his college classmate to accompany him to Moscow. Kosty didn't agree with his new boss politically while they were in graduate school and hadn't changed his opinions or orientation since. About politics, he kept his opinions to himself and his mouth shut. His selection at the Embassy, he knew, would be a feather in his career cap and he was determined to stick it out...two years couldn't be that bad, he figured. Besides that, his wife, Shelly, was pleased as punch at the opportunity to meet and be cozy with all sorts of important people she would meet or entertain in this exotic location.

As Woods began once more to apologize for the delay in commencing the briefing, the door to the conference room opened and a man and woman entered. The man was dressed in the uniform of a Russian FSB colonel.

"Gentlemen," began Woods, with an obvious sigh of relief, "let me first introduce Miss Charlotte Waggner who represents the Jonathan Banks Corporation, a private intelligence group in the United States; she has been assisting in this project." Charlie nodded her head and quickly sought out a chair at the table. After she was seated, she shook her shoulder-length blond hair and looked up squarely at each member of the assembled group in turn. This was what Charlie liked; the delayed entrance to the meeting made her feel even more important. That had been Deiter's idea to gain an impact and she simply went along with it. She relished the attention and smiled to herself as Woods continued. "And this, in spite of the uniform, is Mr. Jack Deiter, recently of the FBI, who arrived just this morning from Baghdad by air, compliments of former Prime Minister Primakov, I might add. He will be the primary operative in this endeavor."

Deiter nodded once to the assembled group and quietly murmured, "Gentlemen," as he sought a seat next to Charlie at the table. He glanced over at Charlie to see a wide smile on her lips. He sensed that Charlie was enjoying herself.

Woods next introduced the others who were seated around the table and then began his briefing. "The mission of this project, as you all know, is to stop Osama bin Laden in his attempts to organize and finance the rebels in Chechnya. In so doing, he will be prevented from perpetrating his continuing terrorist activities against the United States as well. The American government and the Russian

215

government are in full accord on the necessity of eliminating this threat."

Looking over at Sarkorosov and nodding, Woods continued, "Thanks to the Russian Department of Internal Affairs, the MVD, and especially Mr. Sarkorosov, we have a locational fix on bin Laden. An operative is even now inside the terrorist's camp and has provided us a picture of the situation. The plan is to infiltrate Jack Deiter into Chechnya and subsequently inside the rebel sector of Grozny. There, he will gain the exact location of bin Laden and…" Woods hesitated, "and neutralize him." Woods knew of Deiter's hesitancy to assassinate bin Laden outright and wanted to circumvent discussion of that subject at this time. "The contact knows bin Laden and has had dealings with him in the past."

"What results are we to expect of this plan?" asked Colonel General Andrei Konykov in a somewhat raspy, deep baritone voice. "The FSB would like to see a…final solution, you realize."

"Osama bin Laden will be neutralized," replied Woods.

"That is not exactly what I meant," growled Konykov.

Woods turned towards Deiter and raised his left eyebrow. "Jack, would you like to expand on this? You had a lot to say on this topic previously as I recall."

Deiter was introspective for a moment and then he slowly rose to his feet. He posed an impressive figure in his uniform. His steely gray eyes looked fixedly out from under arched black eyebrows and roamed from face to face. He leaned forward and placed his hands on the table with his fingers poised in the form of tents and looked at the group. "Gentlemen, I am not an assassin." He let that statement sink in for a moment. "But, at this time, I want nothing more than to eliminate Osama bin Ladin as a source of trouble to both the United States and Russia...and the rest of the world." There was an uneasy stirring among some of those seated around the table as Deiter paused. "I have my own reason for ensuring that this will be done, and I assure you that it will be done. If there is anyone who doubts this, I would like to hear your doubts now." He waited, moving his gaze around the table. There was silence. It was apparent that those around the table knew Deiter's reputation and his recent loss at the hands of bin Laden.

Woods stood up and cleared his throat. "Uh, what Jack means is that he will make every attempt to capture bin Ladin so that the man will stand trial either in the United States, Russia, or the International Court. If that should fail, he will make sure that the terrorist is terminated rather than let him escape to a safe environment." That seemed to satisfy those around the table and there was a visible relaxation of tensions.

"Deiter will fly into Chechnya on a Russian resupply plane. He will then find his way into Grozny and through the Russian lines to the source of the rebel resistance. There, he will change his identity and wait at a drop-off location to meet with the Russian contact and gain access to bin Laden. He will then confront bin Laden and bring him through the rebel lines to Russian control. The FSB will be waiting at the predetermined contact point and will gain custody of the terrorist; they will transfer him to Moscow by air. The determination of where his subsequent trial will take place will be decided at that time; the important thing now is to get him into custody or to terminate him."

Sarkorosov leaned back in his chair and foppishly motioned at Deiter, as though he were some minion not worthy of his attention. "I am still a bit confused as to why an American is needed to apprehend or eliminate this terrorist. Some of my people could do it as easily."

"Then why haven't they, Mr. Deputy?" inquired Woods.

"Uh…" the politician paused to think of the proper response to the embarrassing question and then continued, "Well, we have made several attempts…unfortunately, he was warned off each time," replied Sarkorosov, with an apologetic shrug.

"I would suspect that there might be someone in your organization who is not quite as anxious as we are to stop bin Laden," observed General Konykov, speaking softly and slowly.

Sarkorosov bristled at the obvious insinuation and was about to bluster at the FSB general when Konykov held up his hand. The Deputy Minister slowly sat back in his seat.

"Perhaps the 'colonel'," Konykov continued, motioning toward Deiter, "is of a better disposition to ensure success." This time it was the general's turn to shrug. "Just perhaps. If not, I am sure that the Interior Ministry will have another opportunity to prove themselves." The general looked at the ceiling and placed his hands together in front of him, fingers pointing upward in contemplation. "In Northern Russia where I was born, there is a fox that is considered as sly and as clever as any person. It has given rise to a saying in that region that to catch a fox one must be a fox." Konykov cocked his head and looked at Deiter. "I have read the 'colonel's' dossier and he impresses me as one who is most like that fox. I would like to take a chance on him."

Hearing no descent, General Konykov leaned forward and placed both of his arms on the table, his hands clasped; he looked approvingly at Deiter through squinted eyes. "Colonel, the FSB will arrange for your flight to Chechnya and return…with or without your prisoner," he growled with a sudden suggestion of a smile. He obviously approved of Deiter as well as the plan.

Woods looked from Sarkorosov to each person seated at the table, ending up with the Ambassador. He received nods from all of them. "Done," he exclaimed, closing the file folder he had before him on the table. The participants at the meeting stood and began to filter out of the conference room. General Konykov waited until Deiter was next to him and in Russian whispered to him that he would be in contact with him shortly concerning the details of the first phase of the operation. Deiter nodded, smiled and took the older man's hand. For the first time in several days, Deiter felt comfortable and fully confident. Konykov turned quickly and left the room.

"You just keep popping up in the damnedest places, don't you?' remarked Hank Henderson as he approached Deiter. The two men shook hands and embraced.

"And where the hell were you when I needed you?" asked Deiter.

"Trying to stop the friggin' cruise missiles!" Henderson replied with a grimace.

"Sorry it didn't work, but it looks like now there's a whole new ballgame," Deiter said softly with a grin.

"I know," replied Henderson, "There wasn't any reason to think we'd ever need to cancel the attack. Also, what we knew about Flight 63 before wasn't the whole story; now we know that bin Laden was the mastermind. Hey, getting Saddam would have been a helluva plus even then, ya know. You did a good job, Jack."

Deiter gripped Henderson on both of his arms, looked him straight in the eye and nodded. "Thanks…uh, I need to talk with you, Hank."

"You staying upstairs?" Henderson asked.

Deiter nodded and motioned to the elevator with his head, "Now's a good a time as any."

The two men walked out of the room, bypassing the opulent frame of Don Adams who was standing in the hallway talking in hushed tones with Ashton Woods. Deiter's eyes landed on Adams for only a moment and took on a look of disdain. Adams looked up and stopped talking as the two men passed him on their way to the elevator. He shrugged his shoulders and whispered something to Woods; he then quickly turned and walked out of the Embassy to a waiting limo.

Charlie stood there for a second, shock frozen onto her face. Following several yards behind Deiter and Henderson, she had been walking past Woods and Adams at the moment of the exchange between the two men. She then regained her composure and turned to assure herself that her reaction had not been noticed and quickly moved closer to the elevator where she waited impatiently for it to open. When it finally did, she slid into it and pushed the button for the fifth floor. The elevator door closed and the car moved slowly upward; she wished for it to go faster, but this gave Charlie some time to think.

Up until this meeting, she assumed that her part in the plan was coming to a close. Now, she didn't know what to do. If she left to go back to Washington and the firm, she would be reassigned. She didn't feel comfortable with what she had just overheard and it had to be something that could harm Jack. She felt that she should stay awhile and see how things developed. Maybe if she talked to Hank Henderson, he'd know more about it. Maybe she didn't hear Adams correctly or heard only a part of the exchange. Somehow she doubted it. At the fifth floor, the elevator came to a sudden stop. Charlie walked out of elevator and quickly down the hallway to their suite. Inside, there was no sign of either Hank or Jack. She rapped on the door to Deiter's room and waited. No response. She rapped again. Nothing. Where had they gone? Were they just ignoring her? Charlie turned and collapsed on the sofa near the window to think. She desperately needed to talk to someone, but only Jack or Hank could really be trusted. Charlie wouldn't have given the overheard conversation any notice at all if Jack hadn't told her about the woman

221

in the garden in Rome. Something was wrong and she needed to find out what it was.

Hank and Deiter sat at a wooden table in the back of a small tavern called the Red Lion Pub located on the southwestern corner of the Mezhdnarodnaya (International) Hotel. The pub was located only about one and a half kilometers west of the U. S. Embassy. In the elevator, Hank had suggested that even in the Embassy, their conversations might not be all that private. He knew of the tavern and it was within easy walking distance from the Embassy. After stopping for Deiter to pick up his overcoat, they walked down the stairs and left the Embassy through a side door. Making their way down Konyushkovskaya Street, past the Mir Hotel, they reached the banks of the Moscow River at Kalioninski Bridge.

The weather was mild for a November day in Moscow and the walk was refreshing for both men. At the bridge, they followed the Krasnoprenenskaya levee along the riverbank west past the White House, the Russian Government Building. After only a few minutes of walking, they had spotted the pub sign with its rampant red lion hanging over the entrance and had made their way toward it.

Deiter's FSB uniform attracted the immediate attention of the owner, and they were quickly seated. A rather well endowed blond waitress with an engaging smile quickly brought them two imported English beers and they finally began to really relax. They spoke in English, both because Hank knew very little Russian and an FSB colonel sitting with a foreigner in a bar in Moscow was still quite above suspicion, even if they spoke in a foreign language.

"Cheers!" said Henderson lifting his tankard of beer.

"Na Zdorovia!" *(To your health!)* returned Deiter in Russian, also lifting his beer.

"That certainly was an interesting meeting," observed Henderson, changing the subject of their discussion they had while walking. They had been talking about what had happened in Iraq and Deiter's flight with Primakov to Moscow. They hadn't gotten around to more recent happenings.

"What was Sarkorosov's problem?" Deiter asked more as a statement of frustration than an actual question.

"My guess is that he was trying to posture himself against General Konykov. I'd say the two of them don't see eye-to-eye on anything."

Deiter took a long drink of his beer. "I'm glad the General's on our side; I'd prefer that to having to rely on Sarkorosov; I don't trust that wimpy lookin' bastard." He then added, "Matter of fact, most of the rest of that bunch can go to hell, too…I'll trust my luck to the ex-KGB guy. Hell, looks like I've done a complete 180…now putting my life in the hands of those who I used to call 'the enemy'…because they're preferable to 'friends.'"

"Oh, I think that most of the rest of them mean well," Henderson replied, "maybe they're just a bit naive, that's all."

"Naive can get you killed," concluded Deiter.

Henderson grinned at that pronouncement and nodded his concurrence. He knew that his friend's opinion couldn't be changed that easily. That's what kept Jack Deiter alive, a healthy skepticism of his fellow man. "So, what's this all about, Jack? You seem as skittish as a colt with a rattler in the stall."

"I can't put my finger on it, but I think that there's more 'make believe' about this whole thing then there is fact."

"Why do you say that?"

"It's almost like the whole thing was planned. Like Rose's plane was supposed to go down to make me more apt to take on Adams' challenge to get Saddam…and then go after bin Laden. Did someone intentionally plan for this to happen? Am I paranoiac, Hank? Did Rose's death do something to me?"

Deiter's questions sat uneasily with Henderson. He remembered his discussion with the tavern owner in Casa del Sol; Rose's meeting in the tavern with the man who resembled a description of Don Adams. And then there were the times that Jack had thought he had seen Rose. How many times? Two…three? Jack had good reason to suspect something. It was time to tell him about Juan Maranda's observations. "Jack, there's something that maybe you need to know…" He was suddenly interrupted by the appearance of someone standing next to their table. The man was tall, clean-shaven and dressed in a dark colored trench coat; blond hair showed from under the traditional mouton ushanka on his head.

"Colonel, if you'll forgive me," the man interrupted while flashing his FSB badge and identification at Deiter. "Colonel General Konykov would like to see you…now; I have a car waiting outside."

Deiter looked up at the man. "I'll be out in a minute," he replied. The man nodded and quickly left the pub.

"Duty calls?" Henderson asked.

"I sure didn't see the tail, did you? Wonder how they found us…"

Henderson shrugged, "Could have been a chopper for all I know. You have to admit one thing, though, if I were in trouble, I'd rather have Konykov's people protecting my ass than Don Adams."

Deiter let out a laugh as he chugged the rest of his beer. "Don't do that when I'm drinking, Hank," he sputtered. "But, I agree!" He nodded at the door to the pub and said, "You know, that guy needs to stop watching spy movies or get a new wardrobe. A trench coat? Give me a break."

Outside the pub, Deiter saw a large black Zil parked next to the curb; the man in the trench coat was standing next to it. As Deiter approached the car, the man held open the rear door. Deiter stepped into the back seat and the man shut the car door behind him. If Deiter had thought that New York City taxi drivers drove recklessly, he hadn't experience the best…or worst of the FSB drivers. They sped through the snow-covered streets of Moscow as though the devil himself was in pursuit.

Ten minutes later, after several close brushes with other cars and a few pedestrians, the high intimidating walls of the Kremlin loomed

Ted Colby

overhead. The Zil headed straight for a portal beneath the Borovitskaya Tower. Deiter felt that he was losing all cognition of the outside world as the car disappeared into the portal and into the cavernous depth of the massive edifice. For the first time that he could remember, he had the feeling that he was drowning as the oppressive and massive structure inhaled both the car and himself.

Charlie sat on the sofa in the suite's common room with her arms around her legs and her face pressed against her knees. She knew she possessed some information that could be vital to the people she cared about and was completely at a loss as to how she could pass on that information without alerting those who might use it inappropriately. Alternately, she paced the room from the window overlooking the river to the door to the hallway and back again. Then she would sit on the sofa again. Finally, she decided that she needed to get some fresh air. She grabbed her coat and headed for the elevator.

Outside the Embassy, she turned right and followed Novinski Boulevard until it came to New Arbat that ran from Arbatskayya Place to the Kalininski Bridge over the Moscow River. Did she want to go to the Arbat section and its antique dealers or towards the river? She decided on the river; the sun was in that direction and it shone brilliantly on her as she walked the tree-lined boulevard. She could feel the warmth of it on her face and it felt wonderful. The trees had long ago lost their leaves and would have looked like spiny skeleton's hands stuffed into the ground except that the ice and snow had coated the branches with a brilliantly white translucent glaze that reflected

226

and refracted the bright sunlight. The trees created a wonderland of brightness along the boulevard, and the sight of them raised her spirits. She hurried across the street that ran along the river, finally slowing down as she reached the levee. A slight rise led her to the embankment just to the right of the bridge; she turned right and starting walking slowly along the river.

Maybe a stroll along the waterway would be pleasant, she thought. The weather certainly couldn't be better for November in Moscow. She was really beginning to enjoy the sudden and unexpected warmth in the Russian capital. There would be time enough to find Jack or Hank later that evening, she rationalized. Charlie stopped and leaned against the railing that followed the pathway in this sector of the levee and served as a protection for pedestrians from falling into the river from the embankment. Closing her eyes, she let the sun fall fully on her face; it felt warm and delicious.

When she opened her eyes, she saw several small ships making their way up the river and she could see crewmembers standing along the railings watching the shoreline. Charlie guessed that they were searching for some human presence along the snow-covered and desolate banks of the river. She waved vigorously at three blue uniformed sailors in heavy peacoats who were standing on the forward deck of a red and white riverboat flying the Russian ensign. She was immediately rewarded by a frantic arm wave in return by all three of them. A smile crossed her face at the antics of the sailors and she sympathized with their yearning for companionship. She sat down on a bench that had been placed along the pathway and remained there for almost a half-hour as the sun drifted lower over the section of Moscow across the river called Victory Park. She remembered in a book she found in the suite that the park had been created in celebration of the Russian victory over Napoleon at the Battle of Borodino in 1812; funny how facts like that burst upon your mind at times. A shiver suddenly ran through her and she pulled her open coat closer around her. At the same time, she became aware of someone standing next to her and slightly back from the wooden bench. She turned quickly to see a tall man dressed head to foot in black fur. He was studying her closely and appeared surprised when she turned to look at him.

"I thought that was you, Charlie," exclaimed Hank Henderson.

"Where'd you get the furry black outfit, Hank? You've been hanging around with Jack Deiter too much," she joked with relief in her voice. "Where'd you go, anyway? I've been looking for you."

"Jack and I figured that the walls of the Embassy had too many ears and the pub down along the river might be a better place to talk."

"Yeah, right," she said with a slight curl in her lip. "I know you two better than that; the fact was you guys just needed a drink."

"Ah, come on, now, Charlie. Give us a break," he replied coming over to sit down beside her on the bench.

"Where's Jack?" Charlie interrupted. "I need to tell him something."

"He got picked up by the FSB and is on his way to meet General Konykov."

"Oh, my God," Charlie whispered.

"What's the matter?" Henderson asked.

"I overheard parts of a conversation between Adams and Woods this afternoon just after the briefing...and I don't know what to make of it."

"If you don't mind, Charlie, would you like to take a walk down to the Red Lion Pub?" Henderson asked. "Even the outdoors have ears in Moscow," he added in a whisper.

Charlie and the general walked slowly along the river embankment; neither one of them said anything. Shortly, they arrived at the same pub that he and Deiter had just frequented. In only a few minutes, they were seated in a booth in the dimly lit pub with a large glass of Guinness in front of each of them. The warmth of the pub felt delightful. They both relaxed and after a few moments sat back to enjoyed the creamy-smooth, dark liquid as it eased a thirst in their throats and brought a sense of well being to them.

"So, tell me what you overheard that made you so uncomfortable," Henderson prodded.

"Truthfully, I don't know if it was the conclusion or the beginning of a discussion. I don't even know if it was the whole discussion itself," she began, leaning forward with both hands holding onto her glass. "Adams seemed to be right up into Wood's face. His expression wasn't very pleasant, either." She paused. "Oh, I checked to see if they noticed if I heard what they were saying; they didn't."

"Go on, what was it?"

"I'm not paranoiac, Hank, and I wouldn't have placed any importance on it at all except for what Jack had told me this morning."

Henderson's interest was suddenly heightened; that was the second time within an hour that someone had used that word. He doubted that it was truly a coincidence. "And what was that?" he responded.

"He told me what he'd seen outside in the garden in Rome. He told me he thought he'd seen Rose."

"Oh? I'm surprised he mentioned it; he seemed to be embarrassed about it at the time."

"It sort of came up when I asked him if he knew who his contact was in Chechnya," she explained. "Anyway, as I passed Adams, he said to Woods, 'You almost botched it in Rome...Deiter mustn't see her again. You see to it.'" She paused and looked directly at Henderson. "Who is this 'she,' Hank? Do you have any idea?"

Henderson shifted in his seat and took a long draft of his Guinness. "Earlier, I was about to tell Jack something when we were interrupted by one of Konykov's men. I never got to tell him." After a moment, Hank continued, "When I went to Costa del Sol to tell Jack about Rose's flight going down, I had dinner by myself in a tavern that the three of us had gone to before. The owner, an old guy by the name of Juan Maranda, knew both Jack and Rose very well. After I had told him about Rose and the plane, he relayed to me that he had seen Rose only a few days before having dinner with a man, a heavy, gray-bearded American."

"Adams?" Charlie interrupted.

"The description fits, but I have no way of knowing." Henderson continued. "Juan didn't seem to like the guy very much." Henderson laughed quietly to himself. "Adams is such a likeable cuss, it could have been him, I guess. If it was, what was he doing talking to Rose? And now, why the Russian woman who seems to look like Rose?"

"I didn't like this before, now I definitely don't like it. You say that Konykov sent for Jack? Does that mean that he's headed off to Chechnya now and not tomorrow?"

"I don't know, but I'd bet on it," he concluded. "Jack didn't say that he'd see me tonight."

Charlie thought for a few moments and then said, "Hank, Jack doesn't know what he's getting into. I'd have felt better if he knew about what your Spanish friend said...you know, about Rose and Adams."

"We're just assuming that it was Adams," replied Henderson. "There's no proof of that."

"We obviously aren't in possession of all the facts, Hank, something else is going on and I'll bet Adams is up to his fat little neck in it."

Henderson chuckled, "I'll second that, but what?"

"Was the plane crash a terrorist act? Is Rose dead? If so, why the lookalike? What was that woman doing in Rome? If she's the contact in Chechnya, why her? What connection does she have and for that matter what connection does Rose…or did Rose have in all this?"

"Wow, Charlie, you got any more questions?"

"Yeah, a whole bunch…I don't like that Woods character either…he's as trustworthy as Adams, the weasel."

"Whew! You're sure in a good mood," Henderson snapped. A look of chagrin then passed over his face and he said, "I'm sorry, Charlie. You're absolutely right; we don't have all of the facts. But, we need to cool it until we do. I'll try to get in touch with Jack, but I don't think I'll be successful without raising a lot of questions…from the people we don't trust."

"I'm glad to know that I'm not the only one that's paranoid," she said with a grin.

Chapter Thirteen

The Fox in Chechnya

Central Airport, Moscow
Early Wednesday morning,, November 24, 1999

The Central Airport in Moscow is located about four to five kilometers northwest of the U. S. Embassy, and is generally regarded as the exclusive domain of the military and the government; no private aircraft or the public has general access. Deiter stood alone on the tarmac beside the unmarked "Cub," an Antonov An-12 Russian military cargo jet. He noticed that from the rear it looked a lot like an American C-130 Hercules. The nose, though, was more pointed than the Hercules. He knew that it was comparable to the Hercules in lift capability and speed. It had been used widely during the war with Afghanistan, and like the C-130, the An-12 could be used in several different roles, such as jamming and electronic reconnaissance. Like its American counterpart in the Western world, most Soviet allies and satellite nations had been supplied with this particular transport aircraft. Deiter noticed one more facet in common with the C-130; this plane obviously was part of the FSB inventory and like similar American aircraft owned by the CIA, it had no markings and was painted a matte black from nose to tail; even the windows were darkened.

Deiter was dressed in the heavy winter camouflage combat uniform worn by the FSB. The black ushanka he wore snuggly down to the top of his ears, contained the FSB double-headed eagle crest in front. He wore a brown shoulder holster containing a nine-millimeter automatic pistol. He looked at his watch; he had been waiting almost ten minutes for someone from the crew to come forward and assist him with his luggage, a large footlocker containing not only uniforms, but also civilian clothes, weapons and ammunition. Deiter surmised that this windfall of gear for his mission was thanks to General Konykov and the intervention of former Prime Minister Primakov.

The previous evening had been an amazing experience for Deiter. At the end of his hectic ride in the FSB's Zil, he had been deposited at the steps of a building deep inside the Kremlin walls. As he stepped out of the car, he was met by a pretty young woman with long dark hair; she had emerged from a large door to the office building just as the car pulled up and appeared anxious to have Deiter follow her inside. Inside the walls of the Kremlin, the wind is channeled along the alleyways and is more piercing than it is in the rest of Moscow. She wasn't wearing a coat and she was shivering. They hurriedly rushed through the entrance and closed the door behind them. Once inside, she calmly introduced herself in Russian; Deiter guessed that she didn't know who he was, but had been instructed to meet a FSB colonel and escort him to General Konykov's office complex. After the niceties were exchanged, she led him up a stairway and through a set of large double doors into the office of the general. Not only was

Konykov a general in the FSB, he was also the senior officer and commandant of the Kremlin, a very trusted and prestigious position.

"Good evening, Colonel." the general said, as he rose from behind his massively carved desk. He quickly put out his hand as he walked towards Deiter. His smile and deportment indicated his sincere respect for the other man. General Konykov was dressed in a dark civilian suit with white shirt and a red tie. Over his left pocket, he wore the red ribbon and star of the Hero of the Soviet Union; in his lapel was a miniature of the winged, double-headed eagle crest of the Kremlin Guard.

"It's good to see you so soon again, Sir," Deiter responded as he accepted the man's hand.

"I have worked out most of the details for your mission," the general responded motioning for Deiter to be seated in a richly padded leather chair placed before the desk. Konykov seated himself behind the large desk and studied the man before him.

Deiter looked around him at the elaborate appointments of the suite that composed the office of the general. The bone white ceilings were high and partitioned off into sections by carved beams. The walls were wainscoted in a rich brown wood with sectors of elaborate wallpaper above. The floors were of hardwood; the only carpeting being under the massive desk in the center of the room and the chair on which Deiter sat. Behind the general were several flags that Deiter guessed were symbols of the man's rank and position. The Russian national colors were among the grouping of flags. The desk drew

Deiter's attention, and he examined it as closely and as quickly as he could. It looked very old and was exquisitely carved. Some of the motifs were obviously of Imperial Russian origin. His inquisitive appraisal was not wasted on the general.

"Do you notice something unusual about this desk?" the general inquired.

"Doesn't look like the product of the Soviet Union," Deiter replied.

"And correct you are," replied the general with obvious pleasure. "It once belonged to Czar Nicholas II. I have a great respect for Imperial Russia, as do most honest Russians. To have this piece of history in this office is of great meaning to me. And by that, I do not mean any disrespect. The czars are a part of our Russian history and a very significant part of it." The general leaned back in his chair and looked up at the ceiling. "Sometimes I sit here at night and hear the advice of those who once occupied these quarters. Royalty once called these rooms their home, you know. Not much has really changed in Russia. We still feel pain and we still yearn for family and home. Russia is more than a political entity; it is a very large family. The land is more precious than gold; it is…Mother Russia."

"I think that I can relate to that in several ways," returned Deiter.

"I know," replied the general, "both as an American…and as a Russian."

Deiter was suddenly quite silent. He stared at the other man.

Konykov leaned forward, smiling. "I know about your heritage...and your parents," he said quietly. "I also suspect that despite your very solid patriotism towards America, you feel a longing, a pull for your roots, your native land."

"Are you a mind reader or a psychic?" Deiter asked.

At this, the general laughed out loud; it was a full and yet kindly and friendly laugh as one is apt to do among old friends. "Neither, my friend, I know of your background and I know what it is to be Russian. It is as simple as that."

Deiter was beginning to like this man more with each conversation he had with him. He smiled and said, *"Touché."*

The general eased himself out of his chair and went over to a heavily carved cabinet against the wall of the office. He opened the double doors in front of the cabinet and revealed a bar with glasses and bottles of liquor lined up across the back. A bowl of ice containing several glasses of vodka was placed in the center of the bar. The general picked up two of the tall thin glasses and handed one of them to Deiter, keeping the other for himself. The general uttered the traditional Russian toast, lifting his glass.

"Cheers," responded Deiter, smiling. He liked this guy, but better yet, he trusted him.

For the next two hours, the general discussed the situation in Chechnya, various contacts who had confirmed bin Laden's presence in or near Grozny, and the terrorist's connection to several bombings in Russia. Several photographs, one taken by satellite, showed bin

Laden and his close associates with rebel leaders. Deiter shuffled through the collection as Konykov provided them to him until he came to one that showed the back of a fairly tall woman. In the black and white shot, he could not tell exactly the color of her hair although he knew it was full and dark, yet not black.

"Do you know who she is?" inquired Deiter, handing the general the photo.

The general took the eight by ten photo and studied it for a moment. "Why yes, she is one of the contacts I mentioned." He then turned a quizzical eye towards Deiter. "You are not familiar with her? She has a Chechen first name, but I don't recall it just now. Her last name was Demidov, I believe. She is not one of my people, so I assumed she was an American."

"Do you know when this was taken?" asked Deiter.

"Look on the back; usually the location and dates of photographs are listed there," the general responded handing the photo back to Deiter. He wanted the American to read the information so that he could evaluate his reaction. He wasn't disappointed, but it still didn't answer Deiter's rather strange behavior towards what seemed to be a routine photograph.

"This was taken only yesterday in Grozny!" Deiter responded in astonishment.

"We are not as backward as we sometimes appear," said the general quietly with a smirk moving across his lips and a twinkle in his eyes.

Deiter suddenly felt uncomfortable and somewhat embarrassed at the insinuation; yet, he knew the general had called it correctly. Deiter smiled back to confirm the general's observation. He turned the photograph over and studied the picture again. The woman had her hair pulled back and hidden by a babushka tied behind her neck. Her build still reminded him of Rose and so did that fashion of wearing her hair. At times, he had seen Rose wear her hair that way when she was "roughing it." What was he thinking? He had to admit that this double was very good indeed if she was passing herself off as Rose. How did Adams ever find her?

"Now, my good friend, what is bothering you? inquired Konykov with a look of honest concern on his face.

"How much do you think you know about me…outside of my dossier, that is?"

"Let me tell you what I do know; maybe that would be easier," the general offered. "Most, you have guessed I already know. You are the son of two Soviet deep agents who defected to the United States. Your origins are Russian and for several generations your ancestors lived in Chechnya. You are a former American Naval officer and FBI agent as well as a CIA operative in your early years. You were married and widowed many years ago and are currently married to one Rose McGuire whom you knew earlier while with the CIA." Konykov smiled proudly at his ability to memorize information and sat back to gauge what effect this might have on his guest.

239

"You're almost correct," Deiter remarked dryly with an expressionless face. "I have been widowed twice; most recently only a few weeks ago. Rose died on Continental Flight 63 from Madrid to Newark...the work of bin Laden."

The general looked shocked and seemed deeply moved by the revelation. He stood up and walked around his desk so that he stood over Deiter. Reaching out, he placed his hand on Deiter's shoulder and quietly said, "We both have lost a loved one to this evil; my oldest daughter, Natasha, was in the apartment building in Volgodonsk when it was bombed in September. Now you know my passion in this mission and I know of yours. This man must face trial and execution in either your land or mine, or he must die. There is no other acceptable outcome."

Deiter stood and placed his own hand over that of the general's and looking him directly in the eyes, nodded his head and quietly whispered, "As you wish, Andrei Vladimirovitch."

The general turned and walked over to the cabinet containing the bowl of iced vodka glasses. He selected two more tall glasses from the bowl and handed one to Deiter. "Once more, my friend, but this time let us drink to the memory of our loved ones," he said. The two men slowly raised their glasses.

"To justice," Deiter said.

"To justice," answered the general.

In this communal drinking of the clear cold spirits, a bond was established between the two warriors. The adversary's fate was sealed. The two men then resumed their examination of photographs, documents, intelligence reports and maps of Chechnya and Grozny.

"I must warn you about something," the general said at one point in their discussion. "Unlike your military, we have many factions. Some will be friendly to you and some will not. In a loose alliance with the FSB troops, who are under my control, are those of the GRU; they are the Ministry of Defense's intelligence forces. They are well trained and disciplined and have been much more effective then even my own troops have been. You must be wary of the Ministry of Interior forces, however, the *Vnutrenniye Voyska* as well as the OMON, or *Otryad Militsii Osobogo Nazncacheniya* and SOBR forces of the Ministry of Internal Affairs; they cannot be trusted. I fear that they have only volunteered to go to Chechnya for the loot and corruption they can find there. I have both *Alpha* and *Vympel Spetznaz* or special forces under my control. I would like to say that they are superior to the GRU, but they are not…they're too political, I'm afraid, but they are loyal to me."

About eight-thirty, there was a knock at the door; it then opened and two waiters rolled in a table set with two dinners into the office. As soon as the waiters left, Konykov motioned to Deiter to be seated. "We can't subsist only on our passion for the mission and vodka; we must have food as well. Bon appetite, my friend."

During dinner, there was no talk of the mission. General Konykov spoke of his boyhood days in northern Russia. His father was a humble farmer while his grandparents had owned considerable land

and at one time were considerably wealthy. His grandfather had fought for the Czar during the Revolution and was killed in 1920 by a marauding band of Bolsheviks. The rest of the family escaped and hid out with sympathetic villagers. The general then changed the topic to Deiter and his family, or what he knew of them. Konykov concluded that Deiter knew only that his parents had lived in Chechnya prior to becoming agents. He didn't even know what their real names were. "Would you like to know about them?" the general asked.

"Of course, but how'd you find out?"

The general only smiled and proceeded to fill in the details of John and Constance Deiter's lives prior to the time they were recruited for the Soviet deep agent project. Their family name had been Demidov, Ivan Romanovitch and Tonya Konstantinovna. "Demidov is a somewhat common name. It is just a coincidence that it also is the same as the woman in the picture which sparked your interest," the general observed thoughtfully. He went on to explain that both of Deiter's parents grew up in and around Grozny; his father was Russian and his mother was both Chechen and a Cossack, or of Christian extraction. Their family had lived in Chechnya since the early 1920's. Deiter's grandfather had been a colonel of one of the Cossack regiments that fought for the Czar during the Revolution. After the fall of the loyalists and dismantling of all military units not integrated into the Red Army, his whole family was forcibly moved to Grozny during the first of many such relocations done by the Communists. Konykov also confirmed that Deiter had been born in the United States. He also said that he had heard that Deiter's parents had been terminated following their defection to the West, as had several other agents since then. "That was a time of paranoia, distrust and very ambitious and unscrupulous men," the general remarked. "I'm not sure we are any better now, but we can try to work together to rid the world of terrorists at least."

Turning to a large footlocker that two soldiers had carried into the room when the waiters came for the remains of the dinner, General Konykov exclaimed, "So, enough of the past; let's continue. Here are several sets of uniforms for you, civilian clothes…you'll need them once you are about to make contact with the rebels…and weapons. I think you will find them satisfactory. Your papers are all in perfect order. They were prepared by the MVD and sent over earlier today."

Deiter checked through the contents of the large footlocker in front of the general's desk. "Who's my first contact?" he asked.

"His name is FSB Major Sergei Borodenko, the only other person who knows who you are and what your mission is. He can be trusted explicitly, for he is my son-in-law, the husband of my late daughter." Konykov smiled with pride and sadness. "He will meet your airplane in Gudermes when you arrive and will be able to direct you further."

"Do you have anything on any other contact?"

The general handed Deiter a folder with a number of photographs and biographical sketches of individuals. Deiter sat down and reviewed each one of them. As he came to the last picture, Konykov leaned over and pointed to it. "The man in the center is Aslan

Maskhadov, President of the Chechen Republic; Major Borodenko will introduce you to him. He is the only person able to turn over Osama bin Laden to you. The man to his left is Abuu Khadzhiyev."

Deiter looked up in surprise. "President Maskhodov? Really, where did these three meet, anyway?" he asked.

"In Leningrad, at the Kalinin Military Academy. They all graduated there in 1981. Abuu left the Soviet Army nine years later and joined Aslan Maskhodov in the Chechen Armed Forces. All of them were friends at the Academy long before General Maskhodov was made Chief of Staff of the Chechen Armed Forces."

"And now they are on different sides," commented Deiter.

"You had a similar war in the history of your country," the general reminded Deiter. "You must realize, however, that my son-in-law is not with the Interior Ministry's forces or with the Army; he is FSB. At times, we in the FSB must look to the greater good of Russia, not at the petty fights in which the other branches of government become embroiled. It has been so since the Cossack Guard, the so-called Secret Police, protected the first czar with their lives. At that time the czar was Russia. Since the Revolution, the KGB, and now the FSB, has inherited the Cossack's responsibility."

The General paused and after he had drained his glass of vodka, he continued. "Sergei has been in constant contact with both of his old friends for months now. Both of them are reasonable men and were devastated when they learned of Natasha's death in the apartment building bombing. They had no responsibility in the bombing; that was Osama bin Laden's doing in an attempt to impress the Chechens."

"These contacts are impressive, when do I leave?" asked Deiter, as he placed the folder with the photographs on the general's desk.

"Tomorrow morning. I have a flight standing by at the Central Airport here in Moscow. You will stay here as my guest tonight, and you will be wakened tomorrow morning in time to join me for breakfast. I will ride with you to the airport. Do you have any more questions?

"Not for the moment; you have been quite through."

"Good, now let us have one more vodka together before we say goodnight," concluded the general grinning as he strode over to the cabinet to pick up two more tall cold glasses.

In the distance, Deiter could see a black van speeding down the freshly plowed tarmac from the briefing building on the north end of the complex. The snow had been piled in six-foot mounds along the entire asphalt strip. The van pulled up to the rear cargo door of the aircraft and five men in dark camouflage uniforms stepped out. Three of them, Deiter assumed to be the captain and cabin crew, climbed into the side hatch and disappeared into the "Cub". The two other crewmembers walked towards Deiter and after saluting him, picked up his footlocker and asked him to come aboard the aircraft as they would be taking off immediately. Deiter complied and swung up onto the ramp that had been dropped at the rear of the aircraft. Inside, he discovered that there were strap seats along both sides of the plane.

He selected a seat nearest the door leading to the cabin area. As he was about to strap himself in, the pilot poked his head around the corner of the doorway and asked if he was all right. Over the noise of the engines, which had suddenly roared into life, Deiter indicated he was fine.

As soon as he had fastened his seat belt, though, the aircraft bolted towards the taxiway and barely slowed as it swung around at the end of the active runway and raced back up the concrete strip to rise above the city. Deiter recalled the ride he had experienced the previous evening with the FSB driver in Moscow and gave a quick prayer that FSB pilots were not of the same ilk. As the aircraft rose abruptly and then banked sharply left, Deiter guessed that the pilot must indeed be related to the Zil driver. It took almost no time at all for them to reach their cruising altitude in a south-by-south-east direction...towards Chechnya.

Deiter had calculated that the flight would probably take several hours and this was confirmed when he climbed into the cabin and spoke with the navigator. The FSB lieutenant told him that his estimate was two hours and forty-seven minutes flying time to the strip outside of Gudermes. They also had been instructed to fly over Grozny to provide the "Colonel" a view of the situation in the city. Deiter thanked the officer, although it was clear that this was not a favor, but an order from General Konykov. They didn't look too happy about the proposition, either. Deiter stayed in the cabin as there was a more comfortable seat next to the navigator's position and he could easily see the terrain ahead and to his left through the cabin windows.

A seemingly endless expanse of white rolling hills spread out as far as he could see. Here and there it was broken up by a section of forest. The trees were covered with snow, yet green growth showed up wherever the wind had blown off the snow or the bright sun softened it sufficiently for it to fall through the branches to the ground. Although stands of hardwood deciduous tree could be seen, they became less frequent as the transport lumbered in flight high over them. Gradually, there were increasing numbers of conifer and other evergreen-forested areas. This then gave way to long white stretches of plains areas that were broken up into cultivated fields on what used to be collective farms.

Remaining in the more comfortable seat in the aircraft's cabin area, Deiter finally succumbed to the demands of sleep. The previous night hadn't been too conducive to rest. Although the accommodations had been more than he could have asked for and the bed sufficiently comfortable, so many other things were going through his mind that after initially dropping off to sleep, he awoke and then dozed fitfully the rest of the night. His head dropped onto his chest and he had been either asleep or dozing for almost two hours when the navigator reached over and shook his shoulder. "Colonel, we are approaching Grozny," the Lieutenant cautioned. Deiter was instantly alert.

Through the windshield, Deiter could just make out the skyline of
the city in the distance; mountains rose to the south and swept across
the entire horizon from east to west. A quick look at the instruments
indicated that they were approaching the city from the east. He
presumed that they has flown over Gudermes and turned to the east to
circle Grozny and would finally return to land at their airfield
destination. The pilot pulled back on the throttle and adjusted the
flaps causing the aircraft to slow; the nose dipped and Deiter could
see that they were losing altitude. At an altitude of one thousand
meters, they leveled off and started their circling to the south. Deiter
understood why the general had wanted him to see the ruins of the
city. Being a generation and a country away from the hatred and
bigotry harbored by both sides, Deiter could feel compassion for all
the combatants of this conflict. He knew that the general looked at the
situation through his personal loss and that of his beloved Russia's
loss of one of its provinces. He also knew that there was more to the
situation than that biased side. The Chechens were prideful, yes, but
they had a real stake in the outcome of the conflict as they had for
hundreds of years. General Konykov's grief was new; the Chechens'
grief spanned generations. Deiter knew that the general wanted him to
see the destruction and grief that this insurrection had caused, yet
Deiter saw more than just that, he saw a people being destroyed.

Deiter's attention was so drawn to the landscape below, and he
almost missed the instructions that the pilot gave to the crew over the
intercom. Out of the corner of his eye, he saw a streak of light spring

from the belly of the aircraft and soar across the panorama below. He shot a questioning glance towards the navigator who smiled and pressed his intercom button. "Flares...to confuse the surface-to-air missiles," he explained.

Deiter nodded; he quickly understood the reticence the crew must have had concerning the order to circle Grozny. This was still a war zone. Flares were launched from the belly tubes of the aircraft at regular intervals as they circled the Chechen capital. This had been a standard practice during the Afghan War and had proved its worth even though it caused many fires in built-up areas. Deiter could see the devastation that had been wreaked against the rebel-held sections of the city. Many buildings were mere shells, and several roads had large craters in them. Nothing could be seen in the form of human beings moving in the streets. Deiter guessed that Russian snipers were keeping the populace at bay during daylight hours. Deiter's briefing by the general had included the fact that rebels for the most part still controlled the city and most of the suburbs.

Suddenly, a different flash caught Deiter's eye. It started in an open area ahead of the aircraft's flight path. He watched transfixed as the brilliant light rose up to meet the circling aircraft. The pilot suddenly banked left and Deiter could hear several flares being fired from somewhere down below in the plane's main compartment. The aircraft then banked right and climbed in altitude. It seemed to be in the throes of a slow-motion dance of death with the missile. Deiter knew instinctively that the outcome was inevitable as he felt a violent shudder accompanied by an explosion heard over the roar of the engines; it had a ring of finality, but not surprise.

The wrenching of his body against his seatbelt restraints dug into his hips and waist as he was thrown against them. A sudden feeling of weightlessness filled him as he saw through the windshield that a view of the ground covered most of the panorama and then all of the view. He knew that they were going in; they apparently had lost control and airworthiness. He hung onto the window frame and the edge of the seat. Seconds went by like minutes as the sequence of events played out before him in slow motion. With superhuman effort, the pilot pulled back on the wheel while the copilot extended the flaps to their maximum. The massive aircraft slowly pulled out of its uncontrolled dive and began to level out. Deiter strained against his belts and managed to see that the terrain below was coming ever closer, but at a slower pace.

Up ahead, he could see what looked like a stretch of railroad tracks. It led over a river and into the center of the city. The pilot guided the aircraft until it straddled the tracks heading in a northwesterly direction. The altitude kept dropping rapidly. Ahead Deiter could see a railway bridge across what he assumed was the Sunzha River. It had a single span; the single trestle was like a horizontal set of parenthesis over the waterway. The pilot pulled up on the wheel and pushed forward on the throttles to increase the aircraft's speed. They barely missed the round steel span on the bridge; the pilot then pushed the wheel forward, easing the lumbering aircraft down. As it touched the railway tracks, he reversed the engines and the plane hit the tracks with a deafening, screeching, and wrenching sound. Flames and sparks spewed from beneath them. They passed by a group of buildings set close to the tracks and were thrown viciously against their restraints as the wings hit the buildings and were torn from the body of the airplane. Absent any lift from the wings, the screeching of metal against metal increased and the helpless, wingless shell rocketed forward over the icy tracks and the new snow. The noise became deafening.

The shell traveled almost three hundred yards more before the wreck twisted to the right and finally began to slow down as it clattered against the wooden ties of the tracks. Deiter could see ahead through the windscreen that they were moving towards what looked like a large open plaza where the tracks divided. One section of track took a decided turn towards the left, the other continued straight ahead. At this point, the aircraft left the tracks in a wrenching motion and hit the ground with a bone-shattering crunch. It finally came to a stop only a few yards from the wall of a large building. They had arrived at the Square of Lenin in downtown Grozny. "Not as I had originally envisioned how I'd get to Grozny," Deiter groaned as he pulled himself upright in his seat. Suddenly, there was a strange quietness over the entire scene. There was no sound, no movement at all; it was as though time had been suspended. Deiter's experience told him that these were the times when the real trouble started.

"You okay?" he asked as he placed a hand on the arm of the navigator.

The man raised his head and to Deiter's surprise, produced the broadest grin that Deiter could recall. "We made it!" the man exploded.

"Did you have any doubt?" asked the pilot as he turned in his seat. "We had better get out of here quickly, though." He then turned and looked at the copilot who was slumped in his seat. He tried to wake him without any success. As he bent to lift the man, he discovered a large piece of glass embedded in his neck. The copilot was obviously dead.

Deiter was closest to the doorway to the center expanse of the aircraft and the forward exit door. He unbuckled his seat restraints and pulled himself through the doorway; his entire body ached from the punishment it had just undergone. The view that came before him was one out of *The Inferno*. Flames were flickering everywhere throughout the wrecked body of the aircraft. Nothing looked exactly as he remembered it. On the right, the exit door had been wrenched from its frame and lay gaping open. He could see the pavement outside through the opening. The smell of distillates was heavy in the air, and he knew that they could explode at any moment. The smell of electrical burning was like acid in his nostrils. A barely visible haze burned his eyes.

He was about to climb out the doorway and jump into the street below, when his eye caught the footlocker that contained his clothing and supplies. He knew that he would need it to complete his mission. Deiter quickly unfastened the buckle on the webbing that held it against the bulkhead and yanked it toward the doorway. The navigator had followed him out of the cabin and saw that Deiter was struggling with the cargo. He motioned Deiter to jump through the doorway and grabbed the box by an end handle. As Deiter hit the ground, he turned and faced his luggage flying through the doorway. He stepped to one side, and the box hit the pavement. Reaching down to grab the handle, he quickly pulled it into an alley and returned to assist the rest of the crew as they climbed out of the aircraft. Flames flickered more brightly inside the chassis of the wreck and the pilot yelled a warning to the crew. They ran swiftly down the alley and turned into the first protected doorway.

The impact of the explosion shattered their senses and dimmed their hearing. Blood began to run from their nose and ears from the overpressure. The force of the explosion was tremendous. Flames blossomed rapidly through the alley that they had just left and scorched the pavement and walls on both sides. When the flames finally subsided, Deiter could barely see through his seared eyes. He lay exhausted against the wall of the building that had protected them from the blast. Through the haze, he saw only three men beside him; one of the crew obviously had not made it down the alley. Again silence reigned in the aftermath of destruction.

Deiter was amazed at how quickly the blazing aircraft burned itself out leaving only a column of heavy black smoke that rose high into the sky. He had been there in the alley only a few minutes when the smoke began to lift sufficiently to allow him to see the street at the end of the alley, though the cloud still masked the noonday sun. The heat from the walls and pavement in the alley radiated the effect of the fire as he eased himself around the corner. He yanked his handkerchief from his rear pocket and placed it over his nose. He could see the carcass of the aircraft smoldering in the street. Here and there flames still flickered throughout the smoking mass. The air was barely breathable. At the end of the alley, he saw his luggage sitting unharmed, but smoking. He quickly approached it, shielding his face from the heat radiating from the aircraft. He could see that the metal footlocker had not caught fire and had evidently protected the contents. He turned back as the other three survivors walked cautiously up the alley toward him.

"We are in rebel-held territory," warned the pilot. "We need to go back toward our lines on the outskirts of the city."

Deiter nodded in concurrence. He reached into his pocket and produced a key to his luggage. Opening the footlocker cautiously with his gloves, he pulled out his civilian clothes, a packet of documents, the sleek black AKM automatic weapon with a collapsible stock and a bandoleer of ammunition. He swung the weapon over his shoulder, the bandoleer over his head, and the bundle of clothing he pushed into a knapsack, which had fortunately been included with the supplies, and threw it over his back. The pilot had moved around the corner of the alley and out into the street heading east towards their original destination. The rest of the survivors followed him. Deiter stopped to adjust the knapsack before heading out into the street. A loud static discharge of machinegun fire interrupted the silence and he could see sparks from the ricochets bouncing off the sides of buildings and the pavement around the smoldering carcass of the aircraft. He eased his head around the corner to see all three Russians lying still on the pavement. Dark red pools already had begun to collect near each body; the warm blood slowly melted the newly fallen snow.

Deiter needed a change in plans…and quickly. He headed back down the alley at a run.

Ted Colby

Chapter Fourteen

Zaira

Grozny, Republic of Chechnya
Wednesday noon, November 24, 1999

Deiter had gone about fifty yards when a door on the left side of the alley caught his attention. He stopped at it and gently depressed the lever on the lock; it responded and the door creaked open. He quickly looked through the doorway to find that there was no one inside and then checked the alley to see if anyone was watching. No one was. He hoped that the building was empty as he slipped through the doorway and closed the door gently behind him. So far, so good, he thought to himself. Considering all the bombs and artillery that had been dropped on the city, Deiter figured that most of the inhabitants had left for the mountains except for the elderly…and maybe some of the small children. The only others he might run up against would be the combatants.

Deiter eased the 9mm automatic from his shoulder holster and looked around him. He was in a hallway of what looked like an apartment building. The door to the alley would have been the rear entrance for getting rid of trash, he guessed. Ahead, the hallway extended to the front of the building that would have an entrance onto a cross street to the one along the railroad tracks. The front door had a window that let in the light from the street out front. To his left, rose a wooden staircase with a railing. The wall under the stairs was paneled in a rich dark wood. There didn't appear to be any damage to this part of the building from the shelling of the city. He walked down the hallway and tried several doors, but all were locked. That was good; he didn't want to occupy the ground floor if he could get to the relative safety of one of the upper floors. In the event he was cornered in the building, a second story location would give him more options for escape. At this point, he needed a place to change into his civilian clothes and think about a new plan.

He crept up the stairway keeping close to the wall. In the distance he could hear artillery dropping somewhere in the city and sporadic gunfire. A window at the top of the stairs provided sufficient light for him to see up the stairway. The second floor had four doors opening off the hallway. He guessed each was an apartment. The two doors at the top of the stairway were locked. He moved down the hallway and tried the room on the left that would look out over the street below. It too was locked. Deiter's guess was that the inhabitants had sufficient time to secure their homes before leaving the city for safety. He needed to find a secure place where he could hide for the moment. An apartment with a window overlooking the street below would give him an advantage. He leaned backward and then threw all his weight against the door. Nothing. He tried again. This time, the lock on the door gave way and sprung open.

Deiter stopped and listened. He detected no sound coming from either the apartment or the rest of the building. He quickly stepped through the doorway and shut the door behind him. The lock clicked indicating that although it had sprung, no real damage had been done to the lock. The apartment wasn't large and, as far as he could determine from his perspective standing in the doorway, had one room off the main room, probably a bedroom. The room he was standing in had a sofa and several overstuffed chairs and appeared to be a living room; a dining and kitchen area was at the far end. It included a stove, a small refrigerator and some cupboards. A table with four chairs was set at the edge of the kitchen area.

Deiter quickly checked the bedroom and satisfied himself that he was alone. The apartment appeared to be occupied, but the inhabitants had obviously left it temporarily. Everything gave the impression that they would at some time return, or at least wanted to return. He quickly stripped off his FSB uniform and donned his civilian attire consisting of a heavy black quilted jacket over a wool shirt with heavy canvas trousers. He pulled a knitted black hat onto his head and stuck his gloves into his jacket pocket. If he were captured, he would be able to explain his presence to the rebels; if he fell into the hands of the Russians, he could demand to be brought to the FSB major who was his contact. He rolled up his FSB uniform and tied it with his belt. There was a bowl of clean water on a sink in the corner of the room. He washed his face and neck and dried himself with a towel that was hung on a peg next to the sink. He felt better.

Deiter had time now to further look around the apartment. In the bedroom, he found several pictures on a small table next to the bed.

One was of a man and a woman. He looked carefully at it. The man was dressed in black and wore the traditional boat shaped woolen papaha, the traditional Chechen hat, on his head. He seemed to be somehow familiar, but Deiter couldn't place him. The woman was of medium height and very pretty. She wore her reddish-brown hair shoulder length and around her head was a babushka that reminded him of the one worn by the woman in the photograph he had seen in Konykov's office. That was it; the man in the picture was also in one of the photographs that the general had shown him, but which one Deiter couldn't remember. Her smile was what particularly captivated Deiter; though; it was warm and showed an inward peace and happiness. He wondered what that smile might look like today.

The sound of the door to the outside hallway opening startled Deiter. He put down the picture frame, turned around and picked up his AKM. He checked the long magazine protruding from the underside of it to make sure it was secure, clicked off the safety, and straightened up to face the intruder. He heard the voice of someone, a female voice, saying something under her breath. It sounded like cursing interspersed with groans and sighs. Whoever she was, she was in the apartment and coming toward the bedroom. As she came around the corner of the doorway, Deiter could see that she was the woman in the picture on the table. She was only an inch shorter than himself; her hair was dark reddish-brown and covered with a dark patterned babushka of the same kind that she had been wearing in the picture. She wore a camouflaged winter combat uniform with a dark red scarf around her neck and a black backpack slung over her shoulder. She was incredibly beautiful and appeared to be in her mid-twenties, maybe pushing thirty. Her eyes were a dark green with bright green highlights that right now were flashing with unmistakable anger.

"Who the hell are you?" she asked as she leveled the older version AK-47 she was carrying directly at Deiter in challenge to his own automatic weapon. "And why are you in my apartment? Oh, I'm not afraid of your gun. The best you have to gain is that both of us will blow each other to hell. Why did you have to spring the lock on my door; how am I suppose to get that fixed, now?"

"I'm sorry, I was coming under fire and needed to get off the streets," Deiter stammered. "I thought the buildings were deserted. My name is Deiter and I am an American. I'm looking for two men, Aslan Maskhodov or Abuu Khadzhiyev; can you help me?" As Deiter phrased the question, he suddenly remembered who the man in the picture was.

"An American? How can I believe you? You look Russian to me. What do you want with the President? Or Abuu for that matter?" she demanded. Her gaze shifted to the picture beside the bed. "Oh, is that it?" she sneered. "You recognized him in the picture and made up that story."

"It sounds strange, I know, but it's the truth," he continued. "I was suppose to meet Sergei Borodenko in Gudermes; he was going to take me to meet with Khadzhiyev who would arrange for a meeting with President Maskhodov."

The woman started to soften her militant attitude and the AK-47 lowered ever so slightly. "Why should Abuu meet with you?" she asked. "Or the KGB, either," she quickly added.

Deiter smiled. She had given herself away by recognizing Borodenko's name; he knew that she too knew the general's son-in-law. "He's FSB now, you know," he said quietly. She lowered her weapon to her side and Deiter did likewise. "He is also concerned enough with what's going on to chance arranging the meeting. We have a common enemy in the terrorists, and for the sake of Chechnya and Russia, these people must be stopped."

"Why you, why an American? What have you to do with this?"

"America has a stake with this terrorist as well, and we have a score to settle with Osama bin Laden; me in particular," he replied. "Help me to find Khadzhiyev."

At first she seemed reluctant, but something she sensed about this man led her to trust him. Her eyes drifted toward the rolled up uniform and to the black ushanka with the FSB crest on it. She looked up quickly toward Deiter. "You lied, you're FSB!" she yelled at him.

"That was my cover. I was suppose to meet with Borodenko; I told you," he replied.

She softened her attitude again. "Well, I can't leave you here; I will take you to Abuu and he will decide what to do with you. How did you get here to Grozny, anyway?"

"The plane that crashed on the railway tracks, I was in it," he explained. "The rest of the crew were shot."

"Yes, I know. We were patrolling this sector when we saw the plane crash. We saw the crew try to escape and killed them," she responded without emotion. "As I was not far from my apartment, I decided to stop by and pick up a few things," she then added, "You're lucky we didn't shoot you. How did you get away?"

"I was slow getting out of the alley," Deiter answered with a weak smile.

"What's your name?" Deiter asked quietly.

At first there was silence, then she replied, "Zaira, Zaira Maskhadov." She said as she turned around and started to pick out items of clothing from a dresser near where she was standing. She stuffed a dozen or so items in her backpack, threw it on her shoulder and headed for the apartment door. "Come with me; I'll take you to see Abuu."

Deiter followed her, carefully closing and locking the apartment door behind him. What the hell just happened, he thought to himself shaking his head. I walked into a strange building, at random broke into a strange apartment and end up with the girl of the guy, who in all of Chechnya, is the one whom I need to contact. And did he hear her right? Did she say her last name was Maskhadov; the same as the President? This has got to be impossibly weird.

"Did I hear you correctly? Is your name Maskhodov, like President Maskhodov?"

"You ask too many questions," she responded. "Yes, he is my father."

"Well, I'll be damned," Deiter whispered mostly to himself.

The sun shone brightly on the city. Deiter looked at his watch; it was almost two o'clock. For the most part, the snow had been blown away by the constant wind into the corners of the buildings and curbs, but it still softened the ruins of the city somewhat. All of the streets were covered with a thin coating of snow. In places, tires from passing trucks had pressed it onto the pavement and had created a hard-packed covering that the sun had difficulty in melting. Deiter noticed that, but for the snow, the city would have appeared totally desolate. Here and there, however, the snow had been violently disturbed by the explosive effect of an artillery shell, which had left in its wake a dark circular scar in testament to the destructive blast. He dutifully followed the woman through the alleys and backyards. He could tell by the way she moved that she was totally familiar with the city. As they alternately walked and jogged toward their destination, he wondered about this woman he was following. She was pretty…no, quite beautiful, actually. One of the things that was so intriguing about her was her eyes and her totally honest expression that betrayed no deceit whatsoever. He had never before seen that in the face of a woman. Deiter became more and more captivated as he followed her toward the outskirts of the city. She obviously was a woman of action and determination. As they talked in low voices, he realized that she was also obviously competent in the ways of street fighting and knew military tactics. Was she really the daughter of the President? Never before had Deiter been so intrigued with a woman, infatuated, maybe, loved, yes, but not intrigued. Deiter shrugged off the thought, though, "Act your age, Jack. She's young enough to be your daughter…if you ever had one," he said to himself. For the first time that he could remember, Deiter fully felt his fifty-seven years. Maybe it was the jogging in heavy clothing, or maybe it was something else. He didn't want to think about it, he had a job to do. He needed to do it and then get back home, alive, if possible.

Zaira didn't necessarily share Deiter's thoughts, however. She had briefly left her team that morning to gather up some of her clothing back at the apartment and ended up escorting an American (she guessed he was truthful about that, anyway) to see Abuu. She wondered if her cousin would be angry at her for doing so. She guessed not; Abuu was brusque, but he was also a fair man and he was very protective of his beautiful favorite cousin. What else was she to do, anyway? Of course, she could have marched this man out into the alley and shot him. That would have been messy and besides, maybe he was here to see her father. He had correctly linked Sergei Borodenko to Abuu and her father. It simply couldn't be some far-fetched plan by the MVD to get at the President, they really weren't that smart. No one knew that she would be in the area of her apartment at that time either, and any MVD plan would have had to include that. She tended to believe…this man. She paused for a moment, because she forgot what he said his name was; she asked him again. He told her it was Jack Deiter. She guessed him to be in his late forties and he was actually quite alluring with his shaved head and dark, arched eyebrows. By the way that he kept up with her, she guessed that he was in very good physical shape as well. There was also a kindness and gentleness about him that surprised her. One didn't get to see much of kindness or gentleness these days, especially in Grozny. She didn't equate gentleness or kindness with softness, though. She had no doubt that this man could pick a fight with the best of them and win.

It had been almost an hour since they had left the apartment and as they slowed to a walk along the Sunzha River heading North, Zaira noticed the ice forming in the waters of the river. It reminded her of the waterfront along the Neva River in St. Petersburg, or Leningrad as it was called in those days. She was barely eighteen when she moved there after being accepted at the Russian Pedagogical University. It had been a happy time there even though the situation in Chechnya had been worsening. By the time she had graduated in 1994, the conflict in her homeland was reaching crisis conditions. She returned to Chechnya just before the Russian Army invaded; she, of course, became a partisan in the local militia. Her father was allied with General Djovkhar Dudaev during the 1994-1996 war with Russia. As Chief of Staff for the Chechen Armed Forces, he helped forge the victory over the Russian invasion, and following talks with former Russian Security Council Secretary Aleksander Lebed, he signed the

Khasavyurt agreements, effectively ending the conflict with Russian troops.

The next few years were spent in relative peace. Zaira had a great deal of pride in her father and what he had accomplished. His election to the presidency in early 1997 only strengthened her respect and pride in this man whom she knew as father and the world knew as a great leader of a new and independent country, the Chechen Republic. In return, this gave her a great deal of respect among her fellow militia.

In some ways, the American reminded her of her father, she thought. She wondered what his connection was with the Federal Security Service. Her mother and her brother and younger sister were now supposedly under the FSB's protection in a dacha near Vladikavkaz. It had been Sergei who had offered them protection and moved them by night to North Ossetia. He had been so considerate and concerned with their safety. If the American were allied with Sergei, he would be on their side. It was impossibly complicated now. It almost seemed that the members of the Russian FSB were at war with the Russian Ministry of the Interior, the MVD. Who had the interests of Chechnya or of Russia in mind in this affair? She didn't know. She also didn't know why this man was interested in their problems, so she asked him.

"Why are you putting yourself in peril by coming here? How does what we do concern you?"

"I have a personal score to settle," he answered simply.

"We all have personal scores to settle here," she chuckled. "How does what we do here involve America?"

"It has nothing to do with either your people or the Russians; it has to do with the terrorist, Osama bin Laden."

"Some here think that he is a hero," she observed quietly, looking up at Deiter.

"He is responsible for killing my wife," Deiter responded.

Zaira was quiet for a moment as they continued walking among the ruins of several buildings. She didn't know if she should inquire any more into the man's reasons. His gentleness, though, led her to believe he was quite sensitive and might respond to honest curiosity. "How did it happen?" she asked quietly.

"He blew up a commercial airliner that she was flying back to the United States."

"Wasn't that just an act of war?"

"For a country at war with the United States, maybe, but not some disenfranchised madman on his personal vendetta," he responded coldly. "He is marked for death."

"And you would kill him? You would be his judge and jury?"

"I plan on bringing him in to face justice. The courts will decide his fate."

They walked on a little further. Neither of them spoke for awhile. She had not told Deiter where they were heading. He understood the reasons why and didn't question her. If for some reason they were captured, his tongue might prove to be looser than hers and therefore more likely to reveal the location of the rebel headquarters.

They entered what at first looked like a graveyard and a memorial of some sort. The tall cement wall surrounding it was plastered red and from a rock pile in the center of the graveyard a large arm holding a sword rose thirty feet into the air. There was an inscription on the wall that Deiter didn't understand. As they walked past it, Deiter looked at Zaira questioningly. "I don't read Chechen. What is this place?"

Zaira smiled, "It's a memorial to Russian repression of the Chechen people." She pointed to the inscription on the wall and said, "It says, 'We should not forget. We should not forgive.' Does that give you a sense of my people's attitude towards the Russians?"

"We are not so different, then," he replied.

They stopped there for a moment to rest and Zaira gave Deiter an abbreviated history of her family and how her grandfather and grandmother had been relocated by the Communists in the early 1920's to a small village in Siberia. It wasn't until 1939 that they were allowed to return to Grozny. When the Germans invaded, they were at first welcomed as liberators from the Russians, but it turned out that they were even worse. The Gestapo treated the Chechens like animals. Then, after the war, they were moved back to Siberia once more along with most of their friends. "We can never forget and to forgive is to cheapen the lives of those who were murdered; this time, it was our families and like you, vengeance is a natural emotion. Can you deny that you feel a need for vengeance?"

Deiter was about to answer when they both heard the noise at the same time. It was like the low distant roll of thunder on a late summer day. They looked around and saw nothing and then both scanned the blue sun-filled sky, but still could see nothing. The sound seemed to come from everywhere and yet from no direction in particular.

"That's gotta be choppers," warned Deiter. As if on cue, two locust shaped forms rose above the high red wall and one cleared the buildings behind them. The two human figures in the graveyard seemed to be the focus of their attention. Deiter immediately recognized the two aircraft ahead of them as Russian Kamov A-50's or "Hokums" as the NATO forces called them. The Russian term was "Black Sharks." They were high performance combat helicopters equipped with cutting-edge day and night capabilities and hard-hitting air-to-air and air-to-surface weapons systems. He wondered how they could have possibly located them; it wasn't like they had been obvious in their movements. The aircraft were the first sign of Russians they had seen that day. On either side of the two aircraft, stubby wings held a brace of four missiles each. The aircraft were painted in camouflage and Deiter guessed that they were MVD close-support aircraft and not FSB that would have been painted black. He figured that the GRU forces would also have had Mi-24 helicopter gunships as that was their main battle copter and not these sophisticated ones.

"This way, quickly," shouted Zaira above the increasingly deafening roar of the aircraft. She sprinted towards the wall and a small entrance no bigger than a hole near the east end. Deiter could hear the sharp crackle of machine gun bursts from the aircraft behind them; they gave a sputtering sound as the rounds hit the ground and moved ever closer to him.

"Deiter!" screamed Zaira as she disappeared into the hole in the wall. "Leave it!"

Deiter swung his black automatic weapon up and pointed it directly at the helicopter on the right. He let loose a stream of bullets, hosing them directly into the intake of the engines on top of the main body of the aircraft. He repeated the same action at the helicopter on the left, emptying the banana clip as he did so. The hot smoking muzzle of his weapon slowly lowered as he accepted his fate without emotion. It was as though time was in slow motion; both aircraft stopped firing. There was only the vibrating chatter of their blades and the roaring of their engines in his ears. His face was grim.

Deiter couldn't bring himself to believe that he was still alive as he saw two human forms leap from the side doors of the aircraft on the right; this was followed by a third person jumping from the aircraft on the left. A brilliant plume of fire erupted from the engines of the first aircraft and slowly traveled forward along the contours of the aircraft towards the weapon encrusted nose. The flame consumed the engines and blade shafts as the entire blazing hulk began to fall slowly to earth like a setting sun. An explosion on the other craft sent a long stream of liquid fuel into the air that arched overhead and onto the falling fireball. When it made contact with the fire, it flashed back overhead and encompassed the second aircraft. The blast wave hit Deiter full on and snapped him back to reality. Prying himself away from the ongoing spectacle, he turned around and dashed towards the hole in the wall. He could hear the chattering of the machine guns of the third helicopter hovering over the buildings as he disappeared into the hole. The impact of rounds hitting against the wall behind him punctuated the closeness of his escape.

In front of him, there was almost total darkness as he stumbled forward keeping his left hand against the wall of what appeared to be a tunnel. How did she know this place existed? He had gone about ten yards when he saw a light off to his left. The floor of the tunnel was fairly smooth, and he was able to pick up speed running while always keeping the light directly in his view. At the entrance to the hole, he paused to see that he was in a fairly large park-like setting. There were many trees and underbrush around him and it continued up to the rear of the wall they had just left. About twenty yards into the wooded area there was a large rock and leaning against it was Zaira, checking her own weapon to make sure there was a round in the chamber.

"That was a foolish thing to do," she said, shaking her head. "You could have been killed for taking so long."

"They're down two aircraft," Deiter replied, shrugging his shoulders.

"You shot them down?" she asked incredulously.

"I didn't like their attitude," he responded, loading a new banana clip into his AKM.

Zaira smiled and cocked her head. "Are you sure you're not Chechen?" she asked.

"Cossack, maybe. I'm not sure anymore."

"That's good enough," she replied. "Where did you learn to do that, Deiter?"

"Jack," he said.

"Jack, jack what?"

"Jack. My name is Jack," he answered.

She nodded. Presently, she stood up and looked around to see if she could see any activity through the trees. Nothing. The sound of the helicopter had also disappeared. There seemed to be nothing but the silence. If there had been any birds around, it was impossible to tell, but for the first time she could remember, the park was quiet. The recent noise must have silenced the birds as well.

"How did they find us?" he asked out loud, yet to himself.

"I don't know; maybe they just stumbled onto us," she replied absently.

"No, they knew exactly where we were. There's no way that they could have planned that ambush without knowing precisely where we were. Unless..." he said speculatively, "unless one of us is bugged." Deiter looked at his jacket and felt the sleeves and the vest portion; nothing there. He next checked the weapon. That obviously was a

KGB holdover armament and must have been in the armory of the FSB for a long time. He doubted the FSB would have placed a bug on him for the MVD to use.

"Come, we have to keep going," Zaira urged as she slung her weapon over her shoulder and started down a path through the trees. Deiter shrugged and followed her. The pathway led through a park that was delightful even though the air was colder here in the shade. In the open areas in which they had been traveling, the sun finally warmed them and was wonderfully welcome. It was obvious that Zaira knew where she was going and the safest way to get there. Deiter wished that he had some idea of where he was and where he was going. It wasn't easy to put his entire trust into someone he had just met, but what choice did he have?.

They soon reached the end of the park and walked through a gate in a stone wall that brought them onto a street that stretched along the river. Deiter checked the skies for aircraft and neither saw nor heard any. Zaira headed up a street between several bombed out buildings. After the serenity of the wooded area, the street spoke of danger and was foreboding. They moved quietly and quickly from one covered position to another. A wind had come up again, dropping the temperature and causing the icy snow that had accumulated in the gutters and corners to blow in their faces and sting their exposed skin. They had gone almost a hundred yards up the canyon-like street when the buildings lost the appearance of devastation that warfare brings to a city; the neighborhood could have easily been as it was a dozen years ago when it was peaceful and safe. It might have been that feeling of safety that led both of them to relax their guard. A noise behind him made Deiter turn to look at the street they had just traveled. Three men stood there with weapons trained on them. They were dressed in the padded camouflaged uniforms of the MVD military. He whispered a warning to Zaira and grabbed her arm to pull her into an alley. She resisted his effort and he noticed that her gaze was locked on the street in front of them; he followed her gaze and then understood why. The remainder of a squad of nine soldiers stood with their weapons at the ready blocking the street ahead of them.

"Oh, shit. Where in hell did they come from?" he asked.

"I think you were right; they were expecting us," she replied. "If we resist, we are dead," she added, her voice carrying a note of deadly resolution.

"Let's bluff our way past them," Deiter suggested. She nodded.

Deiter lifted his arm and waved. "Hello there, how's it going?" he shouted. Zaira waved and smiled at the now advancing soldiers.

The response came from the tall powerfully built man in the center of the group. In Russian, he ordered them to drop their weapons and fall to the ground with their hands over their heads. Deiter didn't like this turn of events. "I need to speak with your commander!" he shouted. Their response this time was silence. That wasn't a good sign, and Deiter knew it. He dropped to the ground, throwing his weapon off to the side and Zaira did likewise. Deiter felt the cold snow sting his face as he lay on the street.

Four of the soldiers shouldered their weapons and walked rapidly towards the two forms on the ground. Two of them quickly stripped Deiter of his holstered 9mm pistol and roughly pulled him to his feet. The other two grabbed Zaira and pulled her up so she stood with both arms pinned behind her. Deiter looked over to see that Zaira's face was defiant yet carried an unmistakable flicker of fear that played in her eyes. There was no conversation between the soldiers. It was as though the scene had been rehearsed and they were only carrying out their part in some somber drama. The leader turned and started walking back up the street. The four soldiers pushed both captives forward to follow the leader as the rest of the squad fell in behind to assure that the captives did not escape them.

The party of soldiers and captives passed by a multistory apartment building in which several soldiers could be seen at the windows throwing valuables to comrades in the street below. From inside came the screams of women, possibly two or three. Then, at one of the windows on the fifth floor, a young girl perhaps thirteen or fourteen years old appeared and acted as though she was about to jump. Strong hands reached out and pulled her back into the room even though she put up a determined struggle. Deiter heard an indignant bellow of a male voice followed by a short burst of gunfire coming from the room. The bellowing voice was silent, but the high pitched screams of the women continued as the group left the scene behind them. Deiter looked over his shoulder at Zaira and their eyes met briefly. Deiter mouthed the words, "Don't worry." Zaira nodded, although her smile was very weak.

The leader looked back at Deiter and ordered the soldier closest to the American to prevent any further communication between the two prisoners. It was then that Deiter first noticed the sickly sweet smell of death that hung heavily on the air. The odor was so overpowering that it could only mean that somewhere nearby there was an accumulation of corpses and that despite the cold, they lay rotting under the bright Chechen sun. They approached a cross street and Deiter could see a large empty lot on the other side of the opposing corner; in it was the remaining camouflaged painted helicopter, its blades turning slowly. As they approached, the engine gave a belch and roared into life. The blades began turning faster and faster. Obviously, the group was expected and they were to be transported somewhere more distant than the outskirts of Grozny. Deiter wished that these were FSB troops, he didn't know what reception he might expect from the MVD contingent. Upon reaching the helicopter, both captives were shoved into the open door of the cargo area and forced to sit on the floor as they were surrounded by the rest of the soldiers to prevent them from escaping or jumping from the helicopter in flight. Deiter decided to delay any additional attempts at conversation with his captors until they were at some type of higher command level.

Ted Colby

Chapter Fifteen

Captives

Grozny, Republic of Chechnya
Wednesday Afternoon, November 24, 1999

The camouflaged helicopter rose slightly off the ground, turned clockwise and tipped forward as it gained speed and transitional lift. The doors were closed against the cold air. Surrounded by the eight soldiers, Deiter quickly became hot; the closeness was suffocating. Despite the oppressively warm air blasting out of a vent near the cabin roof, he could feel Zaira shiver beside him, The smell of rotting corpses was now replaced by the odor of the sweating soldiers around them mixed with the smell of aviation fuel from the aircraft. Deiter wondered in a detached way if Russian soldiers ever bathed during the winter months.

As best Deiter could judge, the helicopter was heading east toward the vicinity of Gudermes. In less than five minutes, they started to descend onto a field just outside a small built-up area consisting of at least a dozen buildings. Deiter could just make out a white, red and blue flag hanging over the doorway of the largest of the buildings as the aircraft glided over the complex. The helicopter rotated counter-clockwise so as to direct the open door toward the cluster of buildings and set down with a sudden jolt. As soon as the motion of the aircraft ceased, the soldiers threw open the side doors and piled out of the

279

aircraft, pushing Deiter and Zaira along with them. On the ground, the two captives were herded at a slow run toward the building draped with the Russian flag.

"Stay here," the tall soldier ordered the remainder of his force as they reached the doorway. The men formed up around the entrance to the building; two faced the doorway with weapons at the ready while the remainder faced outward. Deiter followed the leader through the doorway; Zaira followed him. At the end of the hallway, they entered a large room. Deiter noticed that there were two windows that faced the rear of the building and one window at the end of the long room that faced the side. In the center of the room was a large desk with a sadly overweight Russian major dressed in dark-blue, office-dress uniform with red trim of the MVD seated behind it. The man didn't look up, but continued to read from a stack of papers placed before him. Deiter figured that this man might be of high-enough rank to listen to his story and this had to be the moment of opportunity when he needed to make his move.

"Major," Deiter began, bringing himself up to as imposing a figure as he could muster. "My name is Colonel Demidov, FSB. I am on a mission for FSB Colonel General Konykov. The mission has the full concurrence of Deputy Assistant Premier Yuri Sarkorosov. I must contact FSB Major Borodenko here in Gudermes and the woman must accompany me." Deiter paused and waited for a response.

It wasn't what he expected. A crushing punch to his kidney from the muzzle of the assault rifle was immediately followed by a smashing blow to the side of his head from the butt of the weapon. He felt himself sink to his knees. The pain was excruciating and he felt his head go light. Deiter felt himself starting to pass out, but struggled to maintain his consciousness. He knew that both of their lives depended on it. Deiter looked up at the major; his eyes shooting a deadly look at the man who continued to ignore him. Deiter guessed that he was supposed to remain silent, but that wasn't his style. Through the pain, he clenched his teeth and whispered, "Is this the way the MVD learned to fight, major? Little wonder you've taken such a beating from the rebels." This time he was ready as the tall soldier brought up his weapon to slam the muzzle down onto Deiter's neck. At the height of the man's swing, Deiter stood up and simultaneously slammed his elbow up into the soldier's crotch. He felt it give. The man's scream jerked the seated officer to attention and he half lifted himself up from behind the desk; his right hand going for the holster on his hip.

"Enough," the major shouted, as he drew his weapon and with both hands held it pointed at Deiter. "Take the woman to the room upstairs; I will entertain the American in the holding cell in the basement." The tall soldier recovered himself sufficiently to grab Deiter roughly by the shoulder and force him towards the doorway where a second soldier joined them. After they left the room, a third soldier came in to grab Zaira by the arm and forcefully shove her out into the hallway and up the stairway to the floor above.

The basement consisted of a large open room that was entered through a door at the bottom of the stairway. As he was pushed through the open door by the two guards, he could see that the walls were of stone and the room had several small rectangular windows near the ceiling; two of them were on either side of the room and one was at the extreme end. Deiter noted that none of them were large enough to provide him an escape route. The first guard closed the door behind them. The only furnishings Deiter could see were a straight-backed chair with arms positioned in the center of the room and a table that contained a box about the size of a small suitcase. From the box came two terminal leads about a quarter of an inch thick and about ten feet long. At the end of the leads were electrical clamps. Deiter guessed that both were meant for him. The tall guard shoved Deiter down onto the chair and both of them secured his arms to the wooden arms of the chair with leather straps. Unexpectedly, his legs were not secured with the straps located on the legs of the chair. One guard grabbed a pail of water and threw it at Deiter, drenching his arms, lower body and legs.

"This will keep you from any more attempts to escape," growled the tall soldier. The other soldier tore the black knit hat from Deiter's head and threw it into the corner. Then, for a few moments there was silence. Both soldiers stood a few feet back from Deiter and faced him with their arms folded in front of them and waited. The door suddenly burst open and the major sauntered, as best his heavy frame would allow him, into the room. He stood between Deiter and the two soldiers.

"I would be happy to inflict any pain you should wish for failing to cooperate," he began. "You will quickly tell me where President Aslan Maskhodov is located and where Osama bin Laden can be found. I know that you have this information." The major folded his arms on his chest, unconsciously mimicking the two soldiers behind him. He waited impatiently for a reply. Obviously, it seemed to Deiter, they knew more than they should have about their captive and the mission.

"Someone gave you some bad information," Deiter said shaking his head.

"I warn you, Mr. Deiter, I am running out of time and so are you…and the woman upstairs."

Deiter was convinced now that someone was intentionally sabotaging the mission, and he guessed that it might be the effeminate Deputy Assistant Premier for Internal Affairs, Yuri Sarkorosov. The thought that even Don Adams might have something to do with it still wasn't out of the question. To his surprise, it appeared that they didn't know who Zaira really was and that was something in their favor at least, although he didn't like the man's threat concerning her. Not much else looked promising. Something else bothered Deiter; except for his 9mm pistol, no one had searched him or asked for his identity papers or Zaira's papers either for that matter.

Deiter shrugged, gave a deep sigh as though giving in and asked the major if he spoke English; he explained that he didn't want what he was to say overheard. He assumed that the MVD soldiers probably knew only Russian.

"Yes, little," the major replied in English with a faint yet cocky smile. It became obvious to Deiter that the MVD, and the major in particular, was jealous of the FSB's role in the project and if they could accomplish what others had not been able to do they would have a political advantage. He realized that this pathetic person wanted to use him to solidify his position and future in the MVD. He also knew that ambition can be the downfall of even the most promising of people, but in the hands of the stupid, it can be disastrous…sometimes for everyone concerned.

Deiter decided to lead the major on an intricate and devious maneuver to stall for time. The MVD knew Deiter was alive and here in Gudermes; that information should eventually get conveyed surreptitiously to the FSB, if they were worth a salt in their field, and Deiter knew they were. In time, the FSB would show up. He resigned himself to the fact that this would be his only hope.

"I had to make contact with a man who was to lead me to the President," Deiter began in English. "I was on my way to meet him."

"Where…you…meet him?" the major asked slowly, pausing over the words.

"I was suppose to continue on the street where your soldiers captured us…they were suppose to find us and bring us to the President."

"And bin Laden?"

"Locating him was to be done through the President's people; they know where he is."

"And…covert agent…you…contact?"

Deiter didn't like the way this guy kept coming up with information from that secret briefing at the Embassy, but he kept up with his story. "I thought that the agent belonged to the Interior Ministry and would contact me when bin Laden was located," he said, sitting up straighter with a surprised look on his face.

The officer now appeared agitated. Deiter knew that what he had said, made sense to the guy, but it didn't help him find out what he wanted. The major suddenly turned and headed for the door. "I…find out what…woman knows. Your stories…best match," he said, over his shoulder. The two soldiers followed him through the doorway and closed the door behind them. Obviously, they were eager to be part of that interrogation. Deiter was left entirely alone.

Deiter didn't feel comfortable with this turn of events. He had thought that his story was playing very well up to that point and could give them some time for the FSB to find them. How would Zaira react? He guessed she would probably not say much at all. He wondered just how good the major was at interrogation. He might be smarter than he appeared. He worried about Zaira, though. He had read about the treatment that Chechen women had received from the Russians and doubted that this bunch was any more disciplined then the rest. Deiter remembered the woman in the apartment building they had passed on their way that afternoon. The threat of rape could be a strong motivator during interrogation, and it appeared to Deiter that the officer was not only desperate to find out the information he wanted, but also would probably enjoy that facet of questioning.

Deiter tested the chair he was strapped to by wiggling it back and forth. The joints were loose, not as loose as he might have liked, but it would have to do.

Chapter Sixteen

The Cavalry

Moscow; the American Embassy
Early Wednesday afternoon, November 24, 1999

Charlie sat on the sofa in Hank's suite with her feet up and her arms around her knees; the position she usually assumed when deep in thought or when she was troubled, and she was troubled about not knowing what had happened to Jack. She looked up at Hank as he paced back and forth in front of her.

"For God's sake, sit down, Hank," she hollered at him.

"I'm worried," he snapped back. "I always pace when I'm worried."

"Is Jack really walking into something, or are we just imagining things?" she asked.

"I don't like the whole thing…it's all Adam's idea and that I know for sure," he said, stopping his pacing and putting his hands on the back of the sofa where Charlie was sitting. "Somehow, I feel he's being set up, but I don't know how or why." He came around the sofa, sat down next to Charlie and took her hand in both of his. "Charlie, you know that Jack's like a brother to me. Despite all that's happened over the years, this is the very first time that I've felt really concerned about his safety. Something is definitely wrong."

"What do we do?"

Henderson thought for a moment and then shrugging his shoulders replied, "Jack trusted General Konykov. If we warn him that we feel something's not right, maybe he'll be able to get to Jack."

"What about the Ambassador or Woods and Adams? Won't they try to stop us? How'll we get to the General?"

"First of all," he answered, smiling at her barrage of questions, "they won't stop us if we don't tell them. Second, I think I know who to contact to get in touch with the General."

Henderson had chatted briefly with Colonel John H. Kosty, the military attaché, prior to the earlier meeting. He found him to be very professional and from some reports, not at all in tune with the way the present administration was handling the Russian situation or with a number of the liberal ideas espoused by those currently in power. He thought it might be worthwhile to broach him on how to contact General Konykov. After explaining this to Charlie, he picked up the embassy phone in the suite and had the operator connect him to Colonel Kosty. The phone rang at the office of the military attaché and the secretary put him through to the attaché.

"Colonel Kosty," Henderson heard at the other end of the phone.

"John, it's Hank Henderson."

"Yes, General, what can I do for you?"

"I'm concerned about Jack Deiter, and I need to talk with you."

"Sure, anytime, Sir. What seems to be the matter?"

"I'd rather discuss it in private."

"Sure, I understand completely."

"Where would be the best place to meet? Oh, I also have Charlie Waggner with me."

"Have you seen the Moscow River in the winter? You know, where the street along the entrance to the Embassy crosses over the bridge?"

"Yes, I know the place. We'll meet you there in twenty minutes, if that's convenient."

"Twenty minutes it is," Kosty concluded.

Henderson relayed his conversation to Charlie.

"I'll meet you downstairs in ten minutes," Charlie said, jumping up and walking over to the door of the suite. "I need to pick up my coat and purse."

Both Hank Henderson and Charlie Waggner were upbeat as they walked down the street leading to the bridge over the Moscow River. The ice glowed brilliantly on the branches of the trees lining the sidewalk. Henderson hoped that Colonel Kosty could arrange a meeting with General Konykov who could get a message to Dieter or stop the project until everything could be sorted out. They arrived at the bridge and once again looked out over the scene they had appreciated earlier and waited for Colonel Kosty to arrive.

After about five minutes, they noticed the military attaché walking down the tree-lined sidewalk from the Embassy. He was dressed in a long dark brown overcoat with a fur cap, he would not have been conspicuous anywhere in Moscow. He crossed the street that ran along the river and walked up the embankment to the couple standing along the riverside walk next to the bridge.

"I love to watch the river," Kosty said. "It adds a bit of peace to the chaos I normally deal with."

"I understand that," Charlie said with a grin. "Colonel Kosty, I'm Charlie Waggner, we didn't really get a good introduction at the meeting." She held out her hand towards him.

"Very pleased to meet you, and the name's John, please." The two shook hands. Kosty turned and looked at Henderson.

"It's your meeting, General; what can I do to help?" Kosty asked.

"Jack Deiter, that's the problem. We think that there's something going on that will end up getting him bushwhacked."

"I wouldn't be surprised at all," came the reply. "The bitter exchange between General Konykov and Sarkorosov didn't end at that meeting, you know."

"Konykov sent a car for Deiter, and that's the last we've heard of him," Henderson replied.

Kosty raised his eyebrows at that revelation, but asked, "What makes you think something's wrong?"

"Charlie overheard a reference to the covert agent who was mentioned in the briefing. The CIA appears to want to keep Deiter from seeing the agent. That doesn't make any sense logically in the situation that he's in. His mission includes meeting the agent."

Kosty thought for a moment. "I see what you mean. I too, thought that the agent was supposed to be the intermediary with bin Laden. If

Deiter now isn't supposed to contact the agent, he has no business down there in Chechnya."

"What's more, I just don't like this disappearing act," Charlie inserted. "It doesn't seem either professional or above board."

"That may be, Ms. Waggner, but it is very Russian," Kosty remarked with a grin. "Sometimes we don't see the purpose behind it, but it's just Russian nature. Everything needs to have a mystery about it and nothing can be played straightforward. From what I know of Konykov, he wouldn't be sacrificing Deiter…it's not his style. What you see, is what you get in Konykov. He may be very Russian, but he isn't deceitful."

"Do you think he knows about the contact and Adams' comment?" Charlie asked.

"Adams?" Kosty shot back at her. "It was Adams you overheard?" He frowned.

"Does that make a difference?" asked Henderson.

"There's something about that guy I don't trust," Kosty replied.

"Join the club," commented Charlie aside.

"I know how to contact General Konykov," Kosty said to Henderson. "Wait for me in your suite and I'll call you. I should know in half an hour. What I say to you on the phone may be a little encrypted, but you'll know what I mean." Kosty shook hands and quickly walked back towards the Embassy. Charlie and Henderson waited until the Colonel was almost two blocks away before starting back. No use making their meeting too obvious.

Later that afternoon, Henderson reinitiated his pacing between the window overlooking the Moscow River and the door to his suite. Charlie regained her position on the sofa with her feet on the coffee table this time. Henderson looked at his watch…it was nearly four-thirty. Kosty had said a half-hour and it had now been almost forty-five minutes. "What's taking him so long?" he questioned impatiently. As if in answer to his impatience, the telephone on the small desk next to the window rang twice. Henderson picked it up. "Yes?"

"General Henderson? This is Colonel Kosty. The tour of the Kremlin that you asked about has been arraigned. How soon can you pick up the limo out front?"

"Wonderful, Colonel. We'll be down in five minutes."

"Do you mind if I tag along? I've never had a full tour, and this may be my only opportunity for awhile."

"Not at all, Colonel, I think that'd be great. See you downstairs." Henderson put down the phone and looking at Charlie, he pumped his arm and said, "Yes!"

General Hank Henderson and Charlie Waggner walked through the main doors of the Embassy and out onto the walkway gracing the entrance. A black Lincoln limousine with the American flag flying from one fender and a red flag with a single white star signifying Henderson's rank on the other fender was waiting for them. Colonel Kosty stood by the rear door of the automobile and saluted when

Henderson approached. He was wearing his Army dress green uniform with an overcoat.

"General Konykov was very receptive to meeting with you when I told him about Deiter. I think he was taken with the man and saw a lot of himself in him," Kosty said, as the three of them settled themselves in the rear of the sleek limo. "I also thinks he knows something of what Deiter's situation is at the present time…or will find out by the time we get there. He has agreed to as much time as we need."

The tall imposing walls of the Kremlin rose before them as they sped through Borovitskaya Place, past the Rashkov House and through the walls at Borovitskaya Tower. The limo turned left at the Cathedral of the Archangel Michael, around the Tsar Bell and headed for the entrance to the Arsenal in the north corner of the Kremlin. At the entrance, the car stopped and the three passengers stepped out and climbed the three steps to the doorway. They were met by a young woman with long dark hair and escorted into the upstairs office of General Konykov.

"Welcome to the Kremlin," the general said in a deep voice. He smiled as he rose from his heavy wooden desk and slowly walked to meet his visitors. "General Henderson, I met your father on two occasions. I'm very pleased to know you as well." He turned to Charlie and took her hand, placing it to his lips. "Miss Waggner, I am so pleased that you could come as well. I was hoping that I would get a chance to see you again." Charlie was getting to like Russia and smiled graciously back at the elderly general. Konykov turned and quickly shook hands with Colonel Kosty acknowledging the presence of the military attaché. After motioning his guests to be seated, he returned to the chair behind his massive desk. He looked from one person to another and finally said, "What can I do for you? Colonel Kosty said you were concerned about the safety of Mr. Deiter."

"We think that someone hasn't been completely honest and above board concerning this operation," Henderson replied.

"No one is ever completely honest," the General replied with a faint smile. "Does this someone have a name?"

"Don Adams for one."

The general's eyebrows went up. "The CIA?" Konykov chuckled. "You think that the 'someone' who isn't being honest is in the CIA?" He shook his head. "I have lived too long, I believe, that I should hear that from an American."

The humor and irony was not lost on the other three. "As strange as that would seem," replied Henderson with a broad grin.

"Forgive an old man who has survived many twists of fate…and betrayal, I might add," the general continued. 'To hear these words from your lips makes me think we have more in common than one might think."

"We need to get word to Jack Deiter that this might be a setup even if he is successful in getting bin Laden," Henderson explained.

"Then rest assured that we will watch him more closely. Now, there is something that your government does not yet know. The aircraft carrying Mr. Deiter crashed in the middle of Grozny about noon today. We haven't been able to find Mr. Deiter, but the crewmembers were found dead a short time ago. They apparently had been shot by the rebels near the crash site. Their wounds were similar to those received in combat; they had not been executed."

Charlie gasped and grabbed onto Henderson's arm. He reached over and placed his hand on hers and whispered, "It ain't over 'till it's over."

General Konykov held up his hand and said, "As we haven't been able to find Mr. Deiter, I must assume he survived. I'm not surprised, and neither should you be, for you know him better than I."

"If you haven't found him, he's alive," responded Henderson, "I do know him."

"Then let's proceed under that assumption," said the general. "We must also assume that there is someone in your government who would just as soon see Mr. Deiter dead as not."

"Yeah, I guess that's what we concluded too," interjected Henderson. "Was he supposed to contact you? We seem to be out of the loop in regard to his status."

"He was supposed to contact my son-in-law when he arrived in Gudermes. We could have easily kept in contact with him then. When I was informed of the aircraft being shot down, I instructed Major Borodenko to search for him. If he has joined the rebels or has been taken captive by them, I have no control over the situation. If he is in the hands of the MVD, I will know shortly; I have ears there."

Prophetically, there was a brief knock at the door and the General's secretary appeared in the slightly opened doorway.

"Excuse me, General," she interrupted, "there is a report from Chechnya."

The General nodded and a uniformed major slipped through the doorway behind the secretary. "We have located him," the officer reported curtly and with some enthusiasm. "He is in the hands of the MVD in Gudermes. There was a woman with him." Charlie registered surprise.

"Do we have sufficient forces to extract them?" inquired the General.

"I believe so."

"Do it," the general ordered. The officer nodded and withdrew from the room sliding behind the still waiting secretary. The General nodded to her and she followed the Major out of the room and closed the door behind her.

"A woman?" asked Charlie, turning to Henderson.

The general shrugged, "He is your friend. You should know more about that than I."

General Konykov stood up and leaned on his desk. "They will see to his safety…and that of the woman who is with him. Do you want to send a message to him for when Major Borodenko releases him?"

"Tell him that Adams doesn't want him to see the woman who is supposed to be his contact; that woman may be the one he was with when he was captured, I don't know. But that's all we can say at this time," replied Henderson.

"I will make sure that he gets the message. Now, there is nothing you can do until he is released and allowed to continue with his mission."

"Would you keep us informed? It may be best to contact Major Kosty. Any direct contact with us may give away our situation," Henderson requested.

"I understand," responded the Russian.

Gudermes, Chechnya
MVD Military Headquarters
Wednesday evening, November 24, 1999

He didn't know if the sound would attract the guards or not, but Deiter stood up while still buckled to the arms of the chair and ran towards the stone basement wall turning his body as it crashed into it. The weakened chair had broken apart and he sprawled on the floor next to the wall. Finally free, he stood up and quickly began to unbuckle the straps that held his arms onto the now disassembled and broken chair. He winced at the pain in his shoulder and back as he did so. He retrieved his black knit hat from the corner. He moved to the door and slowly and quietly tried the handle. It moved down and he could hear a quiet "click" as the latch opened. He waited a moment and then slowly opened the door. He had half expected a guard to have been waiting outside the doorway, but the hallway was empty and in the descending darkness of the evening hours, the hallway was beginning to show ever-deepening shadows. He moved to the bottom of the stairs, stopped, and listened to the sounds of the building. In the distance he could hear voices coming from somewhere in the upper floors. He heard a female voice painfully crying out between the lower angry and threatening male voices. Deiter knew that he had to move quickly if he was to prevent something from happening to Zaira.

He moved silently up the stairs and into the hallway of the ground floor. The noises came from the floor above him. As he rounded the corner leading to the upper floor, he noticed a light coming from a slit in the doorway of a room on the left-hand side of the hallway. He crept up to the edge of the door and looked in though the partially open door. There were two soldiers there; one lying on a rather large sofa and the other curled up in a chair. Both seemed to be asleep. Deiter opened the door, hoping that it would not creak in the process. It didn't, and he slipped inside. On a table was an AK-47 assault rifle. He quietly slid over to the table and picked it up, checking to make sure it was loaded and the safety off. The soldier in the chair posed the most danger both from his size and his proximity to the door. Deiter lifted the rifle and brought the butt end down sharply into the man's neck. There was a double sound of a dull thud of the iron butt plate of the rifle hitting flesh coupled by a crack of exploding bone. Deiter swung around to see the soldier on the bed beginning to rise up with a half-conscious look of stupor on his face. One more swing of the rifle and the second man never regained consciousness. Deiter leaned over the man and pulled out the automatic pistol inside the holster on his belt. It was then that Deiter recognized that the man was an MVD lieutenant. He relieved him of the weapon. Now sufficiently armed, he headed out of the doorway and up the stairs. He took the stairs two at time and followed the sound of the voices. Deiter reached the door of the room where the voices originated. He eased open the door and glanced inside. He saw the major standing with his hands on his hips watching the tall soldier just as the man struck Zaira across the face.

299

"We have delayed long enough," the major said, in a cooing voice. He had a leering smile on his face as he began to unbuckle the belt that held his holstered pistol. He motioned to the tall soldier who was standing over the woman to leave them. The soldier let go of the woman's arm and straightened up. Nodding with a grin, he moved backward towards the door to the room. He kept looking from the woman on the floor to the major.

"She certainly is a fine looking Chechen bitch," he remarked as he backed towards the door. "Maybe later, Major, I might be able to continue the interrogation alone," he added as a question. The major jerked his head toward the door, but smiled his concurrence. The soldier opened the door and started to back out into the hallway while still leering at the woman on the floor. She was the last thing he saw in this life. The butt of a rifle smashed his neck and his body crashed the door wide open. Deiter stood holding the AK-47 aimed at the major. The officer's mouth opened and then closed again as he watched Deiter step over the body of the tall soldier.

"Zaira, can you get up?" Deiter asked.

She jerked suddenly and lifted her head from the floor to look at Deiter. A faint smile crossed her bruised face. "Jack," she managed in a whisper.

At the movement and sound of her voice, the major's attention suddenly and briefly switched to the woman's form on the floor. His eyes never saw the blow of the rifle muzzle as it smashed into the Adam's apple in his neck. The simultaneous thud and crack announced the death of the arrogant major. Deiter knelt down beside Zaira as she struggled to rise. He put an arm around her waist and brought her to her feet. She swung towards him and wordlessly threw her arms around him and nestled her head in his shoulder, sobbing.

Noises from the hallway outside caused Deiter to swing around and bring his weapon to bear on a form now standing there in the open doorway. Deiter started to wilt at the sight of a Russian officer standing in the doorway with his pistol drawn.

"Sergei!" Zaira exploded in relief. At that, Deiter lowered his weapon and Zaira staggered toward the officer.

"Zaira, are you all right?" the officer asked as he reached out for her and wrapping his arms around her, held her closely. She nodded in an affirmative response as she collapsed in his arms. "I would have never forgiven myself if the daughter of my friend had been hurt." He turned toward Deiter. "Mr. Deiter, I presume?" the major asked smiling.

"And who are you?" Deiter asked in reply.

"Major Borodenko, FSB. Had a helluva time finding you. By the look of things, I suppose we shouldn't have worried," he remarked in perfect English as he looked at the two bodies on the floor. "I saw what appears to be your handiwork downstairs as well."

Deiter smiled and managed to say, "The US cavalry comes to the rescue again."

"But, I'm not cavalry, I'm FSB," the Major said seriously, a confused look on his face.

"That's okay, right now, it's just as good," responded Deiter.

Chapter Seventeen

Fox Hunt

FSB Headquarters
Gudermes, Chechnya
Early Thursday morning, November 25, 1999

The accommodations weren't exactly five-star, but they were better than how he had expected to spend the night strapped to the interrogation chair in the basement of the MVD headquarters. Deiter had slept soundly on the metal military cot provided him by the FSB on the third floor of their Gudermes Headquarters. He had shared a room with three other officers, but under the circumstances, it was the best accommodations that they had to offer. Zaira had been quartered in a separate small room by herself next to the one that Deiter occupied. To her, the accommodations were better than those she had been used to the last few months; at least they were private.

Deiter stretched and finally threw off the heavy woolen blanket and sat up on the edge of the cot. It was barely light outside, but he could see well enough to gather up his coat, hat and weapons. As he slung the AK-47 over his shoulder and pushed the pistol into his belt, he ambled out of the room and headed downstairs to where he knew there would be someone awake in the operations center. He rubbed his hand over his beard and wished he had the backpack he had rescued from the crash the previous day; it had a razor in it and his toilet articles. When one gets used to shaving each day, it's hard to go unshaven in public. He supposed that he could grow a beard, but he didn't know how that would go with his completely shaved head, which also needed some attention, he noticed as he stroked his scalp with his hand.

"Mr. Deiter, you slept well, I hope?" asked Major Borodenko, as he leaned against the desk pulling on his boots. He was alone in the room that served as the FSB Operations Center. Deiter could see from the unmade cot against the back wall that Major Borodenko had apparently spent the night there in the communications area.

"Thank you, Major, quite well under the circumstance."

"We must continue with the mission, if you're up to it," the major said.

"So how do we contact the President?"

"I think your lady companion may be of the most help," Borodenko replied. "I don't know how you ever came to meet her of all people in Chechnya; you must have outrageous luck."

"I think she found me," said Deiter softly.

"Well, I know that Zaira will be able to contact her father. I was prepared to make contact with several rebels whom I know, but this is much quicker and more direct."

Deiter observed the young major. He was an honest and good-looking officer, but there was also a certain sadness in his eyes that suggested a sense of hopelessness and discouragement. Maybe, Deiter thought, what he saw in the major's eyes was just what others saw in his eyes. He remembered what General Konykov had said of Borodenko's young wife, the general's daughter, being killed in the terrorist bomb attack on the apartment complex. Deiter understood, if anyone could, the emotional stirrings in this young man. Deiter felt much the same. He thought that maybe there might well exist a bond between them. He guessed that the general had briefed Borodenko on Deiter's situation.

"Major, I'm a bit bewildered and concerned over the way this mission has gone so far," Deiter said, as Borodenko was finishing dressing. "I can't fully understand why the plane was shot down and then the two of us captured. The MVD must have known where we were all along."

"I have thought on that as well," Borodenko observed. "Have you thought about a bug?"

"Yes, I did a quick check and found nothing, but I did notice that the MVD didn't search me...other than disarming me...nor did they take my papers or Zaira's identification. They didn't even look at them. They knew me, but I'm convinced that they really didn't know or care who she was."

"And now they will never know, thanks to your handiwork back at the MVD Headquarters."

"That needed to be done; not that I enjoyed it...well that MVD major was a little too arrogant for my tastes and maybe he deserved what he got. Besides, he wasn't planning on being a gentleman with

Zaira. But you're right, I wonder if there's still a locator planted somewhere?"

Deiter looked through his pockets again and came up with his identity papers and the badge that identified him as an FSB colonel. All of his clothes had been provided by the FSB. What was there that hadn't been provided by the FSB, he asked himself. "My papers!" he exclaimed suddenly and placed them on the desk. General Konykov had told him that the MVD had prepared his documents; he guessed that included his FSB badge as well. Carefully, he spread them out on the desk and turned over each piece of paper. Nothing. He looked at the FSB badge, which was in a red felt folder. He took the badge out and turned it over. Glued to the inside of the pin was a small square chip of microboard. He pried it out of the badge with his fingernail and held it up for the major to see. He was about to crush it when Borodenko reached out his hand and stopped him.

"What's the matter?" Deiter asked.

"Why don't we send it on a long trip?" the major asked smiling, his left eyebrow lifting.

Dieter grinned; he liked the way this man thought. Borodenko called for a guard and quickly gave him instructions as he handed him the microchip. The man saluted and disappeared down the hallway.

"Now you must get to the President and find out what he knows about bin Laden," Borodenko said, as he closed the door to the Operations Room. "Would you like to wake up Zaira? I think she has had enough rest."

"Do you know her well?" Deiter asked casually.

"We have mutual friends from our days in St. Petersburg," he replied. "I knew her father there before and respected him then as now. I met Zaira in 1996 and she and…and Natasha, my wife, became friends."

Deiter nodded, remembering what General Konykov had told him of their relationship. Not wanting to press the man any further, he opened the door to the Operations Center, walked out into the hallway and headed upstairs to the room that Zaira had entered the night before. At the door he knocked three times and called out her name. "Zaira…Zaira, are you awake?"

"Come in, Jack, I was just on my way downstairs."

Deiter opened the door and put his head through the opening. "How are you this morning? Sleep well?" he asked.

Zaira was on her way towards the door when he opened it, and she met him at the doorway itself. "Yes, thank you for asking, Jack. We have a lot to do today; come on," she said, as she pushed on by him and pulled on his arm. The two of them quickly descended the stairway and went into the Operations Center.

"Good morning, Sergei," she announced, as she entered the operations center.

"It looks like you're feeling better this morning, Zaira," he responded. As she looked up at him, he saw the black eye and red welt on her forehead and the cut on her lip. He winced. "Your eye looks bad, Zaira, does it hurt you much?" he asked. She didn't answer. "Did you sleep well?"

"Yes, some, I'll be all right." She then brightened. "I will see Father today," she said. "It has been weeks since I've seen him and I miss him. He always makes me feel good."

"How will you contact him?" Sergei asked.

"I think I know where he will be or at least Abuu will know where he is. Then Jack and I will go see him."

"Do you mind if we keep an eye on you while you are out in the city? I'd hate for the MVD to detain you again."

"It really is best you don't, Sergei; we are supposed to be the enemy, you know," she said with a glint in her eye. "Anyway, I know where Abuu Khadzhiyev will be and my father shouldn't be too far from there. If you need to contact us, you can do it through Abuu using his new cell phone," she said, writing down a number on a piece of paper and handing it to the major. "You know, Sergei, the fact that the FSB is sympathetic to us won't play very well in Moscow."

"The FSB does what is in the best interest of Russia. Our organization has been doing that since the early czars. Sometimes that means doing what is unpopular," he replied with a scowl.

He turned to Deiter and explained, "There are several factions in Chechnya. There are those who wish their own republic, and we recognize their legitimate concerns; then there are those who want a fundamentalist religious republic and force everyone to follow their brand of religion, these are enemies of Russia, and the United States, I

308

would think. Finally there are those who wish only to make money illegally and deal in power. Those people are dangerous to us all and the real enemy of both Russia and Chechnya."

Zaira put her arms around Sergei and hugged him. He enveloped her with his arms and laid his chin on her head. "Zaira, what am I to do with you?" he asked.

"Trust me," she said, "Simply trust me…as Natasha did."

Major Borodenko turned to Deiter. "There is a truck parked outside standing by to carry you both part of the way. You and Zaira should get a bite to eat at the kitchen next door first and…and then watch over her."

Deiter nodded. "I will…thank you, Sergei."

As Zaira and Deiter were leaving the room, Major Borodenko called after them, "Oh, I almost forgot, Jack, your friend General Henderson sent a message to you through General Konykov." Deiter stopped and turned around still holding the door open. "He said that they have information that someone will try to keep you from seeing the woman contact with bin Laden's camp. I don't know what that means, but they seemed concerned that it may spell trouble for you. Be careful." Deiter waved his hand in acknowledgement as he left.

"What's that all about?" asked Zaira, as they walked out of the FSB Headquarters and crossed the alley to the next building.

"I don't know, Zaira, but there has always been something wrong with this plan. Henderson was trying to warn me about something, but I'm convinced that even he doesn't seem to know what it is."

They had a breakfast of bread covered with ground meat in a flour and gravy sauce with an egg perched on top. It reminded Deiter of the old US military standby called SOS which has been translated as Same Old Stuff or Shit on a Shingle depending on how proper one wanted to be. Afterwards, both of them checked their weapons to make sure that they had sufficient ammunition and that both their automatic weapons and their pistols were loaded. Satisfied, they climbed into the half-ton FSB vehicle Sergei had promised them and instructed the driver to head westward toward Grozny.

It took them almost an hour to get to the city center. Their final destination was the western side of the city. It was almost ten-thirty that morning when they once more were walking through the center business district of Grozny. Deiter kept a watchful eye behind them as they moved silently through the streets. Unlike the last time they had ventured through the capital, he didn't feel as though they were being watched. He guessed that Borodenko's diversion of sending the soldier off to send the microchip on a trip to a distant location was working. He smiled to himself to imagine the consternation that might be causing the MVD.

Early afternoon found them standing in the street on which the rebel headquarters was located. The building was a nondescript newer ten-story building constructed out of reinforced concrete during the latter days of the Soviet Union. What it lacked in beauty of design, it compensated for with shoddy construction. The entrance was plain and unpretentious, just a set of heavy glass doors opening up onto a lobby. As soon as Deiter and Zaira entered the doorway, a soldier dressed in a camouflaged combat uniform approached them and asked their business. Zaira explained who she was and that she wanted to see the President. The soldier seemed flustered and hesitated. Zaira put her hands on her hips and gave an exasperated sigh; the soldier then quickly keyed a small radio he carried on his webbing and after a few moments received instructions to lead them to the underground command center.

A tall bearded man was leaning over a map board as they entered the Operations Center. He quickly straightened up and walked around the large table in the center of the room and approached the two people who the guard had deposited at the door. "Zaira," he said smiling. "I haven't seen you in weeks."

"Hello, Abuu, I have missed you; how are you, my dear, and how is your family?"

"They are safe and well the last I heard. I understand that your family is in the care of the FSB; do you think they will be safe?" he said, taking both of her hands in his.

"They are with loyal people. As long as they stay out of reach of the MVD or the paramilitary, they are safe."

"And who is this?" he asked, motioning towards Deiter.

"This is Jack Deiter. He is an American working for the CIA. He is here to help."

Abuu Khadzhiyev looked suspiciously at Deiter. "And how exactly does he do that and what does he want?" he asked Zaira.

"Is it still an insult to talk about another, especially a man, while he is present; or is the new order you defend absent of such pleasantries?" Deiter asked, his steel gray eyes closed to a slit as he challenged the bearded man.

"I didn't know you spoke Russian…most Americans can't," Abuu replied.

"Would it have made any difference? It would have been polite to have asked."

"Enough, what is this?" interjected Zaira, grabbing the taller man's arm. "Jack is a friend; he saved my life and destroyed two MVD helicopters yesterday and killed most of the MVD operations staff in their own headquarters. What is it Abuu? What is the matter with you?"

"I didn't know that. I'm sorry. It has not been easy lately; we have lost many of our comrades."

Deiter put out his hand to the Chechen and smiled. "I have heard of you and the work you've done. I am pleased to meet you." The two men shook hands, and the tension seemed to ease somewhat for the moment.

"I must contact my father, Abuu; do you know where he is?"

"He is due to return about noon today. You can wait for him here if you like," he replied. Then turning to Deiter he asked, "What is so important that you need to speak with our president?"

"Major Borodenko was supposed to have brought me to you to set up a meeting with the president. That was before my plane was shot down, and I met Zaira. He must have told you of my mission."

"You are the one Sergei mentioned who is looking for Osama bin Laden?" Abuu asked.

"Yes, and I will explain our plan when I meet with the President." Deiter responded.

"Mr. Deiter," Abuu said in a soft voice so as not to be overheard, "later today we are expecting Shamil Basayev to visit us here. Your mission will not sit well with him as he was one of the ones who sought out bin Laden's help; maybe it would be best if you and Zaira were not here when he arrived."

At the mention of Basayev's name, Zaira's face turned dark and a frown replaced her usual smile. "What's that pig doing coming here?" she demanded of Abuu.

"Your father is hoping to lessen the rift between them and try to convince him that he shouldn't make any more raids into Dagestan." Abuu turned to Deiter and added, "Shamil's attack into Dagestan, and especially the cruelty he displayed there as well as the bombings in Moscow, Buynaksk and Volgodonsk, caused the Russians to invade Chechnya again. We could have remained at peace with Russia, had it not been for him."

Deiter had read about Shamil Basayev. He was a man to be respected for his devotion to the cause of Chechen independence, but was also one to be questioned for his methods. He has sided with the

313

Wahhabi warlords who want to establish an Islamic republic in Chechnya. A link to bin Laden didn't surprise Deiter at all. Some reports already charged that he was getting financial backing from bin Laden.

"He may be a good source to locate bin Laden," observed Deiter.

"You also have a way of asking for trouble," returned Abuu, as he scratched his beard and looked askance at the American.

"Terrorism is a mark of desperation and hopelessness," replied Deiter. "Whatever this war has done, and I realize it has caused a lot of misery, you have the means to overcome both desperation and hopelessness. You are a brave and honorable people. Don't let the barbarism of some of the Russians change that."

Abuu stared at the American for a moment and then said quietly as he turned his head in a display of disgust, "And what have you suffered for all this?"

"His wife was killed by them, Abuu. He has a reason to hate as much as you," Zaira said, sharply, grabbing onto his arm and turning him to face her. Her eyes blazed with anger.

Abuu looked at her and then at Deiter. His eyes dropped and then he looked at Deiter once more. "I'm sorry, again, I did not know...I did not think..."

"I understand. You didn't think an American could ever be affected by what goes on here. There is misery enough to go around for all of us, Abuu. No man's suffering is any less important than another man's suffering...we all have been hurt," Deiter replied.

"Nevertheless, Shamil is no one to bait; he can be…irrational at times."

"I understand, Abuu. I've heard what he did at the hospital in Budenovsk four years ago, I know he can be vicious," replied Deiter. He remembered that in that savage raid, Basayev put innocent hostages along the windows to discourage the Russians from shooting. Over a hundred of the hostages were killed. "Can he be encouraged to give us at least a clue as to bin Laden's whereabouts?"

"Possibly, he thinks everyone should welcome bin Laden as a friend of Chechnya. He wants to establish an Islamic government here. But, you mustn't be involved; you must let me do it…and only after we get the President's approval.

Deiter nodded his concurrence. If he were going to be successful, he'd have to surprise bin Laden. So far, he believed that the various factions of bin Laden's forces didn't know that he was after the terrorist. He wanted to keep it that way.

It was well past noon when Abuu looked at his watch. Deiter could see the concern on his face. He didn't feel it safe for the American, especially one in the company of the President's daughter, to be there when Shamil arrived. He was about to say something to Zaira when a noise diverted his attention to the doorway. Two officers in Chechen uniform walked in and took up positions on either side of the doorway. After a few moments, a slightly built man with a gentle face and easy smile walked into the Operations Center. He wore a black jacket with zippered pockets and a lamb's wool collar. On his head was a traditional Chechen papaha that matched his collar and looked as though it were being propped up by his somewhat large ears. He might have even been to some people, a comical figure except for the extreme respect exhibited by everyone present. Deiter had no doubt that this was the revered Chechen president, Aslan Maskhadov.

"Father!" Zaira exclaimed.

"What are you doing here, lovely one?" the President asked as he opened his arms to his daughter.

"On Chechen business, as usual," she replied, as she gave him a warm embrace. "We've been waiting for you."

"We?" the president asked, as he lifted her chin and looked into her eyes.

"Yes, Father," she said, as she withdrew her arms from around her father and looked at Deiter. "Father, I would like to introduce Mr. Jack Deiter of the American CIA. He is here on very urgent business and needs to speak with you."

Deiter stepped forward and put out his hand towards the president. "It's an honor to meet you, Mr. President," Deiter said.

"And you, Mr. Deiter. If my daughter tells me that you have urgent business, then I am required to listen. May I ask how the two of you met?" he asked, still holding on to Deiter's hand.

"He saved my life, Father," Zaira interjected.

"Then that grants you an uninterrupted audience, Mr. Deiter. No father can refuse such a gift. Let's go into the conference room," he replied, motioning towards a door on the other side of the Operations Center.

The conference room was simple with plain painted walls and appeared to be left over from what might have been a corporate headquarters office. A large oval conference table surrounded by wooden chairs with plush leather seats was the central fixture of the room. As soon as they were seated around the table, President Maskhadov opened the discussion with a question about how his daughter had been endangered.

"I suppose that too was my fault, Mr. President," Deiter offered.

"You place her in danger and then rescue her?"

"No, Father, that's not the way it was...I don't think," she responded hesitantly.

"Mr. President, I was sent here on a mission. By outrageous luck, I stumbled into your daughter's apartment while evading your troops. Then she surprised me by coming home. After explaining my mission, she agreed to bring me to meet you."

"That's when we were captured by the MVD, but not before he shot down two Russian helicopters," she interjected again.

"He what?" the President asked.

"But then Jack freed himself, killed several Russians and saved me just when the MVD were about to..." She hesitated.

Maskhadov then raised his hand as though to call for an end to the story. "I won't ask any thing more. I will simply thank you, Mr.

Deiter." The President shifted his position in the chair and then asked, "What is your mission and what do you ask of me?"

Deiter took a deep breath and started. "I'm sure that you know that a certain person who we have classified as a terrorist is supposed to be in your country now. That person is Osama bin Laden. My government wants him for the murder of many innocent people and the attempt to commit more murders. I have been sent to apprehend him and bring him back to face these charges. That is where I need your help or at least your sanction."

Aslan Maskhadov sat back in his seat and stared at his hands that were spread out on the conference table. He looked at his daughter with a grim face and sad eyes. After a moment, he sighed and straightening up in his chair looked at Deiter who was seated next to him.

"My American friend," he began, "did you know that the symbol of Chechnya is that of a wolf or in our language, a *Borz*? It is in our emblem, and it is in our hearts and our traditions. The lion and the eagle are the symbols of strength, but they attack only the weak animals. The wolf, however, is the only beast that dares to attack a stronger animal. Her lack of size is compensated for by her extreme daring, courage and adroitness. If she loses the struggle, she dies silently, without expression of fear or pain, and she dies proudly, facing her enemy. The appreciation for a boy's adroitness and courage is linked to the saying: 'He was nursed by the she-wolf'. Also, there is only a she-wolf referenced in the Chechen language. As the Chechen national anthem says 'Chechens were born at night when the She-wolf whelped,' and in one folk song there are the words 'She-wolf whelps at night, when Mother gives birth to a Chechen child'.

Mr. Deiter, you seek here not a wolf, but a fox. I am convinced that you wish us no harm; but you are on a foxhunt. I believe also that you may have even been deliberately set to find this fox. I know that your country has been of considerable help to us financially and we are thankful. We know that you do not side with those who would want to destroy us or to enslave us. But, what am I to do? This man whom you seek has offered his help to us and he is, as we are, true believers in the Prophet Muhammad. Why should we believe you or help you and not him?"

This was the type of argument that Deiter really didn't want to pursue. "His way is one of indiscriminate terrorism against the innocent. Is that the way of the true warrior, to war against women and children? I notice that you restrict your raids to military targets, but Osama bin Laden prefers to deal in the shock value caused by the death of the innocent and the noncombatant. He showed that when he financed Basayev in his attack on Dagestan and the ravaging of the hospital in Budennovsk. He seeks a personal vengeance, not justice." Deiter paused and waited for the answer that would tell him what this man's deepest convictions really were.

"Concerning your last statement, Mr. Deiter, do you not also seek vengeance?"

"I did, but not now. I have not come here to kill the man, but to bring him to justice."

Zaira reached out for her father's hand and gripped it tightly. "Father," she said softly, "Jack's wife was on the aircraft that bin Laden bombed over the Atlantic Ocean last month. He too has suffered from terrorism as our people have."

"I see, so there is some vengeance left, isn't there?"

"I was asked to come here to kill bin Laden. I am not an assassin, so I refused and accepted only the task of bringing him to justice. What happens to him then is up to an international court. I have been with the FBI, I have been a policeman too long to do anything else," Deiter explained.

"Mr. Deiter, I sympathize with your disdain for terrorism. I have refused to use it as a national policy; without it, our cause is just and pure. To advance that cause through such means is against our traditions and the Qur'an. You must understand, though, that there are those among us who do not necessarily agree with me. These people are not my political supporters, they are…or have been, my political opponents. Should they ever learn that I have secretly condoned your mission, it would allow them a tremendous political advantage. They would attack me mercilessly."

"I understand," Deiter replied.

"Therefore, I cannot help you, but neither will I prevent you from carrying out your mission. I am assuming that you must have the backing of the FSB; that's good. When the time comes, we will back away. I will tell Abuu to be sensitive to that. He tells me that Shamil Basayev will be here soon. You had better leave before he arrives. He mustn't get wind of your presence here."

"Thank you, Mr. President, that's as much as I could have asked of you. I won't ask anything further."

The Chechen leaned back in his chair and looked at Deiter for several moments. He then quietly began speaking in an earnest tone, but in the manner of a professor. "We, the Chechens, are Muslims by the will of Allah the Compassionate, the Merciful. Constantly over the last 400 years, we have been victims of the Russian State's policies of genocide. Since the 17th century, we have been fighting the brutal Russian aggression and their policy of genocide, which has never shown mercy for our men nor for our children and women.

However, despite being heavily outnumbered and constantly outgunned, we have never surrendered to Russia. Neither have we signed any document accepting the Russian rule over the land given to us by the Almighty Allah. By the end of the 19th century, the Czarist Russian aggression and its attempt at genocide decreased the population of Chechnya to an estimated 50,000 souls. On 23 February 1944, the Soviet Union deported the whole Chechen nation to Northern Kazakhstan. Half of the approximately 500,000 Chechen nation perished during the deportation."

"I am aware of that, Mr. President," interrupted Deiter.

"Let me finish, please," the President responded, reaching out and placing a hand on Deiter's arm. "Next June, I will address the Islamic

Conference of Foreign Ministers. There, I will tell them what I tell you now. In 1994, the Russian Federation launched a new aggression and renewed genocide against the Chechens; this ended in August of 1996 with a humiliating defeat of the Soviet Army. Twelve percent...over 120,000 of the Chechens were murdered in this war.

In September of 1999, Russia began a new war and renewed genocide against Chechnya; this has been going on now for more than three months. The Russian Army has already murdered thousands of Chechen civilians.

Frankly, I am at my wits' end to understand the Russians. I have constantly proposed to the Russian Federation that a cease-fire be introduced and to begin political negotiations with the view of establishing a long-lasting peace in the Northern Caucasus. Unfortunately, the Russians have refused to agree to these offers. Thousands of Chechens, male and female, have been tortured, raped and murdered in the so-called 'filtration camps,' which can only be compared to the Nazi concentration camps in the Second World War. Even Chechen children from the age of ten and older are being detained, tortured, raped and murdered. All of these inhuman acts of violence are still continuing.

We do not ask for weapons or for soldiers. What we ask for is political, diplomatic and legal support. We need for other countries to apply economic and political bilateral and multilateral sanctions against the Russian Federation. You must remember that any inflows to the Russian State budget helps to finance the genocide of the

Chechen People. We need for the Russians to observe the Geneva Conventions in Chechnya; we ask that they treat Chechen soldiers as prisoners of war within the meaning of the Geneva Convention and that they cease and desist from committing all acts of genocide against the Chechen."

He paused a moment before continuing. He could see that Deiter fully comprehended what he was saying. "Mr. Deiter, tell your government…ask your government to use their legal authority as a member of the United Nations to initiate the creation of an International Tribunal for War Crimes committed in Chechnya by the Russian Federation. Finally I appeal to your government to recognize the Chechen Republic of Ichkeria as a *de jure* independent state." The President sighed and sitting back in his chair, he looked at Deiter intently. "You must go back to your leaders in Washington, Mr. Deiter, and tell them what I have told you and tell them what you have seen here."

"Trust me, Mr. President, I will."

"Good," responded Maskhadov. "Perhaps by assisting you in your mission, your country will recognize our situation." He paused for a moment. "But, there is one thing that I must speak with you about alone, Mr. Deiter." Turning to Zaira, he said. "My darling, will you leave the two of us for a moment?" Zaira looked from her father to Deiter and then back at her father once more, nodded and left the conference room.

As soon as Zaira had closed the door behind her, Maskhadov leaned forward and placed a hand on Deiter's shoulder. "One last thing, my friend, I know that my daughter will be going with you in your mission. Take care of her; she means very much to me." Deiter nodded solemnly in accepting the charge of the President. Something inside him, though, left him uncomfortable. He hadn't been there when Rose needed him or Sally, his first wife for that matter. How could he really guarantee the safety of another human being ever again?

Deiter followed the President out of the conference room and joined Zaira who was talking with Abuu and another man in the Communications Center. The man was somewhat heavy with a long and harrowed looking face. Zaira turned to Deiter as he approached and said, "Jack, this is General Mumadi Saydayev. I have been telling him of our escape from the MVD." As the two men shook hands, Zaira turned to Deiter and added, "General Saydayev has been a good friend and ardent supporter of my father for several years now." The two men exchanged pleasantries, and began a discussion of the war. Zaira gently took Deiter's arm and indicated that she wanted to have him meet someone else. He excused himself to General Saydayev and followed her. They headed straight toward a young tall man who displayed a significant aura of importance. Zaira walked up to him as he was in discussion with another man who seemed to be distracted and irritable.

"General Khachukaev, may I introduce a friend of Chechnya, Mr. Jack Deiter of the American CIA."

The general seemed credibly surprised, but extended his hand. "I'm pleased to meet you, Mr. Deiter. I assume that you are here on business with the President because you have such a beautiful and well connected escort."

"General Khachukaev is one of the bravest of our army," Zaira explained. The general laughed and, holding her head gently with both hands, bent down to kiss her on the forehead.

"She overstates things sometimes, but she is too beautiful to contradict," the general replied.

"I have heard of your victories, General," Deiter said, as he shook hands with the battle hardened veteran of the first Chechen war. "Especially the tactics you used against tanks. My very good friend, General Hank Henderson, of the American Army, has told me of your exploits. I am pleased to meet you at last."

The general turned to introduce his partner in conversation. "I must introduce you to our new Minister of Defense," the general said, motioning to the man next to him. "This is Mohammed Yambiev."

"I am pleased to meet you, Mr. Deiter. I hope that what you see here will allow you to convince your government that we need their support if we are to survive this latest attack."

"I am also pleased to meet you, and rest assured that I will provide my superiors with a clear picture of your situation." The Defense Minister smiled and thanked Deiter for whatever message he could deliver. He then excused himself saying that he must meet with the president in private. He walked over to President Maskhadov, and the two men disappeared into the Conference Room and closed the door behind them.

As they were about to linger in further discussion with General Khachukaev, Abuu came over and whispered something into Zaira's ear. Her eyebrows raised in alarm, and she reached over for Deiter's arm. When she touched him, he turned toward her, and she whispered into his ear, "Shamil Basayev is coming; we have to go out the back entrance, now!"

Offering their apologies to General Khachukaev, they walked quickly to the door next to the conference room that led to a hallway and stairway in back of the building. Once in the alley out back, Zaira pulled Deiter's arm and headed for a doorway in the building across the alley. Upon reaching the metal fire door, she tried the door latch and it opened. She went inside and Deiter followed her.

"I will show you a safe place," she whispered, as they moved down a darkened hallway. They reached a set of stairs located next to a set of elevators. "We have disconnected the elevator…it's safer that way and we can control who comes into this building."

"And what is this building?" Deiter asked.

"It used to be home, part of it…for awhile, anyway," she replied. "We used to live here after the '96 war."

"Your family?"

"Yes. It has been left pretty much the way it was when we were here, but it was also our hidden home. Our official home was elsewhere in Grozny…nearer the buildings of the government. We rarely were there, though, except for State occasions."

They walked up to the fifth floor and Zaira opened the fire door to the hallway inside. She poked her head around the corner and seeing no one, went into the hallway, turning to make sure that Deiter was following her. They walked down the hallway to a door that was set back from the line of the hall and had the emblem of the State of Chechnya emblazoned on it. There was a keypad next to the right side of the doorway, and Zaira opened the cover and punched in a set of numbers. When a green light appeared over the keypad, she dropped the cover and reached for the brass door lever. Deiter followed her into through the doorway and into the entranceway of a large apartment.

"Home," she said with a grin, spreading her arms and swinging them around as to introduce the apartment.

"Looks comfortable," Deiter observed nonchalantly as he closed the door behind him.

From the entranceway, the apartment opened up to a expansive reception area with high ceilings and several sets of sofas positioned in conversation clusters. Impressive paintings adorned the walls. A large fireplace was at the end of the reception area, and a large carved Seal of the State of Chechnya was centered above the mantle. A Chechen flag stood on a staff to the right side of the fireplace. On either side of the reception area, hallways led to the end of the floor. Deiter guessed that the apartment extended throughout the expanse of the entire fifth floor and maybe to the floor either above or below the apartment. He could see additional doors down both hallways. In the corner of the rear wall to the left of the fireplace there was a set of double doors that Deiter guessed led to the kitchen and servants' areas.

"Come," Zaira urged, as she started toward the hallway to the right. "Our family's private sector is down here." Deiter followed her. At the end of the hallway was a door on the left-hand side. She opened it and went inside. Deiter followed.

"For the first time today, I feel safe," she observed, whirling around in a playful dance and finally plopping herself down on an overstuffed sofa. "Jack, come on in and relax."

The living room area was well decorated and comfortable. Deiter found an empty chair and fell into it, all the while looking with admiration at the enthusiasm of his hostess.

"Nice place you have here," he observed, stretching out on the ivory colored overstuffed chair.

"This won't be here for long, you know, Jack," she replied solemnly. "The Russians will not be happy until they have completely flattened Grozny. This place will be gone like the rest of the city. We Chechens have been resurrected from the dead much to often to suit them. They marched us off to Siberia and put us in railway cattle cars and separated us from our homeland, yet we have always returned."

When she had finished her tirade, there was an awkward silence as Zaira looked down as though in contemplation of the sad, but resolute, past of her people. After a moment, Deiter cleared his throat and said in a lighter tone of voice, "Do you think that someone left some food here? I'm starved."

Zaira brightened as though thankful for the change in topic, and as she got to her feet said, "Let's go look, I'm sure there is something. We may be here a long time and have to stock up if we have no food." The servant's kitchen produced a sufficient supply of bread and condiments as well as a number of cans of soup, one of which Zaira heated on the stove.

After they had eaten, Deiter stretched back in his chair. He thought that perhaps he knew Zaira enough to ask her a sensitive question about her people. "Where is the loyalties of the various factions of Chechnya, Zaira. It seems as though everyone has their own agenda without considering the country or the people as a whole."

A dark and worried look came over her face. "You know that we have many different factions here in Chechnya. I think you also appreciate that there is still what might be called a 'warlord' faction of men with strong personalities and even stronger egos present and active in the region. The religious faction is being used by some of them as a rallying call by those who wish to consolidate power unto themselves. These people are not truly clerics or holy men, but use the faith of the people to forward their own ambitions and agenda. This faction teaches that the whole world must be converted to Islam, by force if necessary, according to the teachings of Allah in the Qur'an. In other words, they want to install absolute control with themselves as the ultimate authority. Any thought of a democracy is out of the question."

"Where do the Arabs, like bin Laden come in?"

"The spoiled rich boy? He wasn't given any real power in his family and now seeks to steal what was never his to have. He was welcomed by those like Shamil Basayev who sought his money to finance their ambitions. Basayev, as head of an Islamic republic, could have absolute power, or so he thinks. We really do not like the Arabs anymore than the Afghans do. You must appreciate that we are a totally different race of people with totally different backgrounds."

Deiter thought about what she was saying and seemed to appreciate better the complexity of the situation. "Will these factions continue to fight each other, or will they finally learn to work together for the common good?" he asked.

She laughed at the question. "That, my dear Jack, is the ultimate question. Those like my father look to a real democracy with specifically delineated freedoms for the people. The thought of using terrorism is abhorrent to them whereas to people like Basayev it is only a tool to achieve an end. The two will probably never work together; one or the other will ultimately survive and the others will be eliminated."

"That doesn't give a very enlightened forecast of the future for Chechnya or the rest of the world, Zaira. Is there a solution?"

"Get rid of Osama bin Laden and the rest of his ilk. Only then, and then alone will honest and compassionate people like my father be able to save this country. That's why my father will help you," Zaira said quietly, as she picked up the remainder of their meal and began to wash the dishes.

Deiter nodded his understanding. He suddenly felt tired; he guessed it was the hot soup and bread. He thanked Zaira for the food and excused himself. Down the hallway, he sought out one of the empty bedrooms in order to rest. He didn't know when he would be called on to exercise his part of the mission and wanted to make sure he was rested and ready for it.

Chechen Armed Forces Headquarters
On the Western edge of Grozny, Chechnya
Thursday early afternoon, November 25, 1999

The Amir of the Supreme *Majtise Shura* of *Mujahideen*, Shamil Basayev walked confidently into the Operation Center nodding to the various people who were assembled there. He was dressed in camouflage battle dress with a visored cap on his head. His heavy black beard gave him a ferocious look that was accentuated by his dark piercing eyes. He stripped off his gloves and slid them into the belt. To no one in particular he demanded, "Where is the President? I am suppose to meet him here."

Abuu walked over to Basayev and explained to him that the President was in conference with the Defense Minister and would be out shortly, that he was expecting him and urgently wanted to speak with him on a number of issues. The warlord grunted and turned his back on Abuu. Looking around the room, he couldn't see anyone whom he particularly wanted to speak with and so he proceeded to study the map on the table in the center of the room.

At that point, a tall red-haired woman dressed in battle dress entered the Operation Center and looked around at the men as though she was in search of someone. She spied Basayev and quickly walked over to him. On seeing her, Basayev's countenance changed and he smiled broadly. "Rooza, it's a pleasure to see you. What do you hear from our mutual friend?"

"Praise be to God, the Cherisher and Sustainer of the worlds, the sheik is well and anxious to meet with you," she replied in a soft voice. "Tell me of what has happened with you since we last spoke." Basayev told her about their incursion into Dagestan. He spent a considerable amount of time describing his "victories," as he put it. He spoke as well of the need to hit the Russians in their safest places far from Chechnya so that their will should be destroyed and their attention diverted from the action in Grozny. They spoke for several more minutes in very subdued tones, and then she nodded and turned as though to leave the room when she was distracted by a new set of voices and the opening of the door to the conference room.

President Maskhadov walked out into the Operation Center followed closely by the Defense Minister. Seeing Basayev, the President smiled and walked over to him. "Welcome, Shamil," he said warmly, while extending his hand in friendship. "We need to talk of friendship and the need to work together. I asked you here so that we could find common ground."

"That clearly remains to be seen," replied the warlord coldly.

The Defense Minister moved closer to the two men. He clearly didn't like that tone of voice used against the president. "What we have seen clearly is that you have caused this catastrophe to be upon us; it would never have happened if you had not made a mockery of our cause in Dagestan. We had a truce with Russia until you had to violate the accord."

"You are a coward," shouted Basayev.

"It is not cowardice to object to the killing of innocent people."

"Are you accusing me of killing the innocent? There are no innocents."

"Yes, I am accusing your support of the *Wahhabi* and are personally responsible for this new war."

"And you are a weakling and a traitor," shouted Basayev pulling his pistol from its holster. "I am surrounded by traitors and infidels." Seeing the unholstered weapon, the Defense Minister reached for his own weapon. Basayev pointed his pistol at the Minister and pulled the trigger. The noise of the weapon shocked those present in the Operation Center into stunned inaction. They simply froze and watched the unfolding action. The round from the pistol embedded itself in Yambiev's upper thigh. The Defense Minister was thrown off balance and rolled to the floor next to the large map table in the center of the room. As he did so, he pulled his automatic from its holster and rolled over and with both hands brought the weapon to bear directly at the warlord. Before the President could stop him, he fired three rounds directly into the stomach of Shamil Basayev. The warlord staggered backward and fell to the floor clutching his abdomen. President Maskhadov shouted for calm and wrested the handgun from the Defense Minister's hand. He then turned toward Basayev and kneeled down to examine the man's wounds. "Send for the medics!" he shouted to those standing nearby." He pulled the weapon from Basayev's hand and tossed it across the room and into a corner.

Maskhadov stood up and asked those in the room for assistance with both of the wounded men. At that point, some of the others began to murmur against Shamil Basayev, as he lay curled up grasping the wounds in his abdomen. The President stopped all disagreement by shouting, "Enough! Don't we have enough Russians to fight that we must now fight among ourselves?"

"It is not us, it is Basayev who is the problem. If it were not for him, we would not be at war again with Russia," said Yambiev as he held his wounded leg.

A swarthy looking man elbowed his way to where the president stood. Looking down contemptuously at the wounded warlord, "For those who don't know me, I am General Salman Raduev. I have recently made an offer to the Russians to execute this terrorist Basayev," he said. "I have made the offer in return for a cessation of all military actions against us that were in retaliation for what this person was responsible. It was he who invited the Shi'ite extremists, the Arabs to the Caucasus and on their advice attacked our ethnic brothers in Dagestan. This criminal must be punished. This is why my men are even now ready to execute Basayev and his followers or to hand them over to the Russian Army. We await only the permission to do so by you, Mr. President. I will even do it now and retrieve the honor of the Minister of Defense for failing to get rid of him when he had the opportunity."

President Maskhadov placed his hand on the general's arm. "Don't we have enough killing? If we should fight among ourselves, it will only make it easier for the Russians to defeat us. We need to talk of working out an understanding and peace among us that we may successfully defeat the Russians and regain our country."

A team of medics appeared at the doorway and was quickly allowed into the room. They immediately began to work on the two wounded men and, when they had done their diagnosis of them, asked permission of the President to remove the wounded to an ambulance for transport to a field hospital. The President nodded approval and the two casualties were carried on stretchers out of the room and into a waiting ambulance that had just pulled up outside the building.

General Khachukaev walked up to President Maskhadov and quietly said, "Mr. President, Aslan…we have been friends for a long time and we are now among friends. Not that long ago I warned against the *Wahhabi* warlords and I swear now that after the war is over, whatever its outcome, the extremists should stand trial for their actions. There will be a reckoning, beginning with that weasel, Shamil Basayev. He is never to be trusted."

Maskhadov placed his hand on the General's arm and calmly replied, "And after a peace is established we will look at the situation, Khizir, and we will do what is right that the honor of Chechnya is maintained in the world."

In the corner of the operations center, the tall woman with red hair slowly edged her way to the doorway and slid out into the hallway without being noticed.

Chapter Eighteen

The Fox's Lair

Osama bin Laden's Headquarters
Just outside Grozny, Chechnya
Late Thursday afternoon, November 25, 1999

He sat cross-legged on a cushion with his hands folded in his lap. Set before him was a small table with several dishes of ethnic Chechen food. On a large plate were two hot *dolma* or cabbage stuffed with *b'aara,* sausages. Two bowls contained *kurznash*, a type of ravioli, and *puluu*, a rice dish with raisins. The meal had been prepared by several of the older women who were part of the contingent of Chechen guerillas who responded to Shamil Basayev. The room itself was simply furnished, but adequate to the maverick millionaire's needs. The white robe he wore flowed down his body and covered his feet on the floor. His head was wound with a white turban. His dark wiry beard had streaks of gray and appeared to have been recently trimmed. At this moment a simple, detached smile graced his face and took on the appearance of a sneer.

Osama bin Laden was in his glory. He was a significant figure in another new Islamic revolution. The principal evils of the world were his adversaries, and he was instrumental in providing the means to confront them pretty much on his terms. The Chechens were at his bidding. With the allegiance of Shamil Basayev and the *Wahhabis,* otherwise known as the "Islamic Cossacks," he was positioned to control the fight against the satanic Russians. The current president of Chechnya was not recognized by Russia and given scarce acknowledgement by even his own people. On the other hand, he had won in Afghanistan and he would now win in Chechnya. He was content for the time being; elimination of the final evil, America, was already in the works. The rest of the world would then fall under the control of Islam, and his power would be vast.

Osama bin Laden was the seventeenth child out of fifty-two born to a wealthy Saudi and his ten wives. His inheritance was estimated at $250 million, which he had used to build his worldwide organization *al Qaeda*, Arabic for "The Base," to support terrorists in Afghanistan, Bosnia, Chechnya and Kenya. He was exiled from Saudi Arabia in 1991 for his support of terrorist groups. From there, he went to the Sudan to further organize his terrorist forces. In 1996, at the end of the Russian-Chechen conflict, the Sudan, relenting to worldwide pressure to get rid of the nests of terrorists in their country, expelled bin Laden and he returned to Afghanistan. There he continued to build camps to train terrorist groups for his international *jihad* or holy war.

During the Soviet Union's decade-long war in Afghanistan, which began in 1979, bin Laden joined the American-backed *Mujahideen* or "holy warriors" who fought the Soviet troops. At that time, the United States assumed that "the enemy of my enemy must be my friend" and supported him during the early 1980's. When the Soviets finally extricated themselves from this very unpopular war in 1989, bin Laden emerged as the leader of a group of battle-hardened veterans and religious fundamentalists who swore vengeance against all non-Islamic governments. When the Americans invaded the "sacred" lands of Islam in the 1991 Gulf War and later Somalia in 1992, his hatred spread from Russia to America, including the world's only remaining super power.

A knock on the door to his apartment caused him to leave his meditation before his meal and he responded, "Come." The door opened and a tall red-haired woman entered. She was dressed in a long light brown dress, belted at the waist with a tooled dark brown belt that matched her calf-length boots. Her red hair was mostly covered by a conventional babushka of deep red and black.

She stopped several feet inside the door and bowed at the waist towards the seated man. "May Allah the Compassionate, the Merciful grant you success, Osama," she said.

"Rooza, come here and sit down," bin Laden responded enthusiastically, as he motioned to an overstuffed green chair facing him. The woman moved gracefully across the floor and seated herself facing the Arab. Rooza Demidov had just returned from a meeting with Shamil Basayev at bin Laden's request.

"It is once more like the time many years ago when we fought together in Afghanistan. It is nice to work together once more. Would you ever have believed back then that I would be here in Chechnya, your country, and still fighting the Russians? But you have news;

what have you heard?" He did not offer her any of the food on the table. It was not appropriate for a woman to dine with a man, even a woman who had been of significant value by assisting him in reaching his ambitions in the past and was even now providing more connections and allies for him.

"I met with Shamil shortly after noon today. He was waiting to meet with President Maskhadov and Defense Minister Mohammed Yambiev," she replied, giving no hint of the confrontation and injuries that had occurred.

"Why does he tolerate those fools?" responded bin Laden. "It would be better if he eliminated them. He and the *Mujahideen* know how to conduct this holy war, this *jihad*. Maskhadov and his kind look at our struggle as simply a war of independence, not the holy conflict on a global scale that it in all reality is."

"I believe he is trying to use them to further our plans," she responded. "I am sure that he realizes what they are and how impotent they are, but it is simpler if they are not fighting against us."

"What else did he have to say?"

"I was in the Chechen Armed Forces Operations Center when I saw and spoke with him. The President and Defense Minister were in closed sessions in the conference room and Shamil was waiting for them to finish. I believe that they were intentionally delaying the meeting just to embarrass him."

"Yes, most probably."

"He was very anxious, but he spoke to me of the raid into Dagestan in August and the need to publicize the *jihad* to free Chechnya from the hands of the Russians and the influence of the Americans. He wants to continue bringing the war to the Russians on their own land and feels that is the only way they will tire of this genocide and leave us alone."

Bin Laden smiled, "He and I think as one. He will bring the war to the Russian people and I will take it to the American people," he observed.

The woman nodded and at his motion continued. "He believes that the *Mujahideen* in Chechnya are still the masters of the situation in spite of the large Russian presence in Chechnya. He feels as though the Russians are exhausted from the fighting, but that the first and second wars in Chechnya are very different. His people have endured great losses, but still have some equal ways to resist the enemy. He is full of confidence. I know you wish to meet with him, but he says he fears that by coming here, the Russian artillery might attack us and the civilians in the vicinity who remain here. He suggested that I act as go-between as it would assure your safety as well. He respects you greatly." She paused to see if the Arabian had any response or questions.

"What of his dealings with the President? It is only the mystique of that wretched man that keeps him in power and that further encourages the Russians in the hope that there will be a settlement favorable to them."

"He spoke in whispers once. He knows that Maskhadov has a personal detachment of only 400 soldiers. The 'irreconcilables' under Basayev's control number two to three thousand. He said that the leaders of the separatists are prepared to kill their 'President' if necessary. Basayev, himself, could give such an order," she concluded.

Bin Laden had been sitting forward, listening intently to her words; at hearing the last sentence, he leaned back and smiled broadly. "He and I are as one."

The woman fidgeted somewhat and looked away from the terrorist leader. "Is something the matter?" he asked.

"Every time I hear about killing and the deaths of innocents, I am saddened," she replied.

"You think as a woman, most honored one, and that is understandable. But these are not innocents, dear Rooza," he responded in a placating tone. "No, not at all. We do not have to differentiate between military and civilian targets. As far as we are concerned, they are all targets." He paused and looked at the woman.

"Let me try to explain. When the atomic bombs were thrown onto the cities of Hiroshima and Nagasaki by the Americans, there were many deaths. At that time, did the bombs differentiate between the military and the women, the infants, and the children? No, of course not. Remember that the British and the Americans all voted for their leaders. That makes them equally responsible and a part of the conspiracy against Islam. No, as far as we are concerned, they are all targets, and this is what the *fatwah* says…The *fatwah* is comprehensive and it includes all those who participate in, or help the Jewish occupiers in killing Muslims. And that includes anyone who is not a believer who is in Chechnya as well." He paused and smiled at her as he would a child.

"You have helped our cause for many years. From the time in Afghanistan when we needed weapons, you were there for us and found us weapons to destroy the Russians. You have now brought me to this place where another Islamic republic will presently be formed on the bones of the Russians. You have been an angel of Allah, Praise and Glory be to Him. Why are you troubled?"

"I keep thinking that there must be another way for everyone to live in peace."

He sighed. "You are a woman, and despite the contributions you have made to our cause, your reaction is expected. In the order of things, it is in fact, quite normal. That is why it has been so ordained that the man must ultimately rule. The truth reasserts itself time after time."

"The Americans have painted you as a terrorist leader."

"We do not care what America says," bin Laden shrugged. "We view ourselves and our brothers like everyone else. Allah created us to worship Him and to follow in his footsteps and to be guided by His Book. I am one of the servants of Allah, and I obey his orders. Among those is the order to fight for the word of Allah…and to fight until the infidels, especially the Americans and the Russians, are driven out of all the Islamic countries. The people of America and now Russia have elected their leaders and those leaders have chosen to defy the wish of Allah." His voice began to take on a higher pitched tone as though he was becoming incensed at having to explain his actions. He almost shouted as he said, "There are no innocent people there; they have made their choice. When they elected those leaders, they ransomed their children in the process. There are no innocents."

The woman showed no emotion; her eyes were lowered; she changed the subject. "Is there a message for Shamil Basayev?" she asked.

"He must rid himself of the cowards that now control the government...and then wrest control for the sake of Islam."

The woman nodded and stood up, moving backwards towards the door. "I will inform Basayev. I must make one more passage of the lines before nighttime. If it were possible for the two of you to meet," she asked tentatively," would you wish such a visit with Basayev?"

"It is always preferred to speak in private with another to discern truth and honesty," he replied, sounding suddenly calmed and more in control.

She nodded once more and opened the door while still facing the seated man. "Do I have your permission to depart?" she asked.

"Rooza," he replied, almost condescendingly, "Allah has granted the Muslim people and the Chechen *Mujahideen*, and those with them, the opportunity to fight the Russians. They will be defeated by Allah, I am convinced. It is simply up to us to allow it. I know that you will be successful in securing a meeting with Basayev. Yes, you may depart."

"Would you be at this place this evening not long after sundown?"

"If you can arrange a meeting, I will be here."

"I will bring him to you tonight."

"Praise be to God, the Cherisher and Sustainer of the worlds, that He made it possible for us to aid the *Mujahideen* in Chechnya. And thanks be to Allah that he has sent another Umm Ammarah to fight with them, first in Afghanistan and now in Chechnya. Do you remember the story of her, Rooza? She was the wife of a brave *Sahabi,* who were among the very few who fought close to the Prophet, peace be upon him, and who shielded the Prophet with their own bodies. Umm Ammarah was asked after the battle what she desired most, and she answered that she wanted to be in the company of the Prophet, in Paradise – and her request was accepted by the Prophet. You, Rooza, are as Umm Ammarah, a fully trained *Mujahidah* (woman fighter for the sake of Allah) of today's *Jihad.* I will tell you a secret; I am, as it were, one with the Prophet, Rooza, reborn to lead Islam back to its golden years and on to its greatest victory. The flag of Islam shall fly over the White House and over Buckingham Palace and every place in the western world. That is the destiny that Allah has shown me, and you are now part of it.

The woman bowed and moved backward in the doorway. As she did so, a hand rested on her right shoulder, and she quickly looked down at it. She saw that the hand was massive and callused and was missing two fingers. She looked up into the fierce brown eyes of a man of perhaps thirty years. His face had a heavy, black beard, and he wore his hair shoulder length. On his head was a black beret with a saying in Arabic script in white across it. He was dressed in heavy camouflaged battle dress. She stiffened and looked back at Osama bin Laden and saw that he was smiling.

"Rooza, this is my old friend and the bravest man in the world, Ibn-ul-Khattab. He fought as a boy with the *Mujahideen* in the Afghanistan *jihad* with me after you left. We have been comrades ever since, and he is here now with us as a general and commander of all of foreign *Mujahideen* forces in Chechnya."

The woman turned around and looked into the face of the man once more. His expression had not changed. She stepped back into the room still facing him. He was handsome, but the look of suffering was behind the fierceness of his eyes. "Khattab," bin Laden said, with a hint of pride behind his words, "this is the woman whom I told you of many years ago, and she is with us once more. She is protecting us and supporting us as Umm Ammarah did the Prophet, peace be upon him, in the great *Jihad*. This is Rooza Demidov."

The look on the large man's face lightened, and she sensed that he almost smiled. "I have heard of what you did in Afghanistan, but that was when I was very young. Forgive me if I say that it is as if you have not aged. It was indeed you and not your mother in Afghanistan, perhaps?"

At this Rooza smiled broadly and bin Laden laughed, loudly. "Come in, my friend. Rooza was about to leave on an important mission, and we two must talk alone," he said to Khattab.

The woman bowed slightly and as the man came into the room, she backed out and closed the door behind her. Bin Laden smiled to himself and stroked his beard, confident in his power and the righteousness of his mission. He would later today meet with Basayev who would lead this people into becoming one more Islamic nation. The woman would see to it and arrange the meeting that would indeed shape his destiny and that of this country. Suddenly, he was famished. He bid his friend to sit and dine with him as they talked. He then reached for one of the two *dolmas* on the dish and transferred it onto his plate. The fragrance of it delighted his nostrils. "Tell me of the news," he requested, as he broke it in half with his fingers and broke off a smaller piece that he stuffed into his mouth.

"If you had told me in Afghanistan that a day would come when we would be fighting the Russians INSIDE Russia, I would never have believed you. In fact, I gave an interview with a reporter just a few days ago and I said much the same thing to him," Khattab responded with the first real vestige of a smile since he entered the room. "I believe it was a good interview and I sent a message and appeal to all of the Muslim world. I said that the Caucasian people are honest in their religion and their return to Allah. The Western World is supporting Russia to wage war against the Muslims once again, even if they are claiming the opposite of that. The offensives that the

Russian forces undertook, such as in Dagestan, were against towns that announced the implementation of the Islamic *Shariah*. Indeed this is a Christian war and crusade against Islam and its people and it is an obligation upon the Muslims, especially the great scholars, to support their *Mujahideen* brothers in the land of the Caucasus."

"Shamil Basayev will be meeting with us this evening…here," bin Laden announced. "Are you able to attend?"

"No, I must return to my command in the mountains south of here. We are set to strike against a Russian column, which is trying to complete the encirclement of Grozny."

Bin Laden nodded his understanding. "I have learned this morning that our war will now be on two fronts. Not only are we inside Russia fighting Russians, but a new plan is being placed into motion even now that will strike the Americans on their own soil. It will take over a year to bring all of the pieces together, but it has begun," he added smiling. "When it is completed, there will be a massive strike against their homeland. When they respond in anger with great destruction, it will unite all of Islam. Victory will be ours and the final *jihad* will begin."

Chapter Nineteen

Tally Ho

*FSB Headquarters
Gudermes, Chechnya
Friday morning, November 26, 1999*

The woman was taller than most of the men who were in the Communications

Center of the FSB Headquarters; she was dressed in the padded camouflage battle dress of the rebel army. Her head was covered with a babushka under a wool cap, but enough hair showed in the back that its striking red color was apparent. An AK-47 was slung over her right shoulder and she was talking to an FSB major in hushed tones out of hearing of the rest of the men.

"What have you to report?" asked Major Borodenko. "I recognize you from the description sent by General Konykov; you must be Rooza."

"We have a location from which bin Laden can be captured."

"When will he be there? We have the team that will execute the mission standing by."

"Tonight...I will see that he's there. There may be one or two bodyguards with him. He is located at this address," she explained, handing the major a small slip of paper. "He is on the second floor of the building. His room is at the end of the hallway. It is best to enter from the alley. After dark, I will mark the third doorway in the alley with a scarf wound around the door handle. The best time is just after dark, about five o'clock. They will not be eating until about eight, so there should not be many other people present." She paused and then said, "If there is something wrong, there will be no scarf on the alley doorway."

"You have done well. I will brief the team on what you have given me."

The woman paused and looked at the major intently. For a reason she could not identify, something deep in her soul wanted to know the identity of those who would attempt to either capture or kill the master terrorist. She let it go and sighed, looking down at the floor. "I have been with these people for almost a month now, night and day. I have been their guide and confidant. But, what they are doing is horribly wrong. Bin Laden is brilliant, but he's also a mad man and he must die rather than risk the lives of the multitudes he wishes to destroy. His dream must never be realized. He thinks of himself as the reincarnation of the Prophet and is anointed by Allah to spread Islam throughout the world. He blasphemes. I hope those whom you have working for you are up to the task. After tonight, I must disappear and have nothing further to do with them. They will suspect that I have betrayed them, and will want to retaliate."

"You will have safe passage to wherever you want; I will guarantee it."

"Thank you. And where should I meet my escort out of Chechnya?'

"Come here after you have assured yourself that bin Laden will be there and you have marked the doorway in the alley. My job will be finished here as well, and I will return to Moscow tomorrow; you can accompany me and I will assure that you get to whatever embassy you want or on a plane to wherever you wish to go." He paused and took her hands in his and smiling said quietly, "General Konykov has been very pleased with your work. Russia thanks you."

The woman nodded and turning on her heel, she quickly walked out of the Operations Center and the building…and then disappeared around the corner.

On his cell phone, Major Borodenko punched in the telephone number he had been given by Zaira and waited for an answer. In less than five minutes the plan had been relayed to Abuu. Borodenko then leaned back against the desk and pondered the situation. He suddenly became concerned for Zaira's safety. Now that Natasha was gone, Zaira was the most precious person he knew. He had a very bad feeling about this. Although he trusted the American, he also knew that one man by himself couldn't control all of the circumstances in this complicated war. If it were needed, he knew that he could call on the strength of the Russian military, but right now, he felt powerless and feared for her safety. A sudden dread and heaviness filled his chest.

In Grozny, Abuu turned to a military clerk and instructed him to go to the presidential apartment and inform the American and Zaira Maskhadov to come to the Operations Center immediately. "Tell them that it's time." The man saluted and quickly left the room.

Osama bin Laden's Headquarters
Just outside Grozny, Chechnya
5:00 PM, November 26, 1999

Deiter and Zaira squatted in the shadows of the alley across the street from the building that housed bin Laden's headquarters. The sun had set, and the shadows were deepening in the street. Lights were now on in the building and periodically they could see movement past the windows on the second floor. According to the information they had received from Major Borodenko, the alley at the rear of the building would have a doorway with a white cloth on it; that would be their entranceway to the headquarters. They had been told that the terrorist's dinner meal would not be served for another several hours and that the time for making their move was quickly approaching.

Deiter looked over at Zaira as she fitted a fresh magazine into her AK-47. He smiled to himself as he noted what a military professional this young woman had become. The combination of warrior and beauty queen was astounding.

It had been decided by the FSB that only the two of them would attempt the abduction of bin Laden. A larger force would easily be detected and a two-person team had a much greater chance of getting away if anything did go wrong. It was obvious that bin Laden and Basayev considered the terrorist's location a total secret and entirely safe. Also, the FSB could disavow any connection with the plot should it be discovered. Two people could do what needed to be done…either capture or kill bin Laden. By a prearranged signal, FSB helicopters would meet them at one of several sites to move them to a safer location. There they would transfer bin Laden to Russian control of the FSB.

"It's time," Deiter whispered to Zaira. She nodded and followed him as he moved across the street and into the alley on the right of the building. It led to the rear of the building that housed bin Laden. They moved quickly into the alley and crouched next to the wall, waiting to see if their movement had been observed. Deiter listened intently, but heard nothing; they had not been detected.

He stood up slowly and walked down the alley looking at the entrances to the building as he passed them. The first one was unmarked, so he went on the second one…nothing there either. At the third doorway he paused and thinking he saw something white in the dim light, he felt the center panel of the door. A piece of white cloth was draped over the door handle. He unwrapped the cloth from the handle, and as he did so, he noticed that it had a fragrance. The fragrance was somehow familiar, but he couldn't immediately place it. He dismissed it as perhaps being a common perfume. He checked to make sure that Zaira was next to him and slowly opened the door.

A hallway stretched out ahead of him and ended at a stairway to the upper floor. Deiter could see why the contact had chosen this entrance to the building; it led directly to the second floor and to what should be bin Laden's room. The two figures quietly moved down the hallway and up the set of stairs to the floor above. They could hear voices from the room at the end of the hallway on the second floor. Deiter cracked the door open slightly and peered into the brightly-lit room. He could see three people. A figure in a long white robe wearing a white turban was seated on a cushion behind a small table. Two others were seated opposite him. Deiter recognized the first man as unmistakably being bin Laden; the other two he assumed were bodyguards. An AK-47 lay on the table in front of the sheik. Deiter turned to Zaira and held up three fingers; she nodded her understanding. Deiter took a deep breath and swung the door open while leveling his automatic weapon on the three people inside the room. Zaira slid into the room behind him and putting her back against the wall, held her weapon on the two bodyguards.

"I am here to place you under arrest, Osama bin Laden." Deiter said to the man in white. He thought at the time that this gave an almost comical theatrics to the moment…maybe something out of a Clint Eastwood movie, but couldn't think of much else to say. "I will not harm you, but you must come with me."

"Who are you to violate this place?" bin Laden asked.

"I guess that I'm your worst nightmare, bin Laden."

A look of contempt crossed bin Laden's face as his hand darted inside his loose-fitting white robe. Deiter caught the glimpse of a black object being withdrawn from the robes at the same time that one bodyguard crouched down and reached for his own weapon as well.

"Bad move, asshole," Deiter murmured as he fired first at bin Laden - a quick burst directed at the Arab's center of mass, - and then at the bodyguard. A bright red stain quickly blossomed against the white of bin Laden's robes, and he fell back with an astonished look on his face. His mouth was framing a curse, but no noise escaped his lips, only a low guttural gurgling sound. The neck of the bodyguard exploded in a massive spray of blood and flesh that sprinkled the wall behind him as the force of the bullets tore the left side of his neck away and threw him backwards against the wall; he slid down to the floor. Deiter heard several other shots and assumed that Zaira had fired at the second bodyguard. Deiter's attention went back to bin Laden who had fallen sprawled on the large overstuffed chair; his eyes wide open and the shock and bewildered look still frozen on his face. Once more, Deiter aimed his weapon at the Arabian; this time with all deliberateness...he had to make sure that bin Laden was dead.

A flash of red hair became framed in the now open doorway to the second room and caught his attention as he was about to pull the trigger once more, and he looked up to stare into the face of a woman. "Rose! My God, Rose!!" he screamed. Behind him in the hallway, a loud voice yelled something in Arabic and his head instinctively swung towards the sound. More guards had heard the shots and were clambering up the stairs and down the hallway. He looked back to the doorway in which he had seen the figure, but there was no one there; she had vanished.

"Zaira, more guards; we'll have to shoot our way out," he shouted, as he swung around to see his beautiful accomplice slumped against the wall, the AK-47 was held limply by her side; a look of shock was etched on her beautiful face. She was staring at something behind him. He swung back around again, this time bringing his machine pistol to bear at whatever it was that had brought out the reaction in Zaira. He saw nothing and turned back towards her. Her expression had not changed, nor the staring blank look in her warm and gentle eyes. Deiter became suddenly aware of the acknowledgement of death. "No!" he screamed. "No, not you too!" But Zaira didn't hear him; she was already dead.

Deiter leaned down and gently closed her eyes and took the AK-47 from her limp hand and brought it up just as the door crashed open and two soldiers stood there with weapons drawn. They were trying to make sense of the scene before them. Deiter loosed a long burst of fire from Zaira's weapon that stopped their rush into the room and sent them sprawling back into the hallway to collide with two more soldiers who had come to back them up. The soldiers' blood splattered on the doorway and the walls of the hallway. Deiter stuck his machine pistol into his belt and carrying Zaira's AK-47 in his right hand, he unslung his own automatic rifle from his shoulder and carried it in his left hand.

More noise and yelling came from down the hallway and from the next floor below. Deiter turned and took one last look back at Zaira's body now slumped in the corner. Tears cascaded down his cheek and a stillborn cry screamed from his throat as he threw himself through the doorway and ran towards the stairway that he assumed lead to the roof. Stopping at the corner near the head of the stairway leading to the lower floor, he looked down. At least six men were charging up the stairs. He swung the mass of his body around and faced the charging squad of soldiers. Both automatic weapons chattered deafeningly sending a volley of withering fire into the charging mass of soldiers…there was no way of escaping Deiter's fury, and the soldiers died on the stairway. Blood splattered on the walls and ceiling and a ripple of a red liquid began to cascade down the stairs as though it was some macabre waterfall. Some hardly identifiable chunks of gray brain matter joined the splashes of blood on the walls and slowly slid down to the steps below.

Only the sound of faraway yelling could be heard after the deafening barrage. Deiter's face was expressionless except for a quiver of his bottom lip. The carnage he wreaked didn't begin to make up for the loss he felt. It would take more deaths than these to compensate…no, there weren't enough of them to atone for Zaira.

He walked steadily up the stairway, through the door opening to the floor above, then up two more stories until he was on the top platform with a doorway leading to the roof. He pressed his right elbow down on the door handle and swung it open; the roof was empty. He quickly moved through the doorway and onto the roof. In the darkness he ran crouched over to the edge of the roofline. There was a three-foot wall surrounding the flat roof of the building. Deiter peered over the wall at the street below; several soldiers were rushing towards the building entrance below. The alley between the building he was on and the one next to it was empty. The other building was about one story shorter and at a distance about ten feet away. Deiter looked back at the door...no one had dared to challenge him yet by blundering up the stairs, but he knew it was only a matter of time. He backed up and sprinted toward the edge of the roof; his foot slammed down on the top of the wall and he jumped. He landed on the lower roof of the building next door and rolled to a stop. At the other end of the building, he noticed that only a few feet separated this building from the next, and sprinting towards the empty space, he jumped to the next building.

He decided it was time to get to the bottom floor and out of this sector of Grozny and pulled open a covered square opening on the roof. It apparently had been used to allow air into the building beneath. Looking inside, he could see that it was dark, there was no telling for sure, but he guessed that it would be only eight feet down to the floor; he slung the rifles on his left shoulder and easing himself through the hole. Gripping the two assault weapons tightly, he dropped through the opening to the floor below. He landed hard and lay there listening for some noise that would tell him that his sudden entrance had been noticed. He heard nothing, no sound to indicate that his entry had been detected. He stood up and made his way through the partial light to the doorway of the room and into a hallway leading downstairs to the ground floor.

At the main door to the building, he paused and looked out. Up the street to the left, he could see several trucks screeching to a stop in front of the building where Osama bin Laden...and Zaira lay dead. The way to the right was clear and he slid through the doorway and out onto the street. He knew that he had to go in an easterly direction to get to one of the rendezvous points or the Russian lines, but he'd have to go west first and circle around to keep away from the building where he had left so much death. He stepped out into the street.

Chapter Twenty

Confrontation

Aboard a NSA flight from Moscow
to Washington, D.C..
Late Sunday, November 28, 1999

Deiter settled into a comfortable seat aboard the NSA flight out of Sheremet'yevo Airport outside Moscow. The 737 had been flown in on a moment's notice especially for Deiter by Hank Henderson. The general had met him at the embassy upon his return from Chechnya and was concerned that there might be some intention by the Russian government to detain Deiter concerning the massacre of a number of Russian soldiers outside of Grozny. Apparently, the Minister of the Interior had demanded an investigation into the circumstances surrounding the deaths of a number of officers and soldiers in the MVD headquarters in Gudermes.

Deiter only knew that he was exhausted from his tour in Chechnya and wanted to get home. What was suppose to be a rather simple mission ended up leaving him with a feeling of grief and unfulfillment. He had not been able to capture Osama bin Laden or to bring him to justice, although he still believed that he had killed him there in that second story apartment. To Deiter, the death of Zaira had been a tragic and heartbreaking conclusion to the mission. She had been as extraordinary as she was beautiful. It had been too soon after

Rose's death to have met such an extraordinary woman, and he was devastated by her death. He grieved for her as he would have any other comrade in combat, yet there was a more poignant feeling of loss that he couldn't quite understand. At the remembrance of Zaira, Deiter simply shook his head; damn it, she shouldn't have been killed like that. It was just another cruelty, one more in a long line of tricks that fate seemed to have played on him in the past.

He leaned back, took a deep breath and chided himself for self-pity. Looking through the window of the airplane, he could see the ramp outside leading up to the forward door just in front of him. At the bottom of the ramp, he could see Hank talking with someone. He appeared to be upset with the person. Deiter stretched to see if he could see whom it was...and then he shrugged and leaned back. He wondered what the hell Austin Woods was doing there. Deiter had last seen Woods at the American Embassy only an hour ago. There hadn't been any problem then, yet it now seemed that something was up and it didn't look good. He hoped it had nothing to do with Charlie; she was supposed to have taken the last commercial flight out of Moscow. Henderson hadn't thought it was wise to try to smuggle her out too; it was hard enough getting Deiter through the gates to where the diplomatic plane was parked and two people would have caused just that much more suspicion.

Hank Henderson swayed as he made his way down the aisle of the 737 as it pulled out of its parking space and headed up the taxiway. He swung into the seat next to Deiter and buckled his seat restraint.

"Hang on, we're getting outta here fast," he remarked.

"Why, what did you do?" Deiter asked casually.

"Not me...you!" Henderson exclaimed. "Your Rambo routine back in Grozny."

"MVD still a little pissed off?"

"To say the least."

"They haven't any cause to be; they shouldn't have tried to torture me. I was willing to let bygones be bygones."

The sleek black aircraft gracefully lifted off the runway and slowly banked west towards the faraway landing strip at NSA headquarters in Maryland. When the pilot announced that they had left Russian airspace, Henderson sighed in relief and turned towards Deiter. "It wasn't just the MVD that was a problem," he said. "Woods told me something else."

"And what was that?" Deiter asked absently.

"You remember what you told me about Zaira's death and the shooting of bin Laden?"

"Yeah."

"And who it was that you said you saw in the other room?"

"Yeah, apparently it was the double that Adams found to represent Rose. I have to hand it to him, she pulled it off very well and succeeded in getting bin Laden into the trap."

"Not quite," Henderson said, stretching back in his seat and taking a deep breath.

"Oh?"

"You know that Adams has always been tricky and even unscrupulous?"

"Yeah, so what else is new?"

"It was Rose, Jack."

Deiter was massaging his neck to ease the stress of the last few weeks when he stopped and froze. He slowly turned towards Henderson and looked at him as though his friend had just spoken heresy. "What?"

"Adams visited Costa del Sol just before Rose left for the States. He wanted her to take just one last mission. He told her it would not take more than a week and would be of enormous benefit to the country. She was the only one who could accomplish the mission because she had known bin Laden back during the Soviet-Afghani war. Bin Laden would remember her and he would trust her because she had helped him before and he thought she was Chechen. Her mission was to lure him to Grozny so that he could be captured or killed."

Henderson paused and looked over at his friend. Deiter was stone faced. "Woods told you that?" Deiter asked with skepticism in his voice.

Henderson nodded, "Yes, but I have corroborative information as well. Back in Spain, when I left you at your villa and went back to the village, I had dinner at the *Casa de Paraiso* and talked with Juan Maranda. He told me that Rose had met someone there who, by his description anyway, must have been Adams. He said that she had mentioned bin Laden's name as he served them lunch. I wasn't sure about any of this until Woods confirmed it. I was trying to tell you what Juan had told me when we were interrupted by Konykov's messenger at the Red Lion Pub."

Deiter nodded that he recalled the conversation. "My God!" he suddenly exclaimed as though the thought hadn't occurred to him before. "Then Rose is alive! Where is she?" he asked, grabbing on to his friend's arm.

"Woods was pretty sure that she made it out, but he hasn't received any confirmation from Adams yet."

"Why did she do it?" Deiter asked reflectively, as he relaxed back into his seat.

"She thought she could do something good, maybe…and maybe also it was one last adventure. Adams can be convincing. He's smooth, you know that."

"Why didn't she tell me?" Deiter persisted.

"My guess is that she wouldn't have wanted to hurt you; you've got to know that, Jack. She knew that you would worry and not want her to go. Woods says that she still doesn't know about the crash of her flight from Madrid; she was on her way to Rome at that time to get last minute briefings before going to Afghanistan. Woods also said that he told her that Adams would contact you if the mission lasted more than a week. He didn't, of course. I think he expected that you'd be killed…more convenient for him. She fully expected to be back in a week and fly straight to Washington to meet you there. The surprise visit to her parents in New Jersey that she concocted was only a cover story. Knowing her, my guess is that she was looking forward to telling you about her adventure. It must have been a real shock when she saw you in bin Laden's apartment."

"Does Adams know that either you or I know of the whole scheme?" Deiter asked.

"No, Woods was very skittish about the whole thing from the beginning. I think he may have gone along with Adams only to protect his job, but he didn't like it. He really is a good sort, you know. He would have no incentive now to tell Adams that either you or I have learned about his whole plan as it would only point a finger at him for compromising Adams."

Deiter slowly leaned back in his seat. "I'll kill that bastard!" he said quietly and solemnly shaking his head. He then turned again towards Henderson. "Did Adams know about the threat to Flight 63?"

Henderson paused and then slowly and carefully said, "Woods said the plan was to get you to set up the plan to kill Saddam and Rose was to lure bin Laden to Grozny so the Russians could get at him. Then he had to change the plan when you ended up in Moscow. He thought that somehow you might stumble on the truth and upset his plans, although he really didn't care if either of you made it out of there alive. As to the flight from Madrid to the States, he had received corroboration at least a week in advance that the flight was being specifically targeted and it fit neatly into his plans. He could have intervened and saved the flight…if he'd wanted to. If he let events take their own course, he would have a good reason for you to want the mission."

"He's guilty of premeditated murder!" Deiter exclaimed.

Henderson nodded, but then added quietly, "No one's ever going to prove it, Jack."

"And 'no one' needs too, Hank, I'll take care of Adams." Deiter murmured in a low voice. He then leaned back in his seat and closed his eyes. A smile came to his lips as he said to himself, "Rose."

Ted Colby

Fort George G. Meade, Maryland
National Security Agency
Early Monday Morning, November 29, 1999

The matte black 737 with no identifying markings touched down smoothly on the NSA runway at Fort Meade, Maryland, and taxied to the end of a side strip of asphalt next to the NSA Headquarters. A black limousine waited at the edge of the strip until the sleek aircraft came to a stop; it then slowly crawled out to where a ramp of stairs was being rolled up to the forward door of the aircraft. The limo parked near the end of the ramp and waited. As soon as the door of the plane opened and two figures started to descend the stairs, the black uniformed driver stepped out of the vehicle and opened the rear door that faced the aircraft.

"Good morning, General," the driver said as he reached for the suitcase in Henderson's right hand. Deiter walked around to climb into the right rear door of the limo. The General slid into the open left rear door and the driver closed it after him.

The drive to Alexandria in the late November morning was very cool, but pleasant. Most of the leaves had fallen from the trees and the stalk bare branches seemed to want to scrape the clouds that drifted by in the bright blue skies. It would be another month before there was any threat of snow in the Washington area, but the coolness of the morning made Deiter long to feel the snow fly by him as he sailed down a ski slope. He had the good opportunity to do a lot of thinking on the plane trip from Moscow about what he wanted to do now that his mission was over. He could walk away and trust that someday Adams would be required to pay for what he had done, but that wasn't Deiter's style. The suffering he had caused Deiter personally was small in comparison to the suffering he had caused the families and loved ones of those on Flight 63. If Deiter had been made judge and jury for Saddam and for Osama bin Laden, couldn't he also do the same to Adams? He had decided to confront Adams and demand that he confesses to knowing about the threat to the flight. What Adams had done to him and to Rose was a personal thing and not within the authority of the courts to remedy. That course of action, Deiter would have to pursue himself.

The limo turned down Prince Street, bounced along the cobblestones and came to a stop in front of number 125. Deiter looked over at Henderson and put out his hand. "Thanks for everything, Hank, really, thanks."

Henderson just nodded as Deiter opened the limo door and stepped outside onto the cobblestones. Deiter closed the door and the limo rolled awkwardly down the street to the stop sign and then turned left and disappeared around the corner. Deiter walked up to the heavily carved door with the two brass lamps framing it; he lifted the fox head knocker, letting it fall three times. After a few moments, Conley opened it.

"Mr. Deiter, sir, I'm very sorry. I wasn't expecting you. Welcome home, sir."

"Sorry I didn't call, Conley. I didn't really have much of a chance and I had a lot of thinking to do."

"Have you had breakfast, sir?"

Deiter brightened. "Could you fix me something, Conley? I'm starved."

Conley beamed, "I'll bring it to you in the study if you'd like, sir." Deiter nodded and walked through the pocket doors leading to his study and office. He sat down at his desk and turned on the computer. The address list of telephone numbers showed him the private number of Don Adams, and Deiter picked up the cordless telephone from its cradle and punched in the number that had come up on his PC screen.

"Adams," the voice groaned breathlessly on the other end of the receiver.

"Deiter...we need to talk."

"Why, nice to hear you're back safely, Jack Too bad about bin Laden...and Saddam." Adams wheezed.

"Good security, Adams, why don't you just take out an ad in the newspaper while you're at it? Now, when and where?"

"Let me get back to you, Jack...terribly busy right now."

"I'll wait only two hours before I start making some other phone calls."

"Let's not be hasty, Jack. I'll be back to you definitely within the hour."

The phone went dead and Deiter returned the receiver to the cradle and leaned back in his chair to wait. The silky Persian black cat jumped onto his lap; he arching his back and looked directly into Deiter's eyes. That was Sam's way of welcoming his friend and master back and saying that he had missed him.

"Hi Sam, a whole lot's changed since we last saw each other." Sam felt it would be appropriate to curl up and lay on his owner's lap and be caressed. He settled down and waited for the scratch on his head that he knew would come.

Later, Deiter finished the last of his breakfast of Eggs Romanoff. He appreciated what he assumed was Conley's wry sense of humor, and wondered if the elderly gentleman really had any idea where Deiter had spent the last few weeks. The poached eggs served with a slice of ham on a grill-toasted French croissant with Hollandaise sauce and topped off with a dollop of black caviar was absolutely delicious. He was just taking another sip of coffee, when the private telephone on his desk rang twice. Deiter swallowed the coffee, wiped his mouth with a linen napkin and reached for the telephone.

"Hello?" Deiter said into the receiver.

"Mr. Deiter?" inquired a female voice.

"Yes."

"This is Mr. Adams' secretary. He said that he would be pleased to dine with you this evening at his place. A car will be at your home at seven tonight to pick you up."

Deiter at first started to protest and then shrugged to himself. "Fine, I'll be waiting," he responded and hung up the phone. He wondered why Adams would send a car for him. Adams could have just as easily given directions to his home. And why would he want to meet at Adams' home? Vowing to think it through further at some later time, he quickly counted the things he needed to do prior to seven that night.

It wasn't a long drive. Deiter had no idea where Adams was living now, and he doubted if he had ever known. Earlier, Deiter had dressed in his charcoal wool sport jacket over a gray turtleneck sweater and a set of charcoal wool pants. No use getting all gussied up just for Adams, he thought. The limo had arrived precisely on time to pick him up. The driver then drove around the block, headed back up King Street past the Masonic Memorial, and finally turned left on West Braddock Road. At seven o'clock in the evening in November, it was, as usual, completely dark. Although Deiter had no idea where he was going, he knew exactly where he was. To his surprise, the limo slowed and turned left through a tall iron gate, which opened as they approached. The driveway wound down towards a large white house that was fully lighted in front. He could see that there were four tall square pillars supporting the front porch in a Mount Vernon style entrance. Deiter knew that the position held by Don Adams in the CIA included a more than adequate compensation, but he never dreamed that a government employee could afford such a grand residence. He wondered if Adams was independently wealthy or had married into wealth. It should be an interesting evening, Deiter concluded.

The limo pulled up in front of the elegant entrance porch to the house and the driver opened the rear door so Deiter could climb out of the car. Deiter was curious as to whether Adams was privately providing such luxuries or whether it came from the CIA. Standing next to the driver, Deiter turned and asked, "Do you work for Adams or the company?"

"I don't believe you need to know," came the reply.

Deiter smiled. "Company man, huh?" he murmured as he strode toward the entrance door. He found a lighted doorbell button and pushed it. Over his shoulder he saw the driver climb back into the limo and pull away just as the entrance door opened.

"Mr. Deiter, I assume?" The question came from a small thin man dressed as a butler who stood in the open doorway.

"Expecting someone else?" Deiter asked.

"No, sir. You and Mr. Adams will be dining alone. Let me show you into the study where Mr. Adams will be joining you presently."

The butler led Deiter down a long central hallway and opened one of a set of tall, heavy double doors leading into the study. As soon as Deiter entered the room, the butler backed out the doorway and closed the doors behind him. Deiter was alone. He looked around the room and found to his surprise that it was very much to his liking. It was a larger, more expensive and more sophisticated version of his own study and office. A fire was blazing brightly in the fireplace at the end of the room. That touch, Deiter especially liked. On two sides of the room there were bookcases that reached the ceiling. Comfortable furniture filled the room and a large desk was set off to one side. On the desk was a rather complicated telephone hookup and Deiter guessed that the large cabinet next to it contained a full computer setup.

In a little over ten minutes, Deiter heard a noise in the hallway outside the study and assumed that he was about to be joined by his host. The wait had been for effect and intimidation, Deiter concluded. It hadn't worked. When the door opened, Adams' rotund figure filled the doorway. Deiter could hear the wheezing noise of heavy breathing even before he could make out the features on the man's face. As the man slowly walked towards him, he saw the familiar, streaked gray beard, the beady eyes and the humorless mouth of Don Adams.

"Jack," Adams said, acknowledging his guest although he didn't attempt to shake hands.

"Dinner wasn't necessary, you know. Just some answers to a few questions."

"Let's not talk about that business before dinner, Jack, it's not in good form. Plenty of time for that sort of thing later."

"Okay, I'll play your game…later."

"So, about bin Laden. Unfortunately, we've not been able to confirm his death."

"It's possible he survived. When I last saw him, his eyes were open and staring at nothing, but I didn't have time to take his pulse."

"There have been a few rumors that he is ill, you know…possibly cancer or kidney disease. I understand that the Taliban and some of his close associates have been detected trying to locate a dialysis machine."

"Lead poisoning would be more like it," Deiter observed. "You know, with a bit more help from you the plan just might have succeeded."

"How can you say that, Jack? I supported the whole operation. But that's a discussion for later." Adams waddled towards an open cabinet containing several bottles of liquor and glasses "Would you care for a drink, Jack?"

Deiter thought for a moment and then relented. "Okay, Jamison, neat, if you have it."

"Jamison it is," replied Adams picking up a bottle from the cabinet, examining the label and then pouring a small glass full with the amber liquid. He handed it to Deiter and turned back to pour himself a martini from a chilled decanter. He deftly speared three olives with a toothpick and added them to the cone shaped glass and then picking it up, turned back towards Deiter. "To your health, Jack," he announced, holding up his glass.

"Na Zdorovia!" Dieter responded, his face deadpan.

Both men sipped their drinks without saying anything. Finally, the awkward silence was broken by Dieter. "Adams, I really haven't got time to play games. And it doesn't require dinner. First of all, I need to know why you sent Rose on that mission, and I want to know why you didn't have the decency to tell me."

Adams at first seemed surprised at the question. He hadn't been informed that Deiter had known that the mysterious agent had been, in fact, Rose McGuire and not a double.

"Oh, is that all?" Adams finally responded. "Well, that's simple enough. I asked her to finish a job that she had started many years ago and she realized that it would be of tremendous value to the country. Didn't she tell you?"

"You know damn well she didn't…you told her not to."

"Did I now?" Adams said, as he raised one eyebrow.

"Yes, because you knew that I'd talk her out of it."

"Um, I did think of that possibility, matter of fact. She may be your wife, but she still has assets and connections that could help the country…and a mind of her own."

"Why me, then? Couldn't you find some thug to do your assassinations?"

"I think you know the answer to that, Jack. But then again, I guess the FBI hasn't been as strapped by the so called "Torricelli Rule, has it? That's Congress' stupid imposition on the CIA to only pay assassins who are upstanding and trustworthy. Did you ever try to find someone to do that kind of work who was a Boy Scout, Jack?" Adams sneered. "I couldn't find a Boy Scout, so I needed to find someone who was very angry, and I found you Jack Deiter."

"And ethics?"

Adams snorted, "Ethics? What has ethics got to do with it? We are in a silent war and have been so for decades."

"And the people on Flight 63? Were they exempt from ethics in your evaluation? Were they soldiers in your silent war?"

"As a matter of fact, they were," Adams replied indignantly. "We are all soldiers in this war. There are no civilians, there are no women and children, there are only targets for the terrorists."

"You are sick," responded Deiter. "That's the same excuse that bin Laden would have used. The two of you make a good team."

"No, that's too easy a diagnosis, Jack. There's more to the equation. We are in a war, like it or not. The enemy tries to strike at our most sensitive points, our families, our national treasures, our national monuments and the structures of our government," he responded. "We have to do whatever is necessary to end it."

"You knew of the threat to Flight 63, and you didn't do anything to stop it. You committed murder of the most despicable nature," Deiter spit out.

"And what would you have done?" Adams responded. "There was a possibility of getting the most sought-after terrorist in the history of this country."

"At the expense of innocent women and children?"

"Aw, Jack," Adams retorted, "what about the Nagasaki and Hiroshima victims? Did all of them deserve death? Did the women and children...especially the children, the innocent little children," he sneered again, "did they deserve an early death?"

"That's an old argument and the traditional, weak excuse for terrorism," said Deiter shaking his head. "You know as well as I do that the only other alternative to dropping the atomic bomb on Japan was to invade the island. That would have cost over a million U. S. casualties and twice that many casualties among the Japanese people. It would have made a wasteland of the whole country and led to mass starvation. The bomb as a demonstration of our will and our capability was the most humane thing to do."

"And your argument has some credibility," Adams shrugged, "but it is not commonly accepted in the rest of the world. They look at it as America's excuse for racial extermination."

"We're not talking about the rest of the world, Adams, we are talking about what you did to a lot of Americans aboard that airplane. That amounted to murder by omission, if nothing else. You failed to act on information you had on the threat. You could have prevented the crash."

"Rubbish. When are you going to accept the fact we are in a war? In war, we do what we must."

"An undeclared war," Deiter reminded him.

Adams shrugged off the possible nuance. "I needed you to complete the plan to get Saddam, and I needed Rose to get bin Laden. The only way you would ever go on that mission was for vengeance and that meant that you needed to think Rose had been killed by terrorists. By letting the terrorists have their way, I got both of you involved. Not an easy chore," he chuckled to himself in a way of self-congratulation. "You need to look at it objectively."

"It won't be me, it'll be public opinion and the press who will convict you long before the courts ever get their hands on you. You will be pilloried well before you get to see a magistrate. Your career is finished, Adams, and the rest of your life is going to be spent behind bars, if you're lucky," Deiter said, setting down his drink and turning to leave. He paused as he came to the double doors to the hallway. "I'll make sure that the media knows all the details of your crime," he added over his shoulder.

"I wouldn't be so quick to do that, you know."

Deiter stopped as he was going through the doorway. "There's something I don't know?" he asked.

"Your wife is an accomplice to the plan as well as you," Adams warned.

"How do you figure that? You lied to her and to me."

"I could implicate her. I am well known and trusted…and I would be believed."

"I don't doubt that you would; you are a sick toad, Adams."

Adams smiled and raised his glass to Deiter. "You are not a winner, Mr. Deiter. Only the powerful prevail and you are not that," he baited.

"Where is my wife?" Deiter suddenly asked.

"She's safe for now, but she needs to stay in hiding for awhile. They believe that she may have betrayed bin Laden and a *fatwa* has already been issued against her by the clergy in the Taliban."

Deiter turned and started to walk out of the room once more.

"Wait," Adams commanded. His hand slid into the inside pocket of his jacket and extracted a small black pistol. As Deiter turned back towards him, he aimed the weapon at the departing man. "Sorry, Jack, I don't want to have you complicate my life," Adams said quietly.

The sound of the gunshot resounded in Deiter's ears and he felt a thud against his shoulder that quickly turned into a sharp pain. The whole reason for the meeting at Adams' home now became clear to Deiter...too late. Adams had intended to get rid of Deiter to protect his complicity in the destruction of Flight 63 and the attack on a head of state, despite the rationale. It would have been much easier to dispose of a body from here. Adams had planned to murder him to maintain the secrecy of his operation...and then who would be next...Rose? Or even Charlie and Hank?

Deiter could tell that the use of weapons was not one of Adams' better talents. Despite the pain, he charged the fat man and bowled him over grabbing for the gun. One twist and it was in his hand and he rolled over and came to his feet once more holding the gun in both hands pointing it directly at Adams. "Now it's my turn," shouted Deiter.

Adams got to his feet in an agile manner that surprised Deiter completely. The man's face behind his beard was a reddish-purple and angry; veins stood out on his forehead. He rushed at Deiter and attempted to wrestle the weapon from him. Deiter shot once, twice, three times into the furious mass of flesh that charged at him and pressed hard up against him, sending him reeling backwards. Adams' hands were at Deiter's throat. Once more Deiter pulled the trigger, sending a final round directly into the large mass as the glaring, sweating fat face pushed heavily against his own face and Adams' thumbs pressed against his throat. Deiter twisted and with all his strength finally wrenched himself away from the man. Adams' massive body fell forward and sprawled out face down on the hard wood floor, his eyes staring at the grain in the wood. The body jerked once more and then finally went still for good.

"Why the hell did you have to do that?" Deiter breathlessly asked the motionless figure. He then looked around him. He knew that the shots must have been heard by the butler or some of the staff. He suddenly became aware that he was now the hunted. The staff would have to explain the dead body of their employer, and at this point, it was his word against theirs. He had to get out of the house fast and find someplace to hide until he could sort all of this out and somehow get exonerated. He threw the gun at Adams' prostrate body and bolted out of the door into the night.

Deiter knew that it would be impossible for him to go home that night and if he were to contact Conley to help him, he would only be making the man an indictable accomplice. He had to go someplace else. Hank Henderson would be willing to help, but he feared that the FBI would think to go there first given their close relationship. The next person that came to mind was Charlie. It would take them awhile to figure her as a possible link and by the time they had located her, he would be gone.

He started walking north towards Old Town Alexandria and the train station. He had to get to Charlie's apartment in Chevy Chase before he lost too much more blood. As he walked, he took out his linen handkerchief and stuffed it down his collar and into the bullet wound. He pressed it hard into his shoulder and winced. Damn, that hurt…I should have finished that drink, he thought as he walked in the shadows down the sidewalk along Braddock Road. He turned right at King Street and finally saw the lights of the train station ahead of him.

After he bought a ticket, he waited only a short time until the train pulled in and he sought a place to sit away from any of the other passengers. Although the bleeding had stopped, the pain persisted and he felt himself getting weaker. He worried at the thought that there might be internal bleeding. The train sped forward towards Chevy Chase, Maryland. Although his eyes were heavy as he leaned back in the corner seat of the car, he didn't dare fall asleep. He stared out into the darkness outside the window as though it were another world and watched the lights of Washington pass by him. If depression had ever hit him, it was here and now. How had so much gone wrong?

Chapter Twenty-one

The Fox at Bay

Bedford Towers, Chevy Chase, Maryland
Late Monday night, November 29, 1999

At 10:30 P. M. Deiter was standing in the lobby of Bedford Towers. From the station, he had hired a cab. Although he knew that a cab would be a weak link in his evasion technique, he didn't want to call Charlie ahead of time…it might be traced from his credit card. He pushed the button for apartment 1320 opposite the typed inscription of "C. Waggner" on the console and waited for what seemed an eternity. A bored and sleepy voice finally answered. "Yes, what do you want?"

"Charlie, it's me, Jack Deiter, I need your help."

"Jack!" she exclaimed, suddenly wide awake. "I'll push the button for you; come on up."

A buzzing noise drew Deiter's attention to the door off to his left and he opened it. He quickly went inside and over to the elevators, pressed the up button and waited. He looked around the lobby for a sign of anyone who might be able to remember that he was there, but the lobby was empty. Finally, the elevator door opened and he quickly slipped inside and soon he was knocking on the door to apartment 1320. It opened immediately and Charlie quickly ushered him in. She stuck her head out of the doorway and looked around the corner to make certain that nobody had seen him either in the hallway or entering her apartment. There was no one there. She closed the door.

"Jack," she said, throwing her arms around him. "I'm glad to see you, even at this hour. What's wrong?"

"I just killed Adams," he said simply.

"Oh, shit," she sighed. "Sit down and tell me what happen. Have you had dinner?" she added.

"I was suppose to have dinner with Adams at his house…until I shot him."

"I suppose that queered the dinner routine?" she asked, suppressing a grin.

"Yes, it sure did. I'm glad you can keep this in perspective," he remarked.

"Jack, whatever happened, I'm sure the asshole deserved it and I'm sure that you didn't do it without provocation."

"You got that right," he responded.

"What are you going to do now?" she asked.

Deiter took Charlie by the arm and leaned on her as they walked into the living room. He collapsed onto the sofa and motioned for her to sit next to him. "I'll tell you the truth, Charlie. I was invited to Adams' home this afternoon after I called him and wanted to meet with him to discuss what had occurred with Rose. I thought that it was strange, but it wasn't until I tried to leave that he pulled a gun on me and shot me as I was standing in the doorway."

"Shot you? Are you hurt?" she asked.

Deiter gingerly slid off his sport coat and threw it into a chair. A circle of blood had spread across his shirt on his left shoulder. Charlie left him and went into the kitchen. "Take off your shirt...if you can," she said over her shoulder. "I'm getting a few things."

"If the bullet's still in there, I'll have to get it out; do you know how to do that?" he asked.

"Let's look at it first before we jump to conclusions," she said, as she came back into the living room. "Here, let me help you with your shirt."

Deiter winced as she gingerly pulled off his turtleneck sweater. As soon as it was off, he sank into the sofa. Charlie quickly examined the wound. She could see the small entrance hole next to the shoulder bone. She turned him around and looked at the back of his shoulder. There was an angry looking dark mass of slightly larger diameter just above his armpit.

"This kinda looks like where the bullet almost went through, unless you got hit in the back as well."

"In a way, that's good. Maybe you can get it out. Otherwise, I'd have to go to an emergency room and they'd report it to the police."

Charlie turned the table lamp up to high and lifted the shade to place more light on Deiter's back. She then prodded the welt on his back. "Does that hurt?" she asked.

"Not really, it just feels numb."

"I can feel what seems to be the bullet just under the skin. It's right there. One more millimeter and it would have gone completely through. Wait here. I have something in my bathroom that will help." Charlie left the room and returned within a few moments. "I want you to take these," she said, holding out two oblong yellow capsules.

"What are they?"

"Percocet. They'll relax you long enough that I can pry into the wound. It's obvious that the bullet didn't hit a bone or anything serious so I'm confident that I can get it out with the tools that I have here."

Deiter looked skeptically at her. "Are you sure you know what you're doing?" he asked.

"First of all," she said with a pouting expression on her face, "you have no choice and secondly the answer is yes, I do know what I'm doing. The bullet appears to be a small caliber and is just under the skin; with the first aid kit I have, I can do it. All I have to do is slit the skin and it will drop out. Relax, Jack. You're in good hands."

Deiter leaned forward onto the cushion of the sofa and said, "Okay, Doc. Go to it and do your thing."

"No need to get sarcastic," she replied, as she held up the capsules and a glass of water. Deiter took the pills and water. "Got anything stronger? I never finished the drink that Adams gave me," he said, handing the glass back to Charlie.

"Alcohol doesn't go well with these pills," she said, pushing the glass back to the reluctant patient.

"How long before they take effect?" he asked, downing the two.

"You never know, but it won't be long. Just lean back and relax."

In about ten minutes, the medicine seemed to have taken effect and Deiter was laying on his stomach on the sofa in a semiconscious state. Charlie examined the dark projection in Deiter's left shoulder again and pressed it. Deiter didn't to respond to her probing the spot. The entrance wound wasn't bleeding badly, which led her to believe that the bullet had not hit any vital vein or an artery.

She dipped a slender boning knife from the kitchen into a bottle of rubbing alcohol and wiped it on a piece of gauze that she had retrieved from the first aid kit. She sliced a small X over the protrusion and placed a piece of gauze over the incision. As soon as the bleeding eased up, she put pressure on both sides of the wound. A small dark conical mass eased its way through the incision and into the gauze. As she squeezed it from the wound, Deiter groaned. The wound began to bleed and she quickly placed a large piece of gauze on it and held it tightly against the now empty hole. After a few minutes, she loosened the pressure on the wound and checked to see if the bleeding had subsided. The bleeding had slowed sufficiently enough for her to take a piece of surgical tape and cut it in butterfly fashion. She squeezed the flesh together and then quickly placed the small strip of tape securely on each side of the hole. Charlie placed a double piece of gauze over it and pressed down against the wound.

After a few moments, she pulled out two short pieces of tape with her teeth and placed them over the gauze. She repeated her bandaging operation on the entry wound. Charlie sat back and looked at her handiwork and the small projectile that she had placed in an ashtray on the table. She was pleased with herself. Now all she needed to do was to wait until the Percocet wore off.

It was almost seven o'clock in the morning when Deiter finally stirred. Charlie noticed his movement and stretched also. She had been sitting with her legs curled beneath her in the chair opposite the sofa on which Deiter had been sleeping. The first thing that Deiter saw was Charlie's smiling face.

"Hi there, big guy. How are ya feeling?" she asked.

"Fine, I guess...Ow!" he exclaimed, as he tried to lift himself up with his left arm.

"I meant to tell you that your left shoulder might be sore. You had a bullet in it, you know,"

"Yeah, so I remember," he said, sagging back onto the sofa. "I take it that you got it out all right?" he asked.

Charlie nodded her head at the ashtray where the bloody small caliber bullet sat. Deiter nodded his appreciation and picked up the projectile. "A .22 caliber?" he said incredulously. "Why the hell was he using a weapon that small if he wanted to stop me? That doesn't figure."

"You feeling well enough to tell me any more about what happened and give me some idea of where we go from here?" she asked.

"Yeah..." he said slowly, as he thought again about the caliber of the weapon Adams had used and then added, "Have you got any coffee, Charlie...and a couple of aspirin? I've got a helluva headache."

"Side effect of the Percocet, it'll go away with a couple of aspirin," she replied getting up and heading for the kitchen. "Do you think anyone has contacted Hank yet?" she asked over her shoulder.

"Hank'll call here when he's notified. That's when you have to be careful what you say to him on the phone," he responded. "It'll probably be bugged."

"You two know each other pretty well, don't you?' she said, when she returned to where Deiter was sitting. Deiter grunted his concurrence. "Here's some aspirin, but I want you to take these antibiotics also. No use letting that wound get infected," she said, handing him several pills and a glass of water. "The coffee's on. It'll be ready in a few minutes."

"They'll most likely want to know why you disappeared," Charlie continued.

"I know, but at the time, I felt like I was all alone in a gang fight. Someone else at Adams' home had to know what he was planning and how he planned to get rid of my body. He sure as hell couldn't have done it all by himself and at the same time explain what the gun shot was all about even if he could hide my body behind a sofa or someplace."

"We need a third party to run interference with the law while we give them time to figure out the truth...a lawyer maybe. Why don't I call my boss, Jonathan Banks? He knows you and he knows Adams, and frankly he despises the guy."

"Good idea, Charlie. He'd be a perfect go-between, if he'll do it. He could even have his corporate legal staff do it."

"I've known Jonathan all of my life; he's a great friend of my father. I'm sure he'll help, Jack."

At eight-thirty, Charlie placed a call to Jonathan Banks on his private line at the JBI think tank. It rang twice and was picked up. "Banks."

"Jonathan, it's Charlie. I need your help."

"Charlie, I heard that you were back. What the hell's the matter? Where are you?"

"I'm okay, I'm in my apartment; it's really about a friend, someone you know."

"How's Jack doing?" he asked.

"I can't keep any thing from you, Jonathan. How do you do it?"

Banks laughed. "The Alexandria police and the FBI are looking for Deiter for questioning about a possible murder. Oh yes, the CIA is also very upset. I was informed late last night. What can I do for you, Charlie?"

"Jack's here. He came in last night with a bullet wound in his shoulder that I fixed up; he'll be okay. He was caught up in something that happened at Don Adams' house and he acted in self-defense. We need a lawyer to contact the FBI and the Alexandria Police to let them know that he's in the vicinity and will turn himself in…when and if it becomes necessary."

"I understand. I'll contact the Director of the FBI and the Chief of Police of Alexandria's finest to put things on hold. Then I'll have our attorney prepare whatever is necessary to assure that Deiter stays free…don't make any more calls, we want to keep his location secret for now and your home phone line free so that I can contact you on a moment's notice, should it be necessary."

"Got it, Jonathan, and thanks." She hung up, smiled and turned to Deiter. "He'll cover everything, but we have to stay quiet and hide out here for awhile."

"You have a great hideout here, Charlie; sure as hell beats an old dirty barn or the swamp anyway."

"Thanks!" she said, looking hurt. "You know, I'd bet that somehow Jonathan gets in touch with Hank and the two of them will work it all out."

"You are the ultimate optimist," he said, shaking his head.

"Jack," she started. "What exactly happened in Chechnya? I know that the mysterious woman agent finally turned out to be Rose…Ashton Woods told me…and that she isn't dead after all, but there also were reports that you were captured by the MVD in Grozny with a woman, although it didn't seem to be Rose. If you don't want to talk about it, it's okay, but I was just curious."

"And the answers are…" he started out with a grin. "Yes, I now know that Rose never was on Flight 63, thank God. She was on her way to Rome for a final briefing before she went to Afghanistan to meet with Osama bin Laden and others she once knew in the Taliban. She was the one I saw on those occasions in Baghdad, Rome and finally in Grozny.

Rose had known bin Laden fairly well many years ago, and this time around, she encouraged him to go to Chechnya to help the rebels. She even made the travel arrangements for all of them courtesy of the CIA...all unknown to bin Laden, of course. Back in the late seventies, she was secretly supplying the Afghan *Mujahideen* with weapons, food and medical supplies to fight the Soviets. Bin Laden thought that she was a Chechen...he had no idea she was CIA.

The woman I was with when I was captured by the MVD was Zaira Maskhadov, the daughter of the president of Chechnya. It's fantastic, I know, but I met her in the middle of Grozny after the airplane I was in crashed and the crew was shot by the rebels. She was taking me to meet her father when we were captured. After I got loose, I freed her and we were picked up by the FSB and brought to safety. Then when we learned where bin Laden was located, the two of us went to capture him...or kill him. Any more people on a mission like that would have been detected, so it was just the two of us. Zaira was killed in the attempt to get bin Laden."

"Jack Deiter, you are simply amazing...the president's daughter?"

Deiter suddenly was silent and Charlie waited a few moments before she asked. "And was she...special to you?"

"Not in the way I think you mean, Charlie; she was just a very wonderful person who didn't need to die in that way. I thought at the time that Rose was dead and it was much too soon for me to have had any romantic feelings. Yet, there was something there that will never allow me to forget her. She was very beautiful and very wonderful. I will remember her forever."

"And Rose, where is she? Is she okay?"

"So I understand, but I've had no contact with her. This is what makes this whole damn thing so horrendous, Charlie. And that bastard Adams was behind it all. He told me tonight that a *fatwa* had been issued against her by the Taliban and she is in hiding until her trail cools off."

"Do you believe him?"

"Strangely enough, yes; that part anyway."

"Do you think she's safe?"

"Not if Adams is still alive and thinks that I'm about to spill the beans about his complicity in flight 63."

"Jack, why don't you go in the bedroom and lie down for awhile. I'll bring you in some coffee, and later I'll have some breakfast for you. You missed dinner last night, you realize," she said with a chuckle.

"Glad you can laugh about it," Deiter responded, as he gingerly got up and headed for the bedroom.

Sometime later, Charlie came in with some coffee and a plate with eggs, bacon and toast. He ate as they made small talk and then Charlie left him alone to get some rest.

Deiter woke up with the strange feeling that what he had experienced the previous night simply hadn't occurred. He couldn't shake the thought. He looked down at the small projectile that had been taken from his shoulder and shook his head. Why such a small caliber and why had he fired only one shot? Adams was a complete asshole, but he wasn't dumb...no, he was smart as a fox. What had really happened? He thought that maybe what he saw and experienced was only smoke and mirrors. He was shaken from his reverie by the ring of the telephone. He heard Charlie answer it in the other room and he was trying to stand up when she opened the door and came in holding the cordless telephone.

"You got that right," she said into the phone, before handing it to Deiter. "It's Hank."

Deiter sat back onto the bed and took the phone from Charlie.

"Hank, you guessed where I was hanging out; do you think anyone else will?"

"Not for awhile. Are you okay, Jack?" Henderson replied.

"Yeah, I'm all right; I've got a good nurse."

"What did you do with Adams? Everyone wants to know?"

"I shot him after he shot me first."

"What did you do with him."

"What do you mean? Nothing, I left him stretched out on the floor."

"And what else did you do?"

"Got outta there as fast as I could…oh yes, I threw that tiny gun he shot me with at him before I left."

"Tiny gun? Not a .357 Magnum?" Henderson inquired.

"No, the bullet that Charlie dug out'ta me looked like a .22 short. Besides, a Magnum would have knocked me on my ass."

"Get some rest, Jack. I'll drop by as soon as I check out a couple of things. When I see you, I'll bring you up to date on what's going on."

"Okay," Deiter responded, pushing the OFF button on the phone. He lay back on the pillow and closed his eyes. "He's going to drop by later on," he told Charlie. "Boy am I tired."

"Get some rest, I'll be in the next room if you need anything," Charlie said as she closed the door behind her.

It was almost three o'clock in the afternoon when Charlie answered the call from the main entrance. In a few minutes, Hank Henderson knocked on the apartment door.

"Hank, what's up?" she asked, as he quickly slid into the apartment.

"Things don't add up. I believe what Jack told me, but that's not what the evidence shows."

"What do you mean?"

Hank walked into the living room and sat down on the sofa. He shook his head. "No one knows what happened to Adams. The authorities all figure Jack got rid of the body somehow."

"How do they know that there is a body?" she asked

"They found some .357 slugs in the wall and the butler and driver swear that Adams and Jack were alone together in the room. It looks bad."

"That's it!" Deiter exclaimed from the doorway to the bedroom.

"Jack," Henderson said getting up from the sofa and walking over to see his friend.

"Are you okay?"

"Yeah, sure, Hank…but that's what's been bothering me. That asshole shot at me with a small caliber for two reasons. One, he didn't want to kill me…or even hit me; he wanted me to grab the gun and shoot him. That's why he charged me. A large caliber gun at close range would do real damage to his miserable flesh even if he did have a flak jacket on. A .22 caliber wouldn't make too much of an impact at all, especially if some of the powder in the shells had been taken out."

"I still don't follow."

"He didn't ask me to dinner to shoot me; he wanted me to get the blame or suspicion for killing him…he wanted to disappear and frame me to put the authorities on the wrong trail until he had time to disappear for good. He figured it would put me out of commission and give him the time he needed. I think that you'll find that his chauffeur and butler know a lot more about all of this than what they're saying."

Henderson walked over to the telephone and punched in a number. "Jonathan, Hank Henderson. Can you check out the possibility that Adams staged the whole affair and is now on the lamb, because of his involvement with the downing of Flight 63?" He paused and then added, "Thanks, I'm over at Charlie's."

"And?" Deiter asked, after Henderson terminated his call.

"And now we wait."

Ted Colby

Chapter Twenty-two

At Home – The Last Chapter

Washington, D.C.
Friday night, December 24, 1999

Deiter felt very tired as he rolled his Jaguar to a stop along the curb in front of his home. He turned off the engine, leaned back in the driver's seat, and closed his eyes. How long ago had he started out on this nightmare? The last three weeks had been the worst time of his life. He had been a prisoner of the press at times and the FBI at others. Finally, they had believed him and located Don Adams in a hotel on the Mayan Riviera in Mexico. A team was sent to bring him back to the United States. The CIA had completed its internal investigation and concluded that Adams had acted without authority. They didn't blame Deiter for Adams' disappearance, but wrote it off as the ex-CIA executive bolting before he was found out and forced to face justice. Adams was being held on obstruction of justice charges and probably wouldn't be free for many years, if ever.

In the end, the FBI decided to drop their investigation and so did the local police. Deiter had just finished a full debriefing from the CIA and felt drained. It wasn't over, though, not until Rose was finally home. He still didn't know where she was or when he could see her. He hated the separation, but understood that they had to make sure that she would never be connected with Rooza Demidov or the plot against bin Laden.

He finally straightened up and stepped out of the Jag. Locking it, he turned toward the door to his home. The brass lanterns glowed softly against the side of the building. He looked at the brass doorknocker and sighed. The head of the fox gleamed in the partial light and seemed to smirk at him. "What are you laughing at?" he asked the figure. He put a key into the door and opened it. At the end of the hallway, he saw a figure framed in the light from the kitchen area.

"Mr. Deiter?" Conley asked.

"Yeah, it's me," Deiter responded softly.

"I'm glad you're home, sir. It's Christmas Eve, you know, and I thought that you might want something special for dessert before you retire."

"No thanks, I just got through with the CIA, and I think that it's finally over. Right now, I'm tired, Conley, really tired."

"I can appreciate that, sir. Have you had dinner?"

"Yes, thanks. I had it with the Henderson's. I'll be in the study for awhile. Why don't you turn in?"

"If you're sure I can't get you anything, sir."

"Good night Conley, and thanks," Deiter concluded.

"Good night, Sir, and Merry Christmas, Sir."

"Yeah, a Merry Christmas, Conley, Merry Christmas." The older man stood there for a moment as though wanting to choose his words carefully.

"There is something else, sir," Conley added.

Deiter looked back at the elderly man, questioningly. "What is it?"

"As I recall, sir, Christmas Eve was suppose to be a special time for you a few years back."

Deiter understood fully what Conley meant, he hadn't forgotten when he was suppose to have met Rose on Christmas Eve after they returned from Rome; but, he recalled, he had waited until past midnight and Rose never showed. How did Conley know about that? "I've waited many a Christmas Eve, Conley." Deiter responded.

"This time, Jack, you won't wait in vain." The feminine voice came from the kitchen behind Conley. "It took me many years, but I finally made it."

Conley stepped aside to reveal Rose standing behind him. Deiter thought he had never seen anything so lovely or welcome in his life. She ran toward him and threw her arms around his neck.

"I couldn't stand it any longer, Jack. I have been away from you too long. I wanted to surprise you, but I'm not very good at surprise entrances."

"Oh, you're good, alright," he replied, "in fact, you're great! Rose, I've missed you so much." Deiter paused and holding her by the shoulders at arm's length, he added, "I don't know whether to kiss you or slap you."

"I recall that I said that to you once," she reminded him. He chose the former.

Conley smiled, and a tear found its way down his cheek. He turned and made his way quietly up to his room. Things were finally back to normal, he guessed, and it pleased the elderly man. He thought about his own dear Millie and vowed to tell her about it tonight before he went to sleep. He often talked to Millie late at night; he knew how it was to miss someone.

Deiter sat down at his desk in the study while Rose sat on his desk next to him. He picked up the telephone and dialed a number he knew from memory. It would be a shame to raise the old man so early on Christmas morning, but maybe the good news would make up for it. He punched out the number for Juan Maranda in Costa del Sol. Deiter hoped that the villa hadn't yet been sold. He smiled at Rose and grasped her hand as he heard the phone ring inside the *Casa de Paradiso*.

Epilogue

Arroyo de la Miel
Costa del Sol, Spain
New Years Day, 2000

The tide had just started to come in when Deiter stepped out onto the deck overlooking the beach. Off to the East, the sun was a brilliant orb just starting its climb over the bright blue Mediterranean. Down the beach a seagull was circling closer and closer to the villa. When it finally came overhead, it started to cry. Deiter felt a presence behind him and looked around to see Rose standing there in her long white nightgown. She was smiling at him as though she was seeing him and admiring him for the first time. He reached out for her and she hurriedly slid into his arms. How long ago, he wondered, was it when he had stood here early in the morning grieving at the thought that he had lost her? Never in his wildest dreams did he ever think that this moment would come again.

"Are you happy?" she asked.

"Happier than I have ever been in my life," he replied.

"It's a new century, Jack," Rose exclaimed, "I wonder what it'll be like. Do you think that the terrorists we tried to eliminate will ultimately win or will we finally live in peace?"

"They're a long way from here, right now, Rose, and I'd like to keep it that way. Hey, promise me that your spying days are over.

That'd be a great resolution for New Year's Day…and for a new century."

Rose grinned and cocked her head like she always did when she knew she could tease someone. She looked up at him and started to giggle as she held him ever closer to her. "You wouldn't be satisfied with that, Jack, I know you better than that."

"Okay, but next time include me in!"

"I promise, Jack, I promise."

The seagull gave a last cry and flew down the beach.

Bibliography

Reported from NAZRAN, Russia. The Chechen commander, Abuu Khadzhiyev, was killed August 9, 2000 in the village of Samashki by Russian paramilitary after they attacked two armored personnel carriers belonging to Interior Ministry troops (MVD)

Urus-Martan, A key aide to Chechen leader Aslan Maskhadov, General Mumadi Saydayev was arrested last night during a special operation carried out by Russian forces, Interfax news agency reported. He is being held in a military prison in an unspecified north Caucasus location. Saydayev was in charge of coordination military actions against Russian forces and is believed to have been involved in most terrorist acts organized by the Chechen guerillas.

Twenty-seventh Session of the Islamic Conference of Foreign Ministers - In a speech to the Conference, the President of the Chechen Republic of Ichkeria, Aslan Maskhadov, outlined the situation between his nation and Russia and asked for the recognition of his nation by the various ministers present.

Report by Erik Batuek, Moscow, January 15, 2000. "Old wounds were re-opened in late December (1999)…when maverick warlord Shamil Basayev was shot three times in the stomach by current defense minister Mohammed Yambiev. The gunfight reportedly broke out after Yambiev attacked Basayev's Dagestani expedition of August 1999 and accused the extremist Wahhabi faction of starting a potentially apocalyptic war. Basayev promptly shot the minister in the leg; Yambiev grabbed his own handgun and fired back. In a more recent development, a letter was published in the Nezavisimaya Gazeta (January 20, 2000) apparently signed by the infamous Chechen general Salman Raduev, offering to execute Basayev in return for an amnesty and $1 million. The letter read, "[We] will cease military action for which Shamil Basayev is responsible. It was he who invited Shi'ite extremists to the Caucasus and on their advice attacked our ethnic brothers in Dagestan. This criminal must be punished. This is why my men are ready to execute Basayev or to hand him over to the Russian Army."

Hong Kong (AP) March 16, 2000 – Suspected terrorist Osama bin Laden, wanted in the deadly bombings of two U.S. embassies in Africa, is dying of kidney disease, a Hong Kong-based newsmagazine reported today.

Bin Laden's kidney disease has begun to affect his liver, and his close associates are trying to obtain a dialysis machine to stabilize his condition, *Asiaweek* said in a press release. It cited an unidentified Western intelligence source.

The Saudi Arabian millionaire, believed to be hiding out in the mountains in Afghanistan, remains mostly conscious and is able to talk and hold meetings, the magazine said.

Kandahar, Afghanistan. AP report Friday, January 12, 2001. "There were reports last year that bin Laden, a millionaire, was suffering from kidney and liver disease. In the footage (shown on Qatare's Al-Jazeera television) he was smiling and appeared healthy."

The footage included Osama bin Laden reciting a poem at the wedding of his son, Mohammed bin Laden on Tuesday, January 9, 2001 in Kandahar.

Azzam Publications. Exclusive Interview with Dhattab, November 20, 1999. "If you would have told me in Afghanistan that a day will come when we will be fighting the Russians INSIDE Russia, I would never have believed you." **[Ibn-ul-Khattab]**

Associated Press, Waiel Faleh, December 19,1999 – Iraq rejected a new UN policy that would return weapons inspectors to Baghdad after a yearlong absence, saying yesterday that it is prepared to face the consequences.

American Rifleman, March 1999 _ "The FBI's New .45 Pistol" The FBI's newest weapon is the M1911-pattern, l45 ACP built by Springfield, Inc. as the "Bureau model and will be issued only to agents in special units such as the elite Hostage Rescue Team and SWAT units sometimes called Critical Response Teams."

Oxford Micro Devices, Inc. – Using Oxford's A236 Video Digital Signal Processor Chip as the CPU and a small fingerprint image sensor, one can build safer guns.

KRT News Service Nov 26, 1999 "CIA drive aims to diversify operations" - Recruiters targeting minorities and women with experience abroad and taste for spying. After years of directors who favored satellites, electronic eavesdropping and other high-tech intelligence gathering over human spies, George Tenet, the intelligence community's third director in six years, is re-emphasizing personnel.

Spokane, Wash, (AP) Nov 22, 1999 "Police tail suspect with satellites" – After the strange disappearance of a man's wife and 9-year-old daughter, investigators turned to a digital-age version of a bloodhound and placed a GPS device in the man's pickup truck and followed his movements for 18 days. It led them to two graves.

Associated Press, Lyoma Turpalov, October 24, 1999, "Chechnya claims it downed 2 Russian jets" - Chechen fighters claimed they shot down two Russian warplanes in separate incidents yesterday and government forces bombed and fired rockets on rebel positions in the breakaway republic.

Reuters; Susan Comwell, Feb. 15, 1999 "Bin Laden reported to have left Afghanistan" Islamic militant Osama bin Laden, hunted by the United States and reported missing by Afghanistan's ruling Taliban, may have left Afghanistan three weeks ago, the editor of an Arabic newspaper said yesterday. Abdel-Bari Atwan, editor of the London-based al-Quds al-Aravi newspaper, said bin Laden's possible destination was Chechnya, Russia's southern region, where Moscow battled separatist rebels. "He has good contacts with them and some of his men have been fighting there," Atwan said.

Kabul, Afghanistan, Zahid Hussain, (AP), Feb 19, 1999 "Many in Afghanistan relieved bin Laden may have left country" – Many people in the Afghan capital were welcoming news that the United States' No. 1 terror suspect Osama bin Laden may have left their homeland for refuge elsewhere.

Sleptsovskaya, Russia; Yuri Bagrov (AP) November 23, 1999, "Russians move to encircle Chechen capital; all-out battle not expected" - Prominent rebel commander Shamil Basayev, brushed off the prospect of peace talks, saying, "I will not negotiate now because there is not a third party nor any guarantees from the international community. With Russians it's impossible to make a deal. Only fighting works." Many Chechens blame Basayev for prompting the war by invading neighboring Dagestan in August, which enraged and terrified many Russians.

TESTIMONY: Colonel John D. Rosenberger, Commander, 11ᵗʰ Armored Cavalry Regiment, before the Military Readiness ubcommittee, Committee on National Security, United States House of Representatives; First Session, 106ᵗʰ Congress, February 26, 1999 - *"Mr. Chairman, speaking for myself, it is a hard thing to watch my Army, the Army that delivered the outcome of Desert Storm, the Army I and many others sacrificed so much to create from the ashes of the Vietnam War, slowly deteriorate from the conditions we've been compelled to endure the past seven years.*

CNN interactive: December 11, 1997 "Farrakhan in Iraq: Sanctions are 'terrorism'"

Baghdad, Iraq (CNN) – During a trip to Baghdad Thursday, Nation of Islam leader Louis Farrakhan denounced United Nations sanctions against Iraq as a "mass form of terrorism." Though the travel ban carries a penalty of up to 12 years in prison, it is rarely enforced. Farrakhan said he does not expect to be charged because he did not use his American passport to enter Iraq. He did not say what document he used to enter the country. Farrakhan's visit received widespread publicity in the Iraq's state-controlled media, with coverage of his visits to hospitals and meetings with senior officials, including Deputy Prime Minister Tariq Aziz.

The Columbus Free Press; November 6, 1996 "Farrakhan in Cuba," Dr. Manning Marable – In his recent visit to Libya, Farrakhan expressed a desire to his hosts that he would like to travel to Cuba. Representatives of the Cuban government were contacted, and Farrakhan was invited to come to the island. His [sic] visit to the Nigerian dictatorship, only months after the execution by that regime of human rights activists, was shameful. Farrakhan is quoted as saying, "President Clinton should remember what happened in Babylon. Those who were responsible for wrongdoing received the hearts of animals in place of human hearts." He added that the United States today suffers from "the same symptoms as ancient Babylon."

Eurasia Insight via RFE/RL, May 5, 2002 By Jeremy Bransten — After enduring months of humiliating setbacks and losses in Chechnya, the Kremlin claimed a major coup last week, announcing that the Federal Security Service (FSB) had succeeded in killing one of the separatists' top commanders — Saudi-born Samir bin Saleh al-Suwailem, known by his nom de guerre, "Khattab." On 26 April 2002, RTR state television broadcast footage showing the body of a man resembling Khattab being prepared for his funeral. This week, the Chechen separatist command and Khattab's family confirmed his death.

Printed in the United States
1258700004B/62-86